NO BARGAIN

"And to what do I owe the pleasure of your company, Mr. Dawson? Let me guess. You're looking for a house to buy and this one suits you just fine." Sarcasm dripped from Jauncey's words.

"No, ma'am, I'm not and this one doesn't."

"And you expect me to believe that?" Her eyes narrowed.

"Only if you want to believe the truth."

"And just what is the truth, Mr. Dawson?"

"I'm only trying to help you."

"Help?" she exclaimed. "No, thank you!"

"It doesn't surprise me you won't accept my offer. If you weren't so damn stubborn, you'd see how foolish you're being. Sell the house! Buy another one, if you want to run a boardinghouse," Matt said.

"What right do you have meddling in my affairs?" Jauncey demanded.

"Because I'm trying to get you out of a bad situation that's only going to get worse." Matt settled his hat squarely on his head. "And a simple thank you would do."

"Thank you! I'll thank you to leave me alone!" Jauncey shouted, slamming the door in his face.

JAUNCEY

Melody Morgan

LOVE SPELL **NEW YORK CITY**

LOVE SPELL®

December 1994

Published by

Dorchester Publishing Co., Inc.
276 Fifth Avenue
New York, NY 10001

Printed in the United States of America.

*A friend is someone who believes in you,
encourages you, and never lets you give up.
Thanks, JoAnne.*

JAUNCEY

Chapter One

Wyoming 1886

Jauncey Devon Taylor stepped through the doorway, her eyes adjusting slowly to the darkness within the huge Victorian house. A slender ray of sunlight ricocheted off the opposite wall. Squinting, she narrowed her gaze on a large painting and, gasping with shock, she stepped back.

There before her disbelieving eyes, painted in truer-than-life colors, lounged a nude woman on a brilliant red sofa. But it wasn't only the initial surprise of seeing the painting that made her clutch at her throat; it was the woman. Jauncey stared at the long, thick auburn curls covering the lower parts of the woman's body while emphasizing her exposed breasts. Dark hazel eyes in a perfect oval-shaped face stared at her from the nearly life-sized canvas.

And it wasn't just the nudity of the woman that shocked her, but that the woman looked like her.

Tentatively, she walked toward the picture, barely aware of the driver she'd hired to bring her here, who was standing in the open door behind her. While light filtered crazily through the fringe on the partially closed drapes, scattering shadows across the painting, Jauncey pursed her lips in concentration.

"Would you like me to bring your trunks inside, ma'am?"

Whirling, Jauncey faced the driver. She didn't miss the look of surprise in his eyes as he stared first at her, then at the picture over her shoulder, and back at her again. A hot flush crept up her neck. Once more she turned to confront the large painting. She would not tolerate such a disgusting display of flesh. It had to come down. Now. Grasping the bottom edge of the unwieldy frame, she struggled to free it from its hook.

"Here," the driver said, hurrying into the parlor, "let me help you." He lifted the picture with some effort, then, his face scarlet from embarrassment, looked askance at her.

"Just . . . just . . . set it on the floor," she said, turning her back while trying to dismiss the unfortunate likeness with an awkward wave of her hand.

She glanced around the stifling, semidark room, annoyed that there was no place to set her trunks even temporarily. Frowning, she studied the haphazard array of clutter lining each wall: spittoons, chairs and tables with empty glasses.

"You may put the trunks in the middle of the

room since it appears to be the only empty space available." With her head held stiffly, she spoke over her shoulder, too uncomfortable to face the silent, and even more embarrassed, driver.

Stepping aside, she kept her eyes averted from the painting while the driver hauled the trunks off the wide porch and through the doorway. But her head turned as though tugged by a marionette's string toward the picture of the auburn-haired woman that was now partly concealed by a chair.

The driver cleared his throat and shuffled his feet while his eyes roamed over the dusty carpet.

"Oh," she said, digging in her reticule. "Thank you." She paid him, waited politely for him to leave, then closed the door quickly. Her shoulders slumped as her head leaned forward against the glass.

"A bordello," she muttered to herself. How could this have happened? Why hadn't somebody told her? But nobody had, not the lawyer who had come to St. Louis, not the ticket man at the train station, not even the driver. All she'd been told was that she'd inherited a large house, one in which she could take in boarders. Indeed! What self-respecting person would want to rent a room that had been used by a fallen woman to ply her trade?

Now that she was alone, she stared openly at the picture. It was her aunt, according to the lawyer, and the previous owner of the house until her death. The resemblance between her aunt and herself was more than uncanny; it was frightening, like looking in a mirror and

11

finding herself transformed into something or someone she abhorred. She forced herself to turn away.

Feeling deceived, disappointed and more than a little exasperated, Jauncey pulled back the heavy drapes from the front windows, allowing more light into the room, then wandered around examining the contents. With one finger she wiped a fair amount of dust from the wooden frame of a small settee. She wrinkled her nose with disapproval. Dust lay everywhere. Beneath her feet the dirty room-size rug had completely lost all traces of color. Brass spittoons were haphazardly placed, and it looked like they had been missed more times than hit. Apparently, the entire house had been untouched since her aunt's death a few months earlier.

Closed doors on each wall suggested this was more of an entrance parlor, obviously where some of the entertaining had taken place. With a determined sigh Jauncey reached for the door nearest to the front door. Gently, she pushed it ajar. It creaked but offered little resistance.

With openmouthed dismay, Jauncey stared into a room that could be called nothing less than a pigsty. Her eyes roved over the floor covered with stacks of clothing, the open drawers of the dresser dripping with unmentionables, and a lumpy brass bed piled with quilts. She'd truly never seen anything like it in her life.

"Who the hell are you?" came a sleepy voice from the mound of bedclothes. "And how the hell did you get in here?" A woman with suspiciously bright red hair in wild disarray blinked at the light cascading through the doorway.

"What . . . What?" a hoarse male voice stammered, muffled by a pillow.

Jauncey's heart skidded to a halt, then thumped wildly. She was appalled at the sight before her, and only one thought entered her head: run! She spun on her heels, slamming the door behind her, gasping in her attempt to escape. But at the front door she stopped, her hand gripping the doorknob until her knuckles whitened. With her eyes closed, she forced herself to stand steady.

Merciful heavens! What was she going to do? Her mind whirled. This *is* a bordello, not was! In all probability, other women like that one occupied other rooms. She squeezed her eyelids tighter and tried to keep from conjuring up similar scenes and worse.

Go! her fearful mind cried. Don't stay in this terrible place. But she didn't pull the door open.

Instead, her mind battled with her emotions. Her mother would have wanted, no, expected her to run as fast and as far from there as she could. But her mother was gone and now it was her own life she had to think about.

With her eyes still squeezed shut, Jauncey weighed her choices. She was twenty-four, well past marrying age, and could endure the embarrassment of continuing to live as a poor relation, or she could take advantage of the chance to make a new life for herself by staying.

She couldn't leave now, not when she had such high hopes of supporting herself and being independent. For too long she had lived on the charity of her family. She couldn't go back; she wouldn't go back!

Straightening her shoulders, Jauncey turned to face the closed bedroom door. Her heartbeat increased to that of a small bird. As she reached out, her hand wavered over the doorknob. But before she touched it, the door opened to reveal the frowzy-haired woman, her faded silk wrapper barely concealing her ample bosom.

She gave Jauncey an assessing glance from head to toe. "You must be Spicie's niece. Sorry I didn't tidy up the place, but I expect with you here I won't have to worry about it." A sarcastic smile tipped one corner of her thin lips puckered with age lines.

"You have assumed correctly." Jauncey's voice was as tight as the corset she wore. "This is no longer a"—she nearly choked on the word—"brothel."

"Is that right?" The woman's eyes became large with faked surprise; then she shrugged her shoulder. "Working for you would probably be worse than working for Spicie." She turned to re-enter the bedroom, where the sound of boots scraped against bare wood.

Jauncey waited, unsure of what to do. Should she begin emptying her trunks or stand sentinel until the woman left? Unable to pretend such nonchalance, she stood straight as a telegraph pole, feeling awkward and uncomfortable.

After a few moments, a tall, brown-haired cowboy slouched through the bedroom door holding his hat. He aimed a small, embarrassed smile in Jauncey's direction, then quickly averted his eyes

14

and stepped around her, crossing to the front door.

"Bill! You damn rustler, you owe me!" came the woman's rough voice.

With a sheepish look on his face, the cowboy walked around Jauncey again, mumbling, "Pardon me, ma'am."

Terribly ill at ease, Jauncey turned her head toward an opposite doorway and studied a long strand of cobwebs.

"Sorry, Ruby," he mumbled, and made a hasty retreat.

When he'd gone, Ruby stood in the doorway half dressed. "If it's all the same to you, I'll come back for my things after I make other arrangements. It won't take long. Ever since Spicie died, Sam's been after me to come work for him at the saloon. Hell, one place is as good as another. And to tell the truth, I'm a little sick of whimpering females."

Ruby expertly manipulated the lacing on the front of her corset. Her voice lowered confidentially. "It's a tough life, dearie, and there ain't no guarantees. A gal has to take what she can when it comes her way." Then she disappeared long enough to finish dressing. Without a backward glance or another word, she walked past Jauncey and out the front door.

No guarantees, thought Jauncey. How true. There had been no guarantee that her parents would live long healthy lives, or that her mother would be able to keep their home near St. Louis after her father died.

Suddenly her head ached and her new black shoes pinched her toes. She sank gratefully into

the straight-backed, cushioned chair near the front
door. Leaning her head back, her eyes closed, she
took a deep breath, held it and exhaled slowly.
Unwillingly her mind played back the scene that
had just happened.

What whimpering females? she wondered.

A soft rustling sound made Jauncey's head snap
forward and her eyes open wide. At the top of the
stairway stood two women. The one who appeared
older was small, her soft, dark curls pulled neatly
away from her face. Her deep brown eyes showed
no curiosity, only blank acceptance. Beside her
stood a taller woman with blond hair. Her large
blue eyes betrayed her wariness, while her slender
hand held tightly to the arm of the other woman.

Slowly they descended the stairs. When they
reached the bottom, dark eyes met Jauncey's,
measuring and steady.

"Hello. I'm Sugar." The older woman's voice was
low and even. "This is Maggie." Neither woman
smiled.

Jauncey rose from her seat, uncertain.

"I'm Jauncey Taylor," she said, her voice sounding strange in her ears.

"We know. Mr. Collins told us you would be
arriving soon." Sugar's face didn't show a hint
of expression, unlike Maggie, who seemed on
the verge of crumbling. Now that Jauncey had a
closer look at the women, she was certain Maggie
was much younger than Sugar, probably about
eighteen.

"You're closing the house," Sugar stated flatly.

"Yes."

At Jauncey's answer, Maggie collapsed on the

bottom step, and buried her face in Sugar's skirts, sobbing.

Well acquainted with grief, Jauncey recognized this as something more—fear. And she understood that, too.

Jauncey watched while Sugar knelt and placed a protective arm around Maggie's shoulders, her voice soft, her brow wrinkled with concern. "I won't leave you. We'll stay together. I promised. Remember?"

At that moment, Jauncey realized that the same fate that had given her a home was taking one away from the two women. How well she knew what it was like to be suddenly without a place to live, the humiliation of becoming dependent on others for food and clothing.

"Sh-h-h, Maggie," Sugar continued in that same soothing voice. Her hand gently smoothed the blond hair, which was all that could be seen from the folds of Sugar's skirts. "Don't worry. It won't be the way it was before you came here. I'll take care of you," she crooned.

Sugar's last statement profoundly affected Jauncey. The muscles in her throat tightened. She swallowed, but a huge knot formed. A sudden need to blink warned her of the moisture beginning to accumulate in her eyes.

"You don't have to leave," Jauncey said just above a whisper.

Sugar's brown eyes lifted, and her hand poised above Maggie's head buried in her dress. She said nothing, but a fleeting look of hope passed across her pale features.

Jauncey grasped the amethyst ring on her right

17

hand and nervously twisted it back and forth. She wondered if her hasty remark would be one she would soon regret.

She stared at the woman a long time before she spoke. "You may stay here if you have no other place to go."

"Do you know what you're saying?"

"Perhaps not completely. We'll each have to compromise and try to work something out that is agreeable to all of us." Jauncey dropped her hands to her sides.

Visibly stiffening, Sugar asked, "Are you saying we can live here on your charity?"

"I'm not offering charity. As I said, we'll work something out."

"Such as?"

"I'm not sure." Jauncey returned to the chair she had momentarily left.

Quiet now, Maggie turned her head to face Jauncey, her tangled blond hair hiding most of her face.

"When I found out my aunt left me a large house, I considered what possibilities it could have for me," Jauncey said. "And a boardinghouse instantly came to my mind."

"A . . . boardinghouse?" Maggie sat up, hiccuping like a child.

"Yes. Certainly three women could manage a boardinghouse." Jauncey pushed down her apprehension and felt the beginnings of a new resolution flowing through her veins. If they really wanted it to work, why couldn't it?

"With reformed prostitutes living in it?" Sugar's words rang with sarcasm.

Jauncey had to agree that Sugar spoke the truth, yet could she possibly run a boardinghouse this large alone? She could hardly afford to hire anyone for more than the cost of room and board. And the work wasn't going to be easy, she reasoned, looking around. The house needed a thorough cleaning and a complete make-over. It would be difficult, to say the least.

"I'm making you an offer. Are you refusing it?" Jauncey spoke in a businesslike tone, looking Sugar straight in the eye.

"Sugar! Don't say no. Please!" Maggie grabbed Sugar's arm, her blue eyes pleading.

Sugar laid her hand over Maggie's. "I can't say no, but this isn't going to be easy."

No, thought Jauncey, it wasn't going to be easy at all. This house had a reputation to overcome. Could she do that with Sugar and Maggie living here? Truthfully, what were her chances of hiring a respectable woman to clean a bordello anyway? Well, there really was no other choice. She needed them and they needed her.

Jauncey rose quickly, not totally at ease in their company. That would take some time, but she would make the adjustment. After all, what else could she do? "Would you mind showing me the bedrooms? Then I can take my things up and get settled."

Sugar nodded, then gently disentangled herself from Maggie. She smiled and smoothed the girl's hair, saying, "Why don't you make us some tea?"

Without a word, Maggie rose and walked toward the back of the house.

Once more Sugar resumed her cool detachment.

"This way," she said, going up the stairs. "There are ten bedrooms upstairs and two downstairs."

Jauncey did not know what the daily charge for boarders would be, but whatever it was times nine rooms had to be enough to make this venture successful. It just had to be.

"Which room is my aunt's room?" Jauncey asked.

"Spicie had the one facing the front of the house. It has its own small balcony over the porch. Would you like to have it?" Sugar asked, looking over her shoulder at Jauncey who followed her up the stairs.

"No," she answered hastily, sorry she had even asked. She wanted nothing more to do with anything that belonged to her aunt than was absolutely necessary.

They walked along the open hall with its banister rail of mahogany overlooking the parlor below. The house had an undeniable beauty that only needed to be uncovered. Jauncey refrained from touching anything, sure that the filth downstairs must also be upstairs.

Sugar led her to a room at the end of the hall furnished with simple oak furniture. A large four-poster bed was neatly made up; a nightstand beside it, a bare dresser with a mirror over it and a large wardrobe completed the decor.

The heavy drapes had been pulled back, revealing a surprisingly clean room. Jauncey almost had the feeling that the room had been prepared for her.

Placing her hand on the smooth wooden post at the foot of the bed, Jauncey said, "It's a lovely room. And so many windows."

The room, located at one of the many corners of the house, had in each outside wall two windows overlooking roofs and the tops of young trees.

"I'm glad you like it," Sugar replied matter-of-factly, then turned to go. "Supper will be ready in about an hour. Would you like some help bringing your things up?"

For a moment Jauncey considered the heavy trunks downstairs. Without a doubt each item would have to be taken out and carried upstairs before the trunks could be lifted and brought up. All her personal belongings were in them as well as her clothes. She hesitated, not wanting to appear ungrateful but not willing to have a stranger sort through her things.

"It's all right, I understand." Sugar's face was as expressionless as a pane of glass, but not nearly as transparent. "Supper will be ready in about an hour," she said again, then left.

Making innumerable trips with heavy loads of clothing had Jauncey sweating beneath her traveling suit in no time. She bit her tongue with each step she took for turning Sugar's offer of help down. By the time she'd finished, she was beyond exhaustion. Even so, she was determined to mark the room as her own by at least laying out a dish of hairpins as well as the hairbrush that had been her mother's.

Next she opened the small chest Uncle Harold had given her before she'd left for Laramie. A derringer, slightly larger than the palm of her hand, lay inside. This was the first gun she'd ever owned, or even held for that matter. She

21

hadn't wanted to accept it, but he'd insisted she would need it if she was going west. In spite of her own misgivings, she'd taken it, but had never loaded it. Closing the lid, she placed the chest on the stand beside her bed.

Satisfied at last that everything had been properly put away, she considered having to make another trip down the stairs for supper, and almost groaned aloud. But the aroma of baking biscuits mingled with the sweet smell of wood smoke made her stomach rumble and reminded her that several hours had passed since she'd last eaten.

Jauncey forced her aching legs to descend the staircase, cross the filthy parlor and enter the kitchen. Standing in the doorway, she glanced around, speechless. The room was immaculate and it was the biggest kitchen she'd ever seen. Large oak cabinets with clear glass doors hung on two walls, and in the center was a long, broad trestle table with a mixture of benches and chairs. But even more commanding was the cast-iron stove, the likes of which Jauncey had never seen. It had eight lids on the top, a hot water reservoir on each side and a warming oven so high she couldn't imagine how anyone could reach the top of it. With a sense of awe, she sat at the huge table, feeling as though she'd walked into someone's private domain.

Maggie dished up three plates of stew and placed a platter of biscuits on the table before seating herself next to Sugar.

Jauncey buttered a biscuit, then took a bite of the most wonderful beef stew she'd ever tasted. By the time her plate was half empty, nobody had spoken a word, and Jauncey offered a compliment. "That was absolutely delicious, Maggie."

But Maggie didn't respond. Instead, she kept her head bent over her plate, chewing quietly.

The awkward silence lengthened. Jauncey glanced from Maggie to Sugar. Surely, they would never get to know each other if someone didn't talk, she decided. But what did they have in common? The boardinghouse.

Taking a deep breath, she said, "I think we should begin getting the downstairs ready tomorrow. Then we'll be able to rent two rooms while we get the rooms upstairs finished." She glanced at Sugar hoping for some conversation. A sigh of relief almost escaped her when Sugar looked directly at her.

"The downstairs will be the most difficult, except for the kitchen, of course," Sugar replied, her soft voice nearly devoid of any emotion. "The side parlor is much larger than the front one. That's where Ruby entertained most of the time after Spicie died."

And where had Maggie and Sugar entertained? Jauncey wondered. Instantly, she brushed the unbidden thought from her mind. She didn't care, and she didn't want to know.

"Tomorrow I'll look over the rooms down here, but I'm too tired to do anything but have a bath tonight. I hope you don't mind if I leave the dishes for you to do. I'll be glad to take double duty another time to make up for it." Jauncey pushed back her chair. Neither of the women voiced an opinion, leading Jauncey to believe they would rather clean up without her.

She left the women busy at their chores and climbed the stairs to her room. In the doorway, she stopped and studied her new surroundings. It would take some time getting used to it. Her room. Her house. It had been years since she'd lived in her own house, and even though Uncle Harold had been nice enough to take her and her mother in, things just hadn't been the same. At least Uncle Harold hadn't made them feel like poor relations. But Aunt Ida hadn't been so kind.

After taking the pins from her hair, Jauncey shook out her braid. Then she removed a clean white nightgown from a drawer and went back downstairs to the room she'd seen off the kitchen containing a tub.

Maggie was working over the few dishes in the sink, and Sugar dipped water from the reservoir on the huge stove.

"Here are a couple of buckets from the reservoir. Add some cold water and you'll be all set," Sugar told her.

"Thank you."

As quickly as possible, Jauncey readied her bath, got undressed and sat in the warm shallow water. It had been two days since Jauncey had done more than wash up, so she relaxed, trickling the water over her arms and shoulders with a cloth. She remained in the water until it cooled and the tips of her fingers wrinkled. Then, picking up a folded towel from a nearby table, she sniffed the fresh odor of sunshine and lemon.

After donning her nightgown, she made sure she left the room just as she'd found it.

She tucked her laundry beneath her arm, and

since Maggie and Sugar had already gone to bed, she put out the lamp in the kitchen. When she reached for the lamp in the parlor, the front door burst open, bringing a sudden gust of damp night air.

Jauncey gasped in alarm, her bare feet immobilized on the gritty parlor floor, her bundle of clothing clutched tightly to her side.

Framed in the open doorway with the inky blackness behind him stood the most fierce-looking man she'd ever seen. In one frightened glance she took in his rugged features, his black mustache, his dust-covered Stetson and his scowling face.

Her heart pounding, her eyes fell to the holstered gun slung low at his hip. A chill raced down her spine as Uncle Harold's words of warning echoed in her head.

With an air of determination, he walked quickly into the room, his boots thudding on the dirty carpet, his spurs jingling softly.

When she looked him full in the face, she saw surprise registered there, but only for a moment. Then the scowl returned while his dark eyes searched the room.

"Business must be slow," he said, looking past her.

"Get out!" she whispered with a mixture of fear and fury.

"Where the hell is Johnny?" The anger in his voice practically vibrated the floorboards beneath her feet. "And don't think I'm leaving without him."

She summoned every ounce of her courage before telling him again, "I said get out!"

"Not until I find him."

Horrified, Jauncey watched while the intruder moved around the parlor, opening doors. Then, standing in the center of the room, he shouted loud enough for every neighbor within an entire block to hear, "Johnny!"

"There's nobody here named Johnny," Jauncey said, trying to keep her voice from shaking.

But he ignored her and took the steps two at a time.

Jauncey raced up the stairs behind him, clutching her clothes with one hand and holding her nightgown up to her knees. "I said get out! Can't you hear?" At the top of the landing she looked for something to give meaning to her threats.

His heavy boots thudded in the hall as he strode from door to door, opening and slamming each one, not bothering to knock on any of them. She barely heard him mutter, "I'll fire him this time, I swear it."

He tried another door, but it was locked. He studied it for a second, then pounded on it with his fist. "Come out of there! Damn it, I know you're in there!" Before he stopped pounding, Jauncey heard the screams, high-pitched and terrified. She knew it was Maggie. Sugar ran down the hall from the other direction to Maggie's room.

Jauncey wasted no time getting to her own room, and to the derringer hidden in the chest beside her bed. She couldn't take time to load it even if she had known how.

Running back into the hall she found the man standing stock-still, looking confused at all the commotion going on around him.

With unsteady hands, she gripped the gun,

pointing it somewhere near the top button of his shirt.

"Now, I said get out!" Raising her voice loud enough to be heard over Maggie's screams and Sugar's pleading through the door, she bravely waved the gun toward the stairs, her eyes riveted on his face.

Oh, how she hoped and prayed he believed the gun was loaded.

"You've got till the count of three," she said, leveling the gun at his forehead.

"One."

Chapter Two

Matt Dawson stared at the gun in the woman's shaking hands.

"Two."

When he looked up, her hazel eyes were large with fright and determination. He moved toward the stairs and went down. She followed him, but kept a safe distance.

He opened the door and stepped onto the porch. Then she called to him, her voice cracking slightly. "Wait!"

Hesitating, he turned to stare at her.

"Just so you know, this is not a brothel anymore. So don't come back." Then she slammed the door in his face. He heard the scrape and clunk as the bolt slid home.

It was the first time in his life he had ever been escorted from a whorehouse at gunpoint. He would have smiled at the thought, except he didn't have any time to waste musing over a good-looking do-gooder. He had to find Johnny.

Settling his hat more firmly on his head, he walked down the front steps. Darkness had barely set in, so maybe he'd find Johnny still at one of the saloons on First Street. Though that part of town had gotten a lot calmer over the last ten years, it was still a good place to get into trouble. Matt quickly mounted his horse and rode toward the center of Laramie.

When he reached the Crisman House, Matt tied his horse in front of it and went inside. His eyes scanned the crowded room. A sudden burst of angry voices drew his attention toward the back of the room and the gaming table, and he knew he'd found Johnny. Matt's spurs rang with each step as he strode purposefully in that direction.

Johnny lounged in a chair, his arm draped across the back, his lopsided smile suggesting an assurance that came from having several stiff drinks under his belt. But the man standing over him wasn't smiling.

"Pay up, I said, or I'll hang your cheatin' hide out to dry!"

"Damn right!" another man said. "Maybe the buzzards would like to have a go at you!"

"C'mon, boys, you know I'm good for it. I always pay up. Eventually." Johnny smiled at the men around the table, lifting his hand in an easygoing manner. "All I gotta do is ask the boss for an advance. So sit down and deal another hand."

Matt stepped to the side of the table just as two other men scraped back their chairs. "Count me out," they said.

"This time they can hang your hide out to dry,"

Matt said, staring down at Johnny in disgust.

Johnny's head rolled back as he smiled lazily up at Matt. "You don't mean it, Boss." Then he leaned forward, his elbows on the table, and picked up a glass of whiskey, absently studying the contents.

Provoked beyond his usual bounds of restraint, Matt knocked the glass from Johnny's hand, sending it shattering against the wall.

"The hell I don't." Matt's voice was low with unconcealed rage.

The smile instantly faded from Johnny's face. He rose unsteadily to his feet, a flash of anger bright in his eyes. "You shouldn't have done that."

Standing at least a head taller, Matt knew he had the advantage when it came to size and strength. But he also knew Johnny held the ultimate weapon.

Matt clenched his fists and ground his teeth for a moment of control. Then his right arm shot out, clipping Johnny neatly on the chin. The surprise of the impact hurled Johnny back, and he appeared suspended for less than a second before he collapsed at Matt's feet. Out of habit Matt dug in his pocket for the money to cover Johnny's losses, then reconsidering, shoved the bills deeper. He'd played this game long enough. It was time for Johnny to start delivering or take the consequences. He lifted the limp body to his shoulder, aware that the entire place had grown unusually quiet as all eyes turned in his direction while he walked out.

Outside, he tossed Johnny across the saddle and led the horse toward the nearest livery stable in search of Johnny's horse. Soon they were heading out of town.

The long ride back to the ranch gave Matt a large measure of satisfaction as he thought about the throbbing headache Johnny would have in the morning, not to mention a gut ache from riding belly-down on the saddle.

Matt had long since had his fill of the cowboy. He wanted more than anything to fire Johnny and send him packing back to wherever he'd come from. But he couldn't. More times than he could count, Matt had wanted to put his fist into Johnny's smirking face, but he knew he'd only be hurting himself in the end. And he was hurting enough as it was with his herds slowly dwindling. Matt had little doubt who was behind it, but without Johnny's help he'd never prove it.

Somehow he had to get this settled, Matt thought. He was fed up with hauling Johnny's worthless backside out of saloon brawls, gambling fights and whorehouses. And tonight had been no different. Except for the whorehouse that was no longer a whorehouse.

Matt relaxed in his saddle, thinking about the woman in the white flowing nightgown with her long, whiskey-colored curls reaching to her waist. He doubted if she realized that the long gown had hid nothing even though she had buttoned it to her neck. Well, she sure had her work cut out for her. He figured it would be next to impossible to convince anyone she wasn't the new madam. Especially when she looked so much like Spicie Belle. But then maybe it was the lamplight or maybe it was being in that house, or maybe it was that long whiskey-dark hair that had made him think that.

31

Melody Morgan

The next morning Jauncey woke to the sound of a steam whistle from the Union Pacific Railroad only three blocks west of her window. For a few moments she wondered where she was and why the room at Aunt Ida's was so different, so much larger and brighter. Then last night's events came rushing back, and with a small shudder she remembered the tall cowboy stampeding through the house. House indeed, she thought with a groan.

Closing her eyes, she laid her arm across her forehead, contemplating the monumental task before her. Heaving a sigh, she threw back the covers. She had no time to waste lying in bed if she intended to be independent with an income of her own.

It was long past daybreak. She hadn't meant to sleep so late. Chances were Sugar and Maggie had already had breakfast and were wondering when she would get up. Jauncey hurriedly pulled on a cotton work dress, buttoning it up the front, then snatched a pair of stockings from the drawer and slipped them on. The buttons on her shoes refused to cooperate with her hurried fingers. She brushed out the single braid she always wore to keep her hair from becoming a mass of tangles during the night, then pinned it up. With a quick glance she surveyed her appearance in the large oak-framed mirror above the dresser. Satisfied that she looked ready to tackle anything, even a . . . bordello, she turned to leave the room.

Jauncey opened the door, startled to find Maggie standing there. "Oh, my!" she blurted out, jumping back.

"I heard you moving around so I knew you were up. I was just coming to make your bed."

Maggie stood the same height as Jauncey, but wouldn't look her in the eye. Instead, she stared over Jauncey's shoulder, giving Jauncey the feeling she should turn around to see who was there.

"That's all right, I can do it. It isn't necessary for you to clean up after me," Jauncey said. "I'm used to doing for myself."

"If you don't want me to, I won't." Maggie turned to leave.

"It isn't that," Jauncey said quickly, not wanting to hurt her feelings. She almost reached out to touch Maggie, but didn't. "I don't think it would be fair to expect you to do what I'm capable of doing."

Maggie shrugged. "There are some warmed-over biscuits and honey on the stove. Coffee, too." She turned and hurried out of sight down the hall.

"Thank you," Jauncey called after her.

What a strange girl, she thought, so timid and afraid. Then she remembered last night's intruder and how frightened Maggie had been. How truly dreadful to be forced into becoming a prostitute. And certainly Maggie'd been forced or why would she be here? She was so young. Jauncey's thoughts turned to her aunt, and instantly the nude portrait came to mind. Now the disgust she'd felt toward Spicie turned to loathing. What kind of a woman would do such things?

Jauncey found the biscuits and honey, and made plans for the day while she sipped her coffee. She forced herself to concentrate on cleaning the huge

33

house, leaving the problem of obtaining boarders for later.

"Good morning, Miss Taylor." Sugar entered the kitchen and filled a cup with coffee.

"Please, call me Jauncey." She would do her best to make things go smoothly between them, and try to forget about how different their lives had been up to this point.

"All right." Sugar sat down.

"I've been making some plans but I'd like your advice." Jauncey hoped they could get started on the right foot by at least being friendly. "If we begin downstairs like we said, which room do you suggest first?" she asked, wiping up the crumbs of her biscuit and dropping them onto her dish.

"We may as well begin with the worst. The larger parlor. But it's also the nicest when it's clean." Sugar rose gracefully from her seat, and led the way through the front parlor.

Jauncey tried seeing both parlors from a businesslike viewpoint. She looked past the spittoons to see the wood beneath the dirt and past the heavy drapes to see the tall beautiful windows. Both rooms were large, and she remembered her reaction to seeing the house when the driver had stopped in front of it. She'd thought she was dreaming. The house was huge, its exterior painted the palest yellow with garnishes of white gingerbread work at peaks and corners. No two parts of the house appeared the same. Scalloped gables, mullioned windows and dormers of different shapes stood out proudly in the rounded roof. The second level sported two small porches with detailed spindlework.

Each corner of the house was either beveled, bracketed or arched in decorative display. The first level boasted a wide, inviting wraparound porch, but the most spectacular feature was the delicate beadwork dripping from the porch roof, surrounded by a large horseshoe-curved strip of wood balanced above the spindle railing. It looked like a beautiful picture frame waiting to be filled.

How different it was from the house's dirty interior, Jauncey thought now as she followed Sugar out of the larger parlor.

For the rest of the day Jauncey and Sugar worked, stripping drapes and moving furniture onto the back porch to be cleaned later. Dust flew and spiders scattered as Jauncey worked beside Sugar in companionable silence.

All afternoon the smell of pot roast and vegetables tantalized Jauncey, and she was grateful when Maggie came to call them to supper. It was the first she'd seen her since their brief noon meal, and she wondered how the young girl had spent the rest of the day.

Sugar lowered herself into a chair with a groan. "Oohh, my goodness, but I ache all over."

"I have to confess," Jauncey said, relaxing her tired muscles, "working in this house has helped me discover parts of my body that I never knew existed." She paused with her fork in midair while heat flooded her face. "I mean, I have aches and pains, too." She stared unseeing at the food on her plate. Peripherally, she saw that neither Sugar nor Maggie had paid attention to her poor choice of words.

The mealtime stretched out interminably, but Jauncey refused to say another word.

Finally, when they'd finished, Sugar spoke. "You haven't seen the rest of the house. Would you like me to show you around?"

"Yes, I would, but I'll help with the dishes first."

"No. I'll do them," Maggie said, standing quickly. She took the dirty dishes to the sink where a large window overlooked the back porch.

This time Jauncey didn't argue since Maggie had her back turned, shutting her out. Instead, she followed Sugar into the entrance parlor.

"You've already seen Ruby's room." Sugar pointed at the front bedroom. Jauncey nodded, unwilling to make it a topic of discussion.

"Back here," Sugar continued, "is another bedroom. Just under the stairs is the door."

This room was located directly behind Ruby's and near the bathing closet. Little cleaning would be needed here, Jauncey noted.

Upstairs, they gave each of the unused bedrooms a quick glance, assessing the amount of cleaning that would be necessary to prepare them for boarders.

Standing in the open doorway of the last room, Jauncey stared at the mahogany four-poster bed. Not all the rooms were furnished the same. Some had brass beds and others had high, wooden headboards, but all had dressers with mirrors and slop jars with cloth cozies on their lids.

Each room was wallpapered differently, too. This particular one had large blue flowers on a white background. On the wall near the dresser a patch of lighter-colored wallpaper and a nail indicated that a picture had hung there. Perhaps a picture of the girl who used the room? Jauncey thought.

Thin lace curtains hung at the single window backed by a heavy shade pulled halfway. Jauncey walked into the medium-sized room, grasped the bottom of the shade, gave it a quick yank, then released it. Instantly it flew to the top of the high window, snapping as it went around and around. Dust filtered down through the evening light and landed silently on the patterned carpet.

"Whose room was this?" Jauncey couldn't believe she'd actually voiced the question echoing in her mind. But it was harder to separate herself from the life that had gone on in this house than she had expected.

"Pearl's."

Pearl, Ruby, Sugar. The names sounded fake, assumed by women living unreal lives. At least, they were unreal to her.

"Did any of the women use their own names?" she asked.

"Yes. Lottie and Mary did," Sugar replied, giving her an unblinking stare.

She had the urge to ask Sugar's real name and how she happened to be here, but she couldn't. She'd already asked more than she really wanted to know.

On the dresser was a pair of spurs glinting as the last of the sunlight streamed in, catching Jauncey's eye as well as Sugar's.

"Those are Matt's. We brought them from your room when we cleaned it. I'm sure he must have others," Sugar said. "At least I doubt if he'll be back after you pointed that gun at him last night."

A small smile lurked at the corner of her mouth.

"I certainly hope not!" Jauncey replied wide-eyed. "It would be too soon if I ever see that man again." Once more Uncle Harold's predictions about the wildness of the West came to mind.

"It's late," she said, deciding to change the subject. "Tomorrow will be a long day. But we ought to be able to finish one parlor and at least get started on the other. What do you think?" Jauncey asked.

"I don't see why not. But I'm sure we'll run out of cleaning supplies before too long." Sugar's demeanor had returned to her former distant coolness.

Nodding her head, Jauncey replied, "I'll go to town the day after tomorrow." She walked the length of the long hall to stand at the top of the stairs with Sugar.

Bone-tired, Jauncey didn't move as she stared below to where orange and gold twilight streamed through the parlor windows, casting long shadows across the floor.

Suddenly, she felt lost and lonely. Nothing was as she'd hoped it would be when she'd first learned of the house. All her dreams seemed to lie scattered and she felt helplessly unable to gather the pieces together. How could she ever put them back into one solid, attainable goal?

While she stood watching, the colors of the evening light slowly dimmed, the unsettling darkness reminding her of last night's intruder. Shaking off her reverie, she hurried down the steps to lock the front door.

"That's a good idea." Sugar followed her. "Ruby's

callers usually begin showing up about now." She picked up a small dark reticule and placed it on the table near the front door. "This is Ruby's. She'll probably be back to get it."

Jauncey disregarded that bit of information, focusing instead on the possibility of more late-night callers. She didn't know if she could go through a reenactment of the previous night. Her throat went dry just thinking about it.

"What should we do if her callers do come?" she asked.

"We'll just tell them that Ruby's over at Sam's Saloon. Most of them probably know it anyway. Ruby has a way of making her presence known."

Sugar seemed so sure, so relaxed that Jauncey was able to calm herself with a deep breath. Nevertheless, she made sure the lamp in the front parlor wasn't lit all evening. No need to encourage anyone, she decided.

After preparing for bed, Jauncey stood before her nightstand and lifted the lid of the chest, staring at the gun with mixed feelings. Deciding to leave the lid open, she blew out the lamp and crawled into bed. As she lay there in the dark, the creaks and groans of the unfamiliar house came alive, until she was certain someone must be trying to get in the front door.

With her heart pounding in her ears, she picked up the derringer and crept to the door, peering into the hallway. Making sure she was alone, she moved cautiously down the hall, flattening her body against the wall at the top of the stairs. Afraid to go to the railing, she listened.

Nothing.

Then she heard it. The sound of boots scraping on the porch. She forced herself to tiptoe to the rail. Below, a shadow appeared at the curtained glass front door. It moved from side to side as though trying to see inside.

"Open up!" a male voice yelled, slurring its words. The man pounded on the door, rattling the glass. "C'mon, Ruby, open the damn door!"

With her knees nearly knocking Jauncey realized it wasn't the intruder from last night.

She held the gun close to her side. If only she had loaded it! Well, there wasn't time now. She would have to bluff her way through this confrontation, too.

She made her way down the dark stairway more frightened than she'd ever been, and stood in front of the door.

"I said open the goddamn door or I'll break it down!"

"He means it." Sugar spoke from the railing overlooking the parlor where Jauncey stood gripping the gun tightly. "It's Bull Face Jack. You might as well open the door."

"No!" Jauncey whispered forcefully. "Tell him to go away because I've got a gun." But what if he broke in and found her with an unloaded derringer? No, she was better off trying to reason with him through the closed door.

Jauncey cleared her throat in an effort to lower her voice to its normal pitch. "Go away. Ruby isn't here anymore."

Silence.

"Well, sounds like you'll do," Jack slurred.

Panicked, Jauncey turned to Sugar. "Now what?" she whispered.

Sugar seemed to float down the stairs, her pale-colored nightgown ghostly in the dark.

"Jack," Sugar began, "Ruby is at Sam's. She said to tell you to meet her there."

"Why the hell won't you open the damn door? It's mighty lonely out here, Sugar."

"The house is closed, Jack. For good. It's a respectable boardinghouse now."

Jauncey stared at Sugar while she waited for his response, her hands icy cold but sweating so badly she could hardly hold on to the slippery gun.

In the quiet stillness Jack howled with laughter, long and loud, making Jauncey jump with surprise. "That's a good one, Sugar." She heard him slap his knee twice. "A boardinghouse," he roared.

Jauncey couldn't believe it. He was making fun of her! But it wasn't funny. Not one bit. She was one step away from going back to being a poor relation, and that wasn't one bit funny!

Jauncey unbolted the door in a flurry of motion and stood before Jack with her gun in both hands. "I already said it once but I'll say it again. Go away. Ruby isn't here anymore."

Jack stood still, his thick form silhouetted in the bright moonlight. "Spicie?" he said, appearing to sober.

"This is Miss Taylor, Jack," Sugar said. "Spicie's dead. Remember? Miss Taylor doesn't want any more callers. Understand?"

Jauncey was grateful for Sugar's intervention.

"Lord have mercy, if you ain't the spittin' image," he said. "A boardin' house, hmm? Well, ma'am, I'm

41

sorry to have bothered you." He removed his hat and backed off the porch. He stumbled on the steps, then made his way down the street, weaving and chuckling as he went.

Weak-kneed, Jauncey knew she couldn't take much more of this. Something would have to be done about getting the word around that the house wasn't a bordello anymore.

But first she was going upstairs to load her gun.

Chapter Three

Jauncey walked west along C Street in the bright sunshine toward Laramie's business district. Turning onto Second Street, she saw one tall building after another for three or more blocks, but it wasn't difficult to spot the large building situated on the corner with "Trabing Commercial Company" emblazoned down its length. The impressive brick front sported tall iron columns with huge plateglass windows on the first floor, and a large projecting cornice topped the building. Sugar had told her to shop there since they would have everything she needed. In a building that size, indeed they would, she thought.

Taking a lace handkerchief from inside her sleeve, she dabbed at her temples. The late morning sun beat down, making her eager to get inside the undoubtedly cool interior.

But just before she turned toward the door, her

eye caught the bright finery of a scantily clad woman standing brazenly in front of a saloon a few doors down on the opposite side of the street. Even though she knew she should ignore the display and go on about her business, Jauncey felt compelled to watch as the woman tossed her black-as-night curls in open flirtation with the tall cowboy beside her. Then to Jauncey's shocked surprise, the woman leaned suggestively against the man and kissed him on the lips.

With a sudden flash of recognition, she knew he was the same cowboy who had barged into her house and stormed up the stairs. Well, she reminded herself, what was so surprising about his open attentions toward a woman like that? He had, after all, burst into her home believing it was a bordello, not to mention the spurs he'd left behind from an earlier escapade.

Casting a derisive parting glance at the pair, she turned away and opened the heavy front door of Trabing's, which set off a little bell bouncing and ringing. As she entered the store she was suddenly surrounded by the smell of new leather, fabric and fresh ground coffee blending into a single pleasing aroma.

Behind the counter a man of medium height balanced a box in midair before sliding it onto the shelf. Looking over his shoulder, he smiled broadly. "Good morning!"

"Good morning." She smiled and crossed the wooden floor to wait before the counter, taking her list from the pocket of her jacket.

"May I help you?" he asked.

Even though she was still a little distracted by

the scene out front, she didn't fail to notice his friendly tone and his twinkling blue eyes. He was slightly balding, which gave his round face an open, honest look.

"Yes," she answered, trying to shake the impulse to look over her shoulder for the tall dark cowboy Sugar had called Matt. "Do you make deliveries? My address is at the top of the list. I've opened a new boardinghouse."

Wondering if he would recognize the location, she held her breath waiting for his response.

He glanced at the slip of paper, but his expression gave nothing away.

"Welcome to Laramie, Miss . . . ?" he asked.

"Taylor," she replied. "Thank you." She smiled gratefully and went on. "I would also like to look at some fabrics and thread."

"Certainly. You'll find our selection is the best in town." He moved from behind the counter and ushered her to a table stacked with bolts of cloth.

"When would you like these delivered?" He waved the list slightly, drawing her attention.

"Sometime today if it isn't too much . . . trouble," she replied, suddenly catching sight of the cowboy just outside the large glass windows.

"I'll be glad to bring them to your place as soon as I finish work today. Will that be all right?" The clerk's voice intruded into her thoughts.

"Yes, yes, of course," she said in a rush, watching the man outside. Practically holding her breath, she hoped he would pass by the store. But to her horror he pushed the door wide and stepped inside.

Just as the bell announced his entrance, Jauncey quickly moved behind the highest bolt of cloth.

"I'll bring everything later this afternoon then," the clerk said. But Jauncey, with her head averted, stared unseeing at the tiny red flowers on the bright blue calico, scarcely hearing him.

"Morning, Matt," the clerk said cheerily, leaving Jauncey at last.

"Morning, Dan." It was the same deep drawl she remembered. Biting her lip, she wished the floor had a trap door she could crawl into and hide.

"Has that barbed wire come in yet?" the cowboy asked.

"Not yet. But there's a shipment due in. Would you like me to send someone out to the ranch to let you know when it does? Keep you from making extra trips for nothing," Dan offered in the same friendly manner he had shown to Jauncey.

"Thanks, but I've got some business to tend to this afternoon. I'll stop by again before I leave for the ranch. If you see Charlie, tell him I'll be at Anderson's Livery."

"Sure thing."

Anderson's Livery! Jauncey dropped her reticule. Those stables were practically across the street from her house. Hastily, she stooped to pick up her purse.

"Miss Taylor, have you found the fabric you wanted?" Dan called.

Flustered, Jauncey straightened up quickly.

"I-I changed my mind," she stammered. "I won't be needing any fabric after all." She didn't know how she was going to get out of the store gracefully, but she had to leave.

At the sound of her voice, the cowboy turned in her direction. She couldn't help staring at his dark-as-midnight eyes. He was just as tall as she remembered, and just as menacing. Certainly he wouldn't remember her, especially since she was now fully clothed. Unable to control it, she felt her face flush clear to the roots of her hair at the thought of her state of undress that night.

"Matt Dawson, this is Miss Taylor. She's new in Laramie. She owns the new boardinghouse on South C."

"We've met." He lightly touched the wide brim of his hat while nodding at her. A smile tipped one corner of his mustache. "The lighting was poor that night, but not so poor I didn't get a good look." His eyes quickly ran over her. "Nice to meet you again, Miss Taylor, under friendlier circumstances."

Now she was totally embarrassed. Out of the corner of her eye she could see Dan's smile turn to a puzzled frown. Friendlier circumstances indeed!

She drew herself up into her haughtiest posture and though it was physically impossible, tried to look down her nose at him. "The circumstances would be the same should you choose to make another such entrance, Mr. Dawson."

A full smile stretched across his tanned face, and tiny sun-lines appeared at the corners of his eyes. He looked as though he smiled often, and she wondered why she'd thought he looked so threatening. "Exactly the same?" he asked, raising his eyebrow. "Then it might be worth it, Miss Taylor. Even with a loaded gun."

Jauncey's eyes grew wide and her mouth dropped open. An added warmth, not caused by the heat of the day, filtered up from her collar. Matt

Dawson would not get away with embarrassing her in private, or in public. She didn't care if he was the most handsome man she'd ever met, and he definitely was. She would unequivocally set him straight.

"Mr. Dawson," she stated emphatically. Then punctuating every few words with the lowering of her voice, she went on. "If you ever so much as darken my doorstep, you may be assured the gun will be loaded." With that she turned on her heel and walked briskly toward the door, her high-heeled shoes tapping smartly on the floor.

"Just a moment, Miss Taylor," he called.

Turning, she watched as he retrieved something from the floor, then two more things, but her mind wouldn't focus on what they were. She wanted nothing more than to be on her way, back to the solitude and protection of her own home.

He continued walking toward her, bending down once more to pick up something else. His hands extended, he said, "I believe these must be yours." A devilish grin spread across his tanned face.

She glanced at the sparkling hairpins, combs, a small tin of rouge and other assorted facial paints. Then she looked at her gaping reticule, the contents exposed, and realized she must have picked up Ruby's, which she had mistaken for her own. Humiliated, Jauncey snatched the items from his hands and stuffed them into the small bag, then whirled toward the door.

At the same moment he reached to open it for her, but in her rush to get away from him, she misjudged the short step outside and turned her ankle. Excruciating pain shot up her leg. She steadied herself by desperately grasping the doorknob.

Furious with herself, she turned her anger on Matt Dawson, who reached out to support her while she wobbled on one foot.

"Don't touch me!" she said with deadly calm, glaring at him. "If you do, I'll scream."

Obviously unafraid of her threat, but looking somewhat abashed, he picked her up in his arms. "I'll take you home." Then turning to Dan, he asked, "Do you have a wagon or a buggy around back I could borrow?"

"Oh, no, you won't! Put me down!" She looked beseechingly at Dan. "Couldn't you take me home?"

"I wish I could." Dan shrugged his shoulders in a gesture of helplessness. "But there isn't anyone else to tend the store."

Jauncey thought that a highly unlikely story, and frowned. And to think she had actually liked the man!

"I'll bring the buggy around front," Dan said, hurrying toward the back of the store.

After one glaring look into the dark eyes of her rescuer, she clamped her mouth shut and looked away in defiance, her arms folded tightly across her chest. The moments turned into minutes that seemed like hours to Jauncey. She knew she must be getting heavy, although he never shifted her weight once, but she refused to take pity on him since the entire calamity was all his fault. His suffering didn't amount to one tenth of hers.

"How's your foot? Do you think it's broken?"

Jauncey detected his note of concern. Let him worry, she thought, and refused to answer.

Matt continued to stand on the steps with the door open behind them as several passersby turned to look at them.

"Put me down," she hissed. "People are beginning to stare, and no wonder." She felt foolish as well as embarrassed. This was all she needed, to be associated with a man who frequented bordellos and consorted with saloon girls in broad daylight! "I said, put me down."

"No."

Dan drove up with an old wagon. "This is all that's back there. Sorry." He looked sadly apologetic. "I hope that back wheel doesn't fall off."

"We'll drive slow. Thanks, Dan. I'll have it back shortly." He easily lifted Jauncey into the wagon as though he hadn't been holding her for the last ten minutes.

She grabbed the bench seat, protecting her painful ankle as much as possible, then sat down. She bit back the "thank you" that nearly slipped from her tongue and watched as Matt Dawson walked around the dilapidated wagon. With just two large steps, he climbed in beside her.

Slapping the reins on the backs of the two horses, he called, "Let's go." They responded by moving slowly, their heads hanging down and bobbing slightly.

Jauncey didn't speak. Why should she? He knew where she lived.

He glanced at her once, but she tipped her nose up and looked the other way.

After several unbearable minutes she asked, "Can't you go any faster?"

"Don't want the wheel to fall off, do you?" he

drawled. "It might take a good hour to fix it."

"I could hobble home at this rate," she retorted, "and be there before you."

"I doubt it."

Finally, they pulled up in front of her house. He climbed down and she slid across the seat toward him. There was no use pretending she could climb down alone since her ankle throbbed mercilessly. So placing her hands on his shoulders, she allowed him to grasp her by the waist and lift her. When her good foot touched the ground, she noticed again how tall he was.

"Thank you," she said curtly.

Immediately he scooped her up and carried her to the front door, where she leaned over to turn the doorknob, then pushed the door wide.

"You can put me down now."

He ignored her demand and carried her into the kitchen, where he carefully sat her on a chair. "Let's take a look at your ankle."

Staring at him in disbelief, she asked, "I beg your pardon?"

He reached for her foot, returning her stare. "I said, let me see your ankle."

Instinctively she pulled it back, bumping it on the chair leg. "Ow!"

"Don't be so bullheaded," he said, grasping her gently by the foot.

She closed her eyes, squeezing them tight to keep from exposing the pain she felt. "First you break into my home, then you injure me and now you insult me."

"I apologize for the first," he said, still holding her foot, "but it was an honest mistake. And I didn't injure you." Then he added softly, "But I do feel partly responsible."

Jauncey's eyes flew open.

He looked directly at her and said, "But the last one is a fact. You are bullheaded."

Before she could reply, he pulled off her shoe and examined her ankle, which had already begun to swell.

"Nothing's broken. It's just a sprain, but you'll have to stay off it for a few days."

"Thank you, Dr. Dawson," she said, sliding her foot from his firm hold. No man had ever touched, or for that matter even looked at, her feet before.

"I'll be back in a few days to check on you," he said, standing.

That made her sit up straighter. "I don't think that will be necessary. I can take care of myself."

"I told you I feel partly responsible." He touched the edge of his hat and turned to leave. "I'll be back in a few days," he repeated with emphasis.

When she heard the front door close she let out an exasperated sigh. She should never have gone to town, at least not today. Now look at her. She sighed again, this time out of regret.

Maybe if she propped her foot up and wrapped it in cool cloths, it would feel better. She removed her stocking, blushing to think she had allowed Matt Dawson to touch her so intimately. Well, no one had to know about it.

Hobbling to the sink where Maggie had fresh, clean towels stacked, she pumped water into a bucket and dipped one of the towels into it, then wrung it out. She hobbled back to the nearest chairs to sit on one and prop her pulsating foot on the other. With her skirts to her knee, she wrapped the towel around her ankle.

"What happened?" Sugar asked from the doorway.

"I had a silly accident and sprained my ankle. At least that's what Dr. Dawson said."

Sugar smiled. "Dr. Dawson?"

"Yes. Remember that man who barged into the house my first night here?"

"Matt Dawson. But he's no doctor, he's a big rancher outside of town." Sugar looked puzzled. "Did he tell you he was a doctor?"

"No. Actually, it's a long story. And the end of the story is, he's coming back to check on my ankle in a few days." Jauncey adjusted the cloth. "He has a guilty conscience."

"I see."

But Jauncey didn't think she did. Well, she was too tired to explain it right now. She'd do it later. Maybe.

"How bad is it?" Sugar asked, bending over Jauncey's injured ankle and peeling back the cloth. "Hmm. There's some swelling, but no bruises. You'll have to stay off your feet for a few days."

"I know," she groaned. "And there's so much work to do. We'll never get ready for boarders at this rate." Jauncey frowned, more irritated than before.

"Sure we will," Sugar replied, then asked, "Did Matt bring you home?"

"Yes," Jauncey answered, wondering how well Sugar knew Matt Dawson. He had seemed very familiar with the house that night, and today he

53

knew exactly how to get to the kitchen. And it wasn't because of the smell of food cooking because Maggie was nowhere to be seen. But remembering his open familiarity with the saloon girl, and the spurs upstairs, she wasn't at all surprised to think he'd been a regular customer here.

She immediately forced her mind away from that thought.

"Where's Maggie?" Jauncey asked.

"She's lying down. She isn't feeling well, but she'll be better by this evening."

Sugar sounded as though it wasn't unusual for Maggie to be resting. She was such a strange girl.

"It's past lunchtime," Sugar said. "Just stay where you are and I'll fix us something."

"I don't want to be extra work for you. I can still polish lamps and other things while I'm sitting."

"We'll manage fine. And if you take care of your ankle, you'll be on your feet in no time."

They ate cheese and fresh bread and drank cool tea, not wanting to start a fire in the stove to make a fresh pot. A piece of pie baked with dried apples made a delicious dessert.

Afterward Jauncey leaned on Sugar and hopped into the larger parlor to sit on the cleaned settee.

"Are you comfortable?" Sugar asked.

"Yes, thank you."

"I'm going to look in on Maggie. We'll find something you can do when I come down," she said, and left.

Jauncey surveyed the room with approval. The fringe had been stripped from the heavy drapes, which had been cleaned, and sunshine sparkled through the windows, glinting off the brass lamp reflectors. She sniffed the pleasant scent of beeswax and lemon and felt the satisfaction of a job well done.

This was her favorite room. She loved the large marble fireplace with the equally large rectangular mirror over it. A basket of kindling sat beside the hearth, though she had yet to light a fire. The room was practically empty except for two comfortable chairs across from the settee. She had visions of a large dining room table with straight-backed chairs beneath the tiered crystal chandelier. As she sat admiring it, sunlight shone through the windows, sending prisms of color winking around the room.

The sound of footsteps on the porch drew her attention, and she glanced into the front parlor hoping Sugar was coming down the stairs. But it looked as though she would have to let the caller in herself. And here she was barefoot. Undoubtedly it was Dan bringing her supplies. In that case, he would certainly understand if she didn't come to the door, so she called out, "Please, just let yourself in."

With her feet stretched out before her on the settee, she tucked her skirt under them as best she could, feeling very awkward. Well, she thought, there was simply no help for it.

The door opened wide, revealing a man impeccably dressed from his brown felt hat to his neatly cut suit. His highly polished boots showed not even a speck of dust, and Jauncey wondered how he had managed that. She couldn't envision this man standing on one foot and polishing the other on the calf of his pant leg. In truth, she wasn't sure one foot would support him.

"My name's J.T. Lawrence," the stranger said, tipping his hat but not removing it. "You certainly make a mighty fetching picture, Miss Taylor, perched on the sofa that way. Mighty fetching." His grin stretched across his face, but didn't reach his eyes. "Now tell me, what's this nonsense I hear about you closing the house?" He lowered himself onto a chair opposite her without waiting to be asked, his cold blue eyes boring into hers.

Jauncey felt overwhelmed, and she knew he wanted her to be. She prickled instantly. "Mr. Lawrence, I do not know you, even though you presume to know me. I resent your coming into my home and acting as though you have a personal interest in it. I do not owe you any explanations, so please, let yourself out. Good day." She knew the color rose high in her cheeks, and her indignation stood out plainly. Good, she thought, let him see I mean business.

"My dear woman, it appears you have not been informed of who I am." Raising his eyebrows he tilted his chin down until it nearly touched his chest.

She folded her hands in her lap and forced herself to stay calm. "You have already informed me, Mr. Lawrence, and it matters not one whit." She would not be intimidated by this man, especially in her own home.

Mr. Lawrence puffed through his broad lips. "I see I will have to explain the situation, since the lawyer has failed to do so."

Panic gripped her. If he told her there had been a mistake and this house was not hers, she simply couldn't bear it. This was her only chance to be independent. She hadn't forgotten, nor could she ever forget, that once she'd owned nothing, not the bed she slept in nor the quilt that covered her. She desperately needed this house, wanted this house, even with all its problems. At least it was hers and she didn't need to look to anyone else for help.

She waited, holding her breath in anticipation of his next words.

"You see, my dear, you do not own this house completely. Spicie was indebted to me for a fair amount of money. And you have inherited that debt. She ran a rather high-society parlor house, if one can say that about parlor houses, but she still had difficulty making the payments. So how can you, Miss Taylor, expect to pay off the debt by converting this to a mere boardinghouse?" He leaned back as far as his portly body would allow and smiled.

Jauncey felt as if someone had thrown her against a brick wall. She inhaled with little gasps, and forced herself to focus on a bit of color splashed on the wall by the chandelier, knowing she could not look at him without going completely mad.

"Get out." Her voice was low as she continued to stare at the color on the wall.

For a moment Mr. Lawrence neither moved nor spoke. Then he heaved himself out of the chair. "Perhaps you need some time to see the error you're making. So I'll leave you to ponder the situation. Please, don't get up. I know my way out."

Jauncey continued to sit in stunned silence after the door closed. She wanted to scream. She wanted to throw something. She wanted to cry.

Large tears welled up, causing the bright spot of color on the wall to blur and spread. Then it came back into focus again as the tears spilled down her cheeks.

She couldn't give in, not now when she was so close to having her dream come true. She had so wanted to be in charge of her own life, not consulting anyone, making her own choices and decisions. And it had almost happened.

Matt didn't know why he was sitting there. Spying, he decided, pure and simple. He'd gone to Anderson's Livery to pick up his horse and to meet Charlie, and had found himself looking at the large yellow house more times than he cared to admit in the last thirty minutes.

Where the hell was Charlie anyway?

Feeling restless, Matt stood, lifting one booted foot to rest on the bench outside the wide barn doors. He leaned his elbow on his knee and pushed his hat to the back of his head, irritated with Charlie and himself.

He'd spent more time than he should have at the marshal's office and it had gotten him exactly nowhere. He hadn't really expected to get much cooperation, but he was tired of waiting while his herds of cattle dwindled before his eyes. He was tired of dealing with Johnny, and wanted an end to the whole thing.

His gaze drifted once more to Spicie's place.

"I'll be damned," he said, planting both feet firmly on the ground. He watched as J.T. climbed the steps, wondering what kind of business the banker from Cheyenne had with Miss Taylor.

Whatever it was, he figured, would be underhanded and to J.T.'s advantage. He frowned, thinking about his own experience with him.

Before long J.T. sauntered out the front door and across the porch with a smile plastered all over his face, obviously pleased with the way things had gone.

Matt had known J.T. would be in town soon, making his business rounds like he always did on his regular visits to Laramie. He also knew J.T. would summon him to the little office he rented in the alley behind Second Street. Matt clenched his jaw just thinking about it.

He felt sure that J.T. had a hand in the rustling at the Diamond D ranch, of which Matt was part owner, and Johnny was his only chance to prove it. Or so Johnny said. Matt knew he should never trust a thief, but the law wouldn't help and he was getting desperate. But if Johnny didn't produce some evidence, and soon, he planned to beat him within an inch of his life.

Matt parked himself on the bench in agitation.

"Been waitin' long?" Charlie asked, coming around the side of the stables.

"Where the hell have you been?" Matt got up, hooked one thumb in his belt, and set his hat squarely on his head.

"Been doin' what needed doin'," Charlie answered, removing his dust-covered hat from his graying head. He beat the hat against his leg, then put it back on. "How about you?" he asked, giving Matt a long measured stare.

"It's been a waste of time," he answered as they walked into the livery and saddled their horses.

"J.T.'s in town," Charlie said, drawing up on the cinch.

"I know. He paid a visit to the new boarding-house. I can't help wondering what kind of trouble he's causing Miss Taylor."

Charlie raised his eyebrow at Matt. "Miss Taylor?"

Avoiding Charlie's gaze, he answered casually, "The new owner at Spicie's." He wasn't in the mood to discuss Miss Taylor and the day's events.

"That explains why I saw Lottie working at Sam's. Have you seen her?"

Matt nodded as he led his horse outside. He wasn't in any mood to discuss Lottie either.

They mounted up and rode toward the business section of town. He wanted to stop at Trabing's just in case his shipment of barbed wire had come in since he'd been there that morning. If it had, he'd take it on back to the ranch. He sure as hell wasn't going to waste any more time in town since he hadn't accomplished anything with the marshal.

Then he remembered he'd told Miss Taylor he'd be by to check on her in a few days. Well, he'd have to come back into town if the wire hadn't arrived.

Matt brought his horse to a halt in front of the store. "This will only take a minute."

"Looks like you're wrong about that," Charlie said, inclining his head in the direction behind Matt.

Turning, he saw J.T. walking toward them.

"Good afternoon, gentlemen," he said, barely nodding. "Matt, I'd like to see you in my office."

Resisting the urge to say no, Matt settled for a hard-edged glare.

"Be there in about twenty minutes," J.T. commanded, turning in the direction from which he'd come.

Matt continued to stare at J.T.'s back, wishing he could ignore the pompous bastard, but he couldn't. J.T. wasn't just a banker who had loaned them money. He was half owner of the Diamond D.

Chapter Four

J.T. opened the door to his office and left it ajar. Being situated in the middle of an alley, surrounded by tall buildings, wasn't something he enjoyed. But the rent was cheap, even though he could barely tolerate the confines of the small airless room on a hot summer day.

He tossed his hat onto the nearby table, careful not to let it fall to the floor so he wouldn't have to bend over to pick it up. In this room any exertion was too much.

Seated, he pulled out a sheaf of papers from a desk drawer and thumbed through them, each one representing a debt owed to him personally. Pleased with the progress he'd made during this trip to Laramie, he set aside those papers referring to businesses and individuals he had yet to contact. That stack was small. In the larger stack were those who owed him smaller amounts of money and had required less time to collect from. There were also the ones he considered to be stupid. Except for Miss Taylor, who was simply naive.

He wrote the word "contacted" at the top of the page, blank except for her name. This loan would take some special thought and he looked forward to spending some time thinking about it, and her.

On top of the smaller stack was Matt Dawson's page, and it wasn't empty by a long shot.

Leaning back in his chair and getting as comfortable as possible, he picked up the paper and went over the columns of figures that were meant for his eyes only. One column tallied the numbers of cattle owned by the Diamond D and their worth; another column tallied the numbers of stolen cattle and their worth. His goal was to shift the majority of cattle into the stolen column, his column.

J.T. grinned in satisfaction. Though the process was slow, it was damned effective. He had Matt hotter than a whore on Sunday, trying to put a stop to the rustling. Why he'd even seen him at Marshal Williams's office today, and laughed out loud at that.

If there was one person who wouldn't lift a finger to help Matt, it was Williams. Especially since J.T. had loaned the man a thousand dollars at the lowest interest rate in town to cover a gambling debt. At least it was the lowest rate for now.

J.T. had developed a simple scheme for simple people, and it worked beautifully every time. Once the debtor missed a payment, J.T. simply gave him a new loan at a higher rate of interest. That way the sky was the limit. If worse came to worst, he took their collateral. Either way, he won. And it was all nice and legally done with a binding contract, for those who could read. For those who couldn't . . . well, that wasn't his fault. He wasted little time sympathizing with those who couldn't look out for themselves.

Which brought him back to Miss Taylor.

He picked up the blank page and stared at it, wondering how well she could look after herself.

Matt stood in the doorway and watched as J.T. put his papers together and stuck them in his desk drawer.

"Come in, Matt. Have a seat."

Matt crossed his arms over his chest. "No, thanks. I like the smell of the air out here better."

"Have it your way." J.T. shuffled some papers on his desk until he held one up. "I just thought since I was in town we could go over a few figures. You know I like to keep up on how our ranch is doing." He glanced at Matt, waiting for a response.

"What figures you got in mind?"

J.T. shrugged. "Well, for one, I'm concerned about the loss of cattle. What have you done about the rustling?"

Matt felt his temper rise. When was this man going to realize he wasn't dealing with a dreamer like Matt's father?

"What do you suggest?" Matt asked, leaning casually against the door frame.

"Perhaps you could talk to the marshal. Or even put up some barbed wire."

Matt felt his muscles tighten, just itching to lay into J.T. The bastard knew good and well he had the marshal right where he wanted him, and as far as the wire went, J.T. knew that wasn't foolproof either. "Or maybe I should just start hanging the first ones I get my hands on," Matt said.

J.T. blanched. "Yes, I suppose if all else fails it could come to that. Especially if the law won't come to our aid."

Then, poking one fat finger into an equally fat chin, J.T. asked, "Haven't you caught anyone yet? I mean, this has been going on now for . . . what, three months?"

If I had, Matt thought, you'd be the first to know. But he said nothing; he knew J.T. was baiting him.

"Well, I suppose you're doing all you can," J.T. went on. "After all, it's only to your advantage to catch them. And of course, mine, too."

"Of course." Matt pushed himself away from the door. He'd had enough.

J.T. rose from his chair. "That's all for now. I'll be in town for another day or so. If anything comes up, contact me. Otherwise, I'll be back at the end of the month."

Matt left J.T.'s office more positive than ever that J.T. was rustling from the Diamond D's herds. And it didn't take a genius to figure out why.

Riding out of town, Matt pushed his horse into a gallop and Charlie did the same. As the speed of the horses increased so did Matt's thoughts. He had to stop J.T., or else he'd be as bankrupt as a dried-up gold mine. Then J.T. could easily buy Matt's share and become the sole owner of the Diamond D. One way or another he had to make sure that didn't happen. They slowed their horses to a walk when they passed through the gates and under the overhead sign that read, "Diamond D Ranch." For a moment pride filled Matt as he took in the single-story ranch house, the building for the blacksmith, the barns for the horses, the wagon shop and the bunkhouses. Surrounding the ranch was grazing land that rolled as far as the eye could see in all directions. A narrow band of cottonwoods bordered the banks of the Little Laramie River as it wound its way unhindered across the open land. Then it meandered up behind the buildings before wandering off again.

No, he told himself once more, tightening his jaw, he had worked too hard to build this ranch, and he wasn't about to lose it.

When they reached one of the barns they were greeted by Will.

"Johnny's been lookin' for you, Mr. Dawson," the sandy-haired young man said, reaching for the reins of Matt's horse.

"Thanks, Will," Matt said. "Let's go up to the house first, Charlie." Johnny could wait. There were a couple of ideas Matt needed to talk over with Charlie, whom he trusted and relied on, before bringing Johnny in on them.

"Take a look," Charlie said, jerking his head toward the rear of the barn. "Your sister's here."

Matt glanced around the barn for Sarah's roan mare. Sure enough, there stood the mild-mannered horse, so unlike her owner, who was neither mild-mannered nor able to stand still.

Matt walked across the dry and dusty yard, a half grin on his face, while Charlie lagged several steps behind.

They entered the house, which was built in the

fashion of a dogtrot cabin, but on a larger scale with a moderate-sized kitchen at the back. A wide center hallway allowed a free flow of air to circulate through the four bedrooms on one side of the hallway and the sitting room and office on the other. Lately the house had seemed bigger and lonelier to Matt, so he'd spent less time indoors and more time on the range.

Almost at the same instant that he closed the door, Sarah appeared in the kitchen doorway, dark as a thundercloud. She wiped her hands on her once-white apron.

"I declare, Matthew Dawson," she said, her tone threatening, "I'm going to have to come over here more often than I do. It looks as though you let the cattle run through this house." Sarah bent her head as though searching for evidence to support her accusation.

Matt smiled. Sarah knew he always scraped his shoes outside. She also knew he did it for her. Although she had a home and family of her own a few miles to the north, Sarah loved this ranch as much as he did, and had made it her personal goal to keep him and the ranch in order.

"Hello, Sarah," he said, leaning down to kiss her cheek where a dark shiny strand of her hair had stuck.

"There's no use trying to butter me up. You know I've got something to say." She pointed a wadded-up rag at him. "And you're going to listen."

Matt followed her into the kitchen and sat on the edge of the sturdy table. He tipped his hat back, patiently waiting for another lecture. Behind him, Charlie shuffled his feet.

"I see Johnny What's-his-name is still here. Matt, I don't like him. Jeff says he's up to no good and worse."

Matt watched her fists clench at her sides. Sarah stood at least ten inches shorter than he, but size had never mattered much to her. Neither did the fact that he was five years her elder. Sarah had long ago put herself in charge of Matt's life. He figured it was her way of making up for the loss of their mother. Somehow the satisfaction she'd gotten out of mothering him more than tipped the scales for her.

Matt waited for her to go on.

"Jeff says you should watch your back whenever Johnny's around, and especially when he isn't." Sarah's snapping dark eyes melted to a warm brown with concern for him. "Get rid of him, Matt," she pleaded.

He knew she was worried and she meant well. So did his brother-in-law. But Jeff and Sarah had a family of their own to look after, and he would not involve them in his problems.

"Sarah," Matt said, grinning. "What smells so good?"

Exasperated, she flung her dust rag at him. "What am I going to do with you?"

"Feed me?" he teased, with a wink.

"Be serious!"

Matt lifted himself from the table and with his hands on her shoulders, kissed her forehead. "You and Jeff worry too much."

Sarah flapped her arms in defeat. "I give up."

But he knew she didn't mean it. She was simply trying a different tactic. Her mother-hen ways had always amused him, and he waited for whatever was coming next.

"Some no-good cowboy is going to kill my only brother while he calmly goes about his business." Sarah brushed him aside and removed a pan of biscuits from the oven, then stirred the thick brown stew bubbling on top of the stove. "But does he care? No!" With her back to Matt and Charlie, she continued talking to herself. "And what about the ranch? Does he care?"

"Yes," Matt answered for her, dead serious.

Sarah stopped stirring and turned to face him.

"I know you do." She laid her hand on his arm. "Even more than Pa did. This ranch wouldn't be half what it is if it weren't for you." Once more her eyes pleaded. "Get rid of him, Matt."

"Not yet."

Sarah rolled her eyes. "Sit down and eat," she ordered, shaking her head.

Matt and Charlie hung their hats on the pegs at the back door while Sarah dished up two plates and poured three cups of coffee. She pulled up a chair beside them and sipped her coffee while they ate.

"You know who's to blame for this mess?" She voiced the question more as a statement of fact.

Matt stopped chewing and frowned at his plate. He certainly did.

"Matthew Dawson!" She skewered him with her gaze. "I'm not talking about Pa. And you've got to stop blaming him for being so . . . trusting. He didn't realize where this would all lead, or he never would have gone to J.T. in the first place."

Trusting? Matt thought. Grant Dawson had been

an idealist. He had based his life and business on dreams, not reality. And reality, Matt knew, consisted of hard work and logical thinking. But in Grant's case, he had left all the logical thinking to J.T. Well, not anymore. Matt stabbed a chunk of beef with his fork. He didn't view life in the same easygoing way his father had.

Evidently, realizing the subject was closed, Sarah sipped her coffee as she related her family's doings. When she finished, Matt pushed back his chair and stood.

"Charlie and I have work to do. Thanks for coming over." He kissed the top of her head and walked down the hall toward his office.

Inside his office, Matt sat at the large desk while Charlie settled into a leather cushioned chair.

The room suggested the presence of Matt's father, from the tall bookcases filled with volumes of leather-bound books to the wine-red softness of the chairs. But it also spoke of Matt's influence, with well-kept ledgers standing alongside the books.

Swiveling his chair to face Charlie, Matt said, "I've got an idea but I want to hear what you think about it."

Charlie slouched and nodded.

"We've got to put some pressure on Johnny," Matt said, keeping his voice low, "or else he's going to keep both hands in the till for as long as it suits him. It's easy to see J.T. plans on continuing to pay him as an informer as long as Johnny tells him what we're doing with the cattle. Which means we're stuck with him."

"I see your point, Matt." Charlie nodded again.

"But how are you going to know when and where J.T. plans to do his thievin' if it doesn't come from Johnny? I know he's been practically worthless, but can you take a chance on what would happen without him?"

"That's what he's been counting on, and it's time we put an end to it. I'm tired of paying him wages for nothing." Matt leaned forward with his legs spread wide, his elbows on his knees, and his fingers laced loosely together. "We've got to set a trap for Johnny and J.T."

"Now you're talkin'." Charlie smiled. "Do you mean, maybe, give him some false information?"

"Exactly." Matt leaned back in his chair, feeling more in control of the situation than he had in months.

Chapter Five

It had been two days since Jauncey sprained her ankle, and she could no more stay off it than she could control her thoughts about Matt Dawson. Mercilessly, his devil-may-care attitude and chivalrous, albeit unwelcome, actions crept into her thoughts while she polished lamps and cleaned the chimneys. And when she waxed the mahogany railing on the stairs, she remembered the way he'd carried her across the parlor so effortlessly. And today, all the same thoughts plagued her again and again.

Forcing her attention to the task at hand, she tugged at the drapes in the entrance parlor without luck. Then standing back, she glared at the hook where it protruded from the top of the window frame. Sugar had taken one pair down without any problem at all by simply using the ladder.

Speculatively, Jauncey eyed it on the front porch. Her ankle didn't throb anymore, she reasoned, even though it hurt some to put her full weight on it for very long. Yet she was determined not to call Sugar from her work, so she dragged the ladder in off the porch and positioned it in front of the tall window.

Without hesitation she climbed the ladder, ignoring the tiny sparks of pain. Thank goodness she could reach the hook, she thought, without going clear to the top. With a hard tug, the drapes tumbled to the floor, and a light dust cloud drifted up, making her sneeze.

"I see you're getting around as good as new," a voice said from the doorway beside her.

Jauncey swung around, nearly losing her balance. She grabbed for the window frame while Matt Dawson grabbed the ladder with both hands.

"Whoa, there! You'd better come down before you fall down."

Immediately bristling, she replied, "It appears to me that accidents, and near accidents, only happen when you're around." She stood clutching the wall, wondering how she could come down the ladder in a ladylike fashion with him watching her.

"Why do you suppose that is?" he asked, grinning.

Distracted enough by her predicament, Jauncey decided she could do without his teasing. Gingerly she placed her foot on the next rung below, completely ignoring his question. When she reached the bottom, he still held the ladder, one hand on each side of her.

73

"You can let go now," she said, still facing the wall, her cheeks flushed.

Slowly, he released the ladder. "I see your foot is mending."

"And quite well, thank you."

"Well, let's have a look just to be sure," he said, pulling up a chair for her.

She stared at him. "I beg your pardon?"

"I want to see for myself. You looked as if you were in pain when you came down the ladder."

"Are you calling me a liar? I'm perfectly capable of telling when I'm well and when I'm not." He was definitely going too far, and she didn't mind telling him so.

"I think you might stretch the truth, but I doubt if you'd lie."

He said the last with such conviction that she let her indignation fade a little.

"You're just bullheaded," he said with a wink.

Jauncey stiffened, her indignation returning in full force. She searched her mind for a fitting retort.

"Don't get so riled. That wasn't meant as an insult." Gently, he pushed her into the chair and knelt before her.

"Just how did you mean it, if not as an insult?" she asked, tucking her sore foot deeper into the folds of her skirt.

He pushed his hat to the back of his head and looked into her eyes. "I just mean you're stubborn. That can be good, sometimes."

She didn't believe stubborn was good anytime, especially when applied to her.

"Let me take a look at your ankle." He leaned

74

toward her, reaching to grasp her foot.

"No," she said. If he wanted stubbornness, he'd get it.

He rested his arm on his knee.

"I told you, I'm quite well. You'll have to take my word for it." She smiled a little smugly. He would have to grab her foot forcefully, and she was sure now he wouldn't do that.

He continued staring at her, a frown settling between his dark brows.

"All right," he said, swinging out of her way to give her room. "But I want to see you walk across the room."

"I will not!" Heat flooded her cheeks at the idea of putting herself on such display.

"I only want to look at your feet." His smile was a little higher on one side, giving the effect of laughing at her.

The man was impossible, she decided.

"Then will you leave?" she asked, standing. Sitting had rested her ankle somewhat, so she felt confident she could walk without a limp.

"Yes," he said, sitting back on his haunches.

Jauncey walked four steps, then turned around. "Satisfied?" she asked, raising her eyebrow.

"You're faking."

"I am not! It feels fine. Now if you'll excuse me, I have work to do." Jauncey stood beside the door waiting for him to leave.

He rose slowly to his feet and paused beside her. Jauncey's heart increased a beat when he stood looking down at her. Neither of them said anything for a moment.

"You know you're wasting your time on this

house," he said quietly. "Why don't you just sell it?"

"That is none of your business." She glared at him. He was more of a busybody than old Mrs. Lange, Aunt Ida's neighbor. It had been difficult to be unkind to Mrs. Lange, but she would have no trouble telling Matt Dawson to mind his own business.

"Hello, Matt," Sugar called, suddenly appearing in the kitchen doorway, her eyes twinkling. "Making a doctor's call?"

"Something like that," he said, returning her smile. "But I'm afraid she isn't a very good patient."

"And you're not really a doctor," Jauncey put in. "I can take care of my own problems, thank you."

"We'll just have to wait and see," he said, his gaze penetrating hers. She had the uncanny feeling he wasn't referring to her ankle. Then he went on. "I'd better be going. Charlie will be looking for me." He touched his hat, nodded to her and Sugar, then left.

Jauncey watched his long even strides as he walked down the street.

"Did he do something to irritate you?" Sugar, asked. "That's not like Matt. He's usually pretty easygoing. And quiet, too."

"Really? You could have fooled me. I'd say he has a tendency to think that his opinion is worth its weight in gold. I don't happen to agree." Jauncey limped to the chair where she'd been sitting. "And I told him so."

"I see. And how is the patient doing?" Sugar asked.

Jauncey gave her a sideways glance, trying to judge her remark, but Sugar only smiled.

"Not as good as I let on, I'm afraid." Jauncey grimaced as she sat in the chair. "I planned a trip to the newspaper to place an advertisement. I suppose it will have to wait until tomorrow."

"At least that long, I'd say. Why don't we get you up to your room? Matt's right, you haven't been off that foot long enough for it to heal."

Sugar helped Jauncey upstairs, getting her settled on the bed.

"How big is Mr. Dawson's ranch? It seems he spends a lot of time in town away from it," Jauncey said, resting her foot carefully on the quilt.

"It's a big spread, but the ranch house is only ten miles or so out of town. So I suppose coming into town isn't too much of a problem."

"Do you know him very well?" Jauncey removed the shoe from her foot and let it slide to the floor. She didn't miss the pause before Sugar spoke.

"Not really." Sugar turned to leave. "I'll bring up something for you to eat so you won't have to walk downstairs."

Sorry that she'd asked about Matt Dawson, Jauncey tried to pretend she wasn't really interested. "Thanks for your help. I'm sure I'll be much better tomorrow."

Better or not, she had to go to town tomorrow, she decided. It was important that she advertise her boardinghouse soon, but more than that, she felt almost desperate to see Mr. Collins, the lawyer. Her sprained ankle had trapped her in more ways than one. Not only was she unable to get as much accomplished as she had hoped, but J.T.'s visit had given rise to a panic she wasn't able to squelch. And if she didn't get something settled soon, she would go out of her mind.

Another sleepless night stretched before her.

Early the next morning, Jauncey flung the covers back to examine her ankle. No swelling. But then there had been very little yesterday. Carefully she put her feet on the floor and stood up. Her heart lifted. Nothing, not even a twinge! Maybe things would go right today. At least it was a good beginning, she thought.

She gave special attention to her clothing, making sure she appeared as much like a businesswoman as possible. Fussing with a few errant curls, she went over in her mind what she would say to Mr. Collins. He had certainly been wrong not telling her that the house was a bordello, not to mention that she was deeply in debt.

Adding an extra pin to the thick knot in her hair, she wondered what she would have done if she'd known the truth. She paused with her hand in midair. She couldn't honestly say.

Satisfied at last, Jauncey arrived downstairs to be greeted by the smell of frying bacon and pancakes.

"You're walking much better this morning," Sugar said, setting the table.

"If I'm careful, and I intend to be, this ankle shouldn't give me any more trouble," Jauncey replied.

After breakfast, Sugar left to resume cleaning the house and Jauncey sat at the long table watching Maggie. Maggie moved soundlessly from the stove to the table, and back again.

"Let me clean up this morning," Jauncey said. "It isn't right that you always do the cooking and cleaning up." Jauncey picked up the dishes and the silverware.

"No. Thank you. It's my job and I like to do it." Maggie gave her a sideways glance, then returned to the stove.

"It doesn't have to be your job, Maggie. I never meant for any of us to do one job all by ourselves." Jauncey spoke softly, sincerely.

"I know you didn't. Spicie gave me this job. She told me I was in charge of all the work in the kitchen."

"You mean you're the one who kept all of this so spotless?" Jauncey lifted her hand to include the windows, cupboards and hardwood floors.

"Yes." Maggie smiled timidly.

"You mean you didn't . . ." Jauncey flushed, surprised at what she'd almost said.

"No, I didn't." Maggie faced Jauncey, her back to the huge stove. Her shoulders straightened a little, causing a lock of golden hair to fall forward.

Jauncey felt her face turn even warmer, but she didn't look away from Maggie. "I'm sorry, I shouldn't have asked."

"I don't mind. Most people think that's why I'm here." Maggie paused briefly, then continued in a rush. "But it hasn't always been that way." She turned away suddenly, closing Jauncey out once again.

Jauncey would have liked to reach out to Maggie in reassurance—for what, she wasn't sure. But she knew any gesture from her wouldn't be welcome.

So instead she said, "It was a delicious breakfast, Maggie." Then she quickly went on to say, "I guess I'll go on over to the newspaper office."

Maggie continued scraping pans, paying no attention to her.

Leaving Maggie to her domain, Jauncey puzzled over the things she'd said. What had the young girl meant by "it hasn't always been that way"? And why did Maggie keep herself so emotionally guarded, as though she protected an inner secret door? Knowing that door was locked especially against her, Jauncey forced herself to concentrate on her task and to leave Maggie to Sugar.

She walked the short distance to the *Laramie Sentinel*, bracing herself outside the door before pushing it open. This was the first step, an important first step, too. She would announce to one and all that her house was indeed a boardinghouse.

Inside, the pungent but not altogether unpleasant smell of ink and oiled machinery surrounded her instantly. A few customers formed a line of sorts, while others gathered to pass the time talking about the unusually warm weather. Dismay enveloped her; they were all men.

"It's goin' to be a dry summer for sure," one old-timer said to the others while craning his neck to glance at Jauncey. "That means we're sure as hell . . . excuse me, ma'am . . . in for an early blizzard."

She shifted uncomfortably when the old man looked at her.

"No," another gentleman, wearing a tailored suit, countered, "I don't agree. We had our bad winter last year. We won't be getting another one for quite a spell." He smiled politely at Jauncey.

The old-timer snorted. "Hell . . . pardon me, ma'am." He glanced apologetically at Jauncey again. "That warn't no bad 'un. You talk about a real toe-freezer, then you're talkin' about back in seventy-one and seventy-two." The old man squared off a shot at the nearest spittoon, making it ring with accuracy. Jauncey gritted her teeth and swallowed hard. "That was one of the worst winters, and we're about due for another."

It appeared as a challenge to the others, one they couldn't seem to resist. The debate continued until Jauncey nearly gave up hope of being waited on.

Then finally the man behind the counter spoke. "You gentlemen won't mind waiting"—he looked at them pointedly—"while I wait on this young woman."

Everyone stepped aside and the old-timer said, "Sure, Harvey. Don't mind a bit."

"How may I help you?" Harvey smiled, showing tiny wrinkles at the outer edges of his brown eyes.

"I'd like to place an advertisement in your paper for my boardinghouse," Jauncey said. Instinctively, she knew several pairs of eyes swiveled in her direction and the room became suddenly quiet.

"Certainly. And what is the name of your boardinghouse and the street address?"

"Miss Taylor's and it's on South C." Jauncey had a picture in her mind of the men standing behind her with their mouths hanging open and their eyes burning holes into her back. She could practically feel the heat.

"South C Street," he repeated.

Melody Morgan

The spittoon rang with the clarity of a church bell.

"And you have rooms to rent." Harvey's pen scratched loudly across the piece of paper. "And what size ad would you like?" He pulled a copy of the *Sentinel* from under a pile of papers and pointed to several ads as examples.

"This one," she said, selecting an average-sized ad. She had to be concerned about the price, at least until she had one paying boarder. "How much will that be?"

He gave the price, and she told him to run it for a month. After she paid him, she turned to confront the men who had listened to her entire business transaction.

Well, Jauncey, she told herself, you had better get used to the stares, at least for a while. Changing the reputation of her house wouldn't happen overnight. Even though she knew that, it still galled her to think she had to prove herself.

Jauncey held her head high, glancing neither right nor left as she walked through the small crowd. "Good day, gentlemen," she said, closing the door behind her.

She left the building and crossed the street while each step on the boardwalk echoed her humiliation. She didn't like being scrutinized, for any reason. It was degrading. And unfair. Her energy increased with each step she took. She could give the credit for her situation to her aunt, and to Mr. Collins. Why couldn't the woman have run a respectable boardinghouse in the first place? But no, she had to own a whorehouse and leave it full of whores!

Jauncey marched up to the door with "Andrew B. Collins, Attorney" painted in bold black letters on the glass, and shoved it open. A single large desk, two straight chairs, and a wall of books occupied the room. The smell of leather permeated the air.

"Mr. Collins," Jauncey called to the startled little man who had been studying the bookshelf. ·

"M-M-Miss Taylor, what a surprise."

Even now, Jauncey noted, he looked as much like a skinny Rhode Island Red hen as he had when he'd perched on Aunt Ida's settee. It was impossible to look at him without wondering where the feathers were. His eyes protruded from his small face and his head was topped with a thatch of red hair. His large Adam's apple bounced nervously up and down.

"What c-c-can I do for you?" He moved from the books to stand behind his desk. "Please. Sit down."

Jauncey ignored the invitation. "What other information have you withheld from me, Mr. Collins, beside the fact that I now own a brothel *complete* with women?" She circled the desk, advancing toward him until he fell into his chair.

"Nothing else. I mean, there isn't anything else. Really." He swallowed hard and his Adam's apple jumped convulsively. "Really," he squeaked.

"Are you sure, Mr. Collins?" Jauncey skewered him with her eyes. "What about a Mr. J.T. Lawrence?"

Mr. Collins pressed back into the depths of the soft chair. "W-What about him?"

"Do I owe him a debt made by my aunt?"

"Let me look at the papers. If you'll just give me a little room . . ."

Jauncey backed up, allowing him space to search through a neatly filed drawer.

"Yes, as a matter of fact . . . you do." He glanced up apologetically at her, his Adam's apple still bobbing.

"Does that give him the right to tell me how to run my business?" An unbidden note of dread crept into her voice.

"Not really. J.T. may want you to think he can bully you into doing things his way, but as long as you make the payments, he can't do anything. Legally."

Relief flooded through her, almost making her weak.

"Sit down, please, Miss Taylor." He smiled entreatingly at her. "Please. I'd like to try to explain."

Jauncey looked at him sharply. She wondered if she could trust what he might have to say. But actually it was the things he didn't say that worried her the most. But deciding she had little choice but to hear him out, she sat stiffly in the chair across the desk from him.

"I know I wasn't completely honest with you, and I'm sorry for that," he said. "Believe me, I've spent many sleepless nights thinking about you and your situation." He fingered the edge of a piece of paper.

"No more than I have, Mr. Collins," Jauncey said, unwilling to accept his apology and assuage his guilty conscience.

"I understand your reservations about anything

I may have to say. But in all honesty, I couldn't bring myself to tell you the truth when I'd finally found you at your Aunt Ida's house." He squirmed uncomfortably on his seat before he continued. "I-I-I could see right away that you were a lady of delicate upbringing and I simply didn't know how to tell you about the brothel"—his eyes wandered away from her—"or Spicie." His ears turned fire red.

"I sympathize with your situation, Mr. Collins," Jauncey said, forcing herself to relent a little in hopes of obtaining more information. "But finding out about the house and my aunt the way I did gave me quite a shock. Surely, you must have known that would happen. You should have been more professional and straightforward."

"Of course, you're right. It's just that it was so ludicrous that you could have an aunt who was a . . . madam." He spoke the word in a whisper.

"It is to me, too." Now it was Jauncey's turn to feel the warmth of embarrassment in her cheeks. "I'm turning the house into a boardinghouse."

"So I've heard. You're to be congratulated for doing our community such a service. Pay no attention to what people say," he said, smiling at her with outright respect and admiration on his face, and even a little infatuation.

"What people?" So everyone *was* talking about her.

"Now don't you worry about that. When they see your intentions they will heartily approve."

"Just what has been said, and who has been saying it?" She didn't know why she should be so angry. After all, she didn't know anyone in Laramie besides Maggie and Sugar. And Matt Dawson.

Mr. Collins fell silent, but Jauncey saw his jaw harden, showing an intense dislike.

"J.T. Lawrence!" Jauncey practically hissed the name. "I will not allow that pompous man to take anything away from me! Not my home or my business." She was on her feet, pacing before the desk. "How much is the debt I owe to his bank?" Jauncey placed both hands on his desk and held her breath.

"You don't owe it to any bank. It was a personal loan." He looked at the papers, then quietly said, "Five thousand dollars."

Jauncey practically collapsed into her chair. "Five thousand?" she whispered. "It may as well be a million."

"The monthly payments are two hundred dollars. For four years." Mr. Collins's words came to her as though through a haze.

"How can I possibly pay it off?" The hopelessness of her situation nearly brought her to tears.

"Part of it is paid. You only have three and a half years to go." He smiled weakly at her. "I know that's little consolation."

"How could my aunt have managed payments on such a large debt? Why did she agree to it?" Jauncey stared at him, hoping for an answer.

"Spicie would have had no trouble making payments. Her income was quite high since her, uh, clientele were well-to-do. J.T. helped out in that area."

"What did she spend the money on, for heaven's sake! Gold chamber pots?" She watched his ears redden again.

"No. At least, I don't think so." He ran a finger inside his high collar, inching his Adam's apple up a notch. "She imported things. Like the crystal chandelier, the wallpaper and carpets."

"And left me with the bill! Why me? Why not one of her 'ladies of the night'? Just because I'm her only living relative didn't mean I would want it!" But she did want it. At least she wanted the house.

"Miss Taylor, you're working yourself into a state. Please, calm down." He half rose from his chair, reaching across the desk toward her in an attempt to comfort her. "You need to consider a plan of action, and you won't be able to do that in this condition."

She clutched her hands together. "You're right. What counts now is that I'm already in this mess. How I got here doesn't really matter." But would she ever get out of it?

"I want to offer my professional services, free of charge."

She could only stare at him.

"It's the least I can do. And it will help me sleep at night." He smiled at her, and she began to feel as though she had a friend. She smiled back, and noticed how little he really did look like a chicken after all.

"I accept your offer."

"The first thing we'll do is keep J.T. from making visits to your home. I will take your payments to him personally so you won't have to deal directly with him."

"How long do I have before the next payment is due?" She prayed she had time to get some boarders.

"About a month."

She had to get home to do some calculating and draw up a budget. She extended her hand, and Mr. Collins took it in a warm grasp. "You can't give up yet, Miss Taylor."

Jauncey only smiled. She didn't want to give up, but how was she going to win this one? All the odds were against her, and nothing was in her favor.

Chapter Six

Jauncey struggled for days with the idea of telling Sugar about her financial situation as the meager amount of money her mother had left her was dwindling. Even if she had never spent a dime of it, it had hardly been enough to put even a dent in her aunt's loan. But what purpose would it serve to spread her depression to anyone else? She had to work this out alone. And since the only thing that alleviated her frustration was work, she immersed herself in it.

"Well, I think it's time to go into my aunt's room," Jauncey said, finishing the last of her morning coffee. "What do you say?"

Setting aside her own cup, Sugar rose, nodding.

On their way through the front parlor, Jauncey glanced around, pleased with the way everything sparkled.

Once upstairs, Jauncey stood inside the large

room and surveyed its contents. Apparently, nothing had been touched since Spicie's death. Even the bed was unmade.

Sugar walked to it and tugged carefully at the lacy white coverlet tangled at the foot. "Spicie was always neat. I know the rest of the house didn't show it, but it's true. When she became ill, Maggie and I spent most of our time either in this room or in the kitchen." Sugar pulled the sheets off. "That's when Ruby took over the house. At that time there were more girls, but they gradually left. Nobody cared to work for Ruby." Sugar piled the bedclothes near the door and stood before Jauncey. "Spicie was a good woman. She understood people, and they liked her."

Jauncey sensed Sugar's need to defend Spicie, so she kept her thoughts to herself. During the time Jauncey had been there, they'd talked very little about her aunt, and not at all about the life she'd lived, which suited Jauncey just fine.

But her curiosity about Sugar had steadily increased. As she watched Sugar open drawers and remove underclothing and small boxes of jewelry, thoughts of the other women who had also lived here suddenly crowded in.

Gathering her courage, she asked, "What's your real name?" Jauncey prepared herself for . . . what? A cool rebuke? Perhaps a quiet dismissal? She wished now she hadn't asked.

Sugar stared at Jauncey a long time before she answered softly. "Virginia. My family called me Ginny." Then she turned away before Jauncey could see anything more than the usual cool exterior Sugar always presented.

"May I call you Ginny? I think it fits you very well."

The other woman turned to face her again, and for the first time a myriad of emotions crossed her features. "I'd like that."

A movement at the door drew their attention.

"What's going on in here?" Maggie entered the room, her voice pitched higher with each word she spoke. "What are you doing?"

"Ginny and I are cleaning the room to get it ready for boarders," Jauncey said as she watched Maggie rush to Ginny's side.

"Sugar, who is she talking about and what is she doing?"

"She's talking about me. Remember? I told you my real name is Ginny." She patted Maggie's hand and led her to the bed to sit down.

"Sugar, you can't let her take these things out of here," Maggie whispered, but not low enough that Jauncey couldn't hear.

"We have to take them out," Ginny replied gently. "If you don't want to help, you don't have to. Why don't you fix yourself a cup of tea and sit on the back steps?"

"Maggie?" Jauncey asked. "Would you like to keep something of my aunt's? You may choose anything you want."

Her large blue eyes fastened on Jauncey.

"Anything," Jauncey repeated.

Maggie rose from the bed and walked to the dressing table, where she opened a small music box. Jauncey watched while she inserted a key and wound it. A lullaby with a familiar refrain tinkled and chimed in the silent room.

From inside the box Maggie took a gold necklace with an amethyst and held it up to her neck. She looked into the mirror above the table, then at Jauncey.

"It's beautiful," Jauncey said. "Would you like to keep it?"

"And the music box, too?" Maggie asked.

"Of course. They're yours. I'll hook the necklace for you," she offered carefully.

"No. I don't want to wear it. Not just yet." Maggie walked toward the door, then turned around. "Thank you."

"I'm sure she would have wanted you to have it," Jauncey said.

After Maggie left the room, Jauncey knew Ginny wouldn't discuss the young girl's apparent problem, so she said nothing. Uncomfortably aware that they hadn't built that kind of a friendship, Jauncey returned her attention to the task at hand.

"I have no idea what to do with all of these things," Jauncey said, staring at the dressers and tables loaded with personal objects.

"I know Spicie kept some of her things up in the attic," Ginny answered. "The stairs are behind the door at the end of the hall next to your room."

"Well, I guess it's the only thing we can do. There isn't any family besides myself and I can't imagine anybody who would really want . . ." Jauncey stopped abruptly, glancing at Ginny. "I just meant that she was . . ." Her voice trailed off and the silence deepened. She didn't know what else to say. She'd spoken the truth. She certainly wouldn't pretend her aunt had been the lady her own mother had been. It was inconceivable they'd even been sisters.

"I'm sorry, Ginny, I know you cared for her." Jauncey honestly hadn't meant to be hurtful.

"It's all right. You never knew her. She didn't even exist for you until a month ago." Ginny started piling dresses from the wardrobe onto the bed.

No, thought Jauncey, Mother had certainly kept that secret very well hidden.

She turned to her aunt's dressing table, gathering a hairbrush, a small glass jar with hairpins, an ivory-handled mirror and two cut-glass perfume bottles into the fullness of her skirts. Jauncey stared at them. Undoubtedly they were imported and very expensive. And so very personal. She tried without success to ignore the uneasiness that surrounded her by just being in this room. Actually, all the bedrooms unsettled her. Once more she forced her thoughts to return to her task.

"Ginny, why don't you carry the jewelry chest and we'll go upstairs to look around first. There's no point in carrying too many things until we know for sure where to put them."

Ginny agreed and led the way.

Jauncey followed her down the hall and around a corner, holding her skirts carefully so none of the items would fall out. A window at the top of the steps lit their way up the enclosed staircase. Dust motes skittered along the floor and through the air when Ginny turned at the top of the stairs and into the attic. Up here the ceiling hung low where no real interior walls existed, only sections created by the dormered windows.

One window overlooked the front porch, and

sunlight filtered through the small colored squares of glass surrounding the larger clear center pane, casting a myriad of colors across a worn piece of carpet. A large broken mirror leaned against one wall, and beside it was a trunk.

Jauncey took her aunt's belongings from her skirts and placed them on the floor. She lifted the heavy lid, finding it almost filled with dresses, a small wooden chest and a picture album.

"I think I can fit all of this in here," she called to Ginny, "but there isn't room for anything else." She laid the comb, brush and mirror in the folds of the dresses and tucked the perfume bottles as well as the jar of hairpins into the corners.

"There's another trunk over here that's practically empty," Ginny called over her shoulder from another dormer. "We could put her clothes in it."

Jauncey didn't answer, but knelt on the carpet before the open trunk and lifted the album. She saw underneath it a framed picture no larger than the palm of her hand with two smiling young girls in it. She stared at it for a long time. She couldn't mistake her mother, who must have been seventeen or eighteen years old, but there were two images of her mother in the picture. Jauncey moved closer to the window. Identical twins! The picture was of her mother and her aunt.

How disconcerting to think that the woman who had lived in this house had looked exactly like Maybelle Taylor. Immediately, her mind went back to the first day she'd walked into the parlor and seen the nude painting. She had not associated the likeness with her mother, probably because of the lewd pose. Well, she thought, this picture

94

explained why Jauncey so strongly resembled her aunt. She replaced the picture in the depression in the clothes where it had rested for so long. Jauncey glanced with disinterest at the picture album and put it on top of the picture, then closed the lid of the trunk with finality. She didn't want to know the woman her mother had avoided for all these years.

"Did you find something?" Ginny asked, walking toward her.

"Nothing important," Jauncey answered. "I think there's plenty of room up here for everything in my aunt's room and anything else we don't want." She tried to keep the hardness from her voice, but wasn't at all successful.

Glancing around the attic with attempted casual interest, she asked, "What happened to the large painting that was in the parlor?"

"You mean the one of Spicie?" Ginny asked.

Jauncey nodded without looking directly at her.

"Maggie and I brought it up here. I didn't think it was appropriate for your boardinghouse."

Jauncey glanced at Ginny. "Thank you." She was grateful for the removal of the portrait, but more than anything she appreciated Ginny's understanding. Not once had Ginny defended the house as a brothel or tried to make her feel uncomfortable the way Ruby had.

Following Ginny down the stairs, she wondered what had happened to turn this woman toward such a degrading way of life. The more she got to know Ginny, the less it seemed she could have been like Ruby.

Melody Morgan

For the rest of the day, as they made trip after trip to the attic, the heat became unbearable. Sweat trickled down Jauncey's chemise and between her breasts, soaking the waistband of her cotton work dress and dirty apron. Her legs ached, and she wondered if she'd be able to take another step.

Finally, when they had finished, she and Ginny sat side by side on the edge of Spicie's bed. Jauncey swiped at a curl clinging to her damp forehead. "That attic is suffocating! But I think the worst is over." She ran her sleeve across her cheek.

"It certainly is!" Ginny agreed, wiping her dirty hand across her brow, looking totally exhausted. "If any part of my body could talk, I'm sure it would complain out loud today."

A low rumble similar to the sound of a solitary washboard rattling around in an empty tin tub echoed from the vicinity of Ginny's stomach. They had forgotten their noon meal.

They looked at each other in surprise.

"Are you hungry?" Jauncey asked, smiling.

"All I have to do is smell Maggie's chicken and I'm hungry, even without working my appetite into a state." Ginny sniffed the air. "Mmm."

"Well, what are we waiting for?"

Maggie was an exceptional cook, and Jauncey thoroughly enjoyed sitting down to the already prepared meal.

"You have truly outdone yourself, Maggie." Jauncey eyed the golden-brown chicken, whipped potatoes with thick gravy and steaming bowl of green beans. "All three of us will soon be too round to walk, let alone work."

Easing into her chair, Ginny moaned, "I can barely move." She gave a tired smile. "But it feels so good to work hard again. Spicie always kept a clean house, but she never made any of us girls do it."

The conversation had suddenly taken an uncomfortable turn and Jauncey refrained from comment, filling her plate instead. She did not think as highly of her aunt as the other two women did. Far from it.

"I don't know about you but I'm ready to call it a day. I just want a long soak in a hot tub of water after dinner," Ginny said, taking another bite.

"I have a few things to do yet," Jauncey said. "So why don't you take your bath first. Just leave the fire going so I can heat up some water later."

They finished their meal in easy silence. With each day there had been less strain in the daily ritual of living together. And even though they were a long way from sharing confidences, Jauncey knew the companionship they'd shared earlier had helped bridge the gap.

Still moaning quietly, Ginny got the necessary buckets of water for her bath. Maggie cleared the table without a word, moving around methodically.

With her hand on the small of her back, Jauncey left the kitchen and slowly went up the stairs. There was no doubt Ginny was right. It had been a lot of hard work, almost more than her body could take.

She entered her aunt's nearly bare room. A fresh

coat of wax on the hardwood floor was all that needed to be done. But it would have to wait for another day.

Then she went to her own room and sat in the wooden chair that faced the window to the north. Jauncey rested her hands in her lap, staring at the rooftops and treetops. Her thoughts returned to the home she'd left years ago where she'd lived with her mother and father on the small farm outside St. Louis. They were wonderful memories. Until her father had died. Then his brother, Uncle Harold, had invited her and her mother to move in with his family. Although she knew the invitation had not been any of Aunt Ida's doing, with her selfish, peevish ways, her mother had insisted it was their only choice. And that was where the good memories ended.

Jauncey pushed herself to her feet, trying to ignore the soreness in her back. A tub of hot water would be wonderful, she thought.

Once downstairs, she found the kitchen empty except for Maggie.

"Has Ginny finished?" Jauncey asked.

"Yes." Maggie sat at the large table. "I put some water on for your bath."

"You didn't have to do that," she replied, surprised. "But I'm awfully glad that you did." Jauncey meant it from the bottom of her heart.

"I don't mind." Maggie got up and walked toward the door. "Good night."

"Good night," Jauncey answered with a small smile. She watched Maggie leave, not knowing what to make of the girl. Everything she did surprised Jauncey. But she had noticed that Maggie responded to her more with each kind word. What sort of life had she led to be so frightened of everything? Apparently, her aunt had played an important role in Maggie's life, but how could it have been a positive one? Jauncey couldn't figure it out; her tired mind wouldn't allow it. A bath and bed was as far as she could think.

Chapter Seven

The advertisement had been in the paper for over a week, and Jauncey felt anxious about not having a single boarder yet. Her small amount of money was almost gone and she could not forget about the payment she owed J.T.

She had put off buying a sign declaring that this was indeed a boardinghouse, but perhaps that had been a mistake. If only she could be sure she would have boarders soon, she wouldn't mind parting with a few dollars for a simple sign.

Ginny had helped finish cleaning the last room that morning. Now there was nothing left to do but wait. Jauncey stared out the front door, seeing nothing and feeling miserable.

"Don't give up," Ginny said, walking up behind her.

"I haven't," Jauncey said. "But I'll admit, I am worried." She still wasn't able to confide in Ginny.

She couldn't tell her that she would be devastated if she lost the house and had to live forever with Aunt Ida. She couldn't admit that she wouldn't be able to bear seeing the sympathy once again in the eyes of her aunt's neighbors, hearing them whisper, "The poor dear." And especially, she couldn't reveal that the idea of never again being in control of her own life was unthinkable.

"Maybe you should put up your sign now," Ginny offered.

"It's been on my mind. How much do you think it would cost?"

"You could start with something that isn't fancy. I don't think that would cost very much. Tom Brailey has a place on Front Street. Spicie had one put up a few years ago, but the town made her take it down." Ginny quickly glanced at Jauncey, laying a hand on her shoulder. "I shouldn't have said that. I know you're uncomfortable when I talk about her."

Jauncey didn't know what to say. She was more than uncomfortable. Her dislike for the woman was growing every day.

"I think you're right," Jauncey said. "Now is the time for a new sign." She pushed aside her nagging worry about money. "I may as well quit putting it off and go down there today. The sooner it's up, the better."

Jauncey concentrated on improving her outlook while she prepared to go to town, taking extra care in her appearance by wearing her favorite deep green dress and a serviceable black hat. Both were simple in design, since she had never been given to frills or frippery. The cage-like bustle had seen better days, and would likely see many more. She wore the only pair of good shoes she had, the same ones she'd worn when she'd sprained her ankle. Thank goodness that was nothing more than an unpleasant memory.

Calling good-bye to Ginny and Maggie, she went out the door, her frame of mind already improving.

Jauncey found the sign shop easily. Stacks of signs lined the front of the building and littered a small side path that was obviously unusable. And she thought it curious that no sign at all hung over the door to announce the owner or his establishment.

A tall thin man wearing an apron came through the wide barn-like doors. The sun beat down on his graying disheveled hair, and he squinted happily at her.

"Howdy," he said, sticking his hand out toward her. "My name is Tom Brailey. But everyone calls me Brailey."

She accepted his hand and smiled.

"What kin I do for you, ma'am?"

"Well, I need a sign for—"

He cut her off by holding up both hands. "No, now let me guess." He scratched his chin and quickly looked her over, head to toe. "Gotta be a dressmaker. Right?" He was so genuine and friendly, she didn't take offense at his forwardness.

Jauncey smiled. "Actually, no, I own a—"

"No, now don't tell me." He scratched his ear. "You own a fine restaurant." He grinned, obviously pleased with his choice.

Jauncey laughed. "I'm afraid you're wrong. I own a boardinghouse."

"That was my next guess." He looked sorely disappointed, and she was almost sorry she had spoiled his fun. "I don't get much practice at guessing, since I know most everybody. I suppose that's why I'm not very good at it." His smile was back, wrinkles and all. "Did I josh ya too much?"

"No, not at all," Jauncey said, liking him more as the moments passed.

"Well, come on in and we'll see if we kin fix up a sign just for you." He stopped dead in his tracks and stared at her. "I didn't get your name, miss."

Jauncey felt a chill in spite of the heat. "Taylor. Jauncey Taylor." Did he, too, associate her with Spicie?

"Well, now Jauncey's a right pretty name. Don't believe I've ever heard it before." He placed a hand on her back and ushered her into the cool building. "Might that be Irish?"

"Yes. My grandmother's name was Jauncey Devon," she answered, surprised at how relaxed she felt talking to him.

"Well, she couldn't have been half as pretty as you."

She couldn't believe she was accepting such flattery from a total stranger. And enjoying it, too.

"Let's see now," he said. "What color did you have in mind?"

Jauncey stared in amazement at the colorful array of signs. Some hung from rafter beams, some leaned against the walls, but all of them were beautiful.

"My house is yellow. But I thought I'd just have a

plain black and white sign." It almost seemed like an insult to ask him to do something so . . . bleak.

"What!" he exclaimed, gawking at her, his shaggy eyebrows lifting in alarm. "Oh, no, that'll never do. Not if you have a yellow house," he said, shaking his head, walking around a pile of paint cans. "Something like this, mebbe." He held up a small sign painted yellow with dark green ivy entwined in the corners, the fancy script letters in the same dark green.

Yes, she thought wistfully, that most certainly would do. But out loud she answered, "I'm afraid I can't afford anything as nice as that, at least not right now."

"Hogwash! This here sign don't cost no more than a plain one and it's a sight prettier. What size is your house?"

Jauncey stared at him for a minute. Was he only pretending he didn't know where she lived? At first she'd thought he didn't want to embarrass her. But now she wasn't sure.

"It's very large," she replied.

"Then it would have to suit the house," he spoke to himself. "Not big enough." He rummaged around until he came up with the size he was looking for, then compared the two signs thoughtfully. "Um-hmm. Should work out just fine. Except for one problem."

"What's that?" she asked, knowing that it didn't really matter anyway because she could never afford such a large sign.

"Well, this here sign was bought and paid for, but I never finished it 'cause the fella died. But I could never take money twice for the same sign."

He stood scratching his ear. "It wouldn't be right."

He pondered the situation. "Only fair thing to do is just charge for my time to paint it." He looked at her, obviously pleased with his decision.

"How much would that be?"

"Not more 'n a couple dollars, I'd say."

A lump formed in Jauncey's throat. He was practically giving the sign to her. She didn't know what to say.

"Sure would be a help to me if you'd take it. Give me a clear conscience again. I've felt like a thief ever since the fella's family refused to take it, finished or not. Then they just up and left town without a word."

"Thank you, Brailey," she said, her voice straining around the lump. She reached in her reticule and gave him the money. When she looked up at him, she had a strong desire to hug him, but instead she said again, "Thank you." She gripped his hand warmly, trying to convey her feelings.

"We'll just put 'Miss Taylor's' in fine script across the top, and 'Boardinghouse' underneath in big bold letters. How does that sound?"

This time she could only nod.

"Shouldn't take too long to get 'er done, then I'll bring it right on over." Brailey walked her back into the bright sunshine.

Finding her voice, she said, "I can't tell you how much I appreciate your generosity."

He waved off her words, seeming embarrassed by them.

"Well, I guess I'll be on my way," she said, and turned to walk down the street toward town. A few yards away she turned to wave at him, and couldn't help smiling to see he still watched her.

With her spirits uplifted, almost soaring, she spoke cheerfully to everyone she passed. As she passed the large buildings the wind picked up, making tiny whirlwinds appear in the dusty main street, only to disappear just as quickly. That was how she felt today, she mused, stepping lightly along the boarded walk. Her cares suddenly seemed to vanish into thin air. It was amazing what a little kindness could do when you needed it most.

She passed one shop after another, taking time to look at the displayed goods in the windows, no longer in the mood to go straight home as she'd planned. She ambled along with no particular destination in mind, wanting only to get to know Laramie better, something she hadn't cared about doing until now.

She was glad to have the wind at her back, propelling her down the street and giving her a little relief from the heat.

Pausing in front of a millinery shop, she looked over several hats, one of which caught her eye—a deep green one with only the slightest adornment on it, a perfect match for the dress she was wearing. She thought about the well-worn black one she now had on and couldn't hold back a sigh.

"Now that little hat was made with you in mind."

Jauncey whirled at the sound of J.T.'s voice.

"Of course, it could stand a few extra trinkets on it," he said, standing so close that Jauncey backed up against the window. "But then," he continued, "they would dull in comparison to you."

Jauncey tried withering him with a look.

"There's no reason we can't be on friendlier

terms, Miss Taylor. Just because I hold the deed to your house doesn't mean we can't—"

Jauncey interrupted him as she inhaled sharply. She couldn't speak or run, so complete was her shock.

"You didn't know?" he said, looking surprised. "Now you'd think Mr. Collins would have told you about that since it's mighty important. But maybe your best interests aren't what matters most to him." He smiled in a way that told her he indeed had her best interests at heart. But she wasn't fooled, not for a moment.

"I have nothing to say to you, Mr. Lawrence." She started to walk away, but he grabbed her arm, holding it gently but tightly.

"I think you're mistaken about that, Miss Taylor. I have a suggestion that will be of great help to you and will ease your mind completely." He glanced up and down the street, saying, "But this isn't the place to discuss business. Don't you agree?"

Jauncey stared at him in disbelief. Did he really think she would discuss business of any sort with him?

"I don't think you understand the gravity of the situation. Surely you're not considering talking this over with that spineless lawyer, are you? How many times has he lied to you already?"

Jauncey jerked her arm from his grasp. "He didn't lie! And I'll thank you to stay out of my business!" But she wondered why Mr. Collins had conveniently forgotten to tell her about the deed. Could she really trust him? Maybe she should look after her own best interests, take care of her own business affairs. At least then she'd know what was going on.

"All right, Mr. Lawrence. I'll listen to your suggestion, but I won't make any decision until I've had time to think it over." She stared him straight in the eye, showing him that he didn't frighten her.

He stepped out onto the sidewalk, pointing with his hat. "This way, my dear."

Jauncey walked beside him, keeping an arm's length between them. They walked along Second Street before rounding a corner. About half a block down, they turned into an alley. Jauncey stopped.

"My office faces the alley, as do many others. You have nothing to fear."

She hesitated, looking into the alley. It was narrow and shadowed by the two- and three-storied buildings on each side. At that moment, a woman and two little girls came from a doorway, carrying hat boxes wrapped with ribbons.

"You see?" J.T. said.

Jauncey raised her chin, hoping he would think she hadn't really been concerned, and bravely stepped into the alley. She walked briskly beside him.

The office was small, with the benefit of only one small window, and he had to light a lamp. The interior was furnished luxuriously with oak, leather and brass.

Removing his hat, he indicated a chair for her, then dropped heavily into the oversized chair behind his desk.

"Now then, Miss Taylor, let's get right to the point." He leaned back in his chair in a casual, almost reclining position. "I have something you want, and you have something I want. That is a sound basis for a deal, don't you agree?"

She refused to answer until she had all the facts.

"I suppose you're wondering what it is you have that I would want." He picked up a paperweight, hefted it in his hand, then moved it to the other side of the desk. "Before we discuss that, let's talk about the possibilities. You have very little chance of making the payments if you run the house as a boardinghouse. Even if you were to fill every room, you would have to charge high rates. So the result of that is losing your house to me."

Jauncey went cold in spite of the stifling office. That would not happen, she vowed, whatever it took.

"Another possibility is running the house as a"— he smiled—"bordello the way your aunt did. Needless to say, she found making her payments to me a trifling matter. And so would you." He paused as though to let that sink in, but Jauncey's mind would not accept his words.

"Have you found any of the records she kept on her business? It was very lucrative. I believe she said her earnings for one week were around a thousand dollars."

Jauncey swallowed her gasp.

"So. You see what you're passing up." He sounded coolly detached.

"So far you haven't offered anything that would 'ease my mind completely' as you said earlier. Therefore, I believe I'll be on my way." She stood, reaching for the doorknob.

J.T. stood also. "You haven't heard the final possibility yet."

Jauncey watched him walk around the desk toward her, and with panic mounting, she slowly turned the doorknob.

"You're a very attractive young woman," he said, reaching for a lock of her hair. "So much like Spicie when she was younger." He held the curl and twirled it around his finger. "I could forget the payments. For a few favors, that is. Just a few."

His hot breath felt moist against her face, and she leaned back until her head touched the wall. A scream rose in her throat, but it became trapped.

"I'm only in Laramie twice a month for a few days. My wife's family lives here, and I have business here. But I could mix a little pleasure with my business where you're concerned." He released her hair and ran his hand up and down her sleeve. "I guarantee it could be extremely profitable for you. Then you could run your house any way you wish."

He pinned her against the wall with his bulk while his hand grasped her breast, kneading it. She twisted her head away, and his large soft lips felt sticky against her neck and her stomach rolled with revulsion.

"Stop!" she gasped. "No . . ."

"Don't act so high-and-mighty with me. We both know you and Spicie were cut from the same cloth." He struggled with her hands while she tried to slap and scratch him. "I'm making a deal with you and I just want to seal it with a sample of what I'll be getting," he grunted, tussling with her.

He grabbed her face to hold it still, and she felt her hat slip sideways. His lips ground into hers brutally, and her fear spurred her into twisting and turning and kicking his shins with as much force as her skirts would allow.

"Let go of me!" She gritted the words out since nearly all her breath was being squeezed out of her. "You filthy . . . pig!" Reaching inside his coat as close to his armpit as she could get with her hand, she grabbed a chunk of flesh and pinched with all her might.

"Dammit, woman!" J.T. yowled, jumping back in pain.

Jauncey wasted no time in opening the door. Fresh cool air hit her face, and so did the chest of Matt Dawson. With a defensive motion, she swung her arm, striking him ineffectually in the ribs. She reeled for a moment, partly from surprise and partly from the aftermath of her struggle.

She stared hatefully at the cowboy, her lip curling in disgust, and a new realization struck her. These two were in cahoots! She should have known! So she hauled off and kicked him, too. With her dignity far from being intact, the most she could muster was a withering glare. Then, on the verge of totally disgracing herself by bursting into tears, she fled down the alley as fast as her shaking legs could take her.

Matt watched her run away, confused by her attack. He had barely had a chance to take in her lopsided hat, swollen lips, and the fierce but frightened look on her face. He scowled at J.T., who stood rubbing the area beneath his arm.

"What happened in here?" Matt asked, a clear warning in his voice. "When did you add molesting decent women to your list of many 'virtues'?"

111

"Decent? Ha! She's a hellcat just like that whore Spicie. Undoubtedly needs a little taming, which I'm looking forward to doing."

That was just the excuse Matt needed. He let his fist fly into J.T.'s broad face. He watched J.T. stumble back into the room, catching himself on the desk.

"What the hell was that for?" J.T. roared, coming up like an enraged bull.

Matt stood over him, clenching his fists, wanting to beat him senseless. "Don't ever lay a hand on that woman again."

"Now, Matt, don't get so riled. We had some business to take care of. She's just a little unfriendly and I only tried to warm her up. That's all." J.T. removed a handkerchief from his pocket and wiped the blood from his nose, keeping a wary eye on Matt's fist.

Matt didn't believe him for a second. If there was one thing you could count on from J.T., it was dishonesty.

"What kind of business?" Matt didn't care if it wasn't any of his concern. He wanted to know.

J.T. raised his eyebrow. "She owes me the five grand that old whore borrowed before she died. We were just setting up payments." J.T. grinned, walking around his desk to sit down. "What the hell brings you here anyway?" he asked, dropping into his chair. "And leave the damn door open. It's hotter than blue blazes in here." He mopped the sweat from his brow.

Matt leaned against the door frame with his arms crossed. He frowned thinking about Miss Taylor and the sort of arrangements that J.T. must have offered. He couldn't understand why a woman like that wanted to reform a whorehouse. This was just the sort of trouble that came from that kind of thinking. And J.T. was the kind of man she'd always have to deal with. Matt doubted that her situation would improve if she continued doing any business with this thieving polecat. Matt wished he'd hit him harder.

"Just thought I'd let you know we lost about a hundred head," Matt said calmly.

"How in hell did that happen?" J.T. roared, suddenly alert, jumping to his feet.

Matt shrugged his shoulders. "I guess they're just smarter than we are."

"Well, what are you doing about it?" J.T. bellowed.

"That's why I'm here. I figured that since you're half owner, you should have to do half the thinking." Matt tipped his hat back and waited.

"I haven't got time for that. I'm a busy man." Angrily, he pointed a finger at Matt. "You figure it out!"

"No reason I should." Matt continued to lounge in the open doorway.

J.T.'s face mottled with anger as he paced the confines of the small office.

Matt enjoyed watching J.T. explode over something not in his control for once.

"No reason? Money!" J.T. bellowed. "My money!"

"Only half of it," Matt reminded him.

J.T. visibly controlled himself. "Where did this happen and when?"

"Did I say lost?" Matt raised his eyebrows in mock surprise. "I meant almost lost."

113

"Almost?"

Matt could see J.T. try to hide his nervousness, so he added to his agitation by saying, "We caught them with their irons hot."

"Who?" J.T. croaked.

"A couple of two-bit drifters. They claimed they didn't know who hired them, until we decided to have a little necktie party." Matt prolonged J.T.'s discomfort by refusing to say anything else.

"Well, who?" J.T. yelled, completely beside himself.

"Evidently they were hired by some rough cowboys who told them not to ask any questions, and they'd get paid when the job was done."

"Dammit, Matt! Who hired them?"

"Don't know yet. Johnny took them over to the marshal's office." Matt pushed his lanky frame away from the door. "Just thought I'd let you know we just might catch that thieving son of a bitch after all."

Matt tipped his hat congenially, and left J.T. to ponder what he'd said.

As he walked down the alley toward the wide street, Matt's thoughts turned to Miss Taylor. He wondered what had really happened before he'd arrived. She should never have gone anywhere with J.T. alone. He would have thought she had more sense. Then he remembered the gun she'd held on him, and shook his head.

He mounted his horse, riding in the direction of the boardinghouse. Tying his horse out front, he took the steps two at a time in unhurried strides. Then he knocked on the door, thinking he probably shouldn't be here but that someone needed to tell her that the sensible thing to do was to sell the damn house before she had real trouble.

The door opened, revealing a familiar face.

"Hello, Sugar. I'd like to talk to Miss Taylor."

"Hello, Matt. Come in. Jauncey's in her room. She had a run-in with J.T." Sugar stepped aside and Matt entered. "I tried to talk to her, but she's too upset to say much. I'm not sure it's a good idea for you to see her now."

Matt walked toward the stairs. He dropped his hat on a chair, ignoring her suggestion. "Which room is hers?" he asked, before going up.

"Lottie's."

He stood outside the open door. She was lying down with a cloth over her eyes and her arm flung across her forehead. He noticed her shoes neatly beside the bed. Then he saw her chest heave with several big sighs. She'd been crying. The image of J.T. forcing himself on her quickly flashed through Matt's mind, and he clenched his fists, wishing he'd done more than just bloody the bastard's nose. At the same time he wanted to shake her for being so naive.

"Go away," she said on an indrawn breath that was so low he barely heard her. "You . . . you shouldn't be . . . in here."

He walked to the side of the bed. "I just wanted to see how you are." Matt didn't know how to ask if J.T. had hurt her, yet he had to find out.

"Why don't you ask your friend?" Jauncey grasped the edge of the quilt and pulled it over her.

She looked so small, like a frightened little bird

with some of the feathers pulled from its wings. The pins had come loose on one side of her hair and the hat was gone. The top button of her dress was missing, and a tear under her arm exposed a patch of soft white skin.

He ignored her assumption that J.T. was his friend.

Matt stood with his hands in his hip pockets. He wasn't sure how to tell her what he'd come to say. He didn't have much experience with women, at least not women like her.

"You know you're dealing with a man who will do anything to get what he wants. Whether it's this house, or you." He shifted uncomfortably on his feet. "Nothing will stand in his way. My advice is to sell while you can, before you're sorry you didn't."

To his chagrin, she rolled onto her side away from him and started to cry. Matt hated it when women cried; he felt so helpless. It was easier to deal with lying, cheating men than with sobbing females. He wanted to tell her that he had hit J.T., but he couldn't say it. So he stood watching her and feeling miserable while she cried.

Suddenly he needed to get out of there, wondering why the devil he'd given in to the desire to meddle in her business.

"I guess I'd better go," he said, backing awkwardly toward the door, watching her shoulders shake.

He strode down the hall and down the stairs, grabbing his hat off the chair and jamming it on his head. He needed space and lots of it. Within minutes, he mounted his horse and rode for the open range.

* * *

J.T. waited long enough to be sure Matt had left town before going over to the marshal's office, where he intended to find out what Williams planned to do about this situation. If Johnny was the one behind this bungled job, he'd make damn sure Williams kept his mouth shut and turned the fools loose. And if not, then he'd see to it the prisoners were no longer a threat to his own plans at the Diamond D.

He entered the dark interior to find Johnny talking in low tones with Williams. Both men turned when J.T. slammed the door.

"What the hell's going on?" he thundered.

"Caught us a few rustlers," Johnny answered, his steely dark eyes unblinking. J.T. knew Johnny feared no man, not even him, and Johnny wanted him to know it.

"Rustlers, you say," J.T. replied, waiting for further information before he said more.

Williams glanced from him to Johnny and J.T. could imagine just what the marshal was thinking. He could easily face a noose around his neck. "Drifters," Williams said happily. "Not from around here."

"Well, glad to hear that." J.T. leveled a look at Johnny. "Sure would hate to think one of our own would do such a stupid thing."

Johnny clenched his jaw while his hand lightly caressed the handle on his gun, then dropped to his side.

J.T. ignored the move. "How about letting me take a look at these desperadoes?"

Williams scooted around the desk and grabbed

the keys from a hook. "This way."

J.T. followed, Johnny behind him. When they reached the two side-by-side cells, he looked the men over. One of the men grinned sheepishly.

"Mind if we have a few words with these pole-cats, Marshal?" J.T. asked. "We won't do them any harm, since they're behind bars." He eyed the grinning one until the smile fell off his face and he backed away.

"Sure thing, J.T. Just give a holler when you're ready to go," Williams said, already halfway out the door.

When the door to the main office closed, J.T. stepped menacingly up to the bars. "What kind of fools have you hired this time?" he said to Johnny, but his eyes bored into the men inside the jail.

Johnny stepped up beside him, grasping the bars with one hand and his gun with the other. "Stupid ones, I guess."

"Wait a minute now, me and Hank done just what you said," one man piped up.

"Keep your voice down!" J.T. whispered. "Unless you'd like to leave town real quick. Feet first."

Both men shook their heads.

"Now tell me what in the hell you were doing trying to steal a hundred head! I thought I made it clear how I wanted this done."

"Johnny here said there was some easy pickin's in this one spot miles from the others so we went and *picked* 'em! How was we supposed to know it was a ambush?" The man glared at Johnny.

"Easy pickings?" J.T. mocked. "And I thought *they* were stupid."

"I can explain—"

118

"You bet you will, Johnny. But not here. First we'll get these jackasses out of jail and send them on their way."

"Now, hold on!" Hank cried.

"You'd rather rot in here?" J.T. asked, smirking.

Both men sat down, closing their mouths.

"That's better." Then he turned to Johnny. "Pay them off and make damn sure they leave town."

Chapter Eight

Three weeks had passed since the incident with J.T. Jauncey had learned a hard lesson, but one that wouldn't need repeating. She'd gone to Mr. Collins and badgered the poor man, until he'd finally convinced her that he was telling the truth. J.T. had lied. The deed to her house was safe in Mr. Collins's office, where it had been since her aunt had given it to him. J.T. must have hoped she would jump at the chance to be out of debt to him, and had played on the fact that Mr. Collins hadn't told her the whole truth in the beginning. If she didn't know it before, she knew now that J.T. was capable of anything.

Well, she told herself, he was not only a liar and a cheat, but he was also stupid. And that gave her heart. Somehow she would outwit him, beat him at his own game if necessary. Even though she hadn't decided exactly how she would do that, hardly a day went by that she didn't consider the possibilities.

Except for today, when her mind was preoccupied with Matt Dawson.

This morning began with Jauncey trying to spend time with Maggie, hoping to draw her out of her shell and into a conversation. But all she'd succeeded in doing was breaking a cup and saucer. She'd finally given up in frustration, retreating to her room.

Throughout the day she found her thoughts constantly straying to Matt Dawson, until she felt sure she was incapable of even the simplest task. She tried dismissing the circumstances that seemed to throw them together, but couldn't.

Now as she sat on her bed, her mind flashed back to the day he'd stood beside the bed, watching her cry like a baby. She'd been too miserable and embarrassed to look at him. When he hadn't denied he was a friend of J.T.'s and had advised her to get rid of the house, it had seemed like a threat. But was it really? She couldn't be sure. His voice hadn't sounded threatening, yet his words had left her cold.

She walked to the dresser and picked up her mother's hairbrush, handling it absently. Then she accidently bumped a dish of pins, and they clattered to the floor. She frowned at the scattered pins and bent to pick them up. There was no point in trying to solve all of her problems in her head, she decided. It only made her fidgety.

Still she continued to think. If only she could do something that would pay her debt and rid her of J.T. . . . if only the sign would arrive . . . if only a horde of people would descend upon her, wanting to rent her rooms . . . If only she could get Matt Dawson out of her mind.

Jauncey put the last hairpin in the dish, which had remarkably not broken, when a loud rapping at the front door reverberated up the stairs. She turned from the dresser after one quick check on her appearance, then dashed down the steps as quickly as her skirts would allow. Ginny had gone to town to do some shopping, which she'd begun doing frequently over the last few weeks, and Jauncey knew Maggie would never answer the door no matter how hard someone pounded.

The raps echoed again before she could compose herself and pull it open. When she opened the door, a little man with a slightly humped shoulder peered at her through thick spectacles.

"Miss Taylor?" he asked in a raspy high-pitched voice. "I'd like to speak to Miss Taylor." His voice was annoyingly insistent.

"I'm Miss Taylor," she said, ignoring his rudeness.

The little man held his brown bowler hat close to his chest and peered past her into the house. "I heard you had rooms to rent. A gentleman in town directed me here. And I must say it was quite difficult to find without a sign in front." His tone was accusing. "May I come in?"

"Of course, please come in." Jauncey stepped aside. She watched him walk in the parlor, turning his head this way and that. Then with nearsighted closeness he scrutinized several objects on a table.

Abruptly turning to face her, he said, "I'd like to rent a room. But I don't want it on the second floor." He eyed the stairs suspiciously.

"We have two rooms downstairs. Would you like to see them?"

"Naturally, I want to see them." He clipped each word efficiently, then closed his mouth into a tight line.

The front bedroom, which had been Ruby's, didn't meet his approval.

"There's far too much sunlight. I don't want to be blinded during the day." He expressed his dismissal of the room with a squeaky "harrumph."

"Perhaps the bedroom behind this one would be more suitable. It's near the kitchen and the bathing closet."

"Bathing closet?" His voice went a notch higher, even though Jauncey would have thought it impossible. "How much is this room going to cost me?" Obviously, he wasn't moving another inch until she told him.

She hesitated a moment while considering whether he would think her price too high. She had discussed it with Ginny and they had decided that the accommodations at her house were as nice as, and in some cases nicer than, those in town.

"Two dollars a day with meals, but no laundry," Jauncey said firmly.

From behind her, Ginny said, "And you won't find better accommodations anywhere."

Jauncey turned to see Ginny stripping her gloves from her long fingers, smiling with open friendliness.

The little man looked from Jauncey to Ginny, then craned his neck at Jauncey. "Are you the owner? That man in town said to ask for Miss

Taylor," he said with a doubtful expression.

"Yes, I am." Jauncey had to control her voice to keep the irritation from it. After all, he was her first prospect and she desperately needed him.

"You're much too young," he said, his bottom lip pointing at her accusingly.

Gawking at Ginny, he asked, "Who are you?"

"Mrs. Marlowe. I work for Miss Taylor."

Jauncey awkwardly gulped down her astonishment. Mrs. Marlowe? Married? She'd never heard of married prostitutes. But then her knowledge about the life of a prostitute was limited. Very limited, she decided.

Ginny led the man into the second bedroom. "Maybe this room will be more to your liking, Mr. . . ."

"Natter. Elmer Natter."

"Mr. Natter." Ginny smiled sweetly at him. "There's very little bright sunlight in here, but still plenty of light to read by. As you can see, the room is a comfortable size. And it's the only room available with a desk and two chairs."

Mr. Natter surveyed the room with the same impolite scrutiny as he had the parlor. "It's much too large. But it will do," he said, then added, looking at Jauncey, "Why didn't you show me this one first?"

Speechless, she could only stare, first at Mr. Natter then at Ginny. Then before she could reply, he turned to leave.

"I must go now and see to my baggage. What time is the evening meal?" He spoke to Ginny, ignoring Jauncey.

"Promptly at five o'clock," Ginny replied.

"Good. Good. It isn't healthy to eat too late in the day. Bad for digestion." He shook his head and patted his stomach in an absentminded fashion.

Jauncey watched him leave the house and carefully negotiate the front steps.

Her first paying customer! She was thrilled. Never mind that he was irritating, disapproving, nearsighted and difficult to get along with. No, those things didn't matter at all, she told herself, staring down the street after him.

Matt Dawson's words rankled in her brain. Sell the house, he'd said. She thrust them forcefully from her thoughts. Ha! she thought, this was only the beginning. Others would come and want rooms. She had to believe that. Yet in her mind J.T.'s face leered at her, and she had to shake her head to rid herself of the image. Soon she hoped to be rid of him, too.

For the rest of the afternoon Jauncey worked at setting up an account book and making plans to fill it.

Mr. Natter arrived at 15 minutes before five with baggage in tow, and promptly disappeared into his room, closing the door decisively behind him.

With only minutes before supper, Jauncey went into the kitchen and found Ginny alone removing biscuits from the sweltering oven.

"Where's Maggie?" Jauncey asked.

"Who's Maggie?" Mr. Natter asked, walking through the doorway.

"She does most of the cooking for us," Ginny answered. "She fixed the meal tonight. I'm just finishing it for her."

"Where did she go?" he asked, his voice as

accusing as it had been earlier.

"She's shy, so she took a tray up to her room. It'll take her a little time to get used to you," Ginny replied, dishing up the thick beef stew.

Satisfied with her answer, Mr. Natter sat down at the table and gingerly picked at his stew and sourdough biscuits. But Jauncey noticed he made short work of two pieces of dried peach pie that he washed down with two cups of coffee. Perhaps Mr. Natter had a sweet tooth, she thought, making it a point to remember.

She and Ginny did the dishes after Mr. Natter retired to his room, his door firmly closed.

"He seems to be a picky eater, don't you agree?" Jauncey whispered.

"Yes. But he does like pie," Ginny whispered back.

"So I noticed. Maybe if we give him pie every night, his disposition will get sweeter," Jauncey said, smiling at the impossible suggestion.

"Do you think so?" Ginny asked. "If that's true, then I think we should add sugar to his stew."

Jauncey made a face and both of them laughed. The barriers between them were coming down, bit by bit.

At the back door a quick knock sounded before it opened.

"Ginny?"

Jauncey immediately recognized the clerk from Trabing's as he poked his head around the corner.

"Hello, Dan, come in. There's a piece of pie for you. And some coffee, too," Ginny said, wiping her hands on her apron.

"Hello, Miss Taylor, hope you don't mind my

dropping by. Ginny fixes a great cup of coffee," he said, winking at Ginny.

"No, of course not." Jauncey watched, surprised, while Dan familiarly pulled back a chair from the table and Ginny poured them each a cup. He sat easily in the chair, facing Ginny and following her every move with his eyes.

"I wanted to stop in last night," he told Ginny, "but we had a shipment come in that had to be stacked in the warehouse. It was late when we finished." He sipped the coffee, still watching her.

"I don't expect you to stop in every night. I know you're busy." But Jauncey could tell by Ginny's voice how pleased she was to see him, and she noticed the change in Ginny's appearance. Her brown eyes had a sparkle that hadn't been there before Dan arrived.

A long silence followed, and Jauncey felt like an intruder. She quickly put the dishes away, making as much noise as she could, mostly to hide her own feelings of awkwardness. Courting wasn't something she was comfortable with; neither was watching it nor being a part of it.

"Would you like some coffee, Jauncey?" Ginny asked.

"Oh, no, thank you. I've got some mending to do, so I'll just go upstairs and get that out of the way."

Dan stood. He was taller than Ginny, but not as tall as Matt Dawson, Jauncey noted.

He smiled, showing even white teeth. "By the way," he said, "how's your ankle? All mended by now, I suppose."

Jauncey colored remembering that day in the

127

store. "Oh, yes. It's fine now."

"Ginny told me when I delivered your supplies that evening how Matt had you all taken care of. I know he felt pretty bad about what happened." Dan frowned with sympathy, leaning on his chair, one hand tucked in his hip pocket.

"Well, that was weeks ago and everything's fine now." Jauncey walked toward the parlor, giving them a small nod of her head. "Well, good night." Then she quickly left the room.

Upstairs, she sat on the bed, still surprised. So they had been seeing each other since she'd hurt her ankle. And that was why Ginny had been doing most of the shopping lately. Jauncey smiled, truly glad for her.

She pulled a basket of mending from under the bed. It was her least favorite chore, but she clenched her jaw and proceeded. And chore it was. Even her usually patient mother had finally given up teaching her anything but the necessary stitches for mending. She knew what a disappointment it had been to Maybelle, so she'd tried to make up for it in other ways. She'd concentrated on the other ladylike habits, such as walking and talking properly, and especially giving careful attention to the way she dressed. These were the things a lady needed to cultivate, her mother had said. And of course, there were other things a lady did not cultivate. But those things were never discussed.

Jauncey sighed. Now she understood perfectly what her mother had hoped to save her from, sitting here surrounded by the very essence of unladylike living. What would her mother have said about her situation if she were alive now?

After 30 minutes of repairing hems, Jauncey was sure she was going blind and her neck muscles would be permanently tensed. She laid the mending aside, feeling as though she had paid some kind of penance for sticking with it for that long. Leaning her head back against the chair, she rubbed the knot at her nape, her mind wandering once again to her debt. She let her hands fall into her lap, and stared at them.

Her amethyst ring winked at her in the lamplight. Of course. Why hadn't she thought of it sooner? Excitement surged through her, revitalizing her instantly. Her aunt had jewelry, lots of it. She'd sell every piece to make the first payment. In her rush to rid herself of all Spicie's personal belongings, she'd overlooked the value of the contents of the chest.

Jauncey rose and took the lamp from the stand. Her shaking hands held the lamp tightly. She opened the door to her room and walked the few steps to the attic. Grabbing her skirts in her hand, she hurried up the stairs.

She held the light high in order to see around the darkening attic. Where had Ginny put that chest? She walked past the trunk where she'd found the picture of the twin girls, knowing it wasn't in there. Another dormer on the far side held several trunks plus numerous other things. Jauncey set the lamp on a sturdy old table and proceeded to open trunk after trunk. Most of them were filled with clothes. Finally, she found the one containing the chest and stacks of letters wrapped in faded pink ribbons. She pushed those aside and lifted out the chest. Oh, please, she prayed, her eyes closed and her heart hammering, let there be something of value in here. Please.

She opened the chest and searched through the contents of gold rings, pendants and pins. Nothing looked especially valuable, no diamonds, no rubies. Maybe she could get something for the gold, if the quality was good. But she was sure it wouldn't be enough. Disappointed, she relaxed her grasp and the chest dropped the short distance into the trunk. It landed with a padded thump on the stack of letters, breaking the ribbons.

Jauncey stared in surprise as the letters spilled out. Some had meticulous handwriting addressed to Miss Spicie Belle Devon. She recognized it as her mother's with its tiny flourishes and even spacing, just as she had tried to teach Jauncey to do. The envelopes mingled with others written in the same style of careful writing, but with larger, more extravagant flourishes. These letters were addressed to Mrs. Maybelle Taylor, but evidently had never been mailed.

Jauncey gazed into the trunk, wondering how two sisters could live such drastically different lives.

She thought about her mother with her tightly bound curls and chest-flattening undergarments. Not once had she ever seen her mother without benefit of high-collared, long-sleeved clothing. Instantly, the naked picture of her aunt came to mind, and her eyes wandered across the attic.

She fought the urge to open her mother's letters. This was no time to dig into the family's skeletons, she decided. The past was gone and had nothing to do with her. She had more pressing matters to attend to.

Reaching into the trunk, she removed the jewelry chest, then closed the lid. Perhaps she could get a hundred dollars for the entire contents. And with Mr. Natter's rent . . . No, it was too late to consider that. She had only one week left before her first payment was due.

At least she had this much, she thought, clutching the chest, whatever it amounted to. Where would she ever get the rest? She had to think of something, she just had to.

Jauncey carried the lamp and chest down to her room. After donning her nightgown and brushing out her hair, she pulled back the sheet and sat on the edge of her bed.

"Jauncey?" Ginny called through the door. "Are you still up?"

"Yes." She forced a note of cheerfulness into her voice and busied herself with braiding her hair. "Come in."

Ginny slipped into the room, closing the door behind her. "I hope you don't mind Dan stopping by."

"Not at all." Jauncey said, surprised that Ginny felt she had to explain. "I think he's very nice." Jauncey wanted to examine Ginny closely for any signs of a true romantic involvement, but restrained herself.

"He is." Ginny stood beside the dresser, her hands laced together. "I didn't really come to talk about Dan." She appeared vaguely uncomfortable, although calm and sedate. "I know Spicie didn't have a lot of money. She said as much before she died. And you haven't had any income, until today. Now, I don't want to pry into your financial affairs, but since Maggie and I are living here, I know we're an added strain on you."

Jauncey hardly knew what to say. The need for someone to confide in had been building for weeks until it was almost unbearable. She hadn't realized just how much until now.

"I do need someone to help me think this money situation through." Jauncey sighed and motioned for her to sit. She explained about the loan, as well as J.T.'s offer. Ginny listened without saying a word. Then Jauncey revealed that he had attacked her, and that she had happened to run into Matt Dawson. When she finished, she wasn't sorry she'd told so much to this woman who had so little in common with her. She actually felt better, relieved.

"Jauncey, I should have warned you about J.T. I feel responsible. If you'd have known the kind of man he is you never would have gone there." Ginny frowned. "I just thought he would limit his visits to the house like he always did, and I could keep an eye on him. I'm sorry." She placed her hand over Jauncey's to comfort her.

"No, it was my fault. I did know, but I was desperate. I wanted to believe his offer would be fair. It was a stupid mistake." She shook her head for added emphasis. "One I'll never make again."

"Thank goodness Matt was there." Ginny sounded relieved. "What did he do?"

"I didn't stay around long enough to see," Jauncey said. She lowered her voice. "I ran, after I kicked him. Hard."

Ginny laughed. "I don't think I'd worry about Matt. It would take more than a kick from a woman to do him much damage."

"Worry? I didn't say I was worried." Jauncey tugged at her hair as she finished braiding it, forcing a smile to prove how little she really cared if she had damaged Matt Dawson.

"Well, I'm just glad you're all right," Ginny said and dropped the subject. "There isn't time to raise enough money for the loan payment. So I want to give it to you."

"Oh, no. I can't. . . ." Jauncey was flabbergasted.

"But you will," Ginny insisted, making it clear by the inclination of her head and the tone of her voice that she would not take no for an answer.

"Ginny, I . . ." She really didn't know what to say. It was so unexpected, and so charitable.

"There's no need to talk about who owes who what. Or else we'll be comparing lists, and I guarantee mine will be longer than yours."

"But I couldn't have done all this work by myself," Jauncey replied. "Really."

Ginny touched Jauncey's shoulder, her sincerity plain in her eyes. "Maggie and I could never repay you for what you've given us. A fresh start, a better chance . . ." Ginny stopped, her chin trembling.

"Thank you," Jauncey said, softly. "I'll pay you back."

"No. And I don't want to hear any more arguments." Ginny faced her squarely. "Agreed?"

Jauncey nodded her head. She felt at least two inches taller without the burden of the payment weighing her down. Instinctively she reached out and hugged Ginny. And Ginny returned it.

"Agreed," Jauncey said.

"Good. Now, I'm going to check on Maggie and go to bed. It will be morning before we know it."

Immediately, her new boarder came to mind.

"Oh, dear! We didn't ask Mr. Natter about breakfast. What time do you suppose he gets up?" Jauncey asked.

"With the chickens, I'd say. But so does Maggie. I hope she'll be able to cope with him tomorrow. Well, good night." Ginny left, closing the door behind her.

Jauncey felt like singing and dancing. She refrained from singing, but couldn't keep from twirling a few times while she hugged herself. She refused to let any nagging thoughts remind her she was now indebted to two people. Sooner or later she would become totally independent and not need anybody's help. And she was sure it would be sooner. She could just feel it. With one more spin, she landed on the bed and stared at the ceiling with her arms spread over her head.

J.T. Lawrence would be so surprised. She considered delivering the payment in person instead of letting Mr. Collins do it for her. The look on his face might be worth the fear of being anywhere near him, she thought. Oh, how much fun it was to contemplate the shock he would show, then the anger. Suddenly, the hairs along her arm raised. No, she decided. She wouldn't make another mistake like the last. Mr. Collins was her lawyer and had promised to take care of it, and she would let him. She would have to settle for the information about J.T.'s reaction secondhand. There was less risk that way.

Rising, she finished her preparations for bed, then climbed between the crisp cool sheets, moving to the center of the bed to stretch out for a good night's rest, something she hadn't had since she'd arrived. Staring into the pitch black room, she sighed.

Safe. That's how she felt.

Safe and secure.

Jauncey awoke once during the night.

Without a moon, the room lay in unrelieved darkness. She listened. Silence. Still drowsy, she decided Mr. Natter must be going out to use the privy. Dreams of peace and security lured her back into their reality. So she closed her eyes and went willingly.

Chapter Nine

In the month since Jauncey had made her first payment to J.T., she had gotten three more boarders, and all of them were men. Two worked at the rolling mills just the other side of the Union Pacific tracks and the third was a shopkeeper waiting for his house to be built. Mr. Natter was still a mystery, keeping to himself for the most part and spending most of the day away from the boardinghouse. Nobody dared ask what he did for a living.

Jauncey set up an office in the front bedroom downstairs, where it was convenient and private. Moving a large desk from Spicie's room had taken some doing, but with the help of two of the boarders they'd succeeded.

She sat at the desk, a cup of coffee perched on a pile of papers, while she went over the figures again and again. No matter how she approached it, she would be short for this payment, too. She leaned back in the oversized wooden chair and sipped the cooling coffee.

She hadn't counted on the appetites of three healthy men. She'd run up an account at the store, something she hadn't wanted to do, but Dan was very understanding. If only it weren't for those dratted payments to J.T., she'd be doing just fine. She plunked the cup down and got up from the desk. How could she get out of this debt?

She thought about her aunt's jewelry. She hadn't taken it to be sold because the next morning the chest had been missing from her dresser. She knew immediately what had happened. Maggie must have made the sound that woke her that night, when she'd come into Jauncey's room and taken the chest. Jauncey hadn't asked her about it, or even checked the trunk to see if she'd put it back. But she was sure the chest was either in Maggie's room or back in the attic. She had decided to drop the matter since Ginny had offered to make the first loan payment with her own money.

But for a few nights after that, Jauncey hadn't slept well, thinking that Maggie might come back into the room. There was something disquieting about having her prowl around while Jauncey slept. But after a while she had relaxed, and now it no longer bothered her. After all, Maggie was harmless.

Sitting at the desk once more, Jauncey glanced over the figures again. They were close, but not close enough. She tapped her finger on the paper in irritation. She couldn't let Ginny make another payment for her. No, she needed a long-term solution. Perhaps she should talk to Mr. Collins.

Leaving her office, she found Ginny with Maggie in the kitchen. Without giving an explanation, she told them she was going to town and would be back shortly.

Another day of bright sunshine greeted her, but at least her clothing didn't stick to her, now that summer was coming to an end. Barely a drop of rain had fallen since she'd arrived, and the thick layer of dirt and dust covering the porch gave testimony to the fact. Everyone talked about the unusual weather, and she had been reassured several times that this wasn't a typical year.

Jauncey admired, once again, the large yellow sign standing in front of her house. A sense of pride filled her at the sight of her name in large letters proclaiming to all that this was her boardinghouse, a respectable business. Brailey had been proud, too, and it was plain to see why. The sign was beautiful. He had stammered when she told him so, and fallen speechless when she kissed him on the cheek.

She really had a lot to be happy about, she reminded herself, and tried to smile at everyone she passed. After all, her situation was much better than when she'd first arrived. Now, most people knew she ran a real boardinghouse. And those who were still suspicious—well, she would be patient and let her reputation speak for itself.

Jauncey had stopped outside the lawyer's office, her hand raised to knock, when a loud crashing noise came from within, followed by an ominous silence. Her heart pounded as she cautiously opened the door.

Looking around with her hand still on the

doorknob, she saw nothing. The door to the back room was ajar, so she decided to see if everything was all right in there. Again nothing. As she turned to go back into the main office, she saw someone lying on the floor in a heap behind the desk.

"Mr. Collins!" she cried, kneeling beside him. Was he alive? He didn't appear to be breathing. In a panic, she opened his shirt collar to help him breathe. Nearly all of the buttons had popped from the stiff white shirtfront, allowing her easy access. She slapped his face lightly.

"Mr. Collins! Are you all right? Please, be all right!" With shaking hands, she pushed and pulled on his cheeks, hoping for some sign of life.

Momentarily he stirred; his eyes fluttered open.

"Ohhh," he groaned. "My head." He touched his face, then rolled his head from side to side. He fingered his jaw gingerly.

"What happened? Who did this to you?" She saw blood coming from a cut just above his ear.

"Ohhh," he moaned, and tried to raise himself on his elbow. "My neck." He grasped the spot where his neck and shoulder met.

"Let me help you. Can you get up?" Jauncey assisted him as much as she could until he was sitting in the chair, his head in both hands.

"You need to see a doctor," she said, still shaken herself.

"Y-y-yes, I'm sure you're right. But first I have to get my bearings." He rolled his head slightly back and forth.

Agitated, she sat across from him in the only other chair.

"Who did this?" she asked, a sense of foreboding thrumming heavily inside her.

"That's not for you to w-w-worry about, Miss Taylor," he said protectively.

"What do you mean?" He was trying to hide something from her.

"Nothing."

"I don't believe you." She narrowed her eyes at him, determined to get to the bottom of this. "Who did this?" she asked, her voice rising.

He squinted painfully. "Not now, please," he whispered.

Deciding to let it slide for the moment, she rose from her seat. "Where's the water and a cloth? We should clean that cut before you walk down the street frightening everyone between here and Dr. Myers's office."

"Thank you." He winced when he spoke. "In the back room."

Undoubtedly the cut would require a few stitches, and she didn't want to detain him from the doctor, but she had to know what this had to do with her. Obviously, it was connected to her in some way.

He leaned back in his chair, holding the wet cloth she'd given him to the side of his head, and sighed.

"Now." She put as much authority into her voice as she could, although she still sympathized with his condition.

His shoulders slumped. "I shouldn't be telling you this." He glanced at her then sighed again. "It was J.T. Not him personally, of course. That's not the way he does things. He prefers to send his messages without drawing too much attention to himself."

"What message?" Jauncey's body alerted to the word.

"He thinks I paid your last payment and he wants to make sure I don't do it again."

"He what?" Instantly she came to her feet. Poor innocent Mr. Collins! "Didn't you deny it?"

"Yes, I did. But his messenger wouldn't believe me."

"Well! He isn't getting away with this! We're going to see the marshal right after you go to the doctor." It was time to put an end to J.T.'s bullying!

"Oh, no, we can't do that!" He straightened and the cloth fell from his face.

"That man has to be stopped! He'll probably do this again, every time I make a payment. I can't have you subjected to this kind of treatment because of me."

Leaning his elbows on the desk with the cloth to his head once more, he said, "But I can't go to the marshal."

She stared at him in disbelief. "Why on earth not?" Then realization struck her. "J.T. threatened you!"

"Not me." He stared at the desk.

"Then who?"

He refused to look at her.

"Me?" Outrage and shock overtook her, draining her until she felt empty.

"He's an unconscionable man. He can't be trusted. Ask anyone who's done business with him." He glanced at her. "Please don't ask me anything else."

Deflated, she dropped into a chair. She felt as though a weight the size of a house sat on her shoulders, and in truth it did.

"What am I to do? I can't give up, I just can't." Her words seemed to echo in the great emptiness inside her.

"Goodness, no." Mr. Collins stared at the cloth, then applied it again. "There is a gentleman who is willing to take over the loan. That means your debt would be to him and you would make your payments to him—through me, of course."

"A bank?" Her spirits rose immediately. Why hadn't she thought of that before?

"No. I'm afraid a bank wouldn't give you a loan of that size, or perhaps of any size, since your business is so, uh, new. I mean, they inquire into the history of the business, and in this case, they would probably look at the history of the house . . . even though that would be unfair. To you." He stumbled over his words and added the last quickly.

"Who is it then?"

"He asked to remain anonymous." Mr. Collins fidgeted in his chair.

"That's absurd. How can I do business with someone I don't even know? This 'gentleman' could turn out to be as bad or worse than J.T. Lawrence, if that's possible."

"I assure you, that's not the case. He's a respected citizen, and his family has been a part of this area for almost as long as Laramie has been here."

"I see. He's so respected he doesn't want to let anyone know he's loaning money to a former . . . bordello." Her voice rose with each word, and she had to catch herself from saying whorehouse.

"Oh, no. You're wrong about that. Matt—" He stopped abruptly, and closed his eyes as if in pain.

Jauncey catapulted from her seat. "Matt? Matt Dawson?"

"Yes," he said in a small voice.

She paced the floor in front of his desk, her temper simmering at a low boil. "Of all the sneaking . . ." He wanted her house! He had said she should sell it. Now he offered to take over the loan, assuming that she couldn't make the payments.

She came to a halt. "No!" she exclaimed, and pounded her fist on the desk.

Mr. Collins jumped. "Why not? I don't understand. Matt would be fair, and you wouldn't have anything to fear."

"Fair! You call wanting my house fair?"

"Please. Miss Taylor." He grimaced with each word she flung at him.

Instantly sorry, she calmed down. "Here I am going on about my troubles when you need to see Dr. Myers. Let me help you," she said when he stood up looking a little shaky.

"Thank you, I just need a moment. I guess my head took quite a thump." He squinted. "It does feel rather like an overripe watermelon. Ready to burst." He smiled weakly at his own humor.

They walked the few blocks to the doctor's office. Surprisingly few people even seemed to notice the bruised condition of Andrew Collins's face. Then, just two doors away from their destination, a woman stepped from a store directly into their path.

"Oh! Excuse—" Jauncey began, then stopped when she recognized the black-haired woman

143

eyeing her. And Jauncey couldn't help returning the stare. Never had she seen a woman in real life so exposed. Her deep purple dress was cut threateningly low at her bosom, while her corset was apparently laced so tightly that her breasts appeared to ready to burst out of it like a cork on a pressured bottle.

"Hello, Andrew," the woman said, her voice low and distinctly provocative.

"M-Miss Lottie," Mr. Collins replied while the tips of his ears turned crimson. "Uh, Miss Lottie, this is Miss Taylor, the new owner of, uh, the b-b-boardinghouse."

"So I've heard." She looked over Jauncey's modest dress once more, then smiled pleasantly. "Welcome to Laramie, Miss Taylor."

Jauncey couldn't brush aside the woman's obvious dislike of her, but then the feeling was mutual. "Thank you," she replied stiffly.

"Well, if you'll, uh, p-pardon us, Miss Lottie, we have an appointment to keep." Mr. Collins tugged at Jauncey's elbow nervously. "Good d-day."

Resuming their walk to Dr. Myers's office, Jauncey kept her eyes trained on the shingle above the door, forcing herself not to think about the unfortunate encounter.

She waited in the outer room wanting to know about Mr. Collins's injuries. Before long the tall gray-haired doctor followed Mr. Collins into the room. He gently clapped his hand on his patient's shoulder.

"You'll have a headache for a while, Andrew, but otherwise you'll be fine. Come back in a few days and we'll take a look at those stitches. In the meantime, stay away from open doors," Dr. Myers said, winking at Jauncey.

She smiled at him, embarrassed at the idea that he might think she was directly responsible for Mr. Collins's condition—even though, in truth, she was.

Outside the doctor's office, Mr. Collins turned to her. "I'll be all right, Miss Taylor. There's no need to worry yourself. I believe I'll just go home and lie down for the rest of the day and take it easy." He touched her arm and smiled.

Jauncey thought he looked so pathetic with a bandage above one ear and trying to smile as though his head wasn't splitting.

"You go on home, too. We'll come up with an answer to your problem," he said reassuringly.

"We should go to the marshal's office and report this."

"I don't think that would be wise. Really. I don't think I could live with myself if I let anything happen to you." He smiled again. "We'll work out something. I promise."

There was nothing else she could do. She said good-bye and walked the three long blocks home, barely noticing the people she passed or the dust that swirled around her when she stepped off the boardwalk to cross the street. She turned her predicament over and over in her mind, searching for solutions. But she had none. She only knew she would not give up her house. Nothing could make her return to Aunt Ida's biting hospitality.

Her mother had suffered quietly, the way she'd believed a lady in her position must. After all, if not for Aunt Ida's generosity, where would they have been? Her father had left her mother very little money, most of which she had saved for Jauncey. Generosity indeed, Jauncey thought. Aunt Ida didn't have one solid bone of generosity in her entire body. Uncle Harold was the one with the kind heart, just like her father. It was one of several characteristics the brothers shared. If not for Uncle Harold, Jauncey would surely have strangled Aunt Ida. She clenched her fist until her nails bit into her palm. How clearly Aunt Ida's words rang in her ears even today. "My dear," she had said often to friends and neighbors, "the difficulties one must bear financially are nothing when compared to the embarrassment of caring for poor relations."

Jauncey had known the remarks were meant for her ears as well as for those of her listeners, since they were never spoken in a whisper.

How well she remembered the long hours in the evenings when she and her mother would sit by the lamp in the room they shared, stitching. A good friend of her mother's had offered to sell the table scarves and napkins that Maybelle worked so diligently to complete. It was a very small income, but at least she contributed something to Aunt Ida's house and kept herself busy.

Jauncey hated stitching of any kind, but never said so. Maybelle would say, "You don't have to help, dear. I'll be able to finish these without any problem. Why don't you read to me?" And Jauncey would take out a book of poetry and read until the rhythm of the words gently removed her growing irritation.

Now, marching along the street, her heels hammering against the wooden walk, she vowed never again to return to Aunt Ida's as a poor relation.

Maybelle had died after taking to her bed with a cough. They had called the doctor finally, in spite of Maybelle's reluctance. She'd had pneumonia. Even then Aunt Ida had complained to her friends of the high cost of doctors and medicine.

Jauncey recalled with gratitude Uncle Harold's sudden and unusual confrontation with his wife.

"Ida, that will be enough!" he'd said.

With her head high, but not as high as Uncle Harold's, Aunt Ida had glared at him. Yet she had never uttered a word as she left the room in a huff.

No, Jauncey would never return to Aunt Ida's unless it was as an independent woman. She would in no way accept the charity of anyone. Not even poor, dear Uncle Harold.

Now, as she stopped in front of her large yellow house, she admired every aspect of it anew. It was beautiful. And it was almost hers. She would not give it up without a fight. Squaring her shoulders, she marched up the front steps. If necessary, she would even take in stitching in order to keep this house.

Lottie stood on the sidewalk before the small frame house with the neat picket fence surrounding it. She'd never been here before, but everyone in town knew where Andrew B. Collins lived. Without even glancing around to see if any prying eyes watched her from behind curtained windows, she walked up to the front door and knocked loudly. When the door opened to reveal the short lawyer in his shirtsleeves, she smiled and said, "Hello

147

again, Andrew. Mind if I come in?"

He reached out and pulled her inside, nearly slamming the door behind her. "W-w-what are you doing here!" he wheezed.

"Andrew, are you all right?" she said, pretending concern. "You look positively apoplectic."

He swallowed with considerable difficulty. "M-m-miss Lottie, you shouldn't have come here in b-b-broad daylight."

"You'd rather I came after dark?" she asked suggestively.

"No! Oh, no, I didn't mean that at all. I mean . . ." He floundered helplessly.

"It's all right, Andrew," she soothed. "I only came by to tell you something; then I'll be on my way."

He relaxed visibly. "Something to tell me?"

She smiled secretively. "You know that nice young woman you were with?"

He nodded, waiting.

"Well, she seems like such a . . . proper kind of woman, well brought up. Refined."

"Oh, yes, she is," he said, smiling.

"And very pretty, too. Don't you think?"

He blushed, then answered, "Yes, I do."

"Well, I've heard that she's smitten with you, Andrew."

His eyes rounded. "She is?"

"Mmmhmm. And I thought, since you were such a nice fellow, that it was only fair to let you know." She fidgeted with her handbag and put on a long face. "Of course, you've heard the other things people are saying. . . ."

"No. No, I haven't. What are they saying?" Concern etched his face.

"Well, I know it's only gossip, and you're such a nice man, but, well . . ."

"But what? Please, tell me. If Miss Taylor is in some kind of trouble I want to help her. I already feel responsible for everything that's happened to her. Tell me. What is it?"

"Well, her reputation has already been besmirched, they say. By you."

"What!" He stepped back in shock.

"Well, she's been seen going into your office all hours of the day. And night."

"That's absurd! Miss Taylor would never—"

"Maybe not, but nevertheless her reputation is suffering. And it's all your fault, Andrew. And hers, too, I suppose, since she's so infatuated with you."

He dropped into a chair. "My goodness. My goodness."

"Well, I'd better be going. I only wanted to help you out. I hope you aren't angry with me. It's just that when I saw the two of you together today, it just seemed like the right thing to do."

"My goodness," he repeated, staring at the floor.

Lottie backed toward the door. "I'll just let myself out. I'm sorry, Andrew, to leave you with such upsetting news."

"Oh," he said looking up, still dazed by her revelation. "I appreciate your concern. Thank you."

"Anytime. Good-bye." And she slipped out the door, hurrying down the street before her laughter escaped and gave her little charade away.

Chapter Ten

Matt sat squarely in his saddle, one hand on the reins and one hand on his thigh.

"How you gonna handle this, Matt?" Charlie asked, clearly anticipating a fight but not sounding much in favor of it.

"I don't know yet."

"You know Johnny told you about it just to rile you."

"It worked pretty damn well, too." Matt clenched his jaw. He'd been hotter than a branding iron in a cottonwood fire when he found out the marshal had turned those rustlers loose. How much more evidence did the man want? It wasn't likely they'd ever catch a cattle thief applying a new brand on top of one of his with the hairs still freshly singed. Not even those fools Johnny hired were stupid enough to get caught doing that. And Matt had no doubt Johnny had hired them for J.T.

"Charlie, I'm betting J.T. will go for bigger stakes this time. But he'll probably make several small attempts just to keep down his chances of getting caught." Matt leveled his hat for better shading of his eyes, and squinted at Laramie in the distance.

"No doubt about it, Matt. He's as itchin' to get at it as a dog with fleas."

With only two weeks until roundup, J.T. would be anxious to pick the cattle directly from Matt's pocket and put them into his own. That would serve two purposes for J.T., Matt thought grimly. Everything he stole would be his. Then he'd watch Matt fold up and sell. Of course, J.T. would be ready to buy.

They rode into town and left their horses in front of the marshal's office. Matt strode across the walk and practically kicked the door open, Charlie right behind him. Several men sat around in silence, their eyes fastened on Matt, but he ignored them and went straight to the man wearing the star.

"Give me one good reason you let them go." Matt stared down at Williams, his voice quiet and low with anger.

"Calm down, Matt. Have a seat and I'll be glad to explain."

"I didn't come here to socialize, Williams." Matt shoved the chair aside. "Just give me one damn good reason why you let those men go."

"Not enough evidence." Williams glared back.

Matt grabbed him by the shirtfront with one hand. He heard several chairs scrape the floor, but nobody interfered.

"You listen to me and you listen good. I've got rustlers hanging around my place picking off my cattle left and right. And it's going to stop." He pulled Williams close enough to hear him breathe. "Either you do something, or I will."

"Are you threatening me?" Williams struggled free. "'Cause if you are . . .'"

"This isn't a threat. I'm telling you how things are going to be." Matt rested his hand on his hip near his gun. "I want those thieves caught. And that includes J.T."

"Now hold on there. That's a pretty strong accusation. J.T. sure wouldn't take kindly to that sort of talk."

Matt narrowed his gaze. "I'll bring them in here one way or the other. And there'll be plenty of evidence."

Williams glared back. "You do anything foolish and you could be swinging from a rope."

"My neck isn't the one you need to be worrying about." With that, Matt turned to leave and Charlie followed him.

Outside, Charlie mounted his horse, and Matt could feel the hole Charlie was staring into his back.

Matt frowned. "I know what you're thinking," he said over his shoulder before swinging up into the saddle.

"Ain't too often you lose your head."

"So don't bother telling me not to." Matt wheeled his horse down the street toward Trabing's, leaving Charlie to follow.

When they were even with Sam's Saloon, Matt caught a glimpse of red standing at the swinging door. He turned just as Lottie lifted her bare arm to flag him down. Reining his horse toward the boardwalk, he heard Charlie mutter a profanity from behind him.

"Matt, what's your hurry?" Lottie asked, moving to stand alongside his horse. "I haven't seen you around for a while. Got time for a drink?" She smiled seductively, leaning forward, giving him a view of her breasts. "And maybe a little afternoon . . . tussle?"

"Sorry, Lottie. I've got business to tend to." After the run-in with Williams, the last thing he had on his mind was an afternoon with Lottie. Actually, he hadn't thought about Lottie for quite some time. Not since Jauncey Taylor had intruded into his thoughts after he'd intruded into her house.

"But Matt, you never come by anymore." She traced a fingernail up his boot to his knee. "You haven't found someone else, have you now?"

He knew he didn't owe her an explanation, so he simply said, "I've been busy."

"Yeah," Charlie cut in, "real busy. So if you'll excuse us, ma'am . . ."

She grimaced at Charlie, but stepped back anyway. Turning to Matt, she said softly, "I've missed you. Don't be such a stranger."

In his gut a warning signal went off. He looked at her face framed by her coal black curls. They'd had good times, but that was all it had been to him. He could see now that it wasn't the same for her.

"He's got work to do and a roundup to git started on," Charlie said, interrupting again. "And if we lollygag around here all day, we'll never git at it."

"Charlie Hawks! Nobody's stopping you from

going about your business!" Lottie shouted. "So go!"

He turned to Matt. "Are we goin' or not?"

"He's right, Lottie. We've got—"

"Fine! Just go!" Angrily, she flounced back into the saloon, hitting the swinging doors hard enough to almost make them fly off.

Matt watched her, wondering how he'd ever let it get this far.

"Humph," Charlie grunted. "Now let's git on with it."

When they stopped in front of Trabing's, Matt said, "You order the supplies. I need to see Collins about some business he was supposed to handle for me."

Charlie didn't say anything as he swung down from his horse.

Somehow Charlie always knew what Matt was doing, and when he didn't approve he didn't mind letting it show. Matt'd learned a long time ago to give Charlie full rein in his opinions, and to keep his own mouth shut. So, doing exactly that, he headed toward the lawyer's office.

He found Andrew Collins at his desk with a bandage over his ear and several bruises on his face, and knew immediately who had paid him an unfriendly visit. He frowned, thinking about the kind of visit J.T. would likely pay Miss Taylor.

"Did she agree to my loan?"

"I'm afraid not, Matt. She's obviously determined to do this by herself. I wish she'd reconsider, but she won't." Collins fidgeted in his chair. "I just couldn't tell her how, uh, ruthless J.T. can be, since she's such a lady."

"I've got another idea I want to discuss with you. Then I'm going to have a talk with her."

A half hour later Matt was knocking on Miss Taylor's front door.

When she opened the door, he noted her look of shocked surprise, but in less than a second the surprise changed to fierce contempt. She jammed her hand onto her perfectly rounded hip, displayed quite nicely by the day dress she wore without a bustle. He heartily approved. Her hazel eyes had a special glow, which was more fascinating than fearsome.

Matt grinned at her.

"And to what do I owe the pleasure of your company?" She quickly released the doorknob and held up her hand. "No. Don't tell me. Let me guess."

Matt rested his weight on one foot and tilted his hat toward the back of his head, studying her. She was a great-looking woman. Nice hair, sort of soft and curly, and eyes that could tell a story without using any words. And the rest of her . . . well, he couldn't take a long look now, but he'd seen enough before to know that everything was as it should be.

"Hmm." She tapped her finger against her cheek. "You're looking for a house to buy and this one suits you just fine." Sarcasm dripped from her words, and her too polite smile stretched coldly across her face.

"No, ma'am, I'm not and this one doesn't."

"What do you mean 'this one doesn't'?" Her smile vanished instantly.

"Just what I said. It's not the sort of house I

would want to buy, if I even wanted to buy one, which I don't." He leaned his shoulder against the door frame. With his finger he absently smoothed down each side of his mustache.

"And you expect me to believe that?" Her eyes narrowed in disbelief.

"Only if you want to believe the truth. Are you going to ask me in? Or do you want the people passing by to hear our conversation?" He aimed his thumb over his shoulder toward the street behind him.

Irritated, she glanced around him, then stepped aside, closing the door behind him.

"Just what is the truth, Mr. Dawson?"

"Matt," he said pointedly. "The truth is, you're being more than a little foolish about not accepting my offer." He leaned toward her in his earnestness to have her understand.

"I have no intention of exchanging one debtor for another." She stiffened her back and stepped away from him.

"That's where you're making your first mistake. J.T. and I are nothing alike. And if you don't know that by now, you soon will." He wanted her to realize that she was in no position to argue. J.T. always got what he wanted, any way he could get it.

"So you didn't come here to buy my house. You came here to warn me about J.T. Lawrence. Isn't that chivalrous of you?" She flashed him a saccharine smile. "Well, you're a little late, in case you've forgotten."

"I haven't. But I figured you must have since you'd rather owe money to him than me." Matt's irritation rose at her stubbornness.

"How I conduct my business and with whom is none of your affair. Mr. Dawson." Her emphasis on Mister irked him.

"It appears you've got more spunk than sense. I don't know how to make it any clearer to you." He tipped his hat back until it was in danger of falling off his head. "J.T. is a dishonest man. He's a cheat and a liar. He always gets what he wants, and if my guess is right, he wants you!" He hadn't meant to shout at her.

"Keep your voice down!" she whispered, turning to look over her shoulder toward the kitchen.

"Why are you being so bullheaded? I'm only trying to help you." He planted his feet firmly, his thumbs looped in his gunbelt.

"Help? I've heard that before!" she exclaimed. "It usually means I give up something in return. No, thank you! I can do this on my own. I've got boarders now, and before long all the rooms will be filled. Money won't be a problem, Mr. Dawson. I intend to pay J.T. Lawrence every penny my aunt borrowed from him." She glared at him with defiance burning bright in her eyes.

Matt glared back at her, glad that he had made arrangements with Collins. She was going to be, as Charlie would say, mad as a skinned rattler when she heard what he was about to say.

"It doesn't surprise me you won't accept my offer. So I left enough money for one year's payments with Mr. Collins, just in case your house doesn't fill up as fast as you seem to think it will."

He watched while everything about her bristled with anger. The color in her cheeks heightened and her breasts rose with the sudden tensing of

157

her shoulders. She took one step toward him, her teeth tightly clenched.

"You did what?" Her voice was low and full of menace.

"If you weren't so damn stubborn, you'd see how foolish you're being. Sell the house! Buy another one, if you want to run a boardinghouse."

"What right do you have meddling in my affairs?" She stood near enough that he could smell the soft scent of roses in her hair.

But he couldn't answer her because he didn't know what to say.

"I have enough complications to deal with; I don't need you to make things worse," she went on. Some of the fire died in her eyes, even though her fists still rested on her hips.

"I'm trying to get you out of a bad situation that's only going to get worse." He settled his hat squarely on his head. "A simple thank-you will do."

"Thank you!" The fire was back. "I'll thank you to leave me alone!" She advanced another step.

He didn't retreat. At this close range Matt could see the tiny lights of amber in her eyes and the thickness of the dark lashes that framed them. Under other circumstances he'd think she was downright inviting. Even kissable.

She glared at him, and Matt's jaw tensed. She could irritate him, but she didn't make him angry. Not really. He hadn't meant to upset her. And now they were getting nowhere fast. He knew he wasn't making things any better by staying.

Abruptly, he touched the brim of his hat. "Charlie will be looking for me." He turned to go, but stopped with his hand on the door when he heard her speak.

"I don't want your money. Or anyone's."

He opened the door, then faced her. "It's there if you need it." And with that he left, closing the door behind him.

When he looked up, there sat Charlie on his horse, leaning on the saddle horn watching him with disgust clearly written on his face. Matt took the steps two at a time and quickly mounted up.

"Figured I'd find you here."

"Well, I don't know why you figured that." But then Charlie always knew what Matt was up to, and for the first time it got on Matt's nerves.

"I got the supplies ordered. One of the boys can come in and get them in a day or so." Then Charlie clamped his mouth shut.

Matt ignored the unasked question hanging in the air. "Let's get back to the ranch. There's a lot to be done before we get the roundup started." Matt reined his horse around without waiting for Charlie.

Jauncey stared at the door without really seeing it. The last thing she needed was more indebtedness.

She walked to the window and watched Matt Dawson climb on his horse. His long leg swung effortlessly up and over the rump of the horse. With a gesture of determination, he tugged on the brim of his hat while holding the reins in his other hand. After the two men spoke he led the way down the street, his broad shoulders visible for quite a distance.

Jauncey left the window and walked into her office. She wouldn't touch his money. Somehow she would manage to get by without it until her rooms were filled; then she'd be all right according to her calculations. And after the roundups were over, she would have plenty of boarders since most of the cowboys would lose their jobs until spring and winter in the towns. Ginny had assured her everything would improve once the cold weather set in.

Chapter Eleven

The long dry summer neared its end, and now that the evenings were cool enough to warrant a fire in the large fireplace, Maggie and Ginny had taken most of the sitting chairs into the large parlor so the boarders could enjoy its warmth. The cheery glow of the firelight made the room a favorite for everyone in the house.

Even Mr. Natter.

From behind her book, Jauncey surreptitiously surveyed him while he read his newspaper, both feet on the floor approximately an inch apart and the paper held an elbow's length from his nose. Generally he cleared his throat once before turning the page, giving it a quick snap to straighten it. Once he had snapped it so hard it tore halfway down the center.

There were now four other gentlemen boarders. Most evenings they sat before the fire, smoking a pipe or just relaxing before going up to bed. As yet, no women had asked to rent a room, but that didn't surprise Jauncey, since few women were financially independent enough to pay for one. And those who were had shops of their own with rooms attached.

Laying her book aside after all the men had gone to bed, she went in search of Ginny. The time was fast approaching when she would need coal for the small heaters occupying each of the bedrooms. Before too long the temperatures would be well below freezing.

She expected to find Ginny and Maggie talking quietly in the kitchen over a last cup of coffee the way they sometimes did. Instead, she found Ginny standing at the sink with her back to Jauncey and Dan close beside her, his arm around her waist.

She watched as he bent his head and kissed the top of Ginny's dark hair. They stood in shadow with only the lamp burning on the table behind them. Ginny raised her eyes to look at Dan, and immediately his arms encircled her in an embrace. Quietly, Jauncey retreated from the doorway just as Ginny let Dan kiss her.

Such an intimate moment, she thought.

The darkened parlor hid Jauncey, and she was thankful they hadn't seen her. Tiptoeing, she went back to the room where the fire still crackled and snapped cheerfully. Sitting on the edge of a chair close to the heat, she stared into the flames.

Whatever Ginny had been, she deserved happiness now. Dan was a good man and it was obvious how much he cared for her. Lately, he had become an expected guest every evening. When he had to work late Jauncey missed him almost as much as Ginny did. Well, she smiled, perhaps not that much.

She sat before the fire until the embers glowed with only an occasional burst of flame. The house was quiet now. Jauncey heard the muffled sound of shoes across the parlor carpet, and turned to see Ginny standing in the doorway.

"Has Dan gone home?" Jauncey noticed the warm flush in Ginny's cheeks and thought she looked becoming.

"Yes," Ginny said, sitting on a cushioned chair near Jauncey.

"You look very happy," Jauncey said, her voice hushed.

"I am. I really am." Ginny looked from Jauncey to the fire. "I didn't think I would ever be this happy again."

"Again?"

Ginny nodded her head, still staring into the glowing coals. She got up and lifted the lid of the wood box, then selected an armful of the smaller pieces of firewood. Gradually, the fire came to life, licking hungrily at the dry wood.

Jauncey watched her move around, performing the chore easily without giving much thought to what she did. Her mind appeared to be miles away. With Dan? Jauncey wondered. Or her life as Mrs. Marlowe?

"You've never asked me how I came to be working here." Ginny raised her eyes to meet Jauncey's.

Feeling a little guilty and surprised that Ginny had read her mind, Jauncey shrugged her shoulders. "I didn't think it was any of my business."

"That's one of the things I like about you." Ginny smiled at her. "You've just accepted us, and trusted us. I can't tell you what that's meant to me. And to Maggie, too."

"I don't see any reason why I shouldn't."

"Not everyone would feel that way, believe me." Ginny settled back in her chair and wrapped her arms around her middle. "There are 'decent' people who don't understand and wouldn't even care to try. They talk about charity and helping their fellow man, but that's all it is, talk."

Jauncey sensed Ginny's need to get rid of . . . what? Pain? Frustration? Anger?

"I spent the first twenty years of my life in Richmond. It was a beautiful city before the war. I was almost thirteen when it was over. Everyone was as devastated as the city, but I was just a young girl taken with all the things that seem so pressing and important to all young girls. I looked beyond the rubble with a hopeful eye to the future. When I was sixteen I met Benjamin Marlowe and I knew I'd found that future." Ginny smiled. The red and gold from the fire reflected in her dark eyes.

"He wasn't happy with the new South and wanted to head west, where it was said a man could start new and get rich in a week. We went to Virginia City, and he worked in the gold mines for someone else. We didn't get rich at all. But I didn't mind. I was with him and I was so happy. When I found out we were going to have a baby . . ." Ginny paused, her voice thick with emotion. "I thought life just couldn't get any better."

Jauncey watched with a dull ache forming in her chest while Ginny brought herself under control.

"We had a beautiful baby boy. He looked just like his father with his curly dark hair and kind of a sideways smile." She stopped. "He came down with pneumonia. It was common. The houses were all so thin they could barely keep out the cold." Ginny got up to add more wood to the fire. "He died. He was only two." She returned to her seat. "I didn't care about anything after that. Not even Ben."

Jauncey reached out and grasped Ginny's hand. "I'm so sorry." She could feel the tears forming in sympathy for the pain this woman had endured.

"I went on living because I had to. As much as I wanted to die, I couldn't. Ben tried so hard to help me, but he worked long terrible hours in the mines and was too worn out. I must have been an awful burden on him. Then there was an explosion. They happened all the time. And Ben was gone."

Jauncey watched as first one tear, then another slid unheeded down Ginny's cheeks.

"Gone." She blinked her eyes and stared at Jauncey as though trying to recognize who she was. "I was evicted from the little house, put out on the streets with no food, no money. But I didn't care. Now I could die, I thought. Just lie down and die, except it wasn't that easy. I wanted to live. Survival is a strong instinct, one we can't control."

Jauncey thought about her mother. She'd done what she had to do for the well-being of her daughter and herself, regardless of the consequences.

"I wandered the streets for two days before a woman offered me a place to live with food and money. In turn she wanted me to work for her as one of her girls. I said yes."

"My aunt?" Jauncey held her breath.

"No. Her name was Cad Thompson. I didn't meet Spicie until a month later."

Jauncey couldn't say anything. Loathing and disgust filled her chest. These women had taken advantage of Ginny during the worst time in her life.

"Nobody else would help me. People passed me on the street and pulled their skirts aside as though I was one of the girls who lived in the cribs. Good, decent people, you would have thought." Ginny wiped her eyes with a section of her skirt, then straightened in her chair. "When I met Spicie, she offered me more money and another town to live in. I wanted desperately to be away from anything that connected me with the past and a life that no longer belonged to me."

Jauncey's thoughts ran back and forth over what Ginny had said. She tried pulling everything together: a normal marriage and family, tragedy upon tragedy. Was this how it was for all prostitutes?

"What about your family back in Richmond? Wouldn't they help you?"

"I didn't have the money to contact them, and by the time I was making some money I was too ashamed of what I'd become. They wouldn't understand. Few people do." Ginny reached out to Jauncey, clasping their hands together. "Very few people do."

Jauncey squeezed her hands in reassurance. Life had been cruel to Ginny, but nobody deserved to pay forever for making a choice to survive.

"That's all behind you now."

"Yes. It is. And now I've got Dan." A new spark shimmered in Ginny's eyes. "He wants me to marry him."

Jauncey threw her arms around Ginny's shoulders. "Oh, Ginny, that's wonderful! I'm so happy for you both."

Ginny hugged her back. "Thank you. But I haven't said yes."

Jauncey faced her. "Why on earth not?"

"Maggie."

She should have thought of that. Ginny and Maggie were very close, almost like mother and daughter except for the slight difference in their ages.

"I really can't leave her. She's so . . ."

"Fragile?"

"Yes." Ginny gazed into the dying fire. The room was nearly dark.

A sudden idea snapped Jauncey to attention. "You don't have to leave her. You and Dan can live here. I could use a man to help with some of the chores like the coal. Unless Dan has his own house."

"No, he doesn't. He lives with his sister and her family." Ginny smiled. "Do you think it would be all right?"

"It is with me." Jauncey brightened. She hated to think of losing Ginny. Especially now. "I wouldn't charge you for anything as long as I could count on the two of you for help when I needed it."

"Of course, you can always count on that."

"Well?" Jauncey waited for an answer, hoping it would be yes.

"I'll have to talk about this with Dan. But I don't

see why he wouldn't agree, at least until we can find a house of our own. And by then you'll be overflowing with boarders."

"Maggie will adjust easier if you stay here. Then, who knows, maybe she'll find a beau." Jauncey didn't really believe the words she spoke. But just the same, she wished they could come true.

"No." Ginny's voice was quiet. "I don't think that will ever happen."

"She's welcome here for as long as she wants to stay, so don't worry about her."

"She's beginning to take to you a little more. You've been so patient with her and that's important. It won't be long before she trusts you completely." Ginny's eyes held a depth of compassion Jauncey had never seen before in anyone.

"I'm sure she will," Jauncey said. A comfortable, sharing silence filled the room. Jauncey stood and rubbed her arms in the chill air. "I think we'd better go to bed before it gets any colder."

They checked the doors and blew out the lamps before going upstairs. At the top of the steps Jauncey turned to Ginny and hugged her tight. "Congratulations. I'm really happy for you."

"Thanks." Ginny returned her hug with a heartfelt sigh. "Good night."

In her own room, Jauncey set the lamp on the bureau. Married, she thought. What would that be like? She looked at her neatly made bed and considered sharing the same covers with a man, possibly the same pillow. No, that wasn't in her future. Her goal was to be independent, not dependent. Even so, she was glad for Ginny.

Quickly, she dressed for bed and blew out the

lamp, then crawled between the cold sheets, huddling in the center for warmth.

The next morning, before daylight, Jauncey wasted no time dressing and getting downstairs to the warmth of the huge cookstove in the kitchen. It was a sharp reminder that she needed to buy coal.

Her boarders sat around the table, drinking their coffee, waiting for breakfast to be served. Maggie worked busily at the stove with her back turned to them as usual.

"I'm sorry I overslept, Maggie. But that bed was so warm I just didn't wake up," Jauncey whispered.

"That's all right. Nobody minded. And Sug—I mean, Ginny helped." Maggie glanced up to where Ginny was taking plates from the cupboard.

"Well, I won't let it happen again. I promise."

When Maggie looked at her and smiled, Jauncey hid her surprise and smiled back.

Soon forks clinked against dishes and "Pass the butter" or "Pass the salt" was spoken in earnest. Then each man went his respective way for the day.

With the rush over, Jauncey and the two women sat down to eat breakfast and relax with their coffee. Mr. Natter was not an early riser, so they had a few minutes before starting on the last breakfast of the morning.

"What are your plans for the day, Jauncey?" Ginny asked.

Jauncey set her cup down. "I want to ask Dan about getting some coal."

"Spicie always got it from Brailey," Maggie offered tentatively.

Jauncey tried not to stare at her. Maggie seldom said five words to her in an entire day.

"Thank you, Maggie. I'll speak to Brailey about it." She pulled her gaze away from the girl. "What about you?" she said to Ginny.

"I think all the lamp chimneys need a good cleaning. And while I'm getting sooty, I might as well look into the heaters in the bedrooms." She wrinkled her nose.

"Wait until I come back and I'll help you."

Ginny nodded in agreement.

Jauncey made a quick trip to Brailey's, and was glad to be back in plenty of time to help with the lamps. She crossed the front porch and entered the house, where the smell of fresh coffee greeted her. Smiling, she walked through the front parlor to the kitchen where she expected to find Ginny.

"That didn't take . . ." Jauncey halted in mid-sentence when she saw the black-haired Lottie sitting at the far end of the table.

"Would you like some coffee?" Lottie asked, rising from her seat and going to the stove, where she refilled her cup.

Speechless, Jauncey continued standing in the doorway.

Glancing around, Lottie went on as though unaware she hadn't received an answer. "Maggie always did keep a spotless kitchen. Funny how some places just always seem like home." She sipped her coffee. "So which one of the boarders has my room?"

Finally finding her tongue, Jauncey replied, "I haven't any idea which room was yours."

"It's the one with all the windows and the big four-poster bed."

Jauncey felt all the blood drain from her face.

Lottie raised her eyebrows and inclined her head slightly. "You have it?" she said with mild surprise.

Until this moment Jauncey'd been able to put behind her the sort of things that had gone on in this house, and especially in her room. But now, standing before her was a very sharp reminder of exactly what had gone on in her room and who had done them.

Taking a step forward, Jauncey stated flatly, "I think you'd better go."

Lottie placed her cup on the table, giving Jauncey a hard stare. "You might have my room and my home, but that's all you're going to get." Then flicking her eyes over Jauncey's tailored if somewhat worn dress, she added, "Matt Dawson isn't the settling kind. And if he were, he'd need a real woman."

And with those words hanging in the air, Lottie crossed the kitchen and brushed past Jauncey into the front parlor, leaving by the front door.

Dazed, Jauncey stood staring at the empty doorway for several long minutes. Gradually her senses returned. That woman had come uninvited into her home for the sole purpose of making it known that she'd laid claim to Matt Dawson. Whatever made her think Jauncey wanted him in the first place? He definitely wasn't *her* "settling kind," not with his meddlesome ways and the penchant he seemed to have for whorehouses. No, sir! she told herself, Miss Lottie could have him, guns, spurs and all!

Shaking her head, she hurried up to her room to put on an old dress and apron, then went in search of Ginny and Maggie.

When they'd gathered all the lamps and placed them on the kitchen table, Jauncey concentrated on the work at hand, forcing her mind away from Lottie's visit.

After they'd finished, Maggie began baking the necessary loaves of bread and assortment of pies. These were the days Jauncey loved best, when the whole house just seemed warmer and friendlier.

Ginny and Jauncey spent the balance of the day tending the little chimneys of the coal heaters and carrying out soot-covered papers. They wore towels tied around their heads to protect their hair as much as possible, but their faces didn't escape the grime.

When they had finally finished, it wasn't long before the evening meal had to be prepared.

"I suppose we'd better get some of this dirt washed off so we can help Maggie with the cooking," Jauncey said, leading the way downstairs. "Mmm. Smell that apple pie!"

"My favorite." Ginny sniffed the air.

They walked into the kitchen, but there was no Maggie. There were three pies on the table cooling, and one of them had a large wedge missing.

The sound of voices coming from the back porch drew them to the partially open door. Sitting on the steps was Brailey, with a piece of pie. Maggie sat beside him.

"Miz Maggie, you shore do make one tasty pie."

Jauncey saw him smile and wink at Maggie. Brailey was probably old enough to be Maggie's father, and he treated her with fatherly affection, obviously something Maggie needed.

"I know it's your favorite," Maggie replied.

"It shore is." He took another bite.

"Afternoon, Brailey," Jauncey called.

He turned halfway around. "Afternoon to you, too, Miz Jauncey. This young lady must make you proud to sit people at your table."

"That's the truth." Jauncey smiled at both of them.

Brailey squinted up at her. "Looks to me like you been hauling a little coal around yourself."

Jauncey put a hand up to her face and laughed. "I might as well have. I probably couldn't get any dirtier."

Brailey handed the empty plate to Maggie. "Well, I'd better get to work. Thank you kindly for the pie."

Jauncey watched Brailey's lanky frame disappear around the corner of the house. Then she turned her gaze on Maggie, who continued to sit with the plate in her hands.

"He's a very nice man," Jauncey said, watching Maggie's eyes follow Brailey.

Maggie turned toward her. "Yes, he is."

Jauncey was never more aware of the change in Maggie than now. Her clear blue eyes held less fear and worry. The fear Jauncey could understand, but worry? Perhaps Jauncey had only imagined it. After all, Maggie had nothing to fear or worry about anymore.

173

"We should ask him to stay for dinner sometime. What do you think?" Jauncey asked.

"I think he would like that. He doesn't have a family." Maggie got up from the step and walked past Jauncey and Ginny into the kitchen.

"He doesn't?" Jauncey asked.

Maggie shook her head. "He told me once he'd had a daughter about my age. She got married young and died in childbirth."

Ginny added, "His wife has been gone for some time."

Maggie busied herself with her pies and bread, closing Jauncey out once more.

Jauncey puzzled over Maggie's reaction to Brailey. She obviously avoided all the men in the boardinghouse, even though none of them had ever said anything unkind to her. But then Brailey had the ability to put anyone at ease.

The sound of voices coming from the backyard drew Jauncey's and Ginny's attention once more. They strained to peek out the door to see who Brailey was speaking to. Then around the corner came Andrew Collins carrying his bowler hat.

"Oh, my!" Jauncey exclaimed with one hand on the towel around her hair and one on her smudged cheeks. Visitors! Today of all days!

Ginny stepped out of view with her back to the wall.

Well, Jauncey thought, she could hardly run off since he'd already spotted her.

"Miss Taylor," he began. "Isn't this a lovely day?"

"Uh, yes, it is. I'm afraid you've caught me at a rather embarrassing moment. I'm covered with soot and I'd like to invite you in, but . . ."

"Oh, I'm so sorry to have come at such an inopportune time." He took a deep breath, then went on. "I only wanted to bring you these."

From behind his hat he produced a bouquet of some of the last lingering wildflowers. With the tips of his ears burning, he handed them to her.

She accepted the somewhat wilted flowers, flushing profusely. "They're lovely. Thank you."

Standing beside her but hidden from Mr. Collins's view, Ginny covered her grinning mouth. Jauncey did her best to ignore her.

"They're n-not as lovely as you are, Miss Taylor," he said softly as his Adam's apple bobbed nervously.

Embarrassed by this sudden show of affection from someone she'd thought of only as a friend, she hardly knew what to say. "Thank you."

"Well, I must be going and leave you to your work. Again I apologize for this unannounced call. The next time I'll send a note ahead and wait for your reply." He bowed slightly from the waist and turned to go.

When he'd disappeared past the edge of the house, she let out a sigh. "Merciful heavens!"

Ginny smiled entreatingly at her. "Wasn't that sweet? He likes you." She took the flowers from Jauncey's hand and pumped water into a glass.

Dropping into a chair at the table, Jauncey stared at the poor wilting flowers Ginny had placed in the glass. "What did I do to encourage him?"

"Love hears and sees what it wants to," Ginny answered. "He is very nice. You could do worse." She smiled.

"Now I feel guilty. You're right." She sighed again

and unbound the towel from her hair. "Actually, he's exactly the sort of man my mother would have chosen for me."

"My guess is that most mothers would."

Nodding her agreement, she wondered how she was going to handle this new development.

After she and Ginny filled the scuttles with coal and carried them up to the rooms, they each took a long hot bath before the boarders arrived home. Jauncey found she could hardly keep her eyes open during the meal, and it was even harder to stay awake while sitting before the fire. Finally, she excused herself and went to bed.

Earlier she had built a fire in the small coal stove in her room, and the warmth of it surrounded her when she opened the door. Dressing in a night-gown wasn't the quick change of clothing it had been for the past several nights, with layers of gooseflesh raised along her arms and legs. Now she could leisurely undress, and she knew the bed would not be as cold either.

Blowing out the lamp, she climbed into bed, knowing it would take only a little of her body heat to warm the sheets. Then she pulled the quilt to her nose and snuggled into the depths of the soft mattress, closing her eyes.

But her mind would not rest. Thoughts of Ginny and Dan getting married kept her awake. Marriage. What would that be like? She remembered Uncle Harold and Aunt Ida and shook her head. That was not her idea of marriage. And she couldn't see Ginny being so obsessively in control of Dan. No, she thought, they would talk and make decisions together. Remembering the scene she'd witnessed,

Jauncey knew sharing and loving came naturally to Ginny, and to Dan, too.

She stretched the toes of her foot tentatively toward the bottom of the bed to check for warmth. Finding it, she rolled onto her back, extending both her legs and wiggling her toes.

Imagine, she mused, being married to Andrew Collins and sharing this bed with him. The idea was too amusing to be considered seriously, although she felt a stab of guilt for making light of his obvious infatuation. She would have to be kind yet firm when she let him know her life held no room for romantic involvement.

Firelight seeped through the cracks of the stove, making patterns that moved lazily across the ceiling. As she stared at them, the light lessened to a warm glow, then suddenly burst into brightness once again. The effect was hypnotizing.

Her eyelids grew heavy and all thoughts of Dan, Ginny and Mr. Collins disappeared, only to be replaced with visions of Matt Dawson standing in her doorway. He leaned casually against the closed door, grinning, his black hair shining in the light like moonlight on coal. He didn't say anything, and she wondered why he had come. Then just as silently, he opened the door and left, closing it with a loud click.

Jauncey opened her eyes at the sound, dispelling the dream. The dark room appeared almost black, since the fire had died to embers. Something had awakened her, something that was not in her dream. She lay quietly, straining to listen. A light appearing beneath her door flickered as though a breeze threatened to put it out, then brightened at the same time she heard another click.

The attic.

Jauncey was sure someone had been in the attic. Maggie? Who else would go up there? What a strange, troubled girl to grieve so long over a woman who had brought her into a terrible way of life. Jauncey watched as the light disappeared. A moment later she heard a door close farther down the hall.

Pulling her legs up to her chest, she lay in a ball, wide awake now. She wasn't afraid of Maggie, not really, but she couldn't understand her. She didn't even know much about her.

For the rest of the night Jauncey rolled around in a bed that had suddenly turned lumpy and uncomfortable. She thumped and punched her pillow, remembering it had once been Lottie's bed.

And what about Matt Dawson?

Her hand stopped in mid-punch.

Had he also spent nights in this bed? With that thought uppermost, she slammed her fist into the center of the soft pillow, then flopped back down to stare at the dark ceiling.

Why should it matter to her? she asked herself.

It didn't, she replied silently. Not one whit.

Chapter Twelve

As usual, Matt kept his eye on Johnny during the entire roundup. At least during mealtimes it was easier to do.

Johnny filled his tin plate with the noon fare and found a place away from the chuck wagon. He sat down cross-legged on the ground and took a bite of the fried steak, chewing it hungrily. When he noticed Matt staring at him, he stopped chewing and stared back.

Matt didn't miss the tightening of the muscles in Johnny's face. He was obviously irritated at being watched. Good, Matt thought, and moved with his plate to where Charlie sat.

Matt scooped up the gravy with his biscuit, but barely tasted it, his mind occupied on trapping the rustlers, and Johnny along with them. He knew that if you turned a caged animal loose, it would run straight for its hole. And Matt was counting on

Johnny to do the same thing, except he would head straight for the rustlers hiding out somewhere.

He'd known for some time that Johnny acted as the go-between, passing information from J.T. to the men Johnny hired. The rustlers would do nothing until they had word from Johnny, and Matt had done everything possible to prevent that from happening. The wear and tear on Johnny's nerves had begun to show.

He watched Johnny get up to fill his cup with fresh coffee, and everyone held their cups out calling the familiar "Man at the pot!"

Johnny slammed the pot down with a splash, yelling, "Get your own damn coffee!" Then he stalked off.

All heads swung in his direction. Matt knew that most of the men disliked Johnny, and few of them hid the fact.

Charlie nodded at Matt and quietly followed Johnny. Placing his dirty dish in the waiting wash pan, Matt ambled behind Charlie. Johnny would have to be guarded real close tonight, Matt thought. Then tomorrow night he would assign Johnny night duty, giving him the opportunity to slip off. And Matt would be ready. More than ready.

Camp for the noon meal had been set up near the river where a few cottonwood trees dotted the banks. But most of their leaves had long since gone, allowing the midday sun to warm anyone who chose to sit beneath them.

Matt hunkered down beside Charlie, his back against a tree. "What do you think?" he asked, nodding in Johnny's direction.

"'Bout to crack like an old walnut that's laid on the ground too long."

"That's what I figure, too." Matt picked up a blade of withered grass and inspected it. "Maybe tomorrow night is all we can hope for, before he really does crack."

"I think you're right." Charlie squinted up at the cloudless sky. "Should be a clear night, if the weather holds. And I imagine it will."

Matt pushed his hat to the back of his head and gazed across the land. This was the second week of the roundup and things were going fairly smooth, considering. The summer had been dry, with less than three inches of rain since spring, and the cattle showed the effects of it. They lacked their usual weight, due to poor grazing. He doubted they could make it through a rough winter, and everyone predicted one, even the Indians on the reservations. Matt didn't hold much with signs and predictions, but thin cows on thinner grass was asking for trouble. He planned to sell everything but the hardiest animals. At least he could minimize his losses that way.

Matt hadn't mentioned this to J.T. He didn't see any reason to alert the man to move any faster in his rustling activity. It would be better to let him think he had all winter to take what was left.

When it was time for the second shift to come in and have their meal, each man on the first shift mounted up, as if on cue, and rode toward the branding pens.

That afternoon Johnny was at the pens with Matt, no questions asked. An open confrontation would do neither of them any good, and both knew it.

Three other outfits were part of the roundup, and each had their own pens for marking the calves that had been missed earlier. Most of the time it wasn't difficult to tell who owned a calf since the mother cow kept close. These unmarked calves were the ones the rustlers preyed upon, since it would be harder to prove the animal wasn't theirs. But the more adventurous thieves didn't mind the risk of branding over an existing well-known brand, like the Diamond D.

Matt had already checked Johnny's saddle for the hidden running iron some cowboys carried. He hadn't been surprised to find that Johnny was too smart for that. Nevertheless, someone had to have one and Matt intended to catch him. Only this time he wouldn't take them into Laramie for the marshal to turn loose. He'd lock them in an outhouse if necessary, until the Cattlemen's Association or the U.S. marshal looked into the matter.

Matt and his men took their turns at roping and wrestling each of the calves while a hot brand was applied. The odor of burnt hair and sweat hung in the dust-filled air.

Each afternoon was a duplication of the previous one. And it ended the same, too, with each man bone tired and desperately in need of a bath.

Immediately following the evening meal, the shift for guarding the cattle was switched. The men coming in first wolfed down their meal and hit the bedroll, knowing their next shift would come all too soon.

Matt jerked his bedroll from the stack on the chuck wagon and spread the tarp on the ground where he could watch Johnny through the night.

After crawling inside fully clothed, he pulled the rest of the tarp over him to keep out the brisk cold wind. In a matter of moments, the warmth generated by his trapped body heat forced his eyes closed.

Thoughts of thick whiskey-colored hair scented with roses nestled inside his brain. Hazily, he wondered if her boardinghouse was prospering or if she had needed the money he'd arranged for Collins to use to cover her loan.

In what seemed only a second later, Charlie was shaking him. "Matt! That varmint's gone. I don't know how he did it, but he did."

Matt awoke with a start and threw back his covers. "Did anyone see him go?" He was on his feet at once.

"Cook said he lit out toward the river about twenty minutes ago."

Furious with himself, he lashed out at Charlie. "Why the hell didn't you go after him?"

"And let you miss out on all the fun?" Charlie grinned. "I gave Ted, Shorty and Buck a good kick to wake 'em."

Matt and Charlie ran for their horses, the others close behind.

For 20 minutes they rode hard along the nearly dry riverbed. Matt slowed, then came to a halt. He listened for the sound of horses and strained his eyes in search of a campfire. Nothing.

They continued on until the wind carried the smell of smoke to them. They couldn't be far away, Matt thought. And they couldn't be too smart, either. They weren't more than five miles from where the herd rested for the night.

Matt motioned for Ted and Shorty to go in one direction while he, Charlie and Buck went the other way. Matt hoped they could circle the camp.

Before long a bright campfire came into view, but at this distance Matt couldn't be sure how many men there were. So he and Charlie left their horses downriver with Buck, giving him instructions to ride in when the trouble began.

Shrouded in darkness, Matt and Charlie crept up to the edge of a copse of trees just behind the camp. No sign of Johnny. Matt wondered if he was making a mistake and wasting his time with nothing more than some drifters.

He studied the two men sitting beside the campfire, on which a tin coffeepot boiled over. One of the men jumped up to grab it from the heat of the fire.

"Ya lazy bastard! Why'd ya let it boil over?" He cuffed his partner on the head, making him duck.

"Touch me again, Hank, and I swear I'll shoot ya!" the other man shouted, reaching for the gun in his holster.

"Christ-a-mighty, what ya doin', trying to get us caught?" Hank said in a loud whisper, his eyes nearly bulging out of his head.

"Aw, ain't nobody out here but a bunch of dumb cattle and a couple of damn fools. How come we gotta sit here?"

"We don't ask questions as long as we get paid. So shut up," Hank said, pouring a cup of coffee.

Matt motioned Charlie to the other side of the trees where he could come up behind the men when the time was right. Matt watched Charlie move over the ground with the agility of a man half his age.

Hank slurped his coffee while alternately sloshing his cup and blowing on it.

"I hate it when ya do that! Ya sound like a damn bull at a shallow waterin' hole."

"Since when did you get such fancy manners?" Hank said, grimacing at his partner.

Matt couldn't believe J.T.'s stupidity in keeping these men on after they'd been caught once. Unless it had been Johnny's idea.

"Shit. Fancy manners is that oversized dandy banker," the partner said. "If he points that fat finger in my face one more time, I'm gonna break it off and shove it up his ass."

"That's some mighty big talk from someone who says 'sir' every time J.T. farts." Hank grinned broadly.

Matt stepped into the circle of firelight, his gun reflecting its glow. "Evening, boys. Coffee still hot?"

Hank whirled, his hand flying to his gun.

"That could be the last move you'll ever make." Matt kept his voice low and steady. "Drop it where you stand." He gestured with his gun. "Your friend, too."

Hank and the other man gently removed their guns and tossed them aside.

"Charlie." He barely raised his voice, his eyes still narrowed on the two men.

Appearing from the other side of camp, Charlie moved out of the darkness toward them, his gun pointed. "What we got here, Boss? Couple of rattlesnakes looking to have their rattlers pinched?"

"Could be."

185

Hank looked from Matt to Charlie with worried eyes. "We ain't done nothin' wrong. We're just havin' a bite to eat and beddin' down for the night; then we'll be movin' on."

"I don't think we can let you do that. Can we, Boss?" Charlie never took his eyes off the men.

Matt pointed his gun in the air and shot once. Hank and his partner jumped, staring hard into the night beyond the trees. Within minutes, the sound of horses thundered closer.

"Ted, bring a rope," Matt said, enjoying the way the men squirmed. "No," he corrected himself, "bring two."

"Now hold on," Hank's partner whined. "You got no call to hang us."

"That's r-r-right," Hank sputtered.

"I think rustling is a pretty damn good reason." Matt gripped his gun firmly and clenched his jaw.

"You got no proof." Hank looked around frantically.

"Don't need any," Matt said. "Buck, tie their hands. Shorty, get their horses."

"Listen, maybe we can make a deal." Hank wet his lips.

"Why should I deal with a dead man?" Matt asked impatiently.

" 'Cause we know somethin' and if you hang us you'll never find out." Hank looked a little more relaxed, as if he were in control now.

Matt glared at him. "I know all I need to know."

"J.T.'s got big plans." Hank's sidekick blurted out. "Big plans."

"That's right." Hank smiled smugly.

Matt wanted to pound that smug look right off

Hank's face, but held himself in check. After all, when he turned these two in, he wanted them each to be in one piece.

"What plans?" Matt swung the knotted rope from his hand like a pendulum.

"You got to let us go," Hank said, his eyes on the rope.

"No deal. Put him on his horse and hold the reins," Matt said to Shorty.

"Wait! What kinda deal do you want?" Hank croaked.

"You tell the marshal everything you're going to tell us." Matt glared at the pair. "It's that or nothing."

Hank hesitated for a moment. "All right. J.T.'s payin' us and some other fella to take your cattle to Cheyenne to sell."

"What else?" Matt had already figured that much. There had to be more.

"He plans on takin' over the Diamond D, only he'll call it the Diamond Circle. He's already got some of your cattle brands burnt over. Then he'll register his brand with the Stock Association and everything will be all legal." Hank swallowed hard. "Ya ain't gonna hang us now, are ya?"

"Charlie, get them on their horses." Matt ground the words out. He'd like nothing better than to see their worthless hides swing, but more than that, he wished it was J.T.'s neck on the line.

"Ya promised!" Hank's partner whined again.

Matt grabbed him by his shirtfront and jabbed his gun into the man's ribs. "One more word and I guarantee you won't make it to town alive." Matt dropped him in the dust.

187

Unable to get up with his hands tied behind him, the man scrambled away from Matt.

"You said another man is involved?" Matt knew it had to be Johnny.

"What's it matter?" Hank looked nervous.

"It matters a lot. Especially to your neck."

"Johnny . . . Don't know no last name." Hank glanced from side to side, peering into the dark.

"How do you happen to know so much about J.T., but not much about Johnny?"

"Sounds peculiar to me, too, Boss." Charlie stood relaxed, one leg outstretched.

Hank shifted his feet, but said nothing.

"I think we ought to loosen that tongue of yours," Charlie said. He stepped closer to Hank with deadly purpose in his expression.

Hank stepped back out of Charlie's reach. " 'Cause that's all Johnny told us!"

"Now why would Johnny tell a couple of no-'counts that much information about J.T. and nothing about himself?" Charlie spoke to Matt as though they were alone, without taking his eyes off the two men.

Matt wondered the same thing. And where was Johnny now? Well, he wasn't taking any chances.

He motioned to the three men with him. "Take these two out to the line cabin on the north range. Don't let them out without a gun in their backs, even for a call of nature. And shoot if you have to."

"Yessir, Mr. Dawson." Buck brought the horses up and helped the men mount. "Y'all heard the man. No funny business if you like your backside all in one fine piece."

"Cover yourselves. Johnny's out there some-where," Matt said quietly to them before climbing onto his horse.

Matt and Charlie headed toward the camp.

"You think you ought to have sent them off that way?" Charlie asked.

"I don't see what choice I've got, since Johnny's probably waiting for the right time to make his move."

"So you're just gonna give it to him?" Disbelief sounded in Charlie's voice.

"That's what he'll think." Matt smiled at Charlie through the darkness. "I want you to go on to camp while I double back to the line cabin. I hope to get there before Johnny. Maybe I can catch three varmints instead of two."

"I don't know about this." Charlie shook his head.

"I do."

They rode on a little farther before Matt turned north to circle in from the back. He could make better time if he didn't have to worry about meet-ing Johnny along the way.

Matt arrived at the cabin and kept a distance of about 20 yards. A north wind suddenly sent clouds scudding across the sky, blotting out the white moonlight. Matt breathed a little easier, thankful for the blanket of darkness.

He peered into the dark while he listened for the sound of a horse. Faintly, it came to him on the wind and he reached for his gun, aiming it in that direction, waiting. His eyes strained through the shadows. Tense, he held himself in check. Maybe it was nothing more than a drifter looking for shel-ter. Suddenly a match quickly flared at the door of the cabin; then the wind extinguished it.

Johnny.

Matt dropped the reins and slid from his horse, easing toward the cabin, his gun ready. When he finally reached the cabin he flattened himself against the side wall and listened.

He heard Johnny bump into a table and dump a chair over.

"Son of a bitch!"

There was no mistaking the voice. It was Johnny.

Before Matt could decide whether to go in after him or wait until the others arrived, the sound of horses burst upon him.

Trapped inside the small windowless cabin, Johnny wouldn't dare make his presence known unless he used the element of surprise.

"Everybody stand still," Johnny said, his voice slicing the night.

Matt kept out of view. At this close range, the darkness was no cover.

"Johnny! We're shore glad to set eyes on you again," Hank said.

"Well, don't be."

"What d'ya mean by that?" Hank sounded worried.

"You're not as stupid as you look, Hank, or are you?"

"J-J-Johnny, Hank's the one. It warn't me," whined the other man.

"Shut up! I'm sick of both of you."

"What ya gonna do?" Hank's voice rose a pitch higher than before.

"Since there ain't no trees to hang you, I guess I'll

just have to shoot you. All of you." Johnny dragged the words out, obviously enjoying the moment.

Matt heard the click of the hammer as it was pulled back. He wasn't about to let Johnny take away his chance of nailing J.T. with Hank and his partner's confessions.

"Don't move a hair," Matt said, stepping into sight. He didn't look at anyone except Johnny, but he could almost feel his own men's relief. "Release the hammer. Real careful, now. I'd hate to put a hole in that nice Stetson of yours." Matt heard the familiar click. "Now drop it, easy."

Johnny did as he was told, glaring at Matt the entire time.

"So you didn't like what these men had to say? Sounds like they were only telling the truth. Why don't you try doing that?" Matt paused. "It might save your neck. Not that it's your neck I'm interested in."

Johnny remained silent.

"Suit yourself." Matt steeled his gaze on Johnny.

"Ted, bring some rope and tie his hands," Matt said. "Then I want you to ride into town and wire Marshal Davis. Tell him to come out to the ranch as soon as he can." Matt turned to Buck and Shorty. "You're in charge."

"Yessir, Mr. Dawson," both men answered.

Matt wouldn't rest easy until he had J.T. under similar circumstances. But this was the best he could do for now. He still had the roundup to finish and the cattle to be sent to market.

After seeing the men secured inside the cabin, and his men positioned outside, Matt headed back to camp.

Chapter Thirteen

Thanksgiving was less than a week away, and the threat of snow hung in the air like frosty breath on a January morning. Jauncey pulled her coat closer. She still hadn't gotten used to the incessant wind.

She wanted this to be the best Thanksgiving possible. Not just for her boarders, but for Ginny and Maggie. And for herself. She looked forward to a time of warmth, friendliness and laughter, something that had been missing from recent Thanksgivings.

Walking along the boarded walk, she stayed as close to the buildings as possible without bumping into the sidewalk advertising signs. Trabing's wasn't far, and she hurried her steps.

A gust of wind blew in the door with her, giving a sudden last lift to her hem.

"Hello, Jauncey. Has it started to snow yet?" Dan came around the counter to greet her.

"Not yet." She smiled a greeting. The wonderful

warmth of the room surrounded her.

"Well, unless everybody's wrong, it'll be here before the day's over."

Jauncey made a face. Dire weather predictions plagued every conversation, it seemed.

"What can I do for you today?" Dan crossed his arms and smiled in his usual friendly way.

"I forgot to ask you last night about ordering some things we'll need for Thanksgiving, mostly for pies and of course the turkey." She removed her gloves and held her hands up to the stove in the middle of the floor.

"One large turkey, delivered." Dan wrote on a tablet while he spoke aloud.

"Do you have currants and raisins this time of year? And maybe some peaches—dried, of course."

"Yes, ma'am, nothing out of the ordinary about that. Miss Spicie used to order all sorts of . . ."

An uncomfortable silence settled between them. Jauncey's difficulty with accepting her aunt had evidently gotten to Dan's ears. That in itself didn't bother her, but she was sorry she made others so uncomfortable.

"Good," she went on cheerily. "I'm planning to have four kinds of pie: peach, apple, mincemeat and pumpkin. Be sure to bring your appetite to dinner."

"There's no question about that," he replied, smiling broadly. "Couldn't find any better cooks in all of Laramie. You ought to invite the public, for a price."

Jauncey laughed. "I don't know if we're up to cooking for that many! With two more boarders, and all men at that, we'll have our hands full as it is. Maggie spent all day yesterday making out this list." She pulled a piece of paper from her pocket and handed it to him.

Dan looked it over. "We've got it all," he said proudly. "When would you like me to bring it?"

"Tomorrow will be soon enough." Jauncey pulled her gloves on and prepared to leave.

"Would you tell Ginny I won't be over tonight?" he said. "We've got a lot of shelves that need stacking." He looked disappointed to miss even one evening with Ginny.

"Of course I'll tell her. She'll be sorry to hear it." At his look of misery, she added, "But she'll understand. Tomorrow night?"

"Without a doubt." He brightened at her words.

Jauncey said good-bye, then tucked her nose into the collar of her coat. Her next stop was to visit Mr. Collins, but the cold made her wish she was going straight home. She had thought long and hard about even asking him to dinner, thereby encouraging his attentions, which she honestly did not want.

And he'd been very persistent. After bringing her the flowers he'd brought her a box of confections, and they'd sat together primly in the parlor sipping tea. It had been so uncomfortable for Jauncey to allow him to call on her that she'd tried, unsuccessfully, to discourage further visits. One time he'd even moved from his seat to plant himself firmly beside her on the settee and taken her hand in his. She'd carefully extracted her hand and brought an end to the visit with an invented excuse.

Now, she was actually inviting him for Thanksgiving. Deep inside she feared it was a mistake, but on the other hand she didn't wish to be unkind to a friend who apparently had no family to spend the holiday with. She would simply have to set him straight at the appropriate time in as gentle a manner as she could. With that settled in her mind, she hurried to his office.

Opening the door, she was ushered in by the wind. Whirling, she closed the door with a loud click.

Andrew Collins appeared in the doorway of the back room, an open book held in his hands. "Why, Miss Taylor! What a lovely surprise!" His beaming features brought a moment of despair to Jauncey.

"But what brings you out on such a nasty day?" he went on.

"Something important. Thanksgiving." She smiled and walked to the small round stove that matched the little room perfectly in size.

"Thanksgiving?" he asked, looking puzzled.

"I would like to invite you to have Thanksgiving dinner with us, unless you have other plans." She sat on the chair near the stove, her hands outstretched toward the heat.

"I-I-I . . . Well, no, I don't have any plans actually."

"There'll be a houseful," she warned him. "We have more boarders now plus Ginny, Maggie and myself, and a friend."

"I would be honored to come to dinner at your house." He smiled. "What time?"

"Noon. That is if the turkey cooperates by getting done on time." She laughed and rose from the chair.

"Uh, may I ask who your friend is? Could it be Matt?"

"Oh, no!" She shook her head vigorously. "This friend is Ginny's, not mine. I don't mean that Matt—Mr. Dawson, is a friend of mine. I mean . . ."

She didn't know what she meant. Mr. Collins had brought up something she'd been thinking about for a long time, but hadn't really been able to sort out. Did Matt Dawson want to be her friend, and was that what he had told Mr. Collins? The last time she'd seen him, he'd offered to help her. If he didn't want to buy her house, what other reason would he have?

"I had no intention of making you uncomfortable, Miss Taylor. Please forgive me."

She knew she'd overreacted. "It's all right. Don't apologize." Jauncey prepared to leave. "We'll expect you for Thanksgiving. Bring your appetite."

"Oh, I will. I will." He opened the door for her, laid his hand on the small of her back and ushered her out the door.

Once more she buried her nose in the collar of her coat, while the wind brought tears to her eyes and she lifted a gloved hand to shield her face.

Peeking through her fingers, she saw J.T. Lawrence coming toward her. Dread filled her. Quickly, she crossed the street and slipped inside the bank. With her attention riveted on J.T., she gave only passing attention to the tellers behind the tall glass windows.

Not until he had passed did she breathe a sigh of relief. But as she watched, he suddenly stepped into an alley. Jauncey squinted and frowned trying to see the shadowy person facing him, but all she could make out was a woman dressed in layers of frills and a short jacket rimmed in fur. Her finger pointed angrily at J.T.'s face.

He puffed up his chest. Then his hand lashed out, thrusting the woman up against the side of a building, while he held his other hand out, palm up. Suddenly, the woman came away from the wall in a wild struggle, spitting into his hand. Carefully, J.T. wiped it on his trousers, spoke a few words and walked away. Apparently shaken, the woman waited in the shadows for a moment before stepping out of the alley.

Jauncey gasped as her hand instantly covered her mouth. Ruby! How unsettling to see those two together. Somehow it seemed like a bad omen, since both of them had a connection with her house in one way or another. She knew she was being ridiculous, but nevertheless, she couldn't shake her feeling of foreboding.

When J.T. and Ruby were no longer in sight, Jauncey hurried out into the cold. More than ever she needed to get home where the fire crackled and Maggie was busy baking bread.

She arrived breathless at her front door, not stopping to admire the beautiful architecture as she usually did even in the cold. Bursting into the house, she went straight to the kitchen.

Maggie and Ginny looked up in surprise to see her standing in the doorway trying to catch her breath.

"What's wrong?" Ginny quickly came to her side.

"Noth . . . nothing. Real . . . really." She laid her

197

hand on her chest, too winded to talk.

Ginny helped her off with her coat, and Maggie poured a cup of coffee from the pot that always sat on the back of the stove nowadays.

"Something is wrong. What is it?" Ginny sat in the chair across from her, rubbing her cold hand.

Jauncey sipped at her cup, wrapping her icy fingers around the warm stoneware.

"I saw J.T. in town. He didn't see me, thank goodness." Jauncey took a deep breath, feeling safer already. "He met Ruby in an alley. He pushed her. Hard." Jauncey took another deep breath. "That terrible man frightens me."

Ginny frowned. "He's not someone you want to make angry."

"I know. That's why I want him to stay away from here, away from me." Jauncey shivered, her body getting accustomed to the warmth. "I avoided him by going into the bank. I'm sure he didn't see me, but I rushed back home anyway."

Maggie put her hand on Jauncey's shoulder, and she in turn looked up at her and smiled. "I'm all right now. I feel foolish for being so afraid when nothing happened."

"You're safe here," Maggie said, her voice calm and quiet.

"You're right." Jauncey sipped her coffee again, then set the cup down. She did feel much better. "I stopped at Trabing's to order the turkey and everything we need for dinner. Oh, Ginny, before I forget, Dan said to tell you he won't be able to stop by tonight."

"He's probably shelving holiday goods." Ginny looked as disappointed as Dan had. She glanced out the door at the scattering of snowflakes being whisked along the ground.

"Dan was right," Jauncey said. "It's starting to snow." She was glad Brailey had taken care of the coal supply. And there was plenty of wood split and stacked outside the back door, thanks to some of the boarders.

"I asked Mr. Collins to come for Thanksgiving and he said yes. That will certainly give us a large gathering and most of them are hearty eaters." Her spirits lifted when she thought about the table filled with good food and sharing it with friends.

A pleasing odor penetrated her senses. "What is that wonderful smell?"

"Cinnamon cakes. But they won't keep until Thanksgiving, even if it weren't for that pesky mouse," Ginny said. "So I thought we'd have them for dessert."

"Mouse?" Jauncey could stand spiders and other crawling insects, but not mice. The hair on the back of her neck lifted.

"Probably 'mice' since they don't live solitary lives. Unfortunately." Ginny carefully opened the oven door a crack to check on the small cakes. "Maybe we should get a cat, one that's going to have kittens."

"You're absolutely right." Jauncey smoothed down the gooseflesh on her neck. "Maybe two mother cats."

They spent the evening the same way as the previous ones, with the men retiring to the parlor after the meal was finished. Then Jauncey, Ginny and Maggie did the dishes, which was no small task any longer. By the time they had finished, the men had already said good night and gone upstairs, each with a pitcher of hot water for washing.

Jauncey peered out the kitchen window. The falling snow, blown by the gusting wind against the windowpanes, served as a curtain. She cupped her hand around her eyes and put her face to the glass, but still she could see nothing but white. Thank goodness the house was not so old that it whistled and creaked in the wind. At least, not much.

Ginny and Maggie had finished with their baths and gone to bed early, while Jauncey waited by the fire for the water to heat for her bath. She was glad for this quiet time. All day the house bustled with activity, and she enjoyed an occasional evening alone.

Listening to the crackle of the wood burning, she mulled over the things that had changed since she'd arrived. Out of everything, Jauncey was the most surprised by Maggie and the way she'd tried to comfort Jauncey earlier, something she hadn't done before.

Then there was the problem of the loan payments. She'd used some of Matt Dawson's money to make one payment, even though she hated doing it. But now she was a little ahead because of it, especially with the two new boarders, and she vowed to pay him back with interest.

She left the warmth of the fire to bring her nightclothes downstairs, deciding that with all the men asleep, she could put on her gown right after her bath so she wouldn't have to undress again in her room.

After filling the tub, she closed the door and hung her dress on one of the many hooks that lined one wall. She hesitated a moment before she climbed in, considering the rose-scented bath salts on the table near the tub. She took only a pinch and sprinkled it over the water, then used her hand to stir it. Only a slight fragrance wafted from the water, so she picked up the box and tipped it to sprinkle in a little more. From the corner of her eye, she saw something gray streak across the floor and under the door. Yelping with surprise, she dropped the entire box into the water. Instantly, the room bloomed with the strong scent of roses, making her wrinkle her nose at the overpowering aroma. Exasperated, she climbed in anyway, knowing she simply could not empty the tub and fill it again. But she definitely would not dawdle in the delicious warmth of the water unless she wanted the scent of roses to linger on her skin and in her hair for days.

After washing her hair, she quickly got out and toweled herself dry. She caught up her hair in another towel, then donned her gown. Full of gathers, it laid against her body in folds.

Jauncey built up the fire in the kitchen stove and sat before it to dry her hair. The strong odor of roses permeated the kitchen. It smelled like a . . . bordello. She frowned at the thought.

Outside, a rattling sound drew her attention and she turned to face the back door. Only the wind against the windows, she decided, and busied herself with adding more wood to the fire. But the sound came again, so she cautiously went to the door. This time the rapping was insistent.

"Jauncey!"

Thinking it was Dan, she threw open the door.

Matt Dawson burst past her, bringing a good part of the snowstorm with him. "A man could freeze to death waiting for you to open the door!" He went directly to the stove, removing his gloves.

Snow clung to the wool of his heavy coat, sifting to the floor when he shivered. She watched while he turned his hands over and over, rubbing them together. Standing off to the side, she had a good view of his profile. He had a strong nose with a thick mustache beneath it. His brows, like his mustache, were white with snowflakes lodged between the fine hairs. He brushed his face with his hand, and the particles of snow sizzled as they hit the range top.

"It's cold enough out there to freeze the . . ." He glanced at her. "I mean, it's damn cold out there."

Jauncey saw the way his eyes quickly took in her attire, and she moved into the shadows, finding a seat at the table. With one slippered foot on top of the other, she pulled them both back into the folds of her gown.

"What brings you out on a night like this?" And why did you come here? she wondered.

He turned his back to the stove, keeping his hands behind him. "Just finished trailing the herd to the railroad. We should have finished sooner." He shivered once more. "Wish we had."

Jauncey wondered if he wanted to rent a room. What would he say when she told him there were none left? Except for her office, of course.

"Would you like some coffee?" she offered.

"I sure would." Then he added, "If it's not too much trouble."

"The stove is hot so it won't take any time at all." She moved self-consciously to the sink and pumped water into the pot. After adding the coffee, she walked the long way around the table, where the room was mostly in shadow, then back again to place the pot on the hottest part of the stove. Quickly she returned to her seat, wishing desperately she hadn't given in to the temptation of wearing her nightgown. Thank goodness she'd at least turned the lamp down low earlier, she thought.

He shrugged out of his coat and hung it on the back of a chair where it would dry, then took his hat off, hanging it on one of the hooks near the door. She watched him turn another chair around and straddle it, resting his arms across the back. The smell of wet wool lay heavy in the room. She could only hope it would cover the strong odor of roses.

"You were drying your hair. You should finish before you catch cold sitting so far from the heat."

"I really shouldn't have washed it when the weather is like this." Pulling her chair up to the end of the range, she worked her wet curls with a towel.

He sat with his head turned, watching her.

She listened to the sound of the wood snapping inside the stove, while the coffeepot on its top bubbled like rain in an empty barrel. Outside, the wind continued to batter the windows. Other than that, there was dead silence.

Moving in her chair to dry the other side of her

hair, she found herself facing him. So she tipped her head slightly away and briskly rubbed one spot until she thought her hair might fall out.

"Doesn't that hurt?" He grinned.

"No." She stopped rubbing. "Well, maybe a little." She smiled back, liking the way he spoke so honestly. Somehow it demanded honesty in return.

Jauncey rose to move the now-boiling pot to a cooler part of the stove, careful not to let her gown touch the hot edge. Moving to a cupboard at the dark end of the kitchen, she removed two cups from a high shelf, then brought them back and set them on the table near him. With a cloth around the handle of the pot, she poured the coffee, and felt his eyes following her every move.

She let the coffee sit, waiting for the grounds to settle. She knew she should have poured cold water into the pot to help them settle faster, but that would have required another trip to the sink.

Carefully, he took a drink. "Ahh. Just what I needed to warm me from the inside out."

She, on the other hand, was plenty warm.

"You're not very talkative," he said, glancing at her through the steam of his coffee. "You're still upset with me, aren't you?"

"No." She smiled again at his point-blank honesty. "Not anymore."

"And you still want to keep this house?"

She bristled slightly, sitting straighter. "Of course I do."

He raised his hand, grinning. "Wait a minute. I didn't mean to pick at a sore spot."

"It isn't a sore spot." She was being defensive but didn't care.

He raised his eyebrows in question, still grinning.

"This"—she flipped a hand, indicating the kitchen—"isn't a sore spot. It's my home, my livelihood, and things are working out fine. Now." She lowered her head, thinking about the money he'd loaned her and how she had used it.

"So you didn't need the money I left with Collins?"

Jauncey returned his stare. "I did. But I'm going to pay you back, with interest. Very soon."

"That isn't necessary." He took another drink of his coffee and placed the cup on the table. He turned around in his chair, his long legs stretched out toward the stove.

"Yes, it is," she said.

"Consider it a loan to a friend." He looked her way. "I do."

"I suppose a simple thank you will do?" She smiled sheepishly, and he smiled back.

She didn't know what else to say, so she tried to relax, sitting back in her chair with her arms folded. "Are you planning to stay in town until the storm passes?"

He nodded, still looking at her. "I was hoping you had an extra bed."

"I'm afraid all I have left is the one in the office, but you're welcome to it. I wouldn't turn anybody away on a night like this." She saw his gaze drop to where her arms lay crossed beneath her breasts. Immediately she uncrossed them, wishing for the hundredth time that she was wearing her dress.

"It could be more than one night if this wind keeps up."

"What about your ranch?" She wondered if he

205

lived alone and who cooked for him.

"Most of the men get laid off for the winter and the rest will be doing the same thing I am."

"And your cattle?"

"Nearly all sold. What's left on the range, I can't do much to help." A worried frown creased the area between his brows.

"You're welcome to stay as long as you need to."

The lamp on the table suddenly sputtered, casting flickering shadows against the walls. Jauncey glanced at the empty base just before it died, throwing them into unrelieved darkness.

"Oh, no," she moaned. "How did I forget to check the lamps today?"

Placing both hands on the table, she stood. Where were the matches? She wouldn't have any trouble finding another lamp, but where were the matches? Groping her way around the table, she kicked a chair leg, stubbing her toe.

"Ow!" She rubbed the bruised toe and proceeded with a little more caution. When she heard his chair scrape the floor, she said, "Don't move! Or I'll end up bumping into you, too."

Hand over hand she continued around the table to the cupboard by the sink. Nothing. Perhaps in a drawer. She opened one after another until her hand brushed something soft and warm, and wiggling.

"Aaahh!" she screamed, jumping back. She heard Matt Dawson scramble toward her and instinctively reached out for him, clutching the front of his warm flannel shirt. His arms came around her. Gooseflesh made the hair all over her body stand on end, and she couldn't control the shiver that rolled over her.

Just as quickly, a door opened and a voice called, "What's going on in there?"

Lord! It was Mr. Natter. His room was so close her scream must have awakened him. If he found her here in the dark with a man, she would be not only mortified but minus one boarder. She raised her hand in search of Matt Dawson's mouth and clamped her hand over it. His mustache tickled her fingers. He was smiling!

"Oh, nothing, Mr. Natter. I saw a mouse and it frightened me, that's all." She tried to make her voice light. "It's all right, now. You can go back to bed."

"You saw a mouse in the dark?" Mr. Natter sounded disbelieving.

Matt's smile broadened under her fingers.

"I saw it just before the lamp went out. But everything is all right now. Really. Good night."

Mr. Natter mumbled something, then closed the door firmly.

Matt Dawson continued smiling while he held her close.

She removed her hand. "It isn't funny!" she whispered.

"A mouse?" The sound of laughter was just beneath the surface.

"Sh-h-h! Yes, a mouse. It crawled over my hand." She shivered again. "I detest the little creatures."

Matt rubbed the middle of her back with one hand, while the other tightened around her waist.

A warm flush crept over her body. "You . . . you'd better let me go, Mr. Dawson."

But he ignored her words and leaned down to nuzzle the damp hair on top of her head. "I told you to call me Matt. And you smell like roses."

"I know . . . Matt." She held perfectly still, realizing he had no intention of letting her go, and realizing she didn't want him to. Never had she been held so intimately and securely. And even though her mind was sending out warning signals, she closed her eyes against the already dark room and gave herself over to the feelings running rampant through her body.

Thrill to the most sensual, adventure-filled Historical Romances on the market today...

FROM ▉ LEISURE BOOKS

As a home subscriber to the Leisure Romance Book Club, you'll enjoy the best in today's BRAND-NEW Historical Romance fiction. For over twenty years, Leisure Books has brought you the award-winning, high-quality authors you know and love to read. Each Leisure Historical Romance will sweep you away to a world of high adventure...and intimate romance. Discover for yourself all the passion and excitement millions of readers thrill to each and every month.

Save $5.⁰⁰ Each Time You Buy!

Six times a year, the Leisure Romance Book Club brings you four brand-new titles from Leisure Books, America's foremost publisher of Historical Romances. EACH PACKAGE WILL SAVE YOU $5.00 FROM THE BOOKSTORE PRICE! And you'll never miss a new title with our convenient home delivery service.

Here's how we do it. Each package will carry a FREE 10-DAY EXAMINATION privilege. At the end of that time, if you decide to keep your books, simply pay the low invoice price of $14.96, no shipping or handling charges added. HOME DELIVERY IS ALWAYS FREE. With today's top Historical Romance novels selling for $4.99 and higher, our price SAVES YOU $5.00 with each shipment.

AND YOUR FIRST FOUR-BOOK SHIPMENT IS TOTALLY FREE!

IT'S A BARGAIN YOU CAN'T BEAT! A Super $19.96 Value!

▉ LEISURE BOOKS *A Division of Dorchester Publishing Co., Inc.*

Get Four Books Totally FREE— A $19.96 Value!

▼ Tear Here and Mail Your FREE Book Card Today! ▼

PLEASE RUSH
MY FOUR FREE
BOOKS TO ME
RIGHT AWAY!

Leisure Romance Book Club
65 Commerce Road
Stamford CT 06902-4563

AFFIX
STAMP
HERE

Chapter Fourteen

Matt wasn't surprised to find how well she fit in his arms, or that she was soft and smelled like roses. But he was surprised that she hardly resisted being in his arms.

Her long hair curled around his hand at her waist, and he tangled his fingers in its damp thickness, remembering well the burnished red-gold highlights reflected by the lampglow.

He blessed the darkness that surrounded them, reminding him of his first attempt ever to kiss a girl. And just like that first time, his heart pounded and echoed in his ears. Loosening his hold on her slightly, he bent to kiss her forehead, then planted light kisses along her nose until he found her mouth. Softly, carefully, he touched his lips to hers. He knew by the way she held her head stiff and straight she had never been kissed before.

Matt brought his hand up her back and under her hair to her nape. While her hands rested lightly on his chest, he pulled her closer. His lips slanted across hers as the tip of his tongue brushed lightly against them. She relaxed in his arms, letting him explore. Carefully, gradually, she opened her mouth and he deepened the kiss without hesitation. She was wonderfully sweet and as intoxicating as the purest brandy he'd ever had. Her arms slid up and around his neck, and he felt the pressure of her full breasts against his chest. Immediately, his arms tightened, straining to bring her closer. He angled his head for better access to the velvety lining of her lips, taking complete possession with a rhythmic motion, and she accommodated him with a turn of her head.

He braced his leg against the edge of the table in order to keep his equilibrium. She'd gone straight to his head and his heart, and if he was to survive at all, he had to come up for air. Pulling away reluctantly, he rested his chin against her forehead, feeling her breath pelt his neck.

Her hand rested soft as a snowflake on his neck. "Do that again." Her voice was a mere whisper.

His hands caressed her back through the folds of her gown. "In a minute." His voice was deep with restraint.

Jauncey placed a hand on his cheek, her thumb stroking the corner of his mouth.

The movement was irresistible, totally provoking, and he lowered his head again when she guided him to her lips. This time there was no hesitation on her part. She gave to him all that he asked, and more.

When his hand cupped her firm breast, she leaned into it, clinging to him as though he were a precipice. She tightened her hold on his neck, swaying slightly.

Matt knew he had to get a grip on the situation or he'd die trying. For a second he considered the alternative. Gently, he released her lips, kissing her face and eyes, trying to lessen his contact with her slowly. His breath came hard and uneven. So did hers.

"Jauncey." Matt tried to pull his thoughts into focus.

"Matt."

"We'd better . . ." He inhaled again the scent of roses redolent in her hair.

"I know." She kissed his chin. "But I don't want to."

"Neither do I."

She sighed, resting heavily against him.

He drew wide circles between her shoulder blades, enjoying the swell of her breasts pushing into the front of his shirt.

"Is this the same gown you wore that first night I came here?" He smiled in the dark.

"Yes."

"I thought so." He paused, remembering that night. "I like it."

She nestled her head beneath his chin.

"Are you getting cold?"

"Um-hm. But I don't mind."

"The fire is getting low." He was reluctant to let her go, but he knew he had to. This was certainly not the place to share any further intimacies, he told himself. And if he was honest, it was not the time either.

Jauncey didn't for a moment regret kissing him

so unabashedly. It was easy to feel that way in the dark, with his arms still around her and her body still aglow. But she wondered how she would face him in the morning at breakfast.

"Matt?"

"Hmm?" He combed his fingers through her hair, kissing her temple.

"How long will you be staying?"

"Are you in a hurry for me to leave?" he teased. "And I thought maybe you were beginning to like me."

"I'm not! I mean, I'm not in a hurry for you to leave."

"So you do like me?" He ran his lips along her jaw, stopping just under her ear.

She couldn't answer. She could only revel in the wondrous new feelings he invoked. When he grazed the rim of her ear with the tip of his tongue, a shower of shivers cascaded over her.

"Jauncey?" he prodded.

"Yes, I like you," she whispered back, not because he had also whispered, but because it was all she was capable of doing.

Matt lowered his head once more. He held her tightly while he plundered her mouth, taking greedily all that she offered. Then he eased away, kissing her chin.

She touched the black wavy hair he always hid beneath his dark hat. It was softer, finer than she'd imagined.

"If the weather's not too bad, I'll head out in the morning."

"Oh." She couldn't hide the disappointment she felt.

"Do you want the fire built up?" he asked.

She glanced at the window, but could see nothing. The wind still slammed against the glass and squeezed under the door, causing a chill to settle around her feet, although her toes were the only part of her that felt the cold.

Jauncey felt him pull away, and longed to have him hold her close for just a few more moments, to feel protected and cared for and safe in a way she never had before. But she'd already acted wanton enough for one evening, perhaps even for a lifetime.

"The fire? Uh, no," she said. "It's late. And I should show you to your room."

She turned toward the cupboard, her hands outstretched. "I've got another lamp over here, somewhere. If only I had a match. . . ."

A sudden burst of flame lit the space behind her. She whirled to see Matt holding a burning match. He grinned at her, his eyebrows raised.

"You should have asked me. No self-respecting cowboy would be caught without a tin of matches."

Jauncey stared at him with her mouth hanging open. He'd had matches all along! She need not have stumbled around looking for one. She saw him shrug a shoulder in apology; then the room went dark again.

"Ow!" Matt shook his burnt finger.

Another match flared. This time he was frowning.

Jauncey squashed a smile and quickly walked to the cupboard near the sink. She chose a lamp with a half-full base and set it on the table near him. He struck another match and lit the lamp.

213

Holding it in front of her, she led the way to the front bedroom-office.

Matt followed, admiring the way the light allowed glimpses of the outline of her body through her white billowing nightgown. He liked the natural glide of her hips, unfettered by confining clothing.

She stopped at the foot of the stairs near a doorway.

Matt looked inside at the desk and chair in one corner and the bed and table in the other. "This will be fine. More than fine."

"I use it as an office for now, but if we get another boarder I'll have to move my desk into the kitchen." She was rambling, and he knew she was uncomfortable.

"This will be the best night's rest I've had in weeks," Matt said. He turned to face her. The lamp reflected the amber depths of her hazel eyes, giving them an inner glow. Her cheeks were flushed and her lips still slightly swollen from his kisses. He took the lamp from her and set it on the desk. Then he placed his hands on each side of her face, his thumbs on her cheeks. Then he pulled back and gazed into her eyes.

"Good night, Jauncey," he said huskily.

"Good night, Matt."

He kissed her quickly, gently, then turned her loose.

She walked from the room and up the stairs without looking back. Not until she was in her room with the door closed did she allow herself to think how close she'd come to spending the night with him.

Her room was not warm, but the low-burning

214

coal fire had taken the bite from the chilled air. As she climbed into bed, she was much too warm inside to mind the cool sheets. Snuggling into the covers, she allowed the overwhelming drowsiness to overtake her. For once she didn't care that her long hair was unbraided and would be full of tangles in the morning.

Matt lay on his back with his hands stacked behind his head. The bed was too damn soft. He was used to the firmness of the rough ground beneath his bedroll. A bed always took some getting used to after a roundup, just like sleeping in his clothes, or without them.

Matt stared into the darkness, listening to the wind's onslaught. He'd been a fool to come here. He could have stayed at the hotel with Charlie, but he had thought about Jauncey for weeks, and had stubbornly clung to the notion of seeing her.

He tossed restlessly.

It was a mistake, kissing her like that. Nice women were different. He rolled the other direction. Hell, what did he know about nice women? The only kind he'd ever been involved with were the ones who'd lived in whorehouses.

He groaned out loud. She'd hate him in the morning. He was sure of it.

Morning found Matt far from rested. He sat on the edge of the bed holding his head. It was still dark and early enough that no one was up yet. He pulled on his clothes and boots as quietly as he could, remembering Mr. Natter. Then he dug in his pockets for money to pay for the room and left it on the bed. Then changing his mind, he had to light a lamp to write a short note using her stationery and put the money with it on her desk. Carefully, he walked to the kitchen and retrieved his coat from the chair. He struck a match to find his hat on the hook. Opening the door, he stepped into the cold wintry air. The wind had died down a little, and great flakes of snow fell like feathers from a hundred pillows. Matt pulled the collar of his coat tight around his neck. He guessed he'd go to the hotel and bunk in with Charlie until breakfast. He walked toward town through the virgin snow with no other footprints to guide his way, only the dark shapes of houses against the whiteness of the night.

Jauncey awoke with the feeling that something wonderful had just happened, or was about to. She stretched and smiled and yawned all at the same time, rebounding into a ball when the cold air finally penetrated her skin. The gray light of dawn filtered through the curtains, and she wondered if Maggie was up yet.

Matt!

Completely awake now, she sat bolt upright in bed. Matt! He was downstairs sleeping in her office. She placed her cool hand to her now-flushed cheek. How would she greet him after last night? Good morning, Mr. Dawson. How do you like your eggs? She flopped back onto the bed and groaned. This was going to be terrible. Maybe he'd say something right in front of everyone, or worse, he'd pretend nothing had happened. She closed her eyes, shutting out that possibility. Perhaps she could stay in

216

bed for the entire day and not have to see him at all. But what if it snowed for days? She couldn't stay in bed the entire time.

Jauncey threw off the blankets and dressed with a speed only a cold room could motivate. She chose a simple dress of dark green. Her fingers were practically numb and blue by the time she had the tangles brushed out of her hair. Quickly, she braided it as best she could and pinned it up with a minimum of pins. One last quick look and she hurried from the room down to the kitchen.

Bless Maggie for being such an early bird, she thought, warming her hands and backside in front of the huge stove.

Jauncey had noticed in her flight down the stairs that the office door was open, but Matt was nowhere to be seen. She waited a little longer.

Maggie came in from the back porch carrying an armload of wood covered with snow.

"Are we the only ones up?" Jauncey asked timidly.

Maggie nodded, dumping her load in the wood box.

Jauncey walked through the parlor, tiptoeing toward the office. She peeked inside. When she saw the bed made up, she knew he was gone. The money on the desk caught her eye, and the note in unfamiliar handwriting drew her to it.

Thanks for the bed.
M.D.

Chapter Fifteen

For three days the snow had fallen with a driving wind, blowing and drifting until crusty banks formed around every corner of the house. Then it had rained, depositing a layer of ice on top of the already hazardous drifts, making a walk outside worse than treacherous. Everyone in her house had made as few trips outside as possible.

Jauncey sat staring out the window, her fingers idly drumming on her desk, the weather a fitting companion for her mood. Ice rimmed the small panes of glass, leaving only tiny holes. She was cold and isolated, she thought, resting her head on her propped up fist. She sighed.

Picking up Matt's note, she read it again, trying to find a message between the lines. Why had he left without saying anything to her? Was he sorry for kissing her? Was he worried she would expect something more? Lottie's words suddenly came back to her: He isn't the settling kind. She laid the paper down. Obviously, he hadn't wanted to see her, whatever the reason.

She moved to the window and placed her warm finger against the thin layer of ice on the inside of the glass. As the ice melted and ran down the pane, it froze again before it reached the wooden sash.

Undoubtedly, he must have had second thoughts about her. And why wouldn't he? On one hand she was Miss Proper, but in his arms she'd acted as though she had the same "loose blood" as her aunt. How could he know what she was really like? After all, she hardly knew the man! Her face burned hotter with that confession.

What really concerned her was how much she had enjoyed kissing him. Never in her life had she experienced anything like it. His arms had been hard and tight around her, while the pressure of his mouth against hers had made her feel cared for and protected. The warmth of that memory mingled now with the lonely coldness of her office, leaving her feeling melancholy.

There's no point dwelling on it, she told herself. She'd made a fool of herself, and worse. Her only course now was to try to put it behind her, and avoid Matt Dawson.

With a determination she didn't quite feel, Jauncey left the room in search of Ginny. Tomorrow was Thanksgiving and she wanted to ask where to look for the good china, if indeed there was any.

Ginny and Maggie sat at the kitchen table going over the menu for Thanksgiving dinner. So Jauncey poured herself a cup of coffee and joined them.

"We're just checking to make sure we haven't forgotten anything." Ginny ran a finger down the list. "Turkey, cornbread stuffing, whipped potatoes, giblet gravy, sweet potatoes, green beans, corn, apple butter, bread, pickled beets, and pies, pies, pies." Ginny sat back in her chair, winded. "Jauncey, are you sure we'll have enough?" Her brown eyes twinkled.

"I know, it's probably more than enough," Jauncey replied. "But with so many men at our table we can't take any chances. Besides, I want word to get around that we serve the best meals in town." She couldn't hold back a smile of pride.

"I'm sure we won't get any complaints from Brailey, especially if Maggie makes his favorite pie." Ginny patted Maggie's shoulder.

"Brailey never complains about anything. He's easy to please." Maggie appeared less self-conscious while in the kitchen.

"We have nothing to worry about," Jauncey said with a good measure of confidence. "Except getting everything cooked on time."

"The bread and pies can be done in the morning, as long as we put them in the tin boxes to keep the mice out of them," Ginny said.

Jauncey sobered, remembering the reason she'd gone into Matt's arms.

"We have to get a cat." Jauncey forced an even tone into her voice. "Where can we get one?"

"Brailey has several hanging around his place," Maggie said, her eyes lighting up.

Surprised at the reaction, Jauncey said, "Good. We'll have him bring two when he comes for Thanksgiving."

She noticed how Maggie contained her happiness by holding her hands tightly clasped in her lap, but her bright eyes gave her feelings away.

A momentary splinter of sunshine stretched across the floor and drew their attention to the window, where it sparkled through the wavy ice.

"Oh, thank goodness! If I had to endure one more day of snow and howling winds, I'd probably lose my mind." Jauncey's spirits rose. "At least now we won't be housebound." Perhaps she'd be able to get her mind on something besides Matt.

The rest of the day passed with preparations for the holiday. Her aunt's beautiful hand-painted china was taken down from the top cupboards and washed, and the lace-trimmed linens packed in a cedar-lined chest were brought from the attic. Jauncey had to laugh as the boarders eyed the delicate china and lace napkins with looks of concern on their faces.

Thanksgiving dawned with gray-tinged clouds hanging low, but nothing could dampen Jauncey's festive spirits. By 11:30 in the morning the house was full of the wonderful smells of roasted turkey and stuffing, and she wondered if hers was the only rumbling stomach.

Brailey arrived at the back door bundled to his ears. He removed his hat and gloves, handing them to Jauncey, then reached in one pocket and pulled out a gray kitten. Then he pulled a yellow kitten out of his other pocket.

Maggie took the kittens, cradling them against her breast. "Oh, Brailey! They're the cutest things!" They attached themselves to her dress with sharp

221

little claws. "But won't they need their mama? They're so small."

"I figure they will. So . . ." He unbuttoned his coat and a yellow furry head peeked out. "Here's their mama."

The kittens climbed to Maggie's shoulders, one perching on each side, while Maggie lifted the mother cat out of Brailey's coat, holding it in her arms. The kittens skidded down the front of her dress mewling to their mother. Maggie laughed aloud, happiness registering on her face.

Jauncey had never heard Maggie laugh until now, and it filled her with warmth just to see her so happy. She watched while the young girl stooped to the floor, depositing her load and trying to disengage tiny claws from her clothing. She looked up at Jauncey and smiled, but said nothing.

"I'm sure they won't go hungry around here," Jauncey said to Brailey. "Especially today."

"Hmmm. The smell of that turkey practically snatched me off my feet and carried me in here when I was clear down the road." His eyes twinkled. "Course, I come willin' so it wasn't necessary."

Jauncey hung his coat and hat on the hooks near the door, smiling at his good humor. He brought sunshine and kindness wherever he went, and everyone enjoyed his company. Today he was dressed in a good-quality homespun suit, and she noticed he had tamed his hair, somewhat.

"We've got plenty of delicious food, Brailey, and Maggie made your favorite pie." Jauncey stepped back and waited for his reply.

But he only nodded, his kind eyes resting on Maggie while she stroked the mother cat.

A knock at the door drew Jauncey's attention, and when she opened it she saw Mr. Collins buried beneath layers of mufflers until only his eyes were visible.

"Good morning," he said, although Jauncey could barely make out his words.

"Come in. Come in." She ushered him in by his heavily bundled arm. "You must be freezing." Actually, she thought he looked as warm as a little bear.

He stripped off a couple layers of clothing, then said, "You can never be too careful in this sort of weather. A person could catch his death."

Soon all the boarders made their appearance. Introductions were made all around and everyone was seated. Mr. Natter took the seat beside Mr. Collins and engaged in a conversation about poor health versus good health. Brailey sat beside the chair where Maggie would sit, and Dan, who had arrived early, sat next to Ginny.

Maggie placed the carved turkey on the table, and Jauncey poured the fresh hot coffee. After they were seated Dan said a blessing; then the food was passed with gusto.

Jauncey thoroughly enjoyed herself. She spoke and laughed with those sitting near her, sometimes getting up to refill a cup or a bread dish. She graciously included Maggie and Ginny when anyone complimented her on the meal and the table. And there were plenty of compliments.

"I declare, Miss Taylor. I haven't had cornbread stuffing since I left Alabama a good many years

223

ago," one boarder said in a Southern accent thick as molasses.

"Maggie is solely responsible for that," Jauncey replied.

"You must have been raised in the South to cook like this, Miz Maggie." The man winked and smiled at her.

Maggie turned pink and kept her head low. But Jauncey saw her brief smile in spite of her attempt to hide it.

The pies brought a chorus of "aahh's" from the men, and quietly spoken "no, thank you's" from the women.

Brailey patted his stomach where the button on his jacket threatened to pop. "I ain't had so much good food since . . . Well, I can't remember just when." He scratched his head a moment, then returned to patting his full stomach.

"Definitely delicious, Miss Taylor. Thank you for inviting me." Mr. Collins carefully pushed his chair back.

"The dinner was good, and on time, as usual," Mr. Natter said, giving his usual compliment, punctuated with the usual clearing of his throat. "But too much pie," he mumbled.

With many groans, all the men retired to the parlor, where a fire blazed in the large fireplace.

Jauncey scanned the table with the leftover turkey, potatoes, vegetables and pies and smiled. What a wonderful day! The dinner had gone just as she'd hoped, with people talking and laughing and having a good time. Perhaps now she could replace those old memories of holidays spent around a table in stiff silence.

"Where do we begin?" Jauncey lifted both hands, but the plea was lighthearted.

"The turkey," Ginny offered.

They made short work of clearing away the few remaining leftovers. Tomorrow they would make turkey and vegetable pies as well as turkey soup with noodles. The bread was safely stored in the tin box, and the pies were covered with dinner plates to protect them from the mice.

Jauncey followed Maggie's gaze to the cats as they warmed themselves beside the large stove. They had filled themselves on scraps from the table, and were washing each other with great concentration.

The three women tied on aprons to tackle the chore of cleaning the dishes and pans, but with Ginny and Maggie to talk to, the time passed quickly and pleasantly for Jauncey.

"What are you going to name the mother cat, Maggie?" Ginny asked.

"Sunshine."

What an appropriate name, Jauncey thought, especially since the cat came from Brailey. "What about the kittens?"

Maggie looked thoughtful. "I don't know. I'll just wait and see what they remind me of."

After the kitchen was cleaned to its normal shine, Jauncey and Ginny joined the men in the parlor while Maggie disappeared upstairs.

Nearly every man was either slouched and asleep or sitting straight with his head nodding. When Ginny placed a hand on Dan's shoulder, he snapped awake immediately. She leaned down to whisper in his ear and Jauncey saw him smile, covering Ginny's hand with his own.

Jauncey found an empty seat near the low-burning fire, after adding more wood to make the flames slowly increase until the room was aglow once again. Soon the added warmth brought a deep vibrant snore from Brailey, and even though the noise was short-lived, it was effective. Mr. Collins's eyes fluttered open. Sheepishly, he glanced around the room, his embarrassment plain on his face.

Jauncey hid a smile behind her hand, afraid she would burst into laughter if Brailey snored one more time.

Another throaty snort burst from the unaware Brailey. Mr. Natter's head snapped to attention, his eyes wide with surprise. Quickly, he adjusted himself and cleared his throat with several noisy harrumphs, pretending innocence.

This time two snorts resounded in rapid succession with an amazing likeness of two pigs at a slop trough.

The look of relief flooding Mr. Natter's face proved too much for Jauncey, and she burst into laughter. She simply could not hold it back.

When she saw Brailey open his eyes and look around puzzled, she laughed all the harder. Before long, Ginny joined in, followed by Dan, who added his hearty laugh.

Brailey smiled at everyone with a sheepish grin. "Have I been entertainin' all of you with my snorin'?"

"I'm sorry," Jauncey managed to get out between bursts of laughter. "We're not really laughing at you." She fought to get a hold on herself.

"Oh, I don't mind. If a little snorin' is all it takes to make you laugh, I'd do it again." He smiled good-naturedly.

"Harrumph!" Mr. Natter cleared his throat in obvious displeasure at the idea, while Mr. Collins ineffectively squelched a smile.

Then one of the boarders stretched and groaned loudly. "I believe I need some fresh air before I end up sleeping the day away." He kicked his friend's boot. "How about you?"

"Yeah, sure. Believe a turn around the block would do me some good."

Once the spell was broken the other men stood. Each offered his thanks for the fine meal, then departed either for the outdoors or his room.

Brailey slipped into his coat and pulled on his gloves.

Maggie appeared in the doorway and stooped to play with the kittens.

"They couldn't have a better home," Brailey said softly to Jauncey.

She nodded and smiled back. "Thanks, Brailey."

Mr. Collins piled on his mufflers after buttoning his coat to the top of his long neck. "Thank you again, Miss—Jauncey, if I may be so bold." He smiled knowingly at her, then wrapped a final scarf around his neck. "The dinner was lovely," he mumbled through the layers.

She made a mental note not to put off much longer that talk she needed to have with him.

Then both men were gone.

Mr. Natter had disappeared as usual, leaving only Dan and Ginny, Maggie and herself.

"Ginny and I are going for a ride. Would the two

of you like to come along?" Dan asked.

Maggie shook her head without looking up.

Jauncey knew the two wanted to be alone, something that was hard to do in this house. "Oh, no, thank you. It's too cold for me." She had no interest in being the third person. Jauncey watched with a mixture of happiness and sadness while Dan helped Ginny bundle up for their ride.

Then they, too, were gone.

Maggie scooped up the kittens and headed for the stairs with the concerned mother cat following close behind.

The afternoon dwindled into the pre-dusk of early evening, leaving Jauncey at loose ends. She didn't think anyone would want more than a little turkey with a slice of bread for supper and maybe some pie. So she added a little more wood to the stove and put on a fresh pot of coffee.

When it finished brewing, she poured a cup and took it to the parlor. Now that everyone was gone the room seemed less cheery. A few more pieces of wood in the fireplace did little to lift her spirits. She sipped from her cup, watching the flames leap up the chimney.

A loud knock at the front door a moment before it was thrust open brought Jauncey to her feet in alarm. Her coffee sloshed, spoiling her dress, but she paid little heed to it. In the open doorway stood J.T. Lawrence, his expression as foreboding as an impending blizzard. Jauncey's heart beat double time, and trembling, she placed her shaking cup on the nearby table. Then, her chin lifted, she stared him in the eye.

"How dare you barge into my house like this.

Get out." She spoke quietly, and with deadly assurance. But inside she quivered like gravy in a bowl.

"Your house?" His tone was full of contempt. "Is it really? And who is making the loan payments, my dear? You?"

She flinched at his words. "What I do is none of your business! I said get out!"

His bulk filled the doorway, and she cringed inwardly at the memory of being trapped against a wall by his body, with his hands wandering over her. She shivered involuntarily.

Stalking toward her, he stopped within a foot of the hem of her dress. Instinctively, she backed away.

"I do not know why you find my arrangements so displeasing." His silky smooth voice belied his obvious intentions. "When I have so much more to offer than that cowboy-rancher."

She jerked her head away when his finger reached out to touch her face.

"There's no reason to be unfriendly," he said, grabbing her by the arm.

She struggled and wrenched herself free. "Take your hands off me!"

"You can stop pretending to be the innocent virgin. I know you accepted Matt Dawson's money and I know he didn't give it to you for nothing." The smirk on his face turned into a menacing smile. "You're just like Spicie."

In a flash, Jauncey's hand whipped out, striking him full on the face. The imprint of her hand burned red against his pale skin.

He grabbed her roughly by the shoulders, pulling her up to his chest, his fingers biting into her arms. "You shouldn't have done that, you little bitch." Then he smiled. "Hasn't anyone told you that I always get what I want?" He smothered her lips with his own, then threw her onto the settee.

Jauncey wiped a hand across her mouth, glaring at him. "Get out!" she whispered fiercely.

"Don't bother to get up. I'll show myself out." He tipped his hat, sneering at her.

Jauncey didn't move for several minutes after the door closed. A spasm overtook her, and she wrapped her arms around her waist to stop it. The man was vile! Disgusting! A tremor shook her again.

Why didn't he just leave her alone? Had she become a conquest for him? Did he want her house that badly? Or was he simply obsessed with owning what he could not have?

"Jauncey?" Maggie whispered.

Jauncey's hand flew to her throat. "Oh! Maggie!" She hadn't seen or heard Maggie come into the room.

"Did he hurt you?" Concern and fear were evident in her clear blue eyes.

"I-I think I'm all right." Her voice was shaking as badly as her body.

"He's a terrible man." Maggie's eyes darted toward the front door.

"And he doesn't hide it very well, either. He wasn't the least bit worried about coming in here even though he knows I have a houseful of boarders. Unless . . ." Jauncey's new thought frightened her as much as J.T.'s presence had.

"He's been watching the house! He knows when

they're here and when they leave." She remembered the night Matt had stayed. "He thinks . . ." She spoke her thoughts out loud, almost forgetting Maggie was there.

Maggie crushed Jauncey's fingers in a tense grip.

Jauncey hadn't meant to alarm her. "It's all right, Maggie. We'll just have to get in the habit of locking the door more often." She rubbed Maggie's arm, trying to soothe her. "I'm all right, really. See?" Jauncey smiled, and it took more effort than she'd expected. She had to get a grip on her emotions and calm down for Maggie's sake as well as her own.

"Let's have a cup of tea and sit in the kitchen." Jauncey put her arm around Maggie's shoulders. Then, on their way past the front door, she locked it.

Chapter Sixteen

Matt pulled the brim of his hat lower, but it did little good against the cold wind. He shoved his free hand into his coat pocket while the other held the reins lightly. His horse picked up the pace as they rode beneath the Diamond D sign. Warmth lay just ahead for both of them.

The trip to his sister's hadn't been his idea since he had a matter to settle with Johnny, but Sarah wouldn't hear of him spending Thanksgiving alone. Her indignation still rang in his ears.

"What? That's ridiculous! Of course you're coming to our house." And that had been the end of it.

So he'd gone. But he'd barely tasted anything. Uppermost in his mind was the fact that Johnny and his cohorts had been released by the U.S. marshal, and he'd only found out about it the day after leaving Jauncey's. He had yet to lay eyes on the bastard. There was little anyone could say or do to rid him of the overwhelming anger that clung to him like smoke over a wet campfire.

He'd listened politely to Sarah and Jeff's conversation, thinking about how much he would enjoy pounding Johnny's face as soon as Johnny returned to the ranch, if indeed he did.

His lack of interest, however, had proved too much for Sarah.

"All right," she'd said. "You might as well say what's on your mind. I'm not leaving you alone until you do." She had crossed her arms as if she had all day.

Matt had frowned. Sarah could wheedle a confession from an innocent preacher if she set her mind to it.

Jeff had sat back with a shrug of his shoulders, and Matt had known he could expect no help from him. So he'd told them that the marshal had turned the thieves loose when they'd denied everything. Not enough proof, he'd said to Matt. It was his word against theirs. And theirs was backed up by J.T. and his money.

Matt had left after that, anxious to get back and tend to the business of Johnny.

Now he rode up to the bunkhouse, where he saw Johnny's horse outside. Matt gripped the doorknob, pushing the door wide, letting a cold wind into the bunkhouse.

Apparently Johnny had enough sense to know he was fired, since he stood folding his few belongings into his bedroll. A smile hovered on his lips. Matt knew Johnny was dragging it out, rubbing it in. It took every ounce of strength Matt had to keep from ramming his fist into that smug face.

"Don't feel so bad, Boss." Johnny grinned up at him, tying the last string on his bundle. "At least you tried."

Matt clenched his jaw, fighting for control. "Don't ever come within a hundred miles of Laramie if you want to be able to walk straight for the rest of your life." His voice was low.

Johnny stood, tossing his belongings onto his back as if he hadn't heard Matt. He looked around at the cowboys who'd stayed on for the winter. Still smiling, he said to them, "Been nice knowin' you, boys."

Johnny walked up to Matt, waiting for him to step aside, but he didn't.

"You heard what I said. I meant it. Just you and me, no witnesses and no J.T."

The wry grin on Johnny's face disappeared. "Don't threaten me. I don't take kindly to it."

"It isn't a threat. It's a fact."

Matt knew Johnny was worried. His kind didn't fight alone, and they didn't fight fair.

As they stood almost shoulder to shoulder, Matt continued to block the way.

"You'd like to fight right now, wouldn't you? With your boys ready to jump in if things get too rough on you," Johnny said.

"They wouldn't lift a finger in a fair fight." Matt never took his gaze off Johnny. "Right, boys?"

Johnny glanced around, his eyes moving quickly from one silent man to another. "I ain't stupid. I don't like the odds."

"The odds won't change. Not tomorrow. Not the next day."

Matt moved about two inches, giving Johnny the go-ahead to leave, and barely room enough to squeeze past him.

After Johnny left, Matt felt some of the tension that had been building inside him for over a year ease. He wasn't worried about having to watch his back. Johnny would look for fresh new territory where his reputation wasn't known.

"Having him gone is like riding out of a prairie dog town with all four of your horse's legs still intact," Charlie said, slouching back in his chair, his feet propped near the hot stove.

The men around him muttered their agreement, nodding their heads.

"As soon as the weather clears a little, Charlie, I'll be going into town to take care of a few things. Why don't you come along?" Matt kept his affairs between the two of them. It was neater that way. And the business he had in mind might require a helping hand.

Matt waited out the weather for two days, then decided it was only going to get worse. So he and Charlie left the ranch, planning on being in town for a while.

Heavy dark clouds scudded across the sky, obliterating the afternoon sun. Matt raised the collar on his coat, thankful that the wind, full of fury and getting stronger, came from behind.

When they arrived in town, they rode up to Sam's Saloon in unspoken mutual consent. Matt's legs were chilled to the bone, and Charlie wasn't much better. He watched as Charlie's usually limber body moved stiffly as he crossed the boarded walk. Upon entering the bar, they were immediately surrounded by a warmth that was unable to penetrate the aura of cold encircling them.

Glancing over the crowd, Matt noticed that nearly every face was familiar. And especially one. She walked with a sway that seemed natural to her line of work, laughing and touching as she went. Even though she was well past her twenties, she was still a very handsome woman. When she saw him enter, she made her way slowly toward him.

"Hello, Matt." Her voice, low and silky, had been cultivated to draw customers. And it worked. "Heard you finished with the roundup awhile back. What took you so long to get in to see me?" She leaned down, looking directly into his eyes, her low-cut dress giving him a view he remembered well.

"Lottie." He smiled.

"What? No excuses?" Her black curls shook when she suddenly straightened.

"No."

She ran a finger lightly down his nose, then stroked his mustache. "Well, you're here now and that's all that counts," she purred. "What'll you have? You know Sam doesn't like us to entertain unless our customers have a drink first."

"Whiskey. Something to warm me up."

"Honey, that sounds like two separate orders." She winked at him. "Be right back."

Matt saw the extra movement of her hips and knew it was for his benefit.

"Is she the reason we rode into town, freezing our tails off?" Charlie jerked his thumb over his shoulder toward Lottie, a disgusted frown on his face.

"No."

236

Lottie brought two whiskeys and set them on the table. "Drink up," she said, pulling up a chair close to Matt's. "We don't want to waste any time."

"I'm afraid we've got business to take care of that won't wait." Matt took a drink. It burned a path to his stomach, sending arrows of warmth throughout his body.

"You mean, you came in here just for whiskey?" She straightened abruptly, surprise and anger registering on her pretty face.

"That's what he means." Charlie tossed back the contents of his glass, gulping for air when he finished.

She threw Charlie a piercing look, then focused on Matt. "Have you forgotten our good times?" she whispered, leaning close. "Matt?"

He looked at her and saw the struggle going on inside her. No matter what he said or how he said it, she was going to be angry with him. He'd never intended this, never even expected it to happen.

"Lottie—" he began.

"Forget it!" she said, jumping up.

Matt swallowed the rest of the whiskey and reached in his pocket to pay for it, adding a little extra for Lottie.

"Thanks for the drink," he told her, then rose from his chair at the same time as Charlie.

Matt tipped his hat in farewell. Charlie didn't.

Before they had taken two steps, Matt turned toward her again. "Has J.T. been in town?"

"What do you want with that polecat?" she asked, her fist on her hip.

Matt knew she'd had more than one run-in with J.T. Her advice for anyone was to stay clear of him.

237

"Have you seen him?" Matt asked.

"He was in here a few days ago bullying some of the girls and acting kind of cocky. Things must be going his way, or else his skinny wife is dishing some out to him." She made a revolting face.

"Thanks, Lottie," he said, grinning.

Outside, Matt and Charlie pulled on their heavy leather gloves and turned up their collars as a few flakes flashed by. Daylight was fast losing ground with the coming storm.

"Let's check J.T.'s office," Matt said.

Hunched down inside his coat, Charlie nodded.

They left their horses in front of the saloon and walked to the alley. Matt hoped J.T. would be there even though he didn't keep regular hours. Most of the time he came and went as he pleased, sometimes staying long past normal closing time. Probably counting the money he'd swindled from rustling, Matt thought.

A light from the small window of J.T.'s office shone into the alley. Matt hadn't been there for a long time, not since he'd run into Jauncey—or rather, since she'd run into him.

Without knocking, he pushed the door open and walked in with Charlie right behind him.

J.T. looked up in surprise. "Well, well," he said, smiling benevolently. "To what do I owe the honor of your presence, gentlemen?"

Lottie was right, Matt thought. He was pretty cocky about something. But Matt hadn't come to exchange pleasantries. "Johnny's fired. And I told him to stay away. I'm here to tell you the same."

J.T. tipped his head back and roared with glee. "Stay away?" He roared again.

Matt kept his fists clenched and his arms crossed, steeling himself against the anger that welled inside him. "I've been contacted by one of the larger outfits around Cheyenne. Seems they expect this winter to break most of the ranchers and they're offering sizable sums to those who will sell. So either you sell to me or I'm selling my share to them."

"Sell?" J.T. stared blankly at him for a moment. "Hell, no! I won't sell!"

"A lot of those fellas wouldn't think twice about stringing you and your hired rustlers up faster than you could get out your wallet. It's been done." Matt let that sink in for a few moments. "I didn't come by just to give you a friendly warning. I hope they stretch your neck three feet. I came to tell you that we're not business partners anymore, one way or the other."

J.T. sat with his hand gripping the arm of his chair. Matt could almost read the other man's thoughts. His double-dealing schemes wouldn't work very well with someone not as honest as Matt. Matt had had him dead to rights more than once, but because he played fair, J.T. had gotten off scot-free.

"You'd never give up the Diamond D," J.T. said.

Matt didn't plan on giving it up; he only wanted to get back what his father had so foolishly given to this man. A few bad years after a rough start had forced Grant Dawson to obtain a loan from the new banker in town. No other bank would take the risk. J.T. had, but the price had been high. Matt had realized after his father's death just how high the price had been.

239

"I'm not giving it up. I'm making a profit," Matt said, noting he had J.T.'s complete attention. "A large profit." He shrugged. "There are other ranches."

"How much profit?"

"That you'll never know."

"Planning on changing occupations, perhaps?" J.T. looked knowingly at Matt. "Like owning a whorehouse?"

"What the hell are you getting at?" Matt's arms fell rigid at his sides.

"I know you're making payments for Miss Taylor. What is she doing for you in return?" J.T. rose, leaning across the desk toward Matt, a leer on his face. "Is she good? Better than Lottie?"

Matt grabbed J.T.'s shirtfront and plowed his fist into J.T.'s soft face. He continued to hold on while he let go with another punch, followed by another. Matt had pulled back for one more when he felt Charlie's restraining arms come around him, holding him back.

"Whoa there, boy, you don't want to hang for this piece of cowshit."

Matt strained against Charlie's grasp, but Charlie refused to turn him loose.

J.T. slumped into his chair, blood running from his nose and mouth. One eye was already beginning to swell. So was his fat nose, Matt thought with satisfaction. What he'd gotten was far less than he actually deserved.

"I'm going to tell you once and only once, you greedy son of a bitch, stay away from Jauncey." Matt roughly shrugged away from Charlie and picked up his hat from the floor. "And you'd better sell out while you're still breathing."

Furious, Matt threw the door open until it slammed against the wall. He strode down the alley heedless of the cold beating against his chest where his coat flapped open in the wind.

Charlie was right on his heels.

"That was just about the stupidest thing I've ever seen you do!"

Matt ignored him and kept walking fast.

"What the hell did you plan to do? Kill him?"

Matt almost wished he had.

"Williams might not care about your cattle thieves, but he sure as hell wouldn't let a murderer go! You know that! What's wrong with you?"

Matt wasn't in any mood to hear sensible talk. Not from anyone. They rounded a corner, heading for Sam's. Finally, Charlie shut up.

They entered the saloon out of breath from the brisk walk in the cold, and dropped into a couple of chairs near the bar. Matt looked around; Lottie was gone. Probably upstairs, he thought.

Ruby walked over and placed a hand on Charlie's shoulder. "What can I do for you?"

Matt watched Charlie brush her hand away.

"We'll have two whiskeys," Matt said, staring hard at Charlie, warning him to behave.

"You boys sure look friendly tonight." The sarcasm in her voice better suited Matt's mood.

Matt downed his whiskey in two gulps. Charlie did the same.

Ruby continued to stand by the table, watching. "Care to talk about it?" She massaged the area between Charlie's shoulder blades.

Why Charlie spent any time with this one, Matt

never could understand. Charlie had spent almost as much time at Spicie's as Johnny. Well, not really, he conceded. God, he felt like a mess. Here he was ready to fight his best friend. And Charlie was his best friend. Always had been.

"This little ole lion cub just tried to take on a grizzly bear," Charlie said to Ruby.

"Sugar, I thought you were a bear." She playfully ruffled his gray hair. "But never a grizzly." Ruby nibbled on Charlie's ear.

"No, I mean J.T."

"You shoulda let him. Nobody would've cared. Might've even done some of us a favor."

Matt didn't much like being called a little lion cub, but it was better than some of the names he was calling himself.

"Charlie . . ." Matt said.

"Forget it," Charlie replied, dropping his head and waving his hand as if to erase the bad feelings that had begun to crop up between them.

"Thanks for keeping your head when I lost mine."

Charlie mumbled something Matt couldn't understand.

Although Ruby was probably right about J.T., Matt knew he wasn't the one to get rid of the man. He should have kept his head. But when he'd said that about Jauncey . . .

"Who the hell is Jauncey anyway?" Charlie asked, practically reading Matt's mind.

"That prissy new boardinghouse owner?" Ruby asked. "Well, she claims it's a boardinghouse, but she's got more men in there now than we ever had." She let out a humorless laugh.

"Her?" Charlie's eyes opened wide. "You nearly knock off someone's face for a woman?"

"Hey! What's wrong with that?" Ruby punched Charlie's arm, but he ignored her.

"Forget about it." Matt had no intention of discussing his feelings about Jauncey in a saloon. "Bring me another whiskey, Ruby."

"Make it two."

"Now that's more like it. You boys get yourselves in a better mood and we can have a good time." She left them to get their drinks.

Matt sat thinking about his problems for a while, and after downing his drink refused any more, figuring he needed a clear head to think straight.

Charlie told him he was brooding. Then finally, tired of Matt's company, he went upstairs with Ruby.

The sky outside turned as dark as Matt's mood and the wind howled through the door every time a customer entered or left. He didn't know how long he sat there, but when he looked up, Charlie was sitting across from him again. Without Ruby, thank God.

A few minutes later a ruckus at the front door drew his and Charlie's attention. Someone had started a fight just as the marshal walked in.

"I didn't come in here to throw any two-bit drifters in jail for fighting but I will if I have to," he yelled above the din.

The saloon quieted.

"J.T. Lawrence has been shot, and I'm looking for the man who did it."

"Is he dead?" someone hollered.

"Yes."

"Aw, don't worry about it, Marshal. Someone just did us all a favor and you know it," said the same voice, followed by others adding their agreement to the rising clamor.

A sinking sensation gripped Matt in the pit of his stomach. Slowly, he and Charlie got up, weaving their way toward the back door through the crowd of people who were trying to get more news.

"Anybody seen Matt Dawson?" the marshal yelled at the same moment Matt closed the door behind them.

"Someone must have seen us leave J.T.'s office," he said to Charlie outside. Damn! he thought. He'd have to stay under cover until things cooled down or until he could find out who'd killed J.T. And that could take awhile considering half the town hated J.T. as much as he did. But none of them had talked as openly against J.T. as he had, so without a doubt Williams would be looking for him first.

Well, he couldn't go back to the ranch, that was for sure, and he wouldn't involve Sarah and Jeff. Then he thought of Jauncey and that big house. If he could get in without her knowing it, she wouldn't get in any trouble with the law.

"I'm going to Jauncey's. Don't come to me, I'll find you later. Stay in town," Matt ordered Charlie, then headed down the alley.

He crossed the street, staying in the shadows away from an occasional lighted storefront. He angled through a backyard, dodging some frozen laundry on a clothesline, until finally he was at the back of Jauncey's house. The darkness hiding him, he waited around the corner near her back porch for the right moment to enter the house.

After what seemed an eternity, someone came out. Only a dim light burned in the kitchen window, and he hoped it was meant to light the way for the old man who had just made his way to the privy. Without wasting any more time thinking about it, he took the steps quickly and bolted through the unlocked door.

The warmth of the room assailed him, along with the memories of the last time he'd been there.

Out of habit, he pushed his hat to the back of his head, scanning the room. It was empty now, but it wouldn't be for long. Spying the open door to the bathing closet, he crossed the room quietly and stepped inside. The large brass tub gleamed in the low lamplight from the kitchen. Slowly, he closed the door.

Chapter Seventeen

Jauncey sat before the fire alone. She sipped the hot coffee, trying to enjoy its warmth. But nothing helped.

She'd sent Dan and Ginny on their way right after the evening meal was over, knowing they were anxious to be off by themselves, and realizing she was terrible company for anyone, even herself.

She set her cup down on the nearby table and, for the thousandth time that day, thought about Matt. A week had passed since he'd been there, holding her in his arms. But it seemed much, much longer. In truth, it was almost as though it hadn't even happened, except in her dreams. And she dreamed about it every night. But obviously she was the only one who did, since Matt hadn't come back.

The mother cat and her two kittens sauntered into the parlor and sat at Jauncey's feet. Sunshine rubbed her face against Jauncey's skirt, closing her eyes with feline delight. One of the kittens jumped onto her skirt, clinging with all of its claws.

"Poor kitty, has Maggie deserted you?"

The kitten meowed pitifully. Jauncey plucked it from the precarious position and held it in her lap. Sunshine leaped onto the settee and stretched herself out comfortably. The other kitten gathered itself for the leap, but didn't seem to have enough courage to try. So Jauncey lifted it onto her lap where the other one sat purring.

"Well, don't worry. She'll be back to her old self before too long, I promise." She stroked each kitten while speaking in a soothing voice.

Jauncey was worried about Maggie. So was Ginny. Every time the front door opened, even if someone only knocked on it, Maggie would jump. She seldom turned her back on any door, and constantly looked over her shoulder when doing dishes. There was no doubt J.T.'s intrusion on Thanksgiving day had affected her as badly as it had Jauncey, but in a different way.

It frightened Jauncey to think he was so determined and sure of himself. She had never before encountered anyone so thoroughly evil. Even Aunt Ida couldn't be called anything more than uncharitable and perhaps a little vindictive. But that was nothing when compared to J.T.

The kittens tired of sitting calmly in her lap and leaped off, drifting to their mother, who patiently washed them while they sprawled over her, purring contentedly.

Then she heard the sound of footsteps, light and quick, running across the front porch. They stopped at the front door.

247

Jauncey rushed to open it but before she could, it burst open and Maggie flung herself into the hallway, whirling to shut the door behind her. She stood with her back to it, facing Jauncey.

"Maggie! Where have you . . ." Jauncey halted. Maggie's eyes were round with fright. "What's wrong?"

Maggie stared back, her chest heaving with every breath.

She put her hand on Maggie's arm. Maggie's whole body shook, but Jauncey knew it wasn't only from the cold. Something had terrified her. Where had she been?

With her hands gripping Maggie's arm, Jauncey calmly said, "Tell me what's wrong, Maggie."

But Maggie only stared, shaking violently.

Jauncey rubbed Maggie's arms, trying to soothe her. She could feel the cold emanating from Maggie's body right through the heavy woolen coat. She reached down to grasp Maggie's hand . . . and instead touched the icy coldness of metal. A gun!

"Maggie!" Jauncey whispered. "Where did you get this?" She pried the gun from Maggie's tightly fisted fingers, and stared at it in the dim light cast from the fire in the parlor. It was *her* gun. The one Uncle Harold had insisted she take. The one she had threatened to use on Matt. Carefully, she put the gun in her apron pocket, her heart pounding like a hundred horses running on frozen ground.

"Maggie," she whispered again, unable to keep the panic from her voice. Dear Lord, what had she done? She clasped Maggie close to her. What had she done?

Jauncey looked around the empty room to make

sure they were alone even though she knew they were.

"Let's get you upstairs to bed. You're shaking all over." She had to think calmly, coolly. She tried forcing the panic from her trembling body for Maggie's sake.

Maggie went with Jauncey like a wooden doll, not seeming to realize what she was doing. They moved through the deepening shadows, up the stairs, inch by agonizing inch, until finally they entered the safety of Maggie's room.

The firelight from the little coal stove flickered around the room, guiding Jauncey to the bed, where she sat Maggie on the edge, talking to her all the while.

"You're going to be all right. I won't let anything happen to you. You're safe here, Maggie, I promise."

Jauncey located the lamp and matches on the dresser, and shortly had it burning. She looked at Maggie sitting on the bed. Her blond hair was loose and straggling around her shoulders. The hem of her dress was torn in three places, and a dark stain stood out like an accusing finger. Blood! Jauncey was sure of it. But whose? She had to stay calm. She had to stay calm.

"We'll just take off that coat." Jauncey pulled Maggie's stiff cold arms from the sleeves.

"Now let's get you out of that dress and into this warm bed." It took every ounce of her strength to keep her own hands from shaking while she removed Maggie's clothing and helped her on with a warm nightgown. Jauncey pulled back the covers and helped Maggie crawl onto the sheets.

249

Sitting on the edge of the bed, Jauncey smoothed the blankets, then gently pushed back the damp hair from Maggie's forehead, stroking the tangled strands.

"It's going to be all right. I promise."

Maggie's eyes held hers. Not once had they wavered since she'd come in the front door, as though trying to draw strength from Jauncey. Yet she noticed Maggie's trembling hadn't lessened.

"I'm going to get another blanket from my room," Jauncey said, quickly adding, "I won't be but a minute."

She hurried down the hall, snatched a blanket from her bed and ran back. Maggie's eyes fastened on her the moment she entered the room.

Refusing to allow herself to glance at the rumpled dress on the floor, she stepped over it. She spread the blanket over Maggie, tucking it in around her body to seal in the warmth.

"I'm going to make you a nice hot cup of tea. It won't take long. The stove is already hot." Jauncey managed to speak with a measure of reassurance in her voice; she hoped it was convincing. "All right?"

Maggie nodded. Relief flooded Jauncey to have her communicate even as little as that.

She went to the door and turned. "Close your eyes and try to rest. I'll be right back."

Maggie obeyed.

Quickly, Jauncey picked up the stained dress, wadding it into a ball. She had to get rid of it. Maggie could never wear it again even if the blood would come out. Stepping into the dark hallway, she closed the door behind her. There was no time to hesitate, no time to think about what she was going to do or what had happened. Her only concern now was Maggie. She ran back to her room and stuffed the dress into the bottom of her wardrobe.

Hurrying from her room and down the stairs, she almost ran around the kitchen, adding more wood to the fire and setting the teakettle on the stove. Only then did she let herself sit at the table, her head in her hands. If only Ginny would come home, she thought. She could help her decide what to do.

The water boiled, and she poured it into the waiting teapot containing the tea. Maggie liked tea. Maybe it would help.

Jauncey stared at the wall, seeing nothing and feeling numb. Absently, she focused on the door to the bathing closet. It was closed. It shouldn't be closed unless someone was taking a bath; otherwise it got too cold in there. She walked to the door and tapped on it.

"Anyone in there?" No light came from under the door, so she turned the knob and swung it wide. Empty. Just as she turned away a hand from the dark room clamped across her mouth and another around her waist, dragging her back. Her breathing labored, she had no strength to struggle.

"Don't scream. It's me. Matt."

She sagged against him with relief, her eyes sliding shut.

Matt held her limp body while he shut the door, enshrouding them in darkness. He noticed she wasn't wearing one of those ridiculous bustles, and by the feel of her, she wasn't wearing a corset

251

either. He turned her toward him and felt her arms go around his waist.

"I'm sorry I scared you. But I didn't want anyone to know I was here," he whispered in her ear.

Matt held her close, smelling the scent of roses he always associated with her. She buried her head in his chest and her breasts pushed hard against him as her arms tightened.

"I didn't even want you to know," he said, rocking her back and forth in a soothing motion. "I need a place to stay for a while. Someplace where nobody can find me. Someone killed J.T. and they think I did it." Matt felt her tense. "I didn't. Not that I hadn't considered it, but I didn't figure he was worth swinging for. But someone finally had enough of his cheating and stealing and put a bullet through him."

She tightened her grip on his shoulders.

"I only need to stay until I find the man who did it."

She didn't say anything, so he asked, "No room available? Is that the problem?" She was taking so long to answer him, he wondered if he'd made the right decision coming here. Her house was doing well, he had to give her credit, and undoubtedly she wouldn't want to jeopardize it.

"Oh, yes, there's room," she finally said. "Of course you can stay. I'm glad you came, really I am."

He nuzzled her hair. "If you think it's too risky I could always stay in your room," he teased, kissing the softness at her temple. "Nobody would look for me there."

Her room? Maybe he was right. Where else could

he stay, in the attic? No, it was much too cold up there. Besides herself, Maggie was the only one who ever went in her room, and Maggie would be in bed for a few days or possibly longer.

But it was so hard to think when Matt was kissing her. Jauncey gave up trying, and turned her lips to meet his. His hand came up behind her head, steadying it while he deepened the kiss. She automatically opened her mouth allowing him entrance, and her world tilted, then swirled around her head and feet. She was lost to everything but his touch.

Matt pulled her closer. He tangled his hands in her hair, loosening the pins, and her hair fell to her waist. His hand searched the bodice of her dress and grazed lightly across her breast.

Jauncey moved to afford him better access to the buttons on her dress, and wished she wasn't wearing the apron.

Reluctantly, Matt lifted his head. His breathing was harsh and fast. "What are you doing with this damn apron on?"

Jauncey tried to control her voice before she spoke. "I always wear one. It keeps my dress clean and the pockets are handy for . . ." The gun!

"Well, the damn dress can go, too." He kissed the side of her face, angling for her neck.

"Wait."

"Wait?" His voice sounded strangled. "Why?"

"Uh, I can't do this."

"Why not?" he asked, nibbling on her ear. "I thought we both wanted to do this."

"Not anymore."

Matt pulled away from her, trying to see her face

in the dark. "Why not?" he asked again.

"Uh, well, I'm not sure." What a stupid thing to say, she chided herself. Especially when she was very sure she didn't want to stop. And the blood pounding through her veins was proof.

Matt's hands ran down her arms, holding her away from him.

"Where can I stay?"

"In my room."

"Your room?"

"Yes, let's go," she said, remembering Maggie lying upstairs, waiting.

He held her hand while he opened the door, checking to make sure the kitchen was empty. Then stepping aside, he let her go around him.

She picked up the teapot and a cup and saucer.

"Are we having tea?" he asked, grinning.

"No. This is for Maggie. She isn't feeling well." Without explaining further, she led the way upstairs.

She walked to her door and turned to him, whispering, "You go ahead. I'll be back after I see to Maggie."

Jauncey pushed open the door to Maggie's room. She was still awake.

"I'm sorry I took so long. I hope the tea is still hot." Jauncey set everything down on the dresser and helped Maggie sit up. "Are you feeling any better?"

Maggie didn't answer, but took the cup in her shaking hand and drank the tea.

"Perhaps we shouldn't say anything about this to Ginny yet." Jauncey had decided that now that she'd learned J.T. was dead, the less people who

254

knew about Maggie's involvement the better.

Maggie just stared at her round-eyed.

"Now isn't really the time to worry about anything. You need some rest." Jauncey took the cup and set it on the dresser again. Then she put both arms around Maggie, hugging her briefly in reassurance. "I'll add some coal to your fire before I go to bed."

Jauncey took the coal from the metal pail and opened the door on the stove to toss it in, then adjusted the damper. She glanced at her hands, dirty from the coal dust, and looked around for something to wipe them with, but found nothing, so she wiped them on her apron. Then she remembered the gun again.

What would she do with it? She couldn't leave it here. But if she took it back to her room, Matt would see it. No, he wouldn't, she argued with herself. If she undressed in the dark, and of course she would, he'd never know.

Jauncey looked at Maggie. Her eyes were closed. Jauncey turned out the lamp and left.

Outside her own door, she wondered what awaited her. Could she really sleep with Matt so close by? She doubted it.

He was sitting in a chair near the stove, his coat on the back of the chair, the lamp on her table burning low.

"I didn't want to search through your things looking for extra blankets," he said, his deep voice barely above a whisper.

"Oh, well, they're in here." She stepped to the trunk under the window, self-conscious about every move, and took out three blankets. "I think maybe you should make a pallet on the far side of the bed in case Ginny should come in. She seldom does. But just in case . . ." Her words trailed off as the reality of his sleeping in her bedroom struck her. What would her mother have said?

Matt stood, and Jauncey laid the pile of blankets on his chair. "I could get you a pillow from the office downstairs if you'd like." She let her eyes trail up his chest until she was looking directly at him.

"Don't bother. I never use one." He half-shrugged. "Habit from sleeping on the ground."

"Oh. Well . . ."

Matt picked up the blankets and spread them alongside her bed, out of sight of the door. He hung his hat on the back of the chair, then stretched out on the blankets, his hands beneath his head.

Jauncey was relieved to see he would sleep in his clothes. What about her? Should she sleep in her clothes? She didn't know if she could undress in the same room even with the light out, but then the cover of darkness would give her the opportunity to hide the gun.

She put out the lamp and walked to her dresser. Lifting the gun from her pocket, thankful Matt was on the other side of the bed, she laid it beneath the underclothes in her drawer. She slid the drawer closed and allowed a small sigh of relief to escape.

Matt listened to her movements. Her skirts rustled softly, and her shoes padded quietly on the carpeted floor. A light feminine fragrance drifted toward him when she opened the drawer, not one he was familiar with, but he liked it. After a while he heard the door open and close, then more rustling of clothes. He smiled when he realized she was undressing in the hall. He would have thought there was more risk in that than staying in the room with him. When she reentered the bedroom he couldn't resist teasing her.

"Is that the same gown I've seen twice now?"

"No," she said, climbing into bed.

Matt knew from her tone of voice she was lying, and he smiled as he listened to her quickly settle in the bed. Strange, he thought. He didn't remember those squeaks.

Chapter Eighteen

The chill in the air woke Jauncey. The room lay dark as pitch, with no telltale flickering light to signal the burning fire. Snuggling down into her blankets, she wondered why they didn't seem as heavy as usual.

With a jolt, she remembered snatching the top blanket from her bed to cover Maggie. Then suddenly the events of the night before crashed in on her. Murder! Jauncey buried her face in her pillow and tried to chase away the torturous thoughts that bombarded her. But it was useless.

She jumped from her bed, her feet hitting the icy cold floor. Shivering in the dark, she fumbled to find the matches to light a lamp. She would have to take over Maggie's chores, which included getting the cookstove going and starting breakfast. Quickly, she pulled a wool dress from the wardrobe. Her gaze landed on Maggie's dress lying in the bottom. Dread washed over her and she closed her eyes, leaning her head against the stone-cold wooden door.

She knew she had to get a grip on herself if she was going to handle this right. But how would she handle it? There was no doubt that Maggie had killed J.T. Matt had said . . .

Matt!

Jauncey whirled to face the floor where Matt had slept the night before. How could she have forgotten? She stepped around the end of the bed, but before she actually saw the empty blankets she knew he was gone.

Gone. Where? She looked the room over for a sign that he'd just stepped out. But his hat and coat were missing; he wouldn't be coming back, not soon anyway. She sank onto the edge of her bed, knotting her gown with her numb fingers. She needed to sort it all out, but she couldn't get a hold on anything. Not her feelings, not her desires, not anything. Unable to cope with so much at once, she focused on Maggie. Somehow Maggie had to be protected.

She dressed with haste, her cold fingers shaking so badly she could hardly button the front of her dress or tie her apron in back. Quickly, she made her bed and put Matt's blankets back into the trunk, then dashed down the stairs to the kitchen.

Jauncey shook down the ashes in the cookstove and removed them. The large supply of kindling was a welcome sight since she had not spent much time getting used to this particular stove. With a few false starts and several adjustments to the dampers, she finally had a good fire going. The chore had temporarily taken her mind off her worries.

She lifted a lid and fed small chunks of wood through the opening. Standing before the stove, holding her hands over it, she shivered. It would take some time before the large kitchen became warm. She had taken Maggie's wool shawl from the peg at the back door when she first came down, and now she drew it closer around her shoulders.

She listened with only half an ear to the snapping and crackling of the stove as it warmed and expanded, her mind on those she cared most about, their guilt and their innocence. How could Matt ever come out of hiding if she didn't tell him what Maggie had done? But how could she tell him, or anyone? Whatever the circumstances, Maggie didn't deserve to hang for J.T.'s murder; Jauncey was sure of that. But neither did Matt. She had to do something . . . something.

"Where's Maggie?" Ginny stood in the doorway, a new sparkle in her brown eyes.

"Oh!" Jauncey clutched her throat in alarm, her legs trembling.

"I didn't mean to frighten you." Ginny looked distressed.

"It's all right. I just didn't hear you come down." She waved her free hand and shook her head to add credibility to her words.

"Are you sure? Is something wrong? Where's Maggie?" Ginny looked around, her movements almost frantic.

For a second, Jauncey was tempted to tell her all that had happened. Ginny would want to know, she was sure of that, but she couldn't bring herself to unload such a burden on her. Ginny had been so happy lately. And the less involved she was, the more truthful she could be if questioned. No, it would be best if Ginny didn't know.

"Maggie isn't feeling well and I told her to stay in bed. I'm sure if she takes care of herself she'll be better soon." Jauncey added more wood and replaced the lid, trying to give the impression there was nothing to worry about.

"Does she have a fever?" Apprehension was still evident on Ginny's face and some of the sparkle had left her eyes.

"Oh, no. Nothing like that. She'll be fine with some rest and hot tea." Jauncey smiled reassuringly, regretting the need to lie.

"I'll go up and see her after we finish breakfast," Ginny said, walking to the cupboard and collecting enough dishes and cups to set the table. "These men have the heartiest appetites I've ever seen."

Jauncey watched Ginny move around the kitchen, oblivious to the cold, humming a fast-paced tune.

"You seem to be in extra fine spirits this cold morning. Does it have anything to do with Dan?" Jauncey said, thankful for the change of subject.

Ginny stepped lightly around the table, setting it while she continued to hum. A broad smile revealing even white teeth was her only answer.

"What is it?" Something was definitely going on. "Ginny?"

"I've decided to marry Dan." She stopped, holding a dish in one hand. "At the end of this week."

This was wonderful news, and Jauncey was truly

happy for Ginny. She pushed her nagging fears for Matt and Maggie to the back of her mind and grabbed Ginny in a fierce hug.

"Oh, Ginny! Where?"

"Here. If you don't mind, that is."

"Mind! Of course I don't mind. I think it's exciting! We have a lot to do. How should we do this? After all, it's your wedding." Jauncey pulled up two chairs beside the stove, one for herself and one for Ginny.

"We only want a simple ceremony, maybe in the parlor, with a preacher. Do you think we could get one to come?"

"My goodness, I don't know why not." Jauncey patted Ginny's hand. "Does Dan have someone in mind?"

"Yes. He's going to ask him today. If he says no . . ."

"He won't say no. Why should he? A man and woman want to be married because they love each other and that's all he needs to consider. And that's pretty obvious." Jauncey leaned forward to hug Ginny's shoulders once more. "I'm so happy for both of you!"

"I haven't felt this way since . . . I can't remember when. The only concern I've got is Maggie. I don't know how she'll take it. Since Spicie died she's been so dependent on me, not that I've minded. I haven't. Her life has been . . . well, difficult, to say the least. I don't know how she's held together. And if I marry Dan I'm afraid she'll think I'm deserting her." Worry plainly showed in Ginny's eyes.

"I'll take care of Maggie, so don't you worry about her. She'll be all right. You'll see." Jauncey hoped with every fiber of her being that her words would be true.

"I hope so." A loud sigh from Ginny echoed Jauncey's own feelings.

The sound of feet on the stairs threw Jauncey and Ginny into a frenzy of action. Jauncey made the coffee while Ginny started frying the bacon. She placed leftover biscuits in the oven to warm, then set them on the table with fresh butter and apple jelly. Soon, eggs cooked to order sat before each man with a large dish of crisp bacon within reach.

Jauncey poured the second cup of coffee while Ginny offered apple pie. Up until now, Jauncey had completed each task automatically. But if she'd had to keep track of who wanted pie and who didn't, she simply would have lost her grip on the whole morning. As it was, she methodically went from cup to cup filling those that were lifted toward her, and wondering where Matt had gone. What if he were seen?

Suddenly she came back to the present when Mr. Natter jumped out of his chair. She had spilled hot coffee over the edge of his cup, uncomfortably close to his hand.

"If you don't mind, Miss Taylor, I didn't get up this early to be scalded by someone who obviously has more important things on her mind than the well-being of her boarders."

"I'm terribly sorry, Mr. Natter. I guess I wasn't paying attention." Jauncey dabbed at the spill with a cloth.

"That is an understatement of the situation." Mr. Natter harrumphed emphatically.

His insistence on having the last word irritated her more than ever this morning. "I really am sorry," she said.

"No doubt."

Jauncey turned her back on him and rolled her eyes, setting the coffeepot on the stove. This was no time to allow his peevishness to get the best of her. It only prolonged the morning, and she wanted it to end as soon as possible. She had more important matters to contend with.

When the men had finally gone, Jauncey made a breakfast of warm milk on toast for Maggie, and a cup of hot tea.

"I'm going to take this up to Maggie. Then I'll come back and help with the dishes." Jauncey spoke over her shoulder as she headed out the door. She didn't want to give Ginny the opportunity to see to Maggie's needs first.

Carefully opening Maggie's door and balancing the tray against her waist, she peeked inside. The room was dark and cold.

"Maggie?" Jauncey whispered. "Are you awake?"

There was no answer, but Jauncey heard the rustling of the bedcovers and knew she was awake.

Jauncey lit the lamp and set the tray on the nearby bedside table.

"I think if you eat this while I light the stove we'll be able to warm you up." Jauncey smiled at the wan face looking back at her. "Here, let me prop you up with an extra pillow."

She quickly adjusted the pillows and bedcovers to allow a minimum of heat loss, then set the tray across Maggie's lap.

Maggie stared at it while the steam formed columns of escaping heat. But she didn't lift a finger.

Jauncey's heart ached for her. She was so young to have suffered so much. And just how much she had suffered Jauncey could only guess.

Without wasting more time, she built a small wood fire in the stove; then when it was hot enough she added chunks of coal. Still, Maggie sat motionless.

Jauncey moved to the side of the bed. "Maggie, you should eat something." She held one of the young girl's hands in her own, warming it.

Frightened eyes the color of a stormy sky turned toward Jauncey, but still she said nothing.

"You don't have to talk about last night. We'll think about it later when you're up to it." Jauncey smoothed the blond hair back from Maggie's pale face. "I promise I'll take care of you." She felt Maggie's hand squeeze hers tightly.

"You don't have to eat this if you don't want it." Jauncey took the tray away. "Maybe later, all right?"

What was she going to do? Should she call Dr. Myers? Maggie was in a terrible state, which was certainly no surprise. She was in a terrible state herself and she hadn't even been there.

"I'll stay with you if you'd like," Jauncey said, adjusting the pillows behind Maggie in an effort to control her thoughts.

Had Matt left in search of the real murderer? If only she could tell him. But she had to protect Maggie.

Matt waited outside Sam's saloon in the dark until one customer came rushing out the back door, obviously late getting home. Then Matt walked through the unlocked door. It was warmer inside, but not much.

He figured Charlie was with Ruby, so all he had to do was find her. He made his way amidst the tables of the empty barroom where a single wall lamp burned low, then climbed the steps to a long dark hallway. Some of the doors had the girls' names on them, and he struck a match to find Ruby's. Finally, he came to one with a large "R" on it. He tapped lightly on the door.

"Charlie?" he whispered. He wasn't in any mood to deal with an irate customer still feeling the effects of too much drinking. He hoped to hell Charlie was in there.

"Charlie!" He spoke louder this time, and movement from inside told him he had aroused someone.

The door opened and a disheveled Charlie stood before him. "Matt! Get in here!" Charlie pulled him inside the warm dark room, then glanced up and down the hallway.

"Nobody saw you, did they? The marshal's lookin' everywhere. Even sent a couple of deputies out to the ranch." He scratched his new growth of whiskers. "Guess they don't give you much credit for being smart."

"Charlie? Who you talkin' to?" Ruby's sleepy voice slurred the words.

"We can't talk with her around," Matt said with a frown. He had no intention of giving anyone the opportunity to turn him in.

"You're right." Charlie lit a lamp and, keeping it low, moved to the bed, leaving Matt in the dark.

Then Charlie shook Ruby to wake her completely. "Ruby, take your blankets and go on over to Lottie's room."

"Like hell." She rolled over.

"Either you go on your own, or I'll take you."

Ruby whirled. From the darkness Matt was startled to see a large bruise on her cheek. He hadn't remembered it being there last night.

"Oh, all right." She grabbed an armful of blankets and moved toward the door. "Just remember you ain't the only man in town, Charlie Hawks. And I don't take kindly to your attitude."

After she'd gone, Matt pulled a chair up to the small coal stove and warmed his hands. The flickering of escaping light reminded him of last night.

He hadn't slept more than a moment or two all night, listening to Jauncey's even breathing, wondering why he'd decided to get her mixed up in this. He could've gone somewhere else. Someone would have hidden him. Like Lottie. But he had discarded that idea as fast as it had come into his head. Finally he'd admitted he'd gone there because he'd wanted to be close to Jauncey. But it was too damn close. And at the same time too damn far.

Charlie dragged a chair next to Matt's, sat down and pulled on his boots. "It appears someone passing J.T.'s last night saw you clip him. And the marshal said he knew you had it in for J.T. for a long time. It was all he needed to get up a posse."

Matt stared hard at Charlie. "That doesn't mean I killed him. What kind of evidence is that? Hell, I could say you were the one who hit Ruby and gave her that bruise if I didn't know better."

Charlie's hardened gaze told Matt that he'd chosen a poor comparison. "You're right. I didn't."

Matt clapped him once on the back in the way of an apology. "I've got to find out who decided to get even with J.T. and is letting me take the blame. Whoever it is isn't going to be glad to see me when I find him. I'll make damn sure of that."

"But where do we start? I don't know anybody who had more enemies." Charlie buttoned his shirt and tucked it into his pants. "I suppose we'll have to start with the obvious."

"Johnny." Matt wondered if it made sense to think Johnny was the obvious culprit. He'd had no quarrel with J.T. that Matt knew of, especially since J.T. had helped him avoid jail. Did he hope to frame Matt by killing J.T.? Somehow that seemed far above Johnny's intelligence.

"No," Matt said thoughtfully, "I think that's the wrong direction. Maybe we need to go to J.T.'s office to see what sort of schemes he was working on. That might tell us who had the most to gain by killing him."

"Could be risky." Charlie looked skeptical.

"So could waiting around to get hung." Matt stood. "The dark will be to our advantage. Let's get going."

The sight of two men leaving the back door of the saloon was nothing out of the ordinary, but they took precautions to stay close to the buildings anyway.

When they arrived at J.T.'s office, it was with grim satisfaction they found the door unlocked and ajar. Matt pulled his gun from his holster. Charlie did the same. A nod from Matt and Charlie kicked the door wide. Nothing but darkness. They waited outside.

After several moments, Matt slipped quickly into the small office. He struck a match. Empty.

"Close the door and cover that window," Matt called, but Charlie had already stretched the curtain across it.

Matt found a lamp and lit it.

"Someone wasn't wastin' no time searchin' for something. I don't think the marshal would leave the door open and do this."

Charlie and Matt glanced around the littered office. Papers were scattered everywhere so that it was impossible to see the top of the desk or much space on the floor.

"Do you suppose they found what they were looking for?" Matt knelt, picking up a handful of papers.

"It's hard to say." Charlie scooped up a few from the desk, laying them down after a quick glance and picking up another handful. "Looks like some mighty important people had dealings with J.T."

Matt ignored Charlie, focusing his attention on the document in his hand; he recognized the signature. Spicie Belle Devon.

"What've you got, Matt?"

"I'm not sure," Matt answered, holding the paper to the dim light. "Looks like some kind of document with Spicie's name on it."

"Well, we know she couldn't have done it," Charlie said, passing it off.

Matt read the first few lines of the paper. Spicie had borrowed five thousand dollars from J.T., payable in installments of two hundred dollars. The rate of interest was extremely high, but that didn't surprise Matt since it was the only way J.T. did business. What did surprise him was that it was marked paid in full. Matt folded the paper and tucked it into his shirt pocket.

"Find anything, Charlie?" Matt asked, rummaging through more papers on the floor.

"Just that a lot of people will be happy to find J.T. out of their lives for good."

Matt agreed with that. He wasn't sorry about it himself. J.T. had swindled and rustled for the last time. Someone had done him a great favor, in one way. And Matt had to find out who, or likely he'd be swinging from a rope.

He brushed his hand along the floor under the mess until he touched something soft. Lifting it, he saw a piece of cloth partially caked with blood. It looked like a woman's handkerchief, small and made of linen with lace edging. A woman. Matt hadn't considered that.

"What do you make of this?" he said, extending the cloth toward Charlie.

"A woman's handkerchief. Where'd you find it?"

"Here, beside the desk." Matt knelt again, scraping everything aside, looking for another clue, something more conclusive. Since nearly all women carried one, the handkerchief could belong to anyone, even Jauncey, but he quickly thrust that thought from his mind.

"Don't look like there's anything else, Matt."

Charlie was right. He might as well give up.

Daylight crept into the winter sky as they closed the door behind them. Thoughts about Spicie's paid loan kept nagging Matt as he and Charlie split up before making their way along the streets back toward the saloon. He needed to talk to Collins.

They arrived at Sam's back door at the same time. Matt put a restraining hand on Charlie's shoulder when he started through the door.

"I can't stay here. I've got to talk to some people."

"Wait a minute, Matt. You can't go out on the street in daylight. Whatever you've got to find out, I'll take care of it. You stay here with Ruby until you can go back to the boardinghouse tonight."

Matt shook his head. "No. I want you to see what the marshal's up to. I'm going to see Collins."

"Collins! Now that's the damnedest thing you've said yet." Charlie looked as though he might just knock some sense into Matt after all.

But Matt just grinned and clapped Charlie hard on the back, and without another word took off down the alley. He had to talk to Collins about the arrangement J.T. had with Jauncey, and find out who else might be involved.

In a short time he was standing before the lawyer's office, slouched against the door, his hat tipped forward over his eyes and his collar up. He waited for about half an hour while the daylight became brighter and brighter before Collins arrived. When he nearly ran into Matt, he jumped back at least a foot.

"Matt Dawson! W-What are you doing here? Don't you know the marshal is looking for you?" Mr. Collins's voice was so muffled by the layers of scarves wound around his neck that Matt could barely make out his words.

"Good news sure travels fast," Matt said, stepping aside. He glanced behind them. "Hurry and open the door."

With fumbling fingers, Mr. Collins finally got the door open. Heavy green shades, pulled to the sills, darkened the interior of the office, and it took Matt's eyes a moment to adjust to the change of light.

"I'll be with you directly," Collins said.

Matt watched the lawyer set about doing the chores he obviously performed every morning. First he raised the shades halfway. Next, he shook the grates in the stove and built a fire with the neatly piled kindling waiting nearby in a box. Then he disappeared into the back room, only to appear again with a coffeepot. He filled it with the water he'd brought with him. After setting the pot on the stove, he turned to Matt.

"What can I do for you?"

Matt stood near the meager heat thankful for even that. He pulled from his pocket the paper he'd found in J.T.'s office, and handed it to Collins.

"What do you make of this?"

Andrew Collins perused the contents of the paper. "Where did you get this?" he asked, his voice strained.

"I can't tell you. Is it legal?"

"It appears to be. But . . ." Collins frowned.

"But what?"

"The date. It's different than the one I've got."

"You've got a copy?" Matt asked, surprised.

"Yes. I was Spicie's lawyer. That's how I came to be Miss Taylor's, too." Collins opened a desk drawer filled with neatly filed papers, flipping carefully through them until he found the one he sought.

"Here it is." He handed it to Matt.

"The dates are different," Matt said. He noted the one with the earlier date had been marked paid in full, while the copy Collins had produced was dated only weeks before Spicie's death, and wasn't paid in full. Matt squinted closely at the paper in the darkened room. Something else was wrong.

"Look real close," Matt said, handing both copies to Collins. "Is there anything else? Or are my eyes . . . ?"

"The handwriting," Collins whispered with dread in his voice. "It isn't the same." He stared at Matt with large eyes.

"That's what I thought. But which one is the real one?"

Collins rummaged through his files quickly, producing another paper. "This is one of Spicie's personal papers. I know the handwriting is hers because I watched her sign it right here in this office."

The lawyer lit a lamp on the desk and laid the two papers one over the other so the signatures were on top of each other, then held them up to the light. They were definitely different. One was smooth-flowing and large; the other appeared forced and exaggerated, but distinctly feminine.

"Forged!" he groaned.

Matt stared at the forged document dated only weeks before Spicie's death. Could she have been so ill it had affected her handwriting? But why would she borrow five thousand dollars when she knew her niece would inherit the debt? It didn't fit Spicie's way of doing things.

"I-I-I should have been more careful." Collins

shook his head in deep remorse. "Miss Taylor has been paying a debt on a forged loan," he croaked.

"Who gave you this paper?" Matt flapped the paper in Collins's face.

With his eyes downcast he said, "J.T."

"What! You accepted a paper from that cheating bastard as a legal document?" The man was incompetent. "An original document from J.T.?"

"My only defense lies in the fact that I was very unsettled by the predicament forced upon Miss Taylor and m-m-myself. It was quite distressing to have to inform a lady of her standards about the . . . house. I truly regret the situation." He practically collapsed into the chair behind him, his head in his hands. "Truly."

The crackling in the stove was like an irritation in Matt's brain, erupting into tiny sparks of anger. He was going to get to the bottom of this. Whoever had done this had intentionally set out to destroy Jauncey, and had undoubtedly set him up as a murderer. J.T. might have started the whole mess, but someone else had obviously finished it. And he had to find out who.

Collins sat rocking his head in his hands. "Careless. I was so careless."

"There's no time for self-pity now, Collins," Matt barked. "We've got to find the woman who forged this paper. She'll have the answers to most of our questions." He pulled the blood-caked handkerchief from a pocket. "Whoever this belongs to has got to know something, if not everything."

Andrew Collins took the cloth from Matt and inspected it, turning it over in his hands.

"This is blood! Where did you get this?"

Matt detected a note of alarm in Collins's voice. Should he tell him anything? Could he be trusted? Matt knew he had no choice. Besides, the lawyer was the only person who could help him at this point.

"I found the paper and the cloth in J.T.'s office. Any ideas who it might belong to?"

"No. I'm afraid I don't. I wish I did." He gave it back to Matt.

Matt wished he did, too.

"I'll think about it, Matt. Give me a little time and something might come to me. Right now . . ." He shrugged his shoulders in helplessness.

Matt nodded his head. "If you want to get in touch with me, tell Charlie. He'll be at Sam's." Matt looked out the front door at the people on the street.

"You can't go out there. You'll be seen." Andrew Collins ushered him into the back room. "You can stay here if you like until it's safe. Nobody uses the back door. It's always locked." He dug in his coat pocket and produced a key. "Here's the key. You're welcome to come and go as you please."

The gesture was one of trust, and Matt appreciated it. He took the key. "Thanks, Andrew. I'll take you up on it. I may have to stay here until it gets dark." Matt looked around. "Is there a place I can stretch out for a few hours? I didn't get much sleep last night."

Chapter Nineteen

Jauncey couldn't get Matt out of her mind. Where was he? Had he been caught? Why didn't he just stay put until she could come up with a solution? Instead, he was out wandering around in the middle of the day, probably in plain sight. She punched the bread dough on the flouring board extra hard.

Between worrying over him and Maggie, who was lying in bed not saying a word, Jauncey was as nervous as a hen with too many chicks.

"Jauncey, you're concerned about Maggie, aren't you?" Ginny asked, standing at the stove where she was making a large pot of venison stew. "I'm worried about her, too. I don't think she's ill. I think it's something else."

Rising panic nearly choked Jauncey. "She'll be all right in another day. I put Sunshine in her room this morning and that seemed to pick up her spirits a little."

"That's just it. Her spirits are so low. I haven't seen her like this since Spicie died." Ginny's frown deepened. "I suppose we should call Dr. Myers, but I don't think Maggie would tolerate him. He might even make her worse."

"She's such a sad person. It breaks my heart to see anyone so frightened of everything. What a terrible life she must have lived." Jauncey punched the dough once more. And how thoughtful of her aunt to keep Maggie in a house like this! she thought angrily.

"It was a terrible life. Worse than you can imagine."

Jauncey turned her head sharply toward Ginny. Was she agreeing that Maggie had been mistreated by Spicie? She watched while Ginny continued stirring the pot, her concern for Maggie evident on her face. It was also evident that the subject of Maggie's past was still not open for discussion.

Well, the past was done, Jauncey decided, and more pressing worries were at hand. Life-and-death worries.

Jauncey shaped the loaves and placed them in the pans, setting them above the stove in the warming oven to rise. She took a damp cloth and covered them, but all the while her mind was preoccupied.

"Dan said this morning that the preacher agreed to come here for the ceremony." Ginny's voice was low, weighted with concern.

Jauncey knew this should be a happy time for Ginny, and turned to her with what she hoped was enthusiasm. "That's wonderful. Have you decided what day?"

277

"We've decided not to wait. We considered the day after tomorrow, but with Maggie not well . . . I don't know if we should. I don't think she's handling the idea very well."

Jauncey realized that Ginny believed Maggie's depression was because of the impending wedding. If only she could tell Ginny the truth. But the truth wouldn't ease anything; it would only make her feel worse. She had to find another way to convince Ginny she was wrong.

Grasping Ginny by the shoulders, she looked her straight in the eye. "Maggie's illness has nothing to do with your marriage. I know it. She wants what's best for you and so do I. Maggie isn't selfish and she would never want to be the cause of your unhappiness."

Ginny stared back at her, large tears glistening in her eyes, threatening to spill over. "I know." Her voice was so tight, Jauncey barely heard the words.

Jauncey clasped her close. "You'll see I'm right. Maggie will be better by tomorrow and she'll be down here for the ceremony the next day. I promise."

One more promise, she told herself, wondering if she could keep this one.

"No more of this," Jauncey said, holding Ginny at arm's length. "We've got a lot of planning to do. My heavens, a wedding right here the day after tomorrow. Imagine that!"

"Oh, no," Ginny objected. "We don't want anything that will take planning. We just want a simple ceremony."

"Of course we'll make it simple if you like, but

no planning? I think not. We'll have a nice dinner after the ceremony with the best china in the house. All the boarders will be included, so we'll have to tell them so they can be in their Sunday best." Jauncey stopped. "Dress! What will you wear? We don't have time to make anything!"

"That isn't important. Really. A new dress doesn't mean anything to me compared to spending the rest of my life with Dan. I have a dress that will do just fine." Ginny smiled and patted Jauncey's hand. "Really."

She knew Ginny was right; she'd feel that way, too.

"Well, then we can go on to the next thing. Which room? In the parlor with the fireplace would be very nice, don't you agree? We could put up the Christmas decorations . . . goodness, we'll have to do that tomorrow!"

"All of this isn't necessary, Jauncey. Can't we do without the decorations and just have a nice dinner?" Ginny raised her eyebrows in appeal.

"All right," Jauncey conceded. "I guess I wouldn't even know where to look for the decorations."

"We could have champagne," Ginny offered. "Spicie had several bottles set aside for special occasions. I'd say this would be appropriate, wouldn't you?"

Champagne. Jauncey had never even seen a bottle of it, let alone tasted it. Her mother had taught her that all spirits were bad, but even if she hadn't, they could never have afforded champagne anyway.

Pushing aside Maybelle's teachings, she said, "It certainly is a special occasion."

279

With Ginny's help, Jauncey returned to the task of preparing the evening meal, with only a few moments taken to peek into the cupboards where the china and crystal lay. Tomorrow she and Ginny would take it all out and wash it in preparation for the wedding.

Jauncey wished she could let the excitement of it overtake her, but her worry dulled the moment measurably.

A knock at the front door brought Jauncey up short. Surely Matt wouldn't arrive in broad daylight, she thought. Wiping her hands on her apron, she hurried to open it.

There standing before her was Andrew Collins, bundled up tight in his many layers of clothing. She forced down the urge to send him on his way, having more important things on her mind than his need to court her.

"Come in, Andrew, before you freeze to death." She stepped aside, closing the door quickly behind him.

"I'm sorry to barge in like this," he mumbled, pulling off his mufflers and coat. "But I wanted to tell you . . . that is, I . . ."

"If you mean about J.T., we've already heard."

"Oh, yes, isn't it terrible. Well, I mean the circumstances at least are terrible. He certainly won't be missed by many people here in Laramie, if any."

"Is there something else?" she asked, noting the worry lines on his brow.

"Yes, yes, there is. But I hardly know how to begin. I . . . I . . . I'm leaving town soon."

Surprised, she replied, "Leaving town?" He looked so sad that she felt guiltier than ever for being unable to accept his attentions and for not telling him. But try as she might, she couldn't think of him as a serious suitor. He might be exactly the kind of man her mother would have wanted for her, as Ginny had said, but the truth was, she had to make her own choices. And right now, her heart chose Matt.

"Yes, I'll be going back to Philadelphia," he said. "That's where I came from. Perhaps I'll open a law office there."

He sighed deeply and she felt another stab of guilt.

"Though I don't know exactly when I'm leaving, I wanted to express my sincere apologies for causing so many problems for you. I never intended to have you hurt in any way." He looked steadfastly into her eyes. "I truly mean that," he said softly.

A lump formed in her throat. "I know," she said, feeling overwhelmingly sorry that they'd met under such difficult circumstances.

"I guess I'd better be going," he said, pulling on his coat. But before he could put on his mufflers she leaned toward him and kissed his cheek.

"Well," he said, glancing at the door. "The weather out here appears only to get worse. At least in Philadelphia I know what to expect." He wrapped all of his scarves around his neck. "I really must be going," he mumbled.

"Be careful, Andrew, and . . . thank you for caring so much."

He could only nod as he opened the door and left.

Jauncey watched him go, feeling melancholy. He meant well, she knew. But a marriage between them would have been impossible, especially when she remembered how passionately she'd responded to Matt every time she was in his arms. Andrew's propriety would have scorned that in a wife, and she would have scorned his inability to deal with life. Closing the door against the cold, she realized that as sorry as she was for him, she knew it was for the best.

Supper that night went as usual except for Jauncey's announcement of the wedding, which met with hearty approval. Two of the boarders offered their talent with bow and fiddle, while a third said he had a harmonica he believed would fit right in.

"Music! That will be wonderful. Won't Maggie love that?" Jauncey asked Ginny.

"Yes, I'm sure she will." Ginny glanced appreciatively around the table.

But Jauncey didn't think she sounded convinced.

"I think I'll go up now and tell her about it," Jauncey said, excusing herself from the table and fixing a tray for Maggie. She had to start getting Maggie prepared to come down to share in the festivities.

She tapped on Maggie's door. "Maggie?" she called, before opening it. "I've got supper for you. I hope you like it."

The room was almost dark. Jauncey was disappointed that Maggie hadn't lit the lamp since she'd hoped for some sign of improvement.

Sunshine lay in a curled heap with her kittens spread around her on the bed, and Maggie's hand was splayed over the pile of fur at her side, fingering the softness. Jauncey set the tray down and stood beside the bed, then lifted the limp bodies of the sleepy cats to the floor, where they arched and stretched.

"I want you to eat some of this and then we have to talk."

Maggie's eyes became large and round.

"Not about the other night," Jauncey added hastily. "About Ginny's wedding."

She helped Maggie to sit up, setting the tray on her lap. Without a word, Maggie took a bite of the bread and a sip of the tea. Jauncey knew she had to be hungry.

"The stew is very good, don't you think? Ginny made it." She watched in silence while Maggie took a bite of the tender meat and potatoes.

Jauncey sighed with relief when Maggie pushed the dish away at least half-eaten. It was a start.

"Remember when Ginny said she was going to marry Dan? Well, they've decided to be married the day after tomorrow. Here." Jauncey waited for the information to register before going on. "She'd really like you to be there. Do you think you can manage it?"

Maggie stared back. Suddenly tears filled her eyes.

"Oh, Maggie, what is it? Tell me. You want Ginny to be happy, don't you?" Jauncey rubbed the back of Maggie's hand in reassurance.

Maggie bit her lip, nodding while the tears streamed down her cheeks.

"There's no need to be sad. Ginny will be very happy. Happier than she is right now." Jauncey took a clean handkerchief from her apron pocket and gave it to Maggie. "That isn't what's bothering you, though, is it?"

Maggie blew her nose, shaking her head.

"Then you're wondering what's going to happen to you, aren't you?"

Her large blue eyes looked back at Jauncey. The pale blond hair haloed Maggie's face in a mass of uncombed curls. She looked so vulnerable.

"You have nothing to worry about. I promised you I would take care of you, and I meant it. This is your home for as long as you want it to be. You believe me, don't you?"

Maggie nodded.

"Will you think about coming down for the noon meal with Ginny and me tomorrow? We'll be getting everything ready for the wedding. Maybe you could help with some of it." Jauncey smoothed the hair back from Maggie's face. "It will be good for you to do something to get your mind off . . . the other night."

Jauncey waited for a sign of resistance to her words, but none came.

Sunshine jumped back upon the bed, leaving the kittens meowing in frustration on the floor, so Jauncey scooped them up and deposited them on the quilt.

She removed the tray from Maggie's lap, wanting to say something more, but nothing came to mind.

"Ginny will be up to see you later," Jauncey said before walking out the door.

But Maggie continued to stroke the mother cat, saying nothing.

When Jauncey arrived downstairs, the men had all gone to the parlor to sit before the fire. Dan was there, too. She watched from the foot of the stairs in the entrance parlor where the darkness hid her. Ginny sat beside him, their hands together in the small space between them, the glow on Ginny's face mirroring the happiness on Dan's.

Jauncey slipped into the kitchen unnoticed, feeling too full of anxiety and downheartedness to be anything but a damper on their cheerful mood. It was best if she stayed away, at least until she could come up with an answer to Maggie's problem and solve Matt's in the process.

With the dishes neatly stacked and ready to wash, she dipped the hot water from the reservoir into the pan in the sink. Slowly she performed the task, her mind going over the possibilities.

If Maggie had killed J.T. in self-defense, then she wouldn't have to worry about the outcome of a trial. But could Maggie stand going through a trial? No, she was sure she couldn't. What were the other options? Let Matt get caught and probably hang for something he didn't do? Her breath caught in her throat. No, never! But he couldn't hide forever, and she held the key to his freedom.

Quickly, she put the dishes away.

Everyone had retired to their rooms for the night except Ginny. Jauncey heard soft voices coming from the other room where Ginny and Dan said good night. Then Ginny stepped into the doorway to say she would look in on Maggie before going to bed.

Alone once more, Jauncey turned down the lamp. With her head resting on her arms, she wondered if Matt would come back tonight. Or could he?

A window rattled against the sudden force of the wind. Another blizzard was coming, at least that's what everyone predicted, and so far they'd been right about the other storms. She'd never seen so much snow as she had since she'd come to Laramie, and the cold was something to be reckoned with. Shivering, she drew her shawl closer about her.

A sound at the back door drew her attention and she stared at the black glass, trying to see into the darkness. The wind, she decided. But a moment later the door opened and closed, bringing a swift movement of cold air rushing along the floor to her feet. Standing there before her was Matt.

Without a second thought, she flew from her chair and into his arms, burying her nose in the rough wool of his coat where the cold still clung. Icy particles of snow melted on her cheeks, but her only thought was that he was safe.

"Missed me, huh?" he said, wrapping his arms around her.

She lifted her face. "I was worried about you. I kept wondering if the marshal had found you." She looked into his dark eyes and found he was smiling at her.

"Not yet he hasn't. And I don't plan on getting caught." Matt glanced around, taking off his hat. "Maybe we should go upstairs before someone has to make a trip out back." He cocked his head toward the door.

"You're right." Jauncey blew out the lamp and took his hand, leading him through the darkened house. The only noises were the small ringing sounds made by the spurs on Matt's boots and the wind brushing against the house.

Inside her room, she lit a lamp while he built a fire. It was a homey gesture, and she liked seeing him kneel before the stove, his hat on the floor beside him, his thick dark hair still imprinted from the band.

"I think it would be a good idea if you removed your spurs while you're in the house," she whispered. "Someone might hear them." She pulled the shawl closer and stood near the tiny bit of heat.

He glanced at her and nodded. Removing them, he laid them on the dresser next to her hairbrush and pins, and then took off his coat and laid it across a chair.

Jauncey watched his every move, welcoming his presence.

"Where did you go today?" she asked.

"I want to talk to you about that." He placed a chair for her before the fire while he leaned comfortably against the dresser. "I talked with Andrew Collins about the loan you've been paying to J.T. It appears to be a forgery."

Jauncey listened, mesmerized by the deep sound of his voice, but heard nothing, relaxed simply by his presence.

Matt stared at her. "Jauncey?"

Suddenly alert, she asked, "Yes?"

"The loan you had with J.T. was forged."

"Forged?" She blinked and sat up straighter. "What do you mean forged? Andrew has the original paper in my aunt's handwriting. He never questioned it before now." Anger prickled along her spine. Anger directed at Andrew B. Collins.

"He should have questioned why J.T. was so

willing to part with an original document," Matt said. "What if it were destroyed?"

How could she have been so stupid! Of course, it couldn't be the original. How could Andrew have been so careless! She jumped from her chair, nearly overturning it.

"Why that chicken-hearted . . ." She wanted to wring his scrawny neck. Just because of him she'd paid that lying thief her hard-earned money, borrowed money from Matt and worried about it to boot!

She felt like a fool. An empty-headed, brainless twit. Enraged, she stared unseeing at Matt. If J.T. weren't already dead . . .

"We found the real one in J.T.'s office this morning. We found this, too." Matt removed the handkerchief from his pocket and gave it to her. "This proves there was a woman there the night J.T. was killed. Maybe she was the one who killed him."

Like the wind pumped from a bellows, the air left her lungs. She could neither speak nor move. The room started to turn and her knees weakened until she dropped into the chair. It was a simple handkerchief with lace edging. She couldn't be positive it was Maggie's but the lace was close to the color of the amethyst necklace Jauncey had given her, Maggie's favorite color.

"You found this in J.T.'s office?" Jauncey forced her voice to sound normal. What other evidence had been left to point a finger at Maggie?

"The office was turned inside out with papers everywhere. It's a wonder we found it."

She took little gasps of air. "Was there anything . . . else?"

"No."

She laid the cloth on the dresser beside his spurs.

"I thought you'd be glad to find out I'm not the one who did it." Matt grinned at her. "The sooner I find this woman, the sooner I'll be out of here and you'll have your privacy back."

"Oh, no. I mean, I never thought you did it, not for a moment. You've got to believe that." She rose from the chair and stood before him, only a handsbreadth away. "I know you'd never do anything like that." She felt herself carried away in the depths of his dark eyes, and placed her hand on his chest beneath his unbuttoned coat. "Never."

Matt grasped her gently by the arms and drew her close. His eyes locked with hers, her lips touched his in soft surrender.

Jauncey pressed both hands against his chest where she could feel the thudding of his heart, her own keeping rhythm. A sensation of warmth and well-being flooded over her. She lifted her arms to his neck, aware only of her need to be closer.

Crushing her to him, Matt drew her deeper into his embrace. His lips moved across hers in gentle persuasion until she opened to him. Then she was lost in the soft tangled dance that ensued.

Pulling back, he nibbled at the corners of her mouth, then at her lower lip.

"You taste like . . ." He kissed her again. "Like a summer day in the mountains."

"I've never been to the mountains," she said, snuggling closer to his body. "Tell me about them."

"Sunshine. Clear mountain air." He tugged at her lower lip. "Flowers. Especially roses. Always roses." He bent his head to once again take full possession of her mouth.

Once more she gave in to the rhythm, letting it take over her mind and body, aware of nothing but the melting warmth seeping into her muscles and bones. With every ounce of strength she had, she moved her hand to rest on his face, wanting to feel the texture of his skin, the silkiness of his mustache.

He lifted his head. "Jauncey."

She opened her eyes. He was saying no, when she was saying yes.

"I don't think you know . . ." he began.

Yes, she did know. Why didn't it seem wrong? By all the standards she'd been given since she was a child, it was supposed to be wrong.

"Matt . . ."

"Don't. You'll be sorry. I know it even if you don't." He kissed her lightly, firmly.

Her mind resisted his words while her body, still flushed with the heat of his kisses, was not willing to return to cool logic.

He kissed her forehead and drew her hand away from where it rested on his cheek, then placed her palm against his lips while his eyes searched hers.

Her fingertips tingled, echoing the more remote parts of her body. The sensation was wonderful and she closed her eyes, enjoying it.

"Maybe I'd better leave," Matt said, backing away.

"No! You might get caught. Besides, I think the storm has gotten worse." As if to lend credence to her words, the wind rattled the panes in the windows while it seemed to shake the house.

"You see?" She waited, breathless.

"I guess you're right." He hesitated.

The stovepipe crackled as flames warmed it quickly, and puffs of smoke from a downdraft filtered into the room.

"I'll just sleep on the floor where I did last night." He made a move toward the trunk.

She raised her hand. "I'll get the blankets. You'll need more tonight."

She handed him the blankets, then added a few more, and he took them, spreading a pallet in the same spot as before. When the light was out and they'd both settled in, Jauncey's thoughts descended on her in a jumble. Protect Maggie. Hide Matt. Forged papers. Matt's strong arms surrounding her. Matt's lips insistent against hers. Happy. Complete. Satisfied.

Chapter Twenty

Jauncey moved through the darkness as though her body was weighted. Still she held Maggie close, pulling her along even though the added burden was almost more than she could bear. Her heart quickened as rapid gunfire sounded in the distance. Then Matt was calling to her.

"Jauncey!" Matt whispered. "Jauncey!" He tugged at her covers from where he lay on the floor until she groaned.

The distant gunfire came closer until it blended with the short knocks on her bedroom door. She was completely awake now, and relief flooded over her. She was safe.

"Are you up?" Ginny called from the other side of the door.

"I'm awake," she answered groggily. "I'll be right down." Contrary to her words, she snuggled farther into the bed, pulling the warm blankets over her head. She really wasn't ready for another day.

"Are you snoring again?" Matt teased softly, grinning.

He heard only a muffled response.

"What was that?"

Jauncey flung the covers back. "I don't snore. You do. I didn't get a moment's rest all night."

Neither had Matt. He tried to ignore the damp chill seeping into his bones. If this floor was any indication of the weather outside, it was damn cold, he decided, getting up.

"I'll light a fire for you," he said. "Stay in bed until I get it going."

"No," she answered, leaving the bed. "I have to hurry down to help Ginny get breakfast for the men. Cold or no cold."

"Well, I'll build it while you get dressed. I promise to keep my back turned," he said into the blackness of the room.

He heard her rummaging through the wardrobe for a dress and her teeth chattering, then the frantic rustle of clothing. He smiled to himself.

"Doesn't it ever get cold where you come from?" he asked.

"N-n-not l-l-like th-this."

Matt held a match to the wick, and the room instantly became a place of glowing light and shadows. She stood completely dressed and buttoned, trying to wind her braid into a circle at the back of her head with shaking fingers. He watched while she stabbed several pins into the braid.

"I'll b-bring you s-some br-breakfast," she said, then hurried out the door. Just as quickly the door opened again. "Don't go anywhere," she whispered.

"I won't," he whispered back. "At least not until after breakfast," he added mischievously.

Jauncey quietly closed the door and rushed down the stairs, her heart thrumming. She was glad he was back where she could keep an eye on him.

In the kitchen Ginny had a fire going and the table set. Jauncey made the coffee and whipped up the batter for the flapjacks, as the men called them. The faster she moved, the quicker her body thawed.

"This is the coldest it's been yet," she said. "Or am I just exaggerating?"

"I believe you're right." Ginny turned toward the frosty windows and nodded. "Look."

Every window was covered with ice on the inside. On the outside the wind howled, making whistling noises wherever a crack afforded the opportunity. Jauncey stayed close to the stove, thankful for its warmth.

Everyone was there for breakfast except Maggie and Mr. Natter, who had usually never eaten this early until just recently. Actually, it had been right after J.T. was shot, Jauncey mused. But today he'd reverted to his old habit of sleeping late. One more thing to be thankful for, she decided.

It was the longest meal she'd ever served. Each man had at least two cups of coffee after eating stacks of flapjacks. Then finally, they bundled up in layers of clothing, hats, gloves and scarves and went off to work. Snow swirled into the kitchen through the open door, thick enough to be swept away with a broom.

"I'll take Maggie's breakfast up to her this morning and build her fire. I'd like to talk to her," Ginny said while she prepared a tray.

Jauncey pushed down her rising anxiety and forced a nervous smile. Everything would be all right, she told herself. She couldn't prevent them from talking forever.

After Ginny left, Jauncey rushed around preparing a tray for Matt and quietly hurried up the stairs. She slipped into her room, feeling like a thief in her own house.

Matt lay across her bed with his boots hanging off the side, his hands behind his head, sound asleep.

She stood motionless beside the bed looking down at him. He was far too tall to fit comfortably in her bed, even if he'd been lying in the right direction. She didn't feel a bit awkward staring at him while he slept. Instead, she relished the opportunity, watching the even rise and fall of his chest beneath the warm flannel shirt. She was drawn to the strength registered in his relaxed face. From there, her eyes wandered to his heavy dark hair, recalling the texture of it when he had held her in his arms and she'd laced her fingers through its blackness.

Suddenly afraid he'd awake and find her staring so blatantly at him, she stepped away from the bed. If her emotions were as plain on her face as they were in her mind, and she suspected they were, he'd know exactly what she was thinking. And she wasn't sure she was ready to deal with that, not now with so much pressing in on her.

From a safe distance, she called, "Matt? I've got

some breakfast for you." When he didn't move, she called again. "Matt?"

Suddenly awake, he came off the bed in a single leap. Startled, she backed into the dresser with enough force to slosh the coffee from the cup.

"I didn't mean to alarm you," Jauncey said softly, concerned that someone might have heard the commotion.

He ran his fingers through his hair. "I didn't mean to doze off. I guess I didn't sleep very well last night." He sank onto a chair near the hot stove.

"I'm not surprised." She quickly glanced at him. "It was far too cold to be sleeping on the floor. Maybe we can work out a way to get a mattress in here for you." She set the tray on the table near him, trying not to show her nervousness. "I don't know if this is still warm. And I'm sorry about the coffee." She looked up from where she bent over the table. Their eyes met and held while her breath caught in her throat.

"Thanks."

She felt rather than heard his deep voice vibrate along every nerve ending in her body. Quickly she turned to the unmade bed, stifling her thoughts. Pulling the sheets and covers neatly into place, she was very much aware that he watched her movements.

Giving the pillow another unnecessary pat before turning to face him once more, she said, "Today is Ginny's wedding day, so we have a lot of preparations to make. I doubt if I'll have many chances to come up here again."

"Ginny? Is that what you call Sugar?" Matt drank

the last of his coffee, watching her over the edge of his cup.

"It's her real name." She glanced at the still-dark iced-over windows. "I hope the preacher won't have any trouble getting here in this weather."

"She's marrying Dan?" he asked.

"Yes. I'm happy for both of them. Ginny deserves a better life and I'm sure Dan can give it to her."

Matt nodded.

"Well, if you're finished I'll take that downstairs."

"Thanks." Matt stood, handing her the tray.

She accepted the tray, then backed toward the door. "You won't be going anywhere today, will you? I mean, the weather is pretty bad."

"No. I'm not at all interested in going out into a Wyoming blizzard."

She smiled. "Good. Well . . ." she began, placing her hand on the doorknob. "I'll be back around noon."

Once she was in the hallway, she closed the door behind her without wasting a moment and rushed down to the kitchen.

Mr. Natter sat at the table drinking a cup of coffee. She couldn't help rolling her eyes toward the ceiling when she saw his stiff straight back, then quickly adjusted her face in the semblance of a smile.

"Good morning, Mr. Natter. I'll have your breakfast in a minute." Jauncey emptied her tray of dirty dishes at the sink.

"Why hurry now," he said in a sarcastic tone.

She ignored him and heated the frying pan, wondering if he purposely irritated her or if it just came as second nature to the man. He was difficult to understand in more ways than one, she decided.

As fast as the stove would allow, Jauncey supplied the two pancakes served with butter but no other topping, just the way he preferred. He received them with the same perfunctory "thank you" she was used to hearing.

But her mind wouldn't focus on Mr. Natter or his supercilious attitude. Her thoughts were on Ginny and Maggie. What was taking so long? What if Maggie told her the truth? There was some relief in the thought of sharing the problem, but it really would be more like unloading a burden onto someone else's shoulders. No, she didn't think Maggie would say anything. Actually, Maggie hadn't spoken a solitary word since that night she'd come through the front door, the gun in her hand.

After finishing his breakfast, Mr. Natter bundled up and trundled off toward town just as daylight brightened the window near the sink. But still Ginny did not come down.

Jauncey washed the last cup and put it away, added more wood to the fire, then looked around the kitchen for something else to do. It was terribly hard to concentrate on anything.

A sound from the doorway drew her attention.

Standing beside Ginny was Maggie with a shaky smile on her face.

"Maggie! I'm so glad you came down." Jauncey felt genuinely relieved to see her up and around and pulled a chair out for her. "You can sit here and dry the china."

Maggie sat down, grasped Jauncey's hand and

gave it a hard squeeze. Jauncey returned the squeeze and smiled reassuringly.

With all the work that had to be done, the morning passed pleasantly enough. Jauncey thought of Matt only once or twice since she knew he was safe. So her attention turned to Ginny, and her efforts went into making the day a happy, memorable one.

By noontime the china and crystal goblets were gleaming, and Jauncey had even located a bottle of champagne for toasting the bride and groom. Everything seemed to be going along right on schedule.

"I say we take some time for nourishment." Ginny dropped into a chair looking exhausted but happy.

"You're right. You sit while I fix something." Jauncey bustled around the stove preparing a simple fare of potatoes, dried beef and carrots. With warmed biscuits and jam, it made a tasty meal.

Every bite Jauncey took brought to mind the problem of getting some food up to Matt. She decided her only chance was to divert their attention.

"Why don't we take our coffee into the parlor by the fireplace?" Jauncey asked, rising from her seat at the table. "I'll make some tea for Maggie and bring it in right after I clear the table."

"Oh, no. We'll help," Ginny protested.

Jauncey put her hands on Ginny's shoulders. "Really, I want both of you to just go in and sit down. I'll be there in no time."

Without further complaint, Ginny rose with her

299

cup and led the way, Maggie following.

Immediately, Jauncey started the tea, dished up a plate for Matt and covered it with a napkin, then cleared the table and checked on the tea. Close enough. With a teacup in one hand and the napkin–covered dish in the other, she went into the entrance parlor. She set the dish on a table near the stairway and carried the cup into the parlor where the two women sat before the cozy fire.

"I hope it isn't too weak," Jauncey said, handing the cup to Maggie.

"Aren't you going to sit with us?" Ginny asked, looking surprised.

"Yes, but first I have something I want to do upstairs." She turned to leave the room, then looked back at Ginny. "Did you tell Maggie about the music we're going to have tonight?" she said, hoping to turn their attention to the wedding and away from her.

"No! I didn't," Ginny exclaimed, and began filling Maggie in on the details.

Jauncey left the room, picking up the dish on her way up the stairs. Standing outside her bedroom door, she tapped twice before entering.

Matt lay stretched out on the bed, his eyes riveted on the door. When she came in he sat up, facing her, watching while she fussed over the tray and napkin, barely looking at him.

She stood with her hands clasped in front of her, feeling uncertain. "I imagine you feel cooped up in this room with nothing to do."

He shrugged. "I've got a lot of thinking to do, so it isn't all wasted time."

She watched while he juggled the dish on his

lap, trying not to spill anything. He looked out of his element sitting on a bed that was obviously feminine, in a room that smelled of sachet. But it crossed her mind that he didn't seem at all uncomfortable with the situation.

"What sort of things are you thinking about?" she asked, wondering if he had any other clues about the woman in J.T.'s office.

"You," Matt replied, taking a bite of biscuit spread with jam.

"Me?" She hadn't expected that answer, and her eyes opened wide in surprise.

"Yes." Matt set the dish aside and swallowed the last of the coffee. He stared at her. "Your stubbornness . . ." He stopped, smiled, then went on. "I mean, your determination has paid off. You've made this house a success in spite of J.T. Most women like you would have given in and gone back to St. Louis."

She smiled, thinking at least he hadn't called her bullheaded, although she wasn't sure what he meant by "women like you." Did he think she fit into a particular class of women? "Would you care to elaborate on that?" She sat on the chair opposite the bed where he half reclined.

"I just meant, I have to hand it to you. I didn't think you were up to the job." He paused, looking at her until she thought he could see into the depths of her soul. "But you've got more . . . determination . . . than any woman I know."

His words conveyed his belief that she was capable of being an independent woman, a woman who could make it on her own, who could beat the odds against her and win.

301

Melody Morgan

A tapping on the door drew their attention and Jauncey jumped from her chair.

"Jauncey, are you all right?" Ginny called.

"Yes. I'm on my way down now."

"The men have come home because of the blizzard."

Jauncey placed her hand on the doorknob. "I was just putting on some warmer clothes." With her ear to the door she listened for Ginny's retreating footsteps, then turned to Matt and whispered, "I guess I'd better go." Then she slipped out of the room.

Downstairs, the men had indeed come home. Stories of frozen stock on the ranges and the fear of lost men occupied the conversation for the rest of the afternoon. Jauncey and the other two women busied themselves with baking bread and pies, and making noodles for the boiling beef simmering on the back of the stove. With everything under control, Jauncey sent Ginny off to bathe and dress for the evening. She herself waited until the last moment to change clothes, wondering how she would manage it with Matt in her room.

Ginny arrived downstairs wearing a lovely deep blue dress fashionably styled with a lighter blue overskirt draped apron-style in the front and gathered over the bustle in the back. Her dark hair, tightly curled and pulled back from her glowing face, looked like a work of art.

"Ginny! You're absolutely beautiful." Jauncey hugged her, then stood back. "Wait until Dan sees you."

"Thank you." Ginny's smile was radiant. "I hope he doesn't have any trouble getting the preacher."

Jauncey walked to the back door and laid her

warm palm against the frosted window to melt an area large enough to see through. She understood Ginny's concern.

The wind blew ferociously across the backyard, piling the snow in banks wherever it met the resistance of an object or a building. She would rest easier when the ceremony was over and the preacher was home again and Dan was safely back.

Maggie had changed her day dress for a simple light mustard satin one. It, too, was fashionable, with a high neck, draped front, and bustle. She looked lovely, but her cheeks lacked their usual rosy color.

Well, Jauncey thought, it was her turn and she couldn't put it off any longer. Climbing the stairs, she searched her mind frantically for a way to surmount this problem without arousing suspicion from the others in the house. She sighed resignedly and tapped on the door before entering.

Matt sat before the fire, his forearms resting on his knees, staring at the stove in deep thought.

"It's me," she said unnecessarily. "I have to get ready for the wedding."

He gazed at her.

"Could you . . . I mean, I have to change clothes." She bit her lip. At least at night she'd had the cover of darkness to hide behind.

Matt grinned. "Would you like me to leave?"

"No! I mean, you can't. The house is full of people."

"You want me to stay then." His grin broadened.

She frowned, her face feeling warm.

"Okay," Matt said. He turned in his chair to face the opposite wall, placing his hat on his head and tilting it over his eyes. Leaning back, he crossed his arms over his chest. "You're safe."

She fumbled through her wardrobe looking for the dark green dress she always saved for special occasions. Then for the hundredth time she silently cursed the ridiculous bustle, but with more passion than ever before. After arranging the dress on the bed in such a way that she could easily and quickly slip into it, she stripped off her apron and work dress. Without taking her eyes off Matt's back, she tied the bustle over her chemise and wiggled her way into the dress. Her fingers fumbled with the row of buttons down the front in her rush to get finished.

"I'm done," she said, standing before the mirror trying to decide if she should take time to take the pins out of her hair and start from the beginning. It unnerved her to have Matt watching, so she brushed at the tendrils and tucked the wisps of hair back into her braid, then patted it, considering it done.

He shifted his eyes to hers when she turned her back to the mirror, and they locked eyes for a moment before she glanced away.

"I wish I could tell you to give Dan and Ginny my congratulations," Matt said. "But I'll save it until I get this thing settled."

Settled. Jauncey thrust all thoughts and worries from her mind in an almost physical fashion by shaking her head. She had Matt here safe and sound, and Maggie was in no imminent danger. This day was reserved for happiness for Ginny, and Jauncey would try her hardest to keep that uppermost in her mind.

"Well, I'd better get downstairs. There are still a few things I have to do." She smoothed her skirt where a persistent wrinkle showed. "I'll bring something up for you to eat when I get a chance."

He nodded, still staring at her.

"Well," she said, smoothing the wrinkle once more. "I'd better go."

She hurried down to the kitchen, where everybody was greeting the preacher and Dan, who had just arrived covered from head to toe with snow.

"It's getting worse by the minute," Dan said with worry in his voice. "I told the Reverend we wouldn't keep him long, then I'd escort him home."

"I'll go with you," one of the boarders offered. "Nobody should be out alone in this."

"Thanks, Bill, I'll take you up on that."

"Reverend, we'll have the ceremony in the parlor near the fireplace. Would you like to warm yourself first?" Ginny asked.

Jauncey watched the short and very round preacher bob his head, rubbing his hands together for warmth as he glanced surreptitiously around the rooms on his way to the parlor. He seemed more than a little uncomfortable and cleared his throat several times.

The preacher spent an inordinate amount of time warming his backside where he could view the contents of the room at will. And Jauncey noted the women didn't escape his perusal either.

At last, he produced a prayer book from his pocket.

"Would the groom stand here. And the . . . bride . . . here."

Jauncey bit her lip in apprehension at the obvious pause, but Ginny's radiant face showed no sign that she'd noticed.

Dan and Ginny stood side by side in the brightly lit room where wall lamps and candles burned. All the men stood in quiet respect for the solemn occasion behind Jauncey and Maggie. Only the sound of the howling wind and the chattering of a loose windowpane could be heard.

The preacher took a piece of paper from inside the bible and read aloud. "Virginia Marlowe. Daniel Smith." He looked at each of them as if to verify the names. They nodded. He cleared his throat.

"Ladies"—he paused, frowning—"and gentlemen, we are gathered here to witness the marriage of this man and this woman according to the holy ordinances of God and man.

"Do you, Daniel, take this woman to be your wife?" He waited for Dan's answer.

"I do." Dan gazed into Ginny's eyes as though they were the only two people in the room.

Jauncey saw the preacher give a slight shake of his head before proceeding.

"Do you, Virginia, take this man to be your husband?"

"I do." Her voice was hushed, full of love.

"Then by the power vested in me by God and the Territory of Wyoming, I pronounce you man and wife. Let no man put asunder what God hath joined together." He cleared his throat again. "You may kiss your wife."

Dan stood holding Ginny's hands between them,

306

smiling down at her. He bent and kissed her lightly, then took her in a fierce hug, kissing her long and hard.

Whistles and whoops of cheer went up from the watching men, who quickly descended on the couple with demands of kisses from the bride. Claps of congratulations landed on Dan's shoulders time after time.

"Congratulations, Ginny, I'm so happy for you." Jauncey hugged Ginny tightly. If she was radiant before, she was positively luminous now, Jauncey thought.

"Thank you," Ginny said, returning the hug.

Maggie made her way to Ginny, smiling. Neither spoke, but they held each other close for several long seconds.

"Well, I guess we'd better get the Reverend home, Bill," Dan said.

There was a bustle of activity as Jauncey, with Maggie and Ginny's help, hurried to put the finishing touches to the meal while the three men went out into the storm.

The table sparkled with Spicie's best china and crystal goblets, the champagne sat in a bucket of snow ready for the toast and the wonderful aroma of food permeated the house. Jauncey felt relieved to see Maggie smile more than she had for days, even though she didn't join in their happy chatter.

When the back door burst open with the returning Dan and Bill, another round of cheers went up. Dan responded by taking Ginny by the waist and kissing her again while Ginny's happy laughter floated across the room.

"A toast!" Bill cried.

Jauncey quickly handed the glasses around and Bill poured the champagne. She stared into the clear liquid where the escaping bubbles popped into the air, and thought how much it resembled the happiness in one's life. She placed her hand over the glass to trap them.

"May your days be filled with happiness and your nights with . . ." He paused awkwardly. "I mean, to your health and happiness."

Masculine laughter filled the air as Bill took a few good-natured jabs in the ribs.

Too embarrassed by Bill's slip of the tongue even to glance around, Jauncey quickly took a sip of the champagne, choking down the urge to cough. She had to swallow hard several times before she could take another drink. Then the warmth flowed down her throat, all the way down, spreading to her nerves, which had been on edge for so long.

It was really very nice, she decided, taking another long drink.

Ginny and Dan took their seats and everyone followed their example. The meal passed amidst laughter and compliments for the couple as well as for the delicious food.

Afterwards the first chairs scraped back were those of the volunteer musicians with promises to return faster than the shake of a leg. Jauncey and the two women helped clear the table and stack the dishes, agreeing they could wait until morning, then joined the men in the parlor.

With the fiddles tuned and spirits high, Jauncey allowed herself to be swept away by the joviality. She clung tenaciously to the laughter and warmth, refusing to let her more serious problems intrude, dancing first with one partner, then another, laughing at the antics of the men who danced with each other. When someone offered her another glass of champagne, she took it, trying to sip it slowly the way Ginny did. Even so, the bubbles threatened to invade her head and she said no to other offers.

It seemed that hours had gone by and her feet felt completely worn out. As the evening wore on, most of the men began sitting out nearly all of the dances. She suspected a bottle of whiskey had made its rounds from some unknown source and had now taken its toll.

When the musicians finally ran out of energy, one by one they wandered off to their rooms, jostling each other with good humor. Dan and Ginny, too, said their good nights and disappeared.

Jauncey gathered up the glasses in an effort to control her wayward thoughts. Maggie had long since gone to bed, obviously not wanting to participate in the dancing, leaving Jauncey to tend to the evening chores alone.

But as the bubbles in her head dissipated, so did the warmth in her body. And suddenly, she was overwhelmed by loneliness. She thought of Ginny, and the happiness that surrounded her now. In comparison, her own life seemed empty.

Jauncey placed the last of the glasses onto the kitchen table, remembering times of happiness in her own past. Those times had been far and few between, and the ones that stood out the most were the ones she'd spent with Matt.

Matt, who was upstairs in her room now.

Jauncey picked up a clean glass, poured some champagne into it, and drank.

Chapter Twenty-one

Matt sat in the dark listening. Fiddle music vibrated up the stairs and the sound of thumping floor boards beneath the weight of the dancers bore testimony to the gaiety below. He pictured Jauncey dancing with some of the boarders, laughing and enjoying the wedding celebration.

All evening she'd been uppermost in his mind. How could he avoid it since he'd spent the entire night and day in her room? Every time he tried to concentrate on the handkerchief he'd found at J.T.'s and who it might belong to, the scent of roses would float across his nose and he'd start thinking of how soft her skin felt. Or he'd remember the night in her kitchen when the lamp went out and how she'd wrapped her arms around his neck, pulling him closer.

Thinking like that would lead to nothing but trouble, he reminded himself. She wasn't like the

other women he was used to. She was nothing like
Lottie. A good woman like her wouldn't appreciate
the sort of thoughts he'd been entertaining. No, she
would toss him out of her room and into the attic,
if not into the street.

Footsteps tramping heavily up the stairs told him
the party was over. Soon he would have to share
another long sleepless night in the same room with
her, and he wasn't looking forward to it.

Minutes passed after the last door closed down
the hall. But she didn't come. He waited, almost
holding his breath, wondering what was taking
so long.

Then he heard the rustle of the green satin dress
which conjured up a vision of her creamy exposed
skin. He heard her hesitate outside the door.

Matt leaped off the bed, careful not to bump into
anything. That wouldn't be hard, he thought with
a wry smile. He'd been cooped up so long he had
the entire contents of the room memorized. He lit
the lamp on the dresser just as she came through
the door.

Her cheeks were flushed and some of the hair
she'd tucked into her braid had fallen loose.

"Sounded like everyone was having a good time,"
Matt said, trying not to notice how well the bodice
of her gown fit her.

"Yes." She raised a hand to touch her hair,
smoothing it back.

"I built up the fire a while ago. It should last."
He crossed his arms and leaned against the poster
at the foot of her bed, pretending a lack of interest
he didn't feel.

"Good."

Silence filled the room.

"You look tired." He also thought she looked wonderful, but didn't say so.

"I am." She heaved a sigh.

He knew that was his fault, too. "I've been thinking. As soon as the weather gets better I'd better leave. I've made things hard for you by coming here."

Her eyes were riveted to his face. "I didn't mean to imply that you're a bother. You're not." She took a step toward him, then halted. "It wouldn't be safe for you to leave."

"You're the one who isn't safe." Matt stepped purposefully toward her, then stopped short.

"I'm not afraid." Her face held a serene, relaxed appeal.

He took her by the waist and pulled her close, grazing his lips across her forehead. "Take down your hair," he whispered, remembering the luxurious feel of it.

She reached up to remove the pins and pulled them out, one at a time, and her heavy braid fell free.

Matt separated the strands, combing his fingers through its thickness, watching as the golden glow from the lamp created living shadows that deepened the color of her whiskey-colored curls.

"You have beautiful hair," he said, lifting her hair and letting it cascade down her back.

Recognizing the surrender in her face, he pushed aside his conscience, refusing to allow it to intrude. He knew what was right and what wasn't, but right and wrong was too simple for what he felt. So, leaning down, he kissed her gently, and she responded by putting her hands on his neck, returning the kiss. With a groan, his arms crushed her to him.

Matt felt a course of fire ignite his body. He pulled away, depositing long and short kisses on her now-swollen lips. The softness of her skin drew him to the hollow of her neck where her pulse beat rapidly. She arched, allowing him access to the vulnerable spot. He reached down to grasp her bottom, but instead found the caged bustle.

"Why do women wear these damned contraptions?" he muttered hoarsely.

Jauncey wanted to say she didn't like them either, but she couldn't concentrate on the right words. Inside her head the sound of her heart pounded, drowning out everything. Matt's lips traced a heated path to the rise of her breasts, then holding her close, he expertly freed each button clear to her waist. Her simple cotton chemise became the only barrier between them. A tingling urgency washed over her as he untied the string and finally cupped the fullness of her bare breast.

His kisses moved lower, while his hand slid to her shoulder, then gently drew her dress back and down her arm, his lips caressing her as he went. Her only resistance was to the thought of "loose women" as it cadenced through her mind. But she thrust the words away, refusing to acknowledge them, giving in to his touch, which was like a match to dry kindling, setting her afire wherever he chose.

Slowly, methodically, he followed the contour of her neck to the line of her jaw, until once again

313

he took full possession of her mouth. The kindled flame grew until it roared in her ears. This was different, oh, so different, from the other times he'd kissed her, and she knew she could refuse him nothing.

He lifted her in his arms with one swift motion, breaking contact briefly while he moved to the bed. There were no doubts for her when his eyes held hers, and he set her on her feet, then slid the gown and chemise completely from her shoulders and arms. He untied the bustle and it collapsed in a rippling mound of green at her feet.

Entranced, she held perfectly still as he grasped her by the shoulders, pulled her close and kissed the tender place where her neck and shoulder met. Her head tilted back and to one side. Never, ever had she felt anything like she did now. What happened outside of her body held no relevance, not the wind, not the snow lashing the side of the house, nor the penetrating heat from the coal stove.

Raising his head to gaze into her face, he combed his fingers through her hair from her temples to the curly ends, draping them like a curtain around her.

"You're beautiful," he whispered, not taking his eyes from hers.

She smiled softly and touched his dark mustache.

He kissed her lightly, then deepened the kiss. The rough flannel of his shirt brushed the tips of her breasts as her arms circled his neck, sending a shiver of anticipation through her.

Matt's hands, tempted by the silky softness of her

314

skin, ran down her sides along the fullness of her breasts to the narrowness of her waist and rested on the roundness of her bottom. From somewhere deep inside him a moan vibrated as he grasped her to him.

He marveled at the velvety texture of her skin, so similar to the roses whose scent always surrounded her. He buried his nose in the sweet-smelling hair at her temple, tracing a line with his tongue along the curves of her ear.

She shivered.

"Matt . . ." Her voice sounded strange, as if coming from a long distance, low and intense.

Without answering he continued kissing her, her cheeks, her eyes and, finally, her mouth. Then slowly, slowly, he lowered her to the bed until they both were stretched out on it. He captured her breast, gently kneading while she arched more firmly into his hand.

Tearing himself away, Matt raised himself on his elbow. He stared down at her in awe of the new feelings springing to the surface. He'd never cared so much for a woman before. Not that he considered himself totally empty of feelings and only seeking sexual satisfaction. But she was different. Something about her stirred him, and stirred him deeply. He wouldn't allow her to question what was happening between them. All he knew was that it was good. And it was right. He placed his finger on her lips and traced their outline. Her eyes were smoldering embers, ready to ignite at the least of his touches. Her breathing came fast and shallow, causing the rapid rise and fall of her breasts.

He sat up, unbuttoning his shirt and pulling it out of his trousers, then slipping it off. He unbuckled his belt and dropped it to the floor.

"I think we should remove these," he said, grasping her shoes and working the buttons until he held them in his hands. He set them aside. "And these." He inched her stockings down the soft fullness of her calves, then grazed the bottoms of her feet with the palms of his hands. She lay with her hands at her sides, her eyes closed, and her hair spread around her fan-like.

Matt stood. His gaze warmly touched all the exposed parts of her body as surely as though he had used his hands. His boots thudded, first one, then the other, onto the floor. She opened her eyes and kept them fixed on his face when he skinned out of his britches and lowered himself onto the bed alongside her. He first caressed her knee, then lingered over her thigh and splayed his hand over the hollow of her stomach.

"Did you know that your eyes tell your thoughts?" he asked, stroking her as lightly as butterfly wings.

Jauncey rolled her head from side to side with the barest of movements, staring into his dark-as-coal eyes. She wanted to reach up and touch the curly hair on his broad chest, but her hand was trapped between his thigh and hers.

"I can almost read your mind."

She blinked her eyes to rid herself of the thoughts running rampant there.

He grinned. "That won't work."

She smiled impishly and closed her eyes. "This will."

"No. Don't close them. I like to see how the deep brown and gold flecks change to amber. Like the end of a sunset." He skimmed a hand teasingly across her ribs to circle first one breast, then the other until her eyes flew open. "Like that." He grinned.

With her free hand, Jauncey reached up and pulled his head down to hers, welding their lips together. He lay across her, clasping both of his hands along the sides of her head, tangling his fingers in her hair. She opened her mouth and he accepted the invitation with an intensity that sent tremors to the center of her being. The fire within her escalated.

Matt raised himself slightly, positioning his body over hers, nudging her legs.

A desperate need arose within her and Jauncey moved in rhythm to that need. Frantically she held him as he showered her face with ardent kisses before possessing her lips once more. They clung together in a wild frenzy as mouths and tongues came together, uniting and separating, and uniting again.

"Jauncey . . ." His voice, broken with restraint, was close to her ear. "I don't want to hurt you."

She thrashed her head from side to side and arched her body toward him in answer to his plea. With mounting passion she welcomed him . . . then suddenly her world was filled with him. Overwhelmed, a cry of pleasure barely escaped her lips.

Together they moved as one, in search of unity, striving, reaching, until they were completely engulfed in the flames fanned by their desire.

Flames that ultimately erupted into a million sparks, leaving both of them seared and sated.

Matt buried his face in the soft curve of her neck, relaxing on top of her, putting most of his weight on his forearms braced on each side of her head.

"God," he said weakly.

"Are you praying for help?" she asked.

He raised his head to look into her eyes. "Not in the least."

She circled his neck with her arms, tracing her nails along the muscles in his back.

He shivered.

"Tender spot?" she asked.

"Right now everywhere is a tender spot." He twined his leg with hers, running his toes along the bottom of her foot.

She shivered.

"Sensitive?" he quipped.

"Mmm. Everywhere."

The room grew darker, and flickering shadows became more pronounced. Suddenly, they were plunged into darkness.

"Uh-oh. Guess who forgot to fill the lamp again?" Jauncey sighed.

"Convenient, I'd say," Matt said, rolling onto his side and taking her with him. "Now I don't have to get up and blow it out."

"I wouldn't have liked that. We would've slept with the lamp burning." She snuggled tightly against him.

He pulled away, tugging the covers from beneath them. "It's going to get cold if we don't crawl inside here." He pulled her close and with his arm beneath her head, drew the blankets over them.

Jauncey settled comfortably against him, lacing her fingers through the fine hairs on his chest, stroking lightly. She felt secure and cared for, something entirely new for her. She relaxed contentedly under the soothing ministrations of Matt's hand gliding over her back, hips and thighs. There was no room for worry, or regret. Nothing existed beyond her cocoon of happiness and the fulfillment of this perfect moment. Nothing.

Chapter Twenty-two

Jauncey awoke with Matt's quiet, gentle breath against her cheek. She lay without moving, listening to the continued beating of the wind while she snuggled against his hard body. Warmth radiated from him to her, making it impossible for her to want to get up.

In the darkness, she pondered the night before. Never in her wildest dreams would she have thought she could behave with such abandon, and enjoy it so thoroughly. She rolled onto her side, facing Matt, her hair falling between them in an immodest barrier. Immediately, the nude picture of her aunt flashed like a bolt of lightning into her brain. With a sudden sharp intake of her breath, she was fully awake. No! she thought, forcing the comparison out of her mind. She wouldn't think that, she couldn't. She squeezed her eyes shut and clenched her fists in a futile effort to banish the unwanted thoughts.

Matt stirred beside her. "Jauncey . . ." His hand skimmed lightly over her flesh, touching, probing, caressing.

Her tense body melted beneath his touch like a cold jar of honey in the warm sunshine. Yet fear clawed at her, making its way into her conscious thoughts. Fear of what lay hidden within her. She struggled against it, and Matt.

"I have to get up and start the fires downstairs. Everyone will want breakfast even though they can't go anywhere." But she knew that was unlikely, especially with all they'd had to drink.

She threw back the covers from her side of the bed and needles of cold pierced her bare skin. When her feet hit the floor they contacted the silky feel of icy satin lying in a rumpled heap.

Matt reached for her arm. "Why don't you stay in bed where it's warm while I build a fire for you? I doubt if anyone will be up this early after a night like last night." He gently tugged at her, his voice warm and low. "I'm sure Dan and Ginny won't be."

She pulled away from his hold more roughly than she intended. "No. You're wrong. Mr. Natter will definitely want his breakfast on time, if for no other reason than to be contrary."

She stumbled over Matt's boots and clothing in search of her chemise, all the while repeating to herself, "I'm not like her. I'm not like her!" She pulled on the chemise and a work dress that she could only feel in the dark, uncaring if it was suitable or not. Her teeth chattered and her fingers shook as she managed her stockings and shoes with great difficulty.

Tossing the covers aside, he sat on the edge of the bed. "Jauncey, we have to talk."

She heard the earnestness in his voice and it frightened her. "No, really, I have to go." She gave up on finding an apron and ran from the room.

Once she was in the kitchen she lit the lamp on the table, barely able to hold the match in her shaking fingers. Next she snatched Maggie's woolen shawl from a peg and flung it around her shoulders, anchoring her long unbraided hair. Then spying a pair of gloves in one of the boarders' coat pockets, she put them on. She bustled around the large cookstove, shaking down ashes and scraping them into a bucket, adjusting dampers and adding kindling. Soon a small fire crackled and snapped.

She stood as close as she could to the stove, but it would take some time before the cast iron warmed enough to give off heat. Although she didn't think anything could remove the chill that had crept into her soul.

She tried to ignore the humiliation and regret that assailed her. But they came at her from every room of this house that had once belonged to her aunt, the madam of a bordello.

Jauncey grabbed the lamp from the table and hurried into the parlor to build another fire. The sparkling chandelier seemed to mock and condemn her. Clean and dust-free, the entire room accused her of pretending to be something she wasn't. She turned her back on it all and faced the cold hearth.

Quickly, she laid the kindling and struck a match to it, watching as the flames devoured the small sticks one at a time. She added larger pieces and the flames grew and heightened, demanding more and more. The fire was insatiable in following the true course of its nature.

What was the true course of her nature? she wondered, staring into the overwhelming brilliance of the orange and yellow flames.

Matt sat in the dark, unmindful of the penetrating cold. What a jackass he was. Irritated, he plunged a hand into the pile of clothes on the floor trying to locate his. She'd reacted just as he knew she would, and he blamed himself. He jerked on his pants and shirt, jabbing its tail into the waistband. He should never have come here.

Completely dressed, he lit the lamp and built a fire in case she needed to spend some time alone in the room. He collected his spurs, hat and coat and headed for the door. Then something caught his eye.

He leaned down to pick up a dress that had been wadded into a ball, and studied it closer. In her hurry to dress and leave, she'd left the door to the wardrobe open and clothing had spilled out. The dress was torn and heavily stained on the front with blood. Prickles of fear covered his scalp. Was she the one? He stood transfixed. Come hell or high water he was going to get to the bottom of this. He threw the dress into the wardrobe and slammed the door. Obviously, she wasn't going to tell him anything since she'd had plenty of chances and passed them all up. He needed to meet with Charlie.

Jamming his hat on his head, he pulled his coat on as he hurried down the stairs. He didn't care if every person in the house heard him.

Matt didn't stop when he got to the bottom, but continued out the front door into the onslaught of snow and wind. Daylight was breaking but there would be no sunshine today. He plunged along marking his path by familiar fences and storefronts until he reached Sam's.

Inside the saloon, the silence was deafening compared to the howling wind outside. He made his way up the stairs, bumping into Lottie in the dimly lit hallway.

"Oh, Matt!" she called out in surprise, wrapping her brightly colored gown tightly around her body, exposing the gentle curve of her hip.

"Where's Charlie?" he barked.

"Don't sound so unfriendly, it's too early for that." She frowned. "He's over at the hotel. He and Ruby had a fight yesterday."

"Thanks." Matt turned to leave, but she grasped his arm.

"What's your hurry? It's not too early for some things, you know." Her voice was silky soft. "At least it never used to be." She leaned against his chest, reaching inside his coat. "We haven't . . . talked for a long time."

"I've got business, Lottie." He had neither the time nor the inclination to discuss his feelings for her, and pulling her arms out of his coat, he headed back down the stairs.

"Matt Dawson! What's got into you?" she called

after him. "It's that girl over at Spicie's, isn't it?"

He stopped and turned toward her. "She isn't a girl, Lottie."

Slowly, she descended the steps until she stood beside him. "Yes, she is." Her hand lifted, then rested on his arm. "She's a foolish, inexperienced girl who couldn't possibly know how to please a man like you."

He stared back at her without saying a word.

Her hand lashed out, smacking him soundly on the cheek. "You son of a bitch. You've slept with her, haven't you? Don't bother denying it. I can see it written all over your face."

"Lottie—"

"Shut up! Just go on and leave me alone! I don't need you. I never did. Hell, I've got my pick of men!" With that she turned and fled up the stairs.

Matt heard her door slam. He had never meant to hurt her, hadn't realized just how involved she'd become with him. When had he ever misled her? He hadn't, he knew it for certain.

He walked to the back door and, lifting his collar against the elements, stepped out into the street, shouldering his way into the wind.

Unable to participate in the cheery conversation going around the table, Jauncey left the warmth of the kitchen to return to her room, where she regrettably would have to face the aftermath of last night. But as she passed through the parlor a knock at the door stopped her. From outside, the dim silhouette of a woman showed through the curtained window. Relieved that it wasn't Matt returning, she carefully opened the door and found the only other person she cared even less to see. Lottie.

"Good morning," the woman said as she breezed past Jauncey without invitation, shaking the snow from her cape.

Startled at first, Jauncey quickly recovered and closed the door against the blowing snow and cold.

"I hope you don't mind, but this will only take a minute." Lottie's tone was brisk and her smile did little to convey true friendliness. "Could we go somewhere private to talk? We have some personal things to discuss and I'm sure you wouldn't want your boarders to overhear us."

"I have nothing to discuss with you," Jauncey replied stiffly. "So if you'll please leave . . ."

"No, I won't leave. And yes, we do have something to discuss." She pulled the hood from her head and moved toward the bottom of the stairs, her gaze traveling upward toward the door to Jauncey's room. "It's rather comfortable, wouldn't you say?"

Her pointed observation jarred Jauncey. Certainly she must be imagining Lottie's implication, she thought.

"I have to say Sam's place has nothing that compares to that room. Or that bed. Spicie definitely knew how to run a house and keep her girls happy." Lottie's gaze turned to focus on Jauncey once more.

Jauncey clamped her lips tight, refusing to be baited.

"Yes," Lottie went on, her voice a silky purr while her hand stroked the smooth wood of the banister. "If we girls were happy, then our customers were happy. Tell me, were you able to make Matt happy?"

Gripped by sudden anger, Jauncey stared at the other woman. "Get out!" she said fiercely.

Lottie turned toward the door. "Oh, I'll be going, all right. But not before I thank you. I can't think of a better way to secure an illicit relationship than to offer your favors to a man like Matt Dawson without benefit of marriage." She smiled happily at Jauncey. "Sort of gives the two of us something in common, wouldn't you say?"

Jauncey seethed with a fury that was fueled by humiliation, but when she spoke it was with deadly calm. "I said get out."

"Ironic, too, don't you agree?" She arched a brow knowingly. "I mean, the same house, the same bed . . . the same man. It seems we have more in common than we ever would have guessed." With a look of triumph Lottie opened the door and stepped outside, closing it firmly behind her.

Stunned, Jauncey stared at the closed door. How could he have confided such an intimate moment with a woman like that? A strange hollowness swiftly replaced her anger, and the need to retreat from any prying eyes forced her to hurry up the stairs to the haven of her room.

Once she was inside, uncontrollable anguish washed over her, and she covered her face with her hands while the depth of her shame overwhelmed her. How wrong she'd been to give in to her desires. Yet, as Lottie had so carefully pointed out, how predictable that it had happened. And in this house, too.

Once inside the hotel, Matt shook the snow from his coat and slapped his hat against his thigh. A small bespectacled man in an equally small bowler hat fixed him with a withering glare, then dusted the flying flakes from own jacket.

Matt stepped to the desk, but the short man was quicker.

"It is imperative that I speak to the owner of this establishment. Today," the little man said.

The clerk rolled his eyes as though he'd been through this before. "I'm sorry. He's out of town."

"Harrumph." The man obviously didn't believe him.

Ignoring him, the clerk turned to Matt. "You looking for Charlie?"

Matt nodded.

"Top of the stairs, number eight."

Matt took the steps two at a time, found the room and knocked.

Charlie opened the door. "Where the hell have you been? Git in here!" Charlie looked up and down the hall before closing the door.

"There's a blizzard going on out there, Charlie, in case you hadn't noticed. Where the hell do you think I've been?" Matt was in no mood to put up with Charlie's bluster.

"Don't tell me about a blizzard. I've been out in it getting some fresh clothes for me and you. I don't mind smellin' like an old bull when we're on the trail, but something about bein' in civilization gives me a hankerin' for a bath and a shave."

"Sounds good to me, too. Thanks." Matt smiled. "I didn't mean to be so short."

"It's the weather," Charlie said, staring out the window. "This one's a killer, Matt."

Matt frowned. He'd managed to put it out of

his mind, knowing there was nothing he could do about it.

"Where are the rest of the boys?" Matt asked.

"Here. They been wonderin' how you're doin'. I told them not to worry."

"They're probably wondering if there'll be a job for them when this winter is over."

"Yeah."

"You aren't worrying about that, are you, Charlie?"

He didn't answer.

"We've been through just as bad only with more cattle on the range than now. And we made it." Matt removed his coat. "I hate to admit it, but if it hadn't been for J.T. I probably wouldn't have sold all the cattle that I did."

"I ain't givin' him credit for anything."

"Well, at least that money is in our pocket instead of dying out there on the range." Matt thought about the cows, and was glad he'd saved only the sturdiest. They'd have a better chance.

"No point in muling around. I'll get that bath ordered." Charlie left the room.

Matt took off his hat and hung it on the back of a chair. He couldn't quit thinking about the stained dress and why Jauncey hadn't mentioned it. Maybe he was on the wrong trail by assuming it was J.T.'s blood. No, something in his gut told him he was right.

After his bath, Matt shaved and put on the clothes Charlie had brought. His appearance improved, but his disposition didn't. He'd been wasting time staying at the boardinghouse. Now he had to find the person who'd murdered J.T.

"Charlie, I can't let this blizzard get in the way. I—"

A knock at the door interrupted them. Matt jumped up from his chair to stand against the wall behind the door while Charlie opened it a crack.

"Collins?" Charlie asked, surprised.

"Have you seen Matt? He said to let him know if I thought of anything about a . . . woman."

Stepping out from behind the door, Matt said, "Come in, Andrew. What have you got?"

With a quick glance left and right, Andrew Collins entered the room. He cleared his throat. "I've spent a lot of time thinking about that handkerchief and to whom it may belong."

"And?" Matt asked, urging him to get to the point.

"Well, I did see J.T. with a red-haired woman. They were across the street from my office and they were arguing. Very loudly, I might add." He twisted his hat in his hands. "I don't know why I didn't remember it before." A puzzled frown crossed his face.

"A lot of women have red hair," Charlie interjected.

"Well, this one used to work for Spicie. I saw her there several times." Andrew blushed to the roots of his hair.

Matt's head swung toward Charlie. "Ruby."

"What?" Charlie exploded. "She's got some tall explainin' to do." He yanked his coat from the back of a chair.

"Hold on, Charlie." Matt grabbed him by the arm. "We've got to figure this out first and we've got to do it right, or else we may not be able to pin her down."

"There's only one way to find out, and that's ask her," Charlie said.

"Ask her what? 'Did you kill J.T.?' or 'Is this your handkerchief?'"

"Yeah!" Charlie shouted, the veins in his neck standing out.

"She's too smart for that. We need something she can't deny."

Stumped, Matt and the other two men were silent.

"The black eye," Charlie said finally, quietly.

"What?" Matt stared at him.

"You remember. You saw it when you found me in Ruby's room the night J.T. was killed."

"Do you remember if she had it earlier that night?" Matt asked. "When we first arrived at Sam's?"

Charlie's brows squeezed together in thought. "When did it happen?"

Matt knew Charlie was on to something. He wracked his brain trying to remember the events of that night. Lottie was there before they went to see J.T. Was Ruby there too? Did she have a black eye then? He couldn't remember.

"She didn't have a black eye until after we'd been to see J.T." Charlie slapped his knee. "I'm as positive of that as I am of having two good legs."

"How can you be so sure?"

"Because I took Ruby upstairs after we got back. There wasn't any black eye then. I would've noticed 'cause we left the light on. And she was in a real

331

big hurry to get rid of me, too. That's when I went downstairs to sit with you, and about an hour later the marshal showed up."

"I'm afraid that doesn't prove anything," Andrew said.

"But after Matt went to Jauncey's I went up to Ruby's room and she wasn't there. So I waited. When she came in, her eye was as black as sin and I asked her about it. She said she ran into the outhouse door."

Andrew shook his head. "It may sound incriminating, but it wouldn't hold up in a court of law, Charlie."

"Well, all we need is to be pointed in the right direction and be on the look out for anything that would be proof," Matt said.

"I wish I could be of some help," Andrew said. Then his eyes lit up. "Maybe you could show her the handkerchief and say that you knew it was hers."

Matt stared at him with new respect.

"Yeah. That would be two things she'd have to lie about and maybe trap herself. It'd be worth a try, Matt," Charlie said.

That was true. But Matt still couldn't get the stained dress in Jauncey's room out of his mind. How did it fit in with Ruby? As much as he wanted to, he couldn't bring himself to tell the other two about it.

"Before we do that," Matt said, "I have some unfinished business to take care of." He gazed thoughtfully out the window.

Charlie stared at Matt. "What?"

"Something I should have done this morning."

Matt picked up his hat and put on his coat. "I'll be back later."

"Matt, if you go out there too many times, someone is bound to see you and report it to the marshal." Charlie looked as if he would block the door.

"Not in this weather."

"Maybe, maybe not."

"I'll take my chances." Matt raised his collar and Charlie stepped aside.

Matt made slow progress through the town to the boardinghouse. By the time he stood on Jauncey's front steps, his hands were almost too numb to knock on the door.

Jauncey opened the door.

"I need to talk to you."

"You shouldn't be out. Someone might see you," she said.

"Can we go somewhere private?" he asked, searching her face for a sign that she didn't hate him for what had happened last night.

"There isn't anyplace." He saw a faint blush stain her cheeks.

Taking her by the elbow, he hurried her up the stairs to her room. Once they were behind the closed door he unwillingly let her go.

"What do you need to talk to me about?" Her tone was flat, unemotional.

He glanced around the room. It was clean and tidy, as though last night had never happened. The familiar scent of roses was strong in the air.

"Tell me what you know about J.T.'s murder."

"What makes you think I know anything?" Her voice was strained.

Matt walked to her wardrobe and opened it. Then

333

kneeling down, he pulled out the dress.

"You went through my things," she said, accusation strong in her voice.

He saw the way she measured her words, controlling her thoughts.

"No. I didn't."

"How else would you have known it was there?"

"It was laying in plain sight this morning when you left the room in such a hurry. Now whose is it?"

She shook her head, refusing to answer his question.

"Jauncey, I have to know."

He watched the battle warring inside her. She clasped her hands tightly together until her knuckles turned white. Who was she protecting? Surely not Ruby.

"I . . . can't tell you." The words came out strangled.

He grasped her by the arms. "You have to tell me."

She struggled against his hold and wriggled free, backing an arm's length away. "I can't."

It was no use. She would never tell him. And the pain in her tear-filled eyes was something he couldn't bear, so his only choice was to leave her and go after Ruby.

Jauncey bit her lip, trying to hold back the sobs that threatened to choke her. Fear and humiliation engulfed her as the tears streamed down her cheeks. When he took a step toward her, she turned her back, hanging on to the post at the foot of the bed for support. One great sob escaped. Then she heard the door open and close. He was gone.

Falling onto the bed, she released the torrent of tears that she'd been holding back, and her body shook with the force. Total abject misery washed over her and out of her until there were no more tears left. She lay in the chilled room, sniffling loudly and taking shuddering breaths. Her face was swollen, she could tell. And her eyes felt like mere slits. She curled herself into a ball and tucked her arms under her as far as she could. She had never been more miserable in her life. Surely things couldn't get any worse.

Exhausted, she drifted in and out of sleep with nothing to show for it except memories of bad dreams. She tried to shake them off, but each time she dozed they sucked her under. Until at last, she fell into a deep sound sleep.

Chapter Twenty-three

Matt entered the hotel room and saw Charlie straddling a chair and Ruby sitting on the bed. She sat with her arms crossed, looking belligerent.

It was as though Charlie had read Matt's mind and had taken Ruby out into the storm to bring her there for questioning. Matt now conceded there was no other way since Jauncey refused to tell him what she knew.

"Hello, Ruby," Matt said.

She raised one penciled eyebrow and slanted her chin downward. "So you want to be civil before you beat me."

Matt ignored her caustic remark.

"Well, you drag me out in a blizzard and lock me up in a hotel room with this grizzly to guard me. What else am I supposed to think?" Her hands flew in frantic motions to indicate her surroundings as she spoke.

336

"That ain't the truth, and you damn well know it!" Charlie all but shouted.

"Then tell me why!"

Matt pulled up a chair and hung his coat on it. "We just have a few questions," he said, sitting down, then leaning his elbows on his knees as he pushed his hat back.

"You know, the marshal's been looking for you. He might be glad to find out where you're hiding," she said slyly.

Charlie glared at her. "You keep talkin' like that . . ."

Ruby tossed her red curls in defiance.

"Nobody's going to do anything." Matt leveled a warning look at Charlie, then turned back to Ruby.

"Looks like you got hit in the eye, Ruby. Must have been a few days ago, judging by the color. How did that happen?" Matt stretched his legs out in front, crossing one booted foot over the other.

"I ran into the outhouse door. Some ass left it open." She said it with such boredom that Matt was sure she'd repeated it more than a dozen times.

"I remember the night you did it. The night J.T. was killed."

"What's that supposed to mean?" She clenched her teeth and jutted out her chin.

"Just a coincidence?" Matt asked, folding his arms across his chest.

"Damn right."

"I don't think so." Matt stood, pulling the bloodied handkerchief from his shirt pocket. "I believe this is yours."

Her eyes widened, but she said nothing.

He unfolded it, revealing the caked blood. "You must have dropped it that night at J.T.'s. Kind of careless of you, Ruby."

Matt saw her swallow hard.

"You're making this up," she said.

He shook his head.

"You think I killed him?" Her rough laughter filled the room. "You give me a lot of credit, Matt. Men tougher than me would've liked to do it." She laughed again.

For a moment he believed her. After all, the dress at Jauncey's just didn't fit in with Ruby being the one. But his gut feeling took over again, or was it his need to keep Jauncey out of it? No, Ruby was bluffing. She had to be. He had one more thing to try.

"Well, I think we should go on over to Andrew Collins's office and look at a few pieces of paper. You know the ones I mean. The original of Spicie's handwriting, and the one you forged for J.T."

Her voice was a whisper when she spoke. "I don't know what you're talking about." But her face said she did.

"What did J.T. promise you, Ruby?" he asked softly.

Suddenly, her face crumpled as she broke into tears.

"It . . . was . . . Maggie . . . all . . . her . . . fault." Ruby continued sobbing into her hands. Nothing she said was intelligible.

Charlie jumped from his chair. "For God's sake, Ruby, stop that caterwaulin'. You'll have everyone in the hotel bangin' on our door."

But she didn't stop.

"Now what'll we do?" Charlie asked, throwing his hands up.

Matt wasn't sure. She hadn't exactly confessed; instead she had as much as accused Maggie. He couldn't believe Maggie could kill anything, let alone a man, and one like J.T. to boot. He was more confused than ever. But what about the bloodstained dress?

There was only one thing to do. Take Ruby to Jauncey's and have the whole thing out in the open.

"Get her things, Charlie. We're going to the boardinghouse."

Charlie helped Ruby on with her coat and wrappings. "I never knew a woman was so full of water." He shook his head.

They struggled through the vicious winds to the boardinghouse, where Matt burst in the front door without knocking.

"Jauncey!" Matt yelled, closing the door behind them.

The scraping of chairs in the kitchen told him everyone was seated at the table for mealtime.

She appeared in the doorway, surrounded by the others. Her eyes carefully scanned Matt, Charlie and Ruby.

Dan spoke first, coming through the crowd toward Matt.

"Matt, are you crazy? The marshal's looking for you, blizzard or no blizzard."

"Not for long. We're about to clear this mess up.

339

Now." He looked directly at Jauncey and saw her face turn as white as the snow outside.

Jauncey thought the floor must surely be moving, and grabbed on to the door frame to steady herself. He must have found out about Maggie, she thought. But what was Ruby doing here?

Jauncey made her way toward Maggie, who had backed up against the wall. How could he do this to Maggie? Certainly he knew how fragile she was.

"All right, Ruby, I want to hear everything. And don't leave anything out." His deep voice clearly held a warning.

Ruby took in a shaky breath before speaking, her eyes cast downward, staring unseeing at the floor. "When you and Charlie stopped in at Sam's that night, I'd heard from Lottie that you'd had a run-in with J.T. Charlie and I went upstairs for a while and he told me how you really lit into J.T."

Matt angled a glare at Charlie, who stared off in the distance looking sheepish.

Ruby continued. "After we'd finished, Charlie went downstairs and I went to J.T.'s office. I thought maybe you had roughed him up enough that he would reconsider and stick to our deal."

"What deal?" Matt asked.

"I . . . forged the paper with Spicie's name. The paper that said Miss Taylor owed him five thousand dollars."

Jauncey was stunned. Could she have heard her right? Ruby had been responsible for the forgery?

"What was the deal, Ruby?" Matt asked.

"He said that I could run the house as owner when he took it away from Miss Taylor."

Fire sparked and leapt inside Jauncey as she took a step toward Ruby.

Matt stretched out his hand and grasped her by the shoulder.

"Go on," he urged Ruby.

"Well . . . he'd took a liking to her and said the deal with me was off. She looks so much like Spicie he was sure the house would be more profitable if she ran it. He even had a few women from Denver ready to come up here and work for him, and her."

Ruby lifted her head defiantly and stared at her. Jauncey bristled at Ruby's words. A madam of a whorehouse! But the memories of last night were so fresh in her mind that she held her tongue.

"So when Charlie said that you had beat J.T., I thought I could get him to change his mind," Ruby went on.

"Were you blackmailing him?" Matt asked.

"No! I was just going to threaten to tell the marshal about the letter I forged. I wasn't asking for money. But when I got there I heard screams. Maggie's."

Maggie wet her lips, her frightened eyes fastened on Ruby. Jauncey saw that she was trembling. She shrugged off Matt's hand and reaching out, grasped Maggie's hand in an attempt to comfort her, but it didn't help.

"J.T. was mauling her, the bastard," Ruby said. "He had his hands all over her, trying to get inside her dress."

Maggie pulled her hand out of Jauncey's and clapped her hands over her ears and squeezed her eyes shut.

341

"I tried to pull him off her, but he backhanded me. That's when I saw the gun on the floor." Ruby stopped for breath. "I picked it up and . . . and I shot him."

Maggie turned and fled up the stairs, her tortured sobs echoing in the suddenly quiet house. Ginny ran after her, while Jauncey stood transfixed, staring at Ruby.

Maggie didn't do it! Ruby did! All along she'd thought Maggie was guilty without even listening to what Maggie might have to say about it. Her feelings ran the gamut from complete relief to overwhelming guilt, then to anger at Ruby.

Turning her rising anger on Ruby, Jauncey said, "You were going to let someone else hang for what you did." She advanced slowly until she stood directly in front of Ruby. "Just to save your worthless hide!" Jauncey's hand ached to slap her.

"Wait a minute!" Ruby cried. "If I hadn't done it, where do you think Maggie would be right now? I'll tell you where! Stark raving mad in a loony house!"

Matt grabbed Jauncey's hand just as it was about to fly into Ruby's face. Quietly, he said, "She's right, Jauncey."

"Or maybe she would have killed him," Ruby yelled. "It was her gun I found so she must have intended to use it when she went there."

That was true. Oh, God, that was true. But one thing Jauncey knew that they didn't; Maggie would have done it for *her*. She had been so upset and frightened when J.T. had come to the house and forced himself on Jauncey, that it must have driven

342

Maggie to take matters into her own hands. Once more guilt overwhelmed her.

Matt wished he could comfort Jauncey, take her in his arms and hold her until her feelings of misery subsided. He wanted to kiss away her hurt and anger, and most of all he wanted to tell her he loved her just as he'd wanted to tell her that morning before she'd jumped out of bed so full of regret. But she had brushed him aside then, and he knew she would again.

A knock sounded at the door and Charlie, standing closest to it, opened it. The marshal, frosted in white, hustled in on a gust of wind, slamming the door behind him. Looking around the room from under the frozen brim of his hat, he gawked at so many people staring at him. Then his eyes rested on Matt.

"I'll be damned," he said. "You're under arrest."

None of them moved or talked. They all just stood staring at him.

Dumbfounded, the marshal glanced around. "What the hell's wrong?"

"It appears, Marshal, that you're arresting the wrong man, uh, person." Mr. Natter shouldered his way past a few of the boarders to stand beside Jauncey and Matt.

"What?" Williams frowned.

"Mr. Dawson isn't the person you're looking for. This woman is." He indicated Ruby with his hand. "Apparently, she's the one I've been searching for, too." He cast a critical eye toward Ruby.

Disbelieving, Jauncey stared at Mr. Natter.

"I was hired as an investigator by the bank in Cheyenne to look into the business affairs of Mr.

J.T. Lawrence. I'm not at liberty to say too much, but I will say that he was certainly an enterprising man, in an unscrupulous way." He harrumphed emphatically with importance.

She couldn't believe her ears. This annoying, contrary little man was trying to catch J.T. and probably have him arrested. She could have hugged him then and there.

"It must have been you who was looking for incriminating evidence in Mr. Lawrence's office and left it in such disarray," Mr. Natter said to Ruby. "Probably searching for the forged papers?"

Ruby nodded, her shoulders slumping.

"Ruby?" the marshal asked. "You killed J.T.?"

"There are extenuating circumstances, Marshal," Mr. Natter said.

She nodded again, realizing there was little use in putting up a fight.

"Well"—the marshall rubbed his gloved hands together—"looks like I was wrong, Matt. I guess I jumped to conclusions. Mr. Natter here has been keeping me posted on his investigations and he said he had a hunch I was wrong.

"All right then. Ruby, you ready?" The marshal helped her wrap herself up against the cold and they disappeared into a sea of white.

Dan clapped a hand on Matt's shoulder. "I sure am glad it's over for you, Matt. Can't imagine how the marshal could have thought you did it."

"We'd had words before. I guess it just seemed logical to him." He spoke to Dan, but his focus was on Jauncey and the cool barrier she'd built like a wall surrounding herself.

She turned her back on Matt, and he watched her

344

go up the stairs, barely aware that Dan had offered him some hot coffee to warm himself before going into the storm. She hadn't even said good-bye.

"No, thanks, Dan. We'll just be on our way while we still can." Matt and Charlie prepared to leave. "Oh, congratulations on your wedding. I heard you and Ginny got married."

"Yesterday." Dan smiled, nodding happily.

Only yesterday? To Matt, last night had been weeks ago.

Jauncey heard the men say good-bye. Then Matt was gone. As she leaned against the outside of Maggie's door, her emotions spun and clashed inside her body in a mixture of relief, anger and shame. And, she realized, something more. Sadness.

The sound of crying through the door shook her out of her misery. She pushed it open and went to stand by the bed, where Ginny sat trying to comfort Maggie. Looking up, Ginny shrugged her shoulders in helplessness.

"I'll take care of her," Jauncey said softly. "You go see to the men's supper. It's probably cold by now."

Ginny left with a reluctant backward look, but Jauncey smiled and waved her on.

When Ginny had closed the door behind her, Jauncey finally spoke again. "Maggie, I'm so sorry. Can you forgive me for thinking you could have done anything like that?"

Maggie rolled over to face her. "I'm not blaming you," she said, sniffling.

"I'd understand if you did."

"No. It isn't you. It's just m-me. When Ruby

345

started telling about him and what he did . . . it all came back like it was happening all over again." A shudder visibly shook her.

"Can you talk about it? Will that help?"

"I don't know." Maggie sniffled. "I don't think so."

"You went to see J.T. because of me, didn't you?" She spoke with a heavy heart.

"Yes. He wanted to hurt you and make you leave here." Maggie started to cry again.

Jauncey pulled her close and hugged her tight. "Oh, Maggie, I wouldn't have left."

"I was afraid of what would hap-happen if you weren't here anymore. I-I couldn't stand to have m-m-men looking at me and t-touching m-m-me." She broke into sobs in Jauncey's arms. "Like J.T. did. I th-thought if he was dead . . . but I c-couldn't do it. I couldn't do it!"

"Shhh. Of course you couldn't." Jauncey rocked her back and forth, speaking quietly. "Of course you couldn't."

Long moments passed while Jauncey waited for her to calm down. She stroked Maggie's hair as she continued to rock her, and thought about the kind of life she must have lived to put such fear into her. Finally, Maggie's sobs subsided.

"When Ruby came," Maggie continued, "I was s-so glad to see her."

Jauncey handed her a clean handkerchief and Maggie blew her nose.

"I had your gun but I dropped it when he . . . grabbed me." A shudder *ran* through her body and tears gathered in her eyes. "He touched m-me and tried t-to rip off my dress. I screamed and

346

screamed; then Ruby s-started pounding on him. But he knocked her on the floor. Then the gun . . . went . . . off." She sobbed anew.

"Oh, Maggie. Poor Maggie. Shhh. You're all right now and he's gone. He can never hurt you again. He can never hurt anyone."

"I felt him . . . jump," she continued. Jauncey sensed her need to tell it all. "Then he fell, taking me with him. I just stared into his dead eyes. I couldn't . . . move."

Jauncey held both of Maggie's cold hands, rubbing them, watching the anguish on her face.

"Ruby pulled me off him and shoved me toward the door. She pushed the gun into my hands and told me to get out. So I ran. I think she was behind me, but I'm not sure. I just kept going." Maggie lay back exhausted, closing her eyes.

"It's over. Try not to think about it," Jauncey said, pulling the quilt across her.

"It is over, isn't it? We're all safe now."

Maggie appeared to drift off, but Jauncey decided to stay with her awhile to make sure she was really all right. Glancing at Maggie's face, she was glad to see some of her color had returned. She wondered for the hundredth time about the role Spicie had played in Maggie's unfortunate life. And, for the hundredth time, she could find no answer to the question of why. Ginny had survived as a fallen woman simply because she was too strong not to. But was that any credit to Spicie? Even though Ginny thought so, Jauncey did not. And what about Maggie?

She lightly ran her hand across Maggie's warm forehead.

347

Maggie's eyes opened. "I'm all right now. Really." Her weak but reassuring smile eased Jauncey's worry.

"Will you be able to come downstairs later?" Jauncey asked.

"Yes. I'll just rest first. I'm suddenly very tired."

"Of course you are." Jauncey rose from the bed. "I'm sure Ginny has her hands full down there with all the men home. She probably can't keep enough coffee made. I guess I'll give her some help." She smiled, relieved to see even a small improvement in Maggie from talking about what had happened.

Jauncey entered the kitchen and saw everyone sitting at the table drinking coffee and discussing the events of the last hour.

"I can't believe the marshal honestly thought Matt could've done it. I think he had a grudge against Matt. And I also think that J.T. had been paying him to keep his nose out of certain affairs," Dan said, finishing his coffee.

"I'm sure he had," Ginny offered.

"I'm not at liberty to say much, but"—Mr. Natter harrumphed importantly—"I can say there weren't too many tills that Mr. Lawrence didn't have both hands in." He tapped his fingers with emphasis on the table. "Not too many."

"How's Miz Maggie doin'?" asked the Southern boarder.

"She's still a little shaken, Bill, but she's better," Jauncey answered.

"Poor girl." He shook his head in sympathy.

A fierce wind shook the house and pounded it with a force it hadn't shown before. Everyone's eyes moved to the rattling back door.

"I sure hope Matt and Charlie made it to the hotel safely," Ginny said, concern in her voice. "This isn't any kind of weather for anyone to be out and about. We probably should have insisted they stay."

"I tried to talk Matt into staying, but he seemed determined to go. Although Charlie did look agreeable to the idea," Dan said.

Jauncey turned her back on the group and pushed the boiling pot of coffee to the coolest part of the stove. She didn't want to hear anything about Matt Dawson. His name alone was too strong a reminder of last night. Even though she'd sensed he felt no regret for what had happened between them, she did. But then why should he? she asked herself. Those moments obviously meant nothing to him, as Lottie had so spitefully but truthfully pointed out.

Now, as she stood near the warmth of the stove surrounded by friends and boarders, she felt cold, miserable and isolated. The freezing storm blowing outside was nothing compared to the one going on inside her, and she wondered if she would ever melt again.

Chapter Twenty-four

Jauncey sat in a stretch of sunshine that came through the kitchen window where it served to lift her spirits a little.

Idly, she drew a pattern around the shadow cast by her coffee cup. It had been ten days since she'd seen Matt. Not that she wanted to see him again. No, she certainly did not, she told herself. But in these ten days, when her thoughts had repeatedly turned to him and the night they'd shared, she no longer wholly blamed him for the way things had turned out. She should have known better than to give in to the yearning within her. As Lottie had said, that alone had brought her to the level of a prostitute. Truthfully, there had been no benefit of marriage or even a promise of marriage, not even the mention of love. She had acted wantonly, just as her aunt would have done.

Now she knew what her mother had tried to save her from by sheltering her. She'd tried to save Jauncey from herself.

Even though she understood everything so much clearer now, her thoughts betrayed her logic, inflicting more pain on her damaged heart by conjuring up images of Matt.

Glancing out into the backyard, she wondered if he was out on the range counting his losses as the boarders said most of the ranchers were doing. And the losses were said to be high, although no one would really know until spring.

She visualized him on his horse, his black Stetson securely on his head, as he scanned the frozen grazing lands that surrounded Laramie for miles. Charlie would be with him, and together they would ride slow and sure until the cold would drive them back to the ranch. Then he would probably stand before a warm stove, rubbing his large capable hands in an effort to warm them. In her mind, the stove was the one here, in her kitchen, which then turned her memories to the night he'd held her in his arms and kissed her for the first time.

"Jauncey," Ginny said. "I think today would be a good day to begin baking for Christmas. What do you think?"

"What?" Jauncey tried to focus on Ginny's question.

"Christmas is only three days away and I know some wonderful recipes that my grandmother taught me when I was a . . ." Ginny frowned at her. "Is something wrong? You've been so quiet lately."

351

"No. It's just the season, I guess."

Ginny sat down. "I know. It has a tendency to take you back to other times. Almost another life, even another person."

Ginny had said it very well. Jauncey did feel as though she was another person. One she didn't know. This person did things she never would have considered doing at one time, and now she must live with the aftermath.

"You're right, let's start baking." Jauncey was determined to improve her spirits. "My mother had a favorite Christmas cake recipe made with molasses and raisins."

"Good!" Ginny bustled around the kitchen gathering her ingredients, humming a tune.

Dan popped his head in the door, grinning ear to ear. "Did I hear someone say cake?"

"You certainly did. Jauncey and I are just getting started and I warn you, the kitchen is no place for amateur cooks."

"Amateur!" He looked wounded. "I'll have you two know that I'm a very capable cook."

"With rabbit stew and biscuits maybe," Ginny teased.

"Oh! You have cut me to the bone." Dan hung his head.

"Only if you insist on staying in the kitchen," she rejoined with mock sternness on her face.

"All right. I'll go peacefully, and in one piece," Dan said, throwing his hands up in defeat.

"That's more like it." Ginny smiled as she watched him retreat to the parlor.

It was plain to see how happy Ginny and Dan were, and her own unhappiness contrasted sharply.

"What was your mother like, Jauncey? You always sound like you miss her a lot," Ginny said.

"I do. She was a kind, hardworking woman. She never complained about the things in life she couldn't change. She just accepted them and made the best of it." Jauncey thought about Aunt Ida and the unkind remarks that went unnoticed by her mother. Or at least she'd pretended they went unnoticed. Jauncey suspected it had been for her benefit that her mother had held herself in check, another example for Jauncey to live by. Nearly everything her mother had done seemed to be an example, and Jauncey had tried to live up to each of them.

Until Matt.

Quickly, she thrust those memories aside.

"I remember when I was a little girl and my father was alive, we'd had a very poor garden and little to put up for winter. Except for potatoes." Jauncey smiled. "Mother cooked potato stew with a lot more potatoes than carrots. We ate potatoes in soups with few other vegetables and fried potatoes in large pieces, small pieces, and sometimes whipped. But she always added some favorite herb to make it taste a little different. Father and I actually thought we were getting a variety." Jauncey laughed.

She did miss her mother, terribly. They had shared so much, talking about the past and keeping it fresh in Jauncey's mind. And of course there had been the future to think about. Her mother had told her of the great hopes she'd had for Jauncey to marry a man for love so she would know the kind of happiness she herself had experienced. But that had not happened.

"Were you the only child?" Ginny asked.

"Yes. I was born when my parents had been married for five years. They'd almost given up hope, Mother said. But then God blessed them with a baby girl, she told me. She always said they'd never minded that I was the only one. Although, I admit, I often wished I'd had a sister to play with." Her smile was wistful. "What about you?"

"Oh, heavens no! I had so many brothers and sisters I'd have gladly given you several. I was halfway between the beginning and the end, as my mother used to say." Ginny laughed. "I always told her I didn't know which was worse, the beginning, which was the older ones who nagged, or the end, which was the ones who always tagged along. But definitely not the middle ones!"

Jauncey laughed with her. "It sounds like a houseful."

"It was. Thank goodness we had a big house."

"Are you and Dan going to go back and see them sometime? I know if I'd had a sister, I'd want to see her. Especially, if it had been a long time."

"We've talked about it. But I don't know."

"You should, Ginny. Families are so important. They support you and love you, no matter what." Jauncey believed that with all her heart. Uncle Harold was the only family she had left, and she knew he loved her even though Aunt Ida dominated him.

"Maybe in the spring. We'll see." Ginny turned back to her mixing bowl. "Now let's get these cakes in the oven."

* * *

The rest of the day was spent making preparations for Christmas. Maggie helped string popcorn and dried apples with cinnamon and make ornaments of hardened bread dough. Jauncey was glad to see her participate and come out of her shell.

A pot of bean soup with a meaty ham bone simmered on the stove, providing a simple but tasty meal for supper. It was not a meal Mr. Natter would have approved of, but he no longer resided at the boardinghouse, having left on the first train headed east as soon as the weather had cleared.

The relaxed atmosphere and the memories of her mother had Jauncey longing for the days of her childhood. Suddenly, her thoughts turned to the letters in the attic, written in her mother's own handwriting, probably telling of the everyday things they'd done.

She couldn't resist the temptation, and after making an excuse, went up to her room for a warm shawl. As she opened the door to the attic, freezing cold air swept down upon her but did not deter her from the search. At the top of the steps, bright sunshine filled the large room. There were no dust motes scooting around in the heavy cold air. She drew the shawl closer as she moved to the dormer that held the trunk with the letters.

The lid was open, exposing the faded ribbons that had tied the letters together, and finding a chair, she pulled it up to the trunk. With one hand, she searched through the yellowing envelopes for the ones her mother had addressed, purposely bypassing the ones her aunt had written.

With great care she opened one. The date at the

top of the page indicated the year she'd turned 14. She read each word, savoring them like the first meal after a fast.

Dear Sister,

We are all well and hope this finds you the same. As regards your concern for Jauncey, have no fear. The illness was light and left no lasting effects. She's a healthy girl with a loving heart and we bless God each day for that.

As for the ring, I will see that she gets it on her birthday as you requested.

Jauncey pondered that last sentence. What ring? She'd never received such a gift for her birthday, and certainly none from her aunt. At that moment the sun caught the amethyst ring on her finger; she stared at the lovely purple glow. Impossible. Her mother had given her that ring when she'd died.

Jauncey picked up another letter dated earlier.

Dear Sister,

John says we cannot accept your gift of money, so I have enclosed it with the hopes it doesn't become lost in the mails. Please understand our position. Even though you sent it for Jauncey, we feel it is unfair to keep it. It is up to us to look after her welfare and we do so with love and happiness, be assured.

A warning spark of fear ignited somewhere near the vicinity of the pit of her stomach, rising to her throat until it nearly choked her. With frenzied control, she grabbed a handful of the letters, looking for the one with the earliest date. Her hands shook so badly, she could barely keep from tearing the paper.

Dearest Sister,
   It is with regret and sadness that I read your letter. I had hoped that when I finally heard from you that the news would be heartening. I'm sorry for your sake that it was not. I wish that I could change your circumstances so that such wonderful news could be exactly that. Wonderful. As it stands, John and I will gladly raise the child as our own.

Panic and fear thrummed in her breast. But I am an only child, she thought, there was no other child! Her eyes scanned the sheet of paper for any important words. Finally, at the end of the second page she stopped scanning and read:

We have only one request and please believe me when I say it is in the child's best interest. We ask that you do not contact Jauncey and tell her that you are her real mother.

Real mother? No! The words screamed in her brain. She dropped the paper as if it had burned her and jumped from her chair, knocking it over. It wasn't true! It couldn't be true! Jauncey clapped her hands over her ears and squeezed her eyes shut, trying to rid herself of the words "real mother."

"No!" she shrieked, unable to hold it in any longer. "It's a lie!"

She backed away from the trunk, horror-stricken, her chest heaving as she tried to hold in her sobs. She stumbled, almost falling in her rush to get away, then caught herself on something. She stood transfixed, staring into the eyes of the nude woman in the life-size portrait.

In a great release, she cried, her entire body shaking with soul-rendering shudders. She ran across the attic, bumping into things she couldn't see because of the curtain of tears that blinded her, and all the while the words "real mother" beat into her brain.

She felt her way down the stairs and into her room, slamming the door behind her, and flung herself onto the bed as the convulsive sobs continued to wrack her body. It wasn't true! Oh, God, it couldn't be true!

Through the sounds of her own grief, she heard frantic pounding on her door and Ginny calling her name.

"Jauncey!" The door flew open and Ginny was at her side. "What's wrong? Tell me! What is it?"

She had no voice for words. Her grief was all consuming. She wasn't Jauncey Devon Taylor. She was simply Jauncey Devon, the illegitimate daughter of a whore. She buried her face in the quilt and released another torrent of tears.

Ginny continued to croon and soothe her, but she paid no heed. Then Maggie joined in an effort to comfort her. But Jauncey ignored them, suffering inside alone.

Time passed, and finally she shed the last tear

her worn-out body could produce and empty shudders shook her when she took a breath. From somewhere above her, a quilt floated into place across her back and a gentle hand soothed her damp brow. Warmth and exhaustion overtook her and she stole away to a place free of cares, a sleep without dreams.

Chapter Twenty-five

Opening her eyes to darkness, she felt constricted from lying in one position for so long while still dressed. She rolled her head to the other side, wondering why she had such a terrible feeling of dread.

Slowly, realization flowed over her and threatened to swallow her up again. Tears filled her eyes and she bit her lip to hold them back. Sniffling loudly, she held her breath.

"Jauncey, are you awake?" It was Maggie's voice, soft and even.

She sniffled again, unable to talk.

"Is it all right if I light a lamp?"

"No. Please," Jauncey whispered, her throat tight. She couldn't bear to face the light. The truth.

"You don't have to say anything. I'll help you into bed. You'll be more comfortable."

Jauncey wanted to thank her, but couldn't.

Maggie undressed her in the dark, Jauncey's body as limp as the sock doll she used to play with as a child. She rolled under the covers, allowing Maggie to tuck them in around her much the same as she had done for Maggie.

She refused to let her mind dwell, or even momentarily light, on the secret she'd discovered. Sometime, maybe, she'd sort it all out. But not now.

Bright morning light shone into her room, and the air was as warm as a summer day. But it wasn't summer because she could hear the snapping sounds of a fire in the stove. And she wasn't at home where it was safe.

Something heavy lay on her feet, and she looked down to see Maggie sound asleep across the foot of her bed, draped with a quilt.

Carefully, Jauncey pulled her feet from under Maggie and rolled to her side.

So many thoughts ran through her head that she couldn't sort them out. Daughter. No, she pushed that one aside. Matt. It was with him that she'd shown who she really was, but she had tried to deny it. The truth had stared her in the face that morning, and deep inside she'd known it even then, but she'd turned away from it. Just as she wished she could turn away from it now.

Stirring slightly, she tried to relieve a sore spot in her backside, but the movement woke Maggie. Her eyes fluttered open, as if she were unsure of her surroundings. When she saw Jauncey watching her, she sat up quickly.

"You're awake. How are you feeling?"

"Better." No, actually she felt numb.

"Jauncey, I know what happened. If you want to talk about it . . ."

"I don't think I can." Tears sprang from nowhere and she raised her eyes to the ceiling.

"When you can, I want you to remember that I'm here. Anytime."

Jauncey licked her dry lips, then bit the bottom one, nodding her head. It was too fresh. Too hurtful.

"I'm going to fix us some hot tea. I'll be right back."

Jauncey nodded again, feeling the trickle of tears on her face.

While Maggie was gone, unbidden bits and pieces of her childhood skipped through her mind. Her father holding her while he rocked in a chair, her mother singing lullabies at bedtime when she was too old for them, sitting in church between them with barely enough height to see over the pew ahead.

She sniffled twice and got out of bed to find a handkerchief in her drawer, then returned to bed, propping herself against the headboard. Glancing at the ring on her finger, she yanked it off and threw it against the door.

Maggie returned shortly with a tray of two cups and a teapot. Moving inside the room, she looked down where the ring sparkled, then stepped over it.

"This tea will help you feel better. I have all kinds, but this one works best."

Jauncey took the cup to please Maggie as much

362

as anything and sipped from it. The light tangy flavor soothed her throat and the aroma pleasantly filled her nostrils.

"How long did you know my..." Jauncey couldn't bring herself to say "mother," so she didn't. "You know."

"A long time." Maggie sipped the hot tea.

"When did you find out about..." Again the words failed her.

"Just before I went to J.T.'s office."

She knew Maggie wouldn't force the issue, and these were only preliminary questions. But she wasn't sure she wanted to go any farther.

"Do you like the tea?" Maggie asked, glancing over the edge of her cup.

"Yes." Jauncey smiled. "Thank you."

After that neither spoke for some time.

"Matt stopped by this morning to see you. Ginny told him you weren't feeling well."

Matt! Why would he come here? Hadn't she made it plain that what they'd done had been a mistake? He'd certainly made his feelings clear when he'd disclosed their night of intimacy to Lottie, even if he didn't know about the encounter between the two women.

"He said he'd stop in later to see how you were doing," Maggie continued.

"I can't see him."

Maggie drank her tea, saying nothing.

After a length of time passed in silence, Maggie gathered up the things for the tray and walked to the door. She bent, picked up the ring, then laid it on the dresser.

"I'll be up later to see if you need anything."

"I'm fine," Jauncey said, forcing a smile.

When the door closed behind Maggie, Jauncey slid down under the covers until they were directly beneath her chin.

She felt guilty; she felt shame; she felt betrayed. Of the three she didn't know which was the hardest to bear.

Two days had passed and Christmas morning arrived. Ginny came in to see her just as dawn was breaking.

"Jauncey?" she called.

Jauncey sat in bed with the lamp burning low. She'd spent the long lonely hours going over every aspect of her life, weighing and measuring the words she remembered, looking at them in a new light.

"It's Christmas. Aren't you going to come down and share it with us?" Ginny asked. "It isn't the same without you."

"I don't know, Ginny." She was beginning to tire of her surroundings, and her search for understanding seemed futile.

Maggie skipped around Ginny and into the room.

"You can't miss Christmas," Maggie insisted.

Jauncey felt like a spoiled child, pouting in her room, waiting for someone to beg her to come down. She hadn't meant to pass on her suffering to anyone else. She only wanted to be alone in her misery.

"I'll start breakfast," Ginny said. "Please, say you'll come down."

"Will you?" Maggie asked.

With little hesitation she replied, "Yes, I will."

"Good," Ginny said, and left.

Taking a piece of paper from her pocket, Maggie handed it to Jauncey. "I have something for you. Promise me you'll read all of it."

Jauncey could tell the paper was important to Maggie by the pleading look in her eyes. She nodded.

When she took the paper she realized it was an envelope folded in half with an unbroken seal. Inside was a letter with the familiar handwriting she'd seen in the attic. Her heart lurched with foreboding, but she took a deep breath, then opened the envelope and read:

To My Baby,

I know you are no longer a baby, but in my mind you are still the bright-haired, smiling child I held in my arms for such a short time. If you are reading this letter on Christmas, then you've decided to stay and keep the house. Somehow I knew you would.

Where do I begin? What can I say? It broke my heart to give you up, even to my dear sister. But what kind of life could I give you? So with regret and longing I sent you to Maybelle. I grieved for days . . . no, for months, for years. So much so, that when Maggie was born . . .

Jauncey looked up from the letter. Maggie stood beside the bed, biting at the corner of her lip, staring down at Jauncey, her blue eyes wide with expectancy. Sisters? Her mind couldn't take it in. She read on.

. . . I searched for a home that would be nearby. A minister placed her with a family on the edge of town, so I was able to watch her grow and love her from afar. I couldn't bear to be separated from another child by so many miles again.

I never saw a picture of you, and can only guess by the letters I received occasionally from Maybelle that you were a beautiful child and now a beautiful woman. I honored Maybelle's wishes to stay away and not contact you, although it nearly tore the heart out of me to do so.

Jauncey stopped reading and reached out for Maggie's hand, pulling her to sit down beside her.

"You knew about this?" Jauncey asked, still unable to believe that they could be sisters.

Maggie nodded.

"How long have you known?"

"About being sisters?"

"Yes." But Jauncey wondered, too, how long Maggie had known she was Spicie's daughter.

"Not until I read the letters in the attic." Then indicating the letter Jauncey held, she went on. "Spicie gave me that one before she died. She said to wait until Christmas to give it to you."

"She didn't tell you anything about me?"

"Not really. She said you were a relative who lived in St. Louis and would be coming to live here. I didn't ask any questions." Maggie looked away. "I wanted to, but she was so ill and I could tell she didn't want to talk about it."

Jauncey grasped Maggie's hand. She had grown very close to Maggie over the past few months, and especially over the last week.

"I didn't know whether you would let us stay. Ruby said you were probably uppity and would make us leave." Maggie turned beseeching eyes on Jauncey. "I didn't mean to be unfriendly when you first came. But I was so afraid."

Jauncey thought back to the day she'd arrived, when Ginny was so distant and Maggie was so terrified.

"I hadn't noticed your ring," Maggie went on, "until the day you gave me the necklace. It was Spicie's favorite stone. I knew then there was a reason why Spicie wanted you here, even if I didn't know what it was. That's when I started looking through the letters."

It was planned, Jauncey thought. Planned to bring them together. For that she could be glad, but still she could hardly forgive the woman for the kind of life she'd led.

"Why do you call her by her name?" Jauncey would have thought Maggie would have called her "Mother," as much as she appeared to love Spicie.

"I didn't find out she was my mother until about six years ago when I was thirteen." Maggie took a deep breath, then expelled it slowly. "I was raised by a woman who loved me and a man who hated me. He drank all the time and beat my mother whenever he felt like it. He left me alone, until my mother died."

Jauncey felt the tremors run through Maggie's body. What had that awful man done to her? She held Maggie's hand tightly.

"Then he began beating me. After a while, he started calling me names like whore and bad seed

367

and . . . other names. I didn't know why he said those things."

Jauncey rankled, wondering how Spicie could let those things happen. If Maggie had lived close by, then Spicie must have known.

"Then one night . . . he crawled into my bed when I was asleep. I . . . screamed . . . and I cried. But he wouldn't listen." She paused while another shudder ran over her. "Then . . . he brought others . . . for money," Maggie said haltingly while she held Jauncey's hands in a death grip.

"Maggie. Don't." Jauncey wrapped her arms around Maggie's stiff body, her own heart breaking. "Don't talk about it." Jauncey hoped with all her might that the man was dead. He deserved to be.

Maggie leaned against her.

"Spicie told me later that when she'd seen the bruises on my face she'd wanted to kill him," Maggie said, her voice muffled.

"How did you come to live here?" Jauncey asked, trying to get her mind away from those terrible memories.

"Spicie sent Brailey and Matt to get me."

"Matt?" Jauncey tried to picture the two of them rescuing a young girl. Yes, she thought, they would do that. Brailey had a heart as big as Wyoming Territory, and Matt wouldn't waste any time getting it done.

Maggie nodded. "He threatened Pa with a rope. Pa believed him. So did I."

Jauncey could imagine that, too. Matt could be dangerous unless he was on your side.

She released Maggie and looked at her. "When did you learn about your real mother?"

368

"When Brailey and Matt brought me here they never said anything about that," she said, taking a relaxing breath. "I was so glad to be away from Pa that I was willing to go anywhere. I knew what this house was and I knew what Spicie was. But she talked nice and she seemed to really care about me." Maggie nervously smoothed the front of her apron. "I never really felt loved before. Ma spent all her time avoiding Pa or doing as she was told, so she had little time for me."

Jauncey was struck by how wrong she'd been about Maggie. She'd been victimized by a man she'd believed to be her father. Their lives had been so different, and Maggie had been the unlucky one.

"Spicie didn't tell me the truth for about a month. We spent a lot of time together getting to know each other." Maggie smiled. "I loved this house immediately, especially the kitchen. She told me it was up to me to see that it was clean and tidy. I helped the cook with all the meals, and when she left I took over. It was wonderful to be loved, to be needed."

It all made sense now, Jauncey thought, her fear of men and her attachment to Spicie.

"Maggie, that's all in the past now."

"I know." Maggie smiled at her. "Now I've got you."

Jauncey smiled back. "I am glad we're sisters," she said straight from the heart. "I'd say this is the best Christmas present I could ever get."

"Before we go downstairs," Maggie said, "there's something else I'd like to give you." She hurried to the door, then stopped, turning back to smile. "Wait right here."

369

In a moment she returned carrying a small cloth-covered book. Handing it to Jauncey she said, "I found this in a small chest. It's about you."

Jauncey could only stare at the little book that was obviously a diary. "I don't know," she began, but inside she did know and the pain was still too raw.

"You should read it." Maggie laid the diary in Jauncey's lap, then gently touched her shoulder before leaving the room.

With one hand she fingered the dull purple cloth. Inside this book, she knew, were the answers she needed, maybe even the explanation why a woman would turn to such a life.

A new feeling of expectancy burgeoned as she opened to the first fragile page and read about the daily happenings in the lives of the twin sisters, including the marriage of Maybelle, at the young age of 17, to John Taylor. But she skimmed those pages in search of something that would deliver her from this remorse. Then she reached a date in the year she was born, and her hand stilled over the page while her heart tripped as she realized she would at last know the truth.

In the same flourishing handwriting she read:

Life is grand! I've never felt so wonderful, the air has never smelled sweeter and I just can't stop smiling. Mama says I need to put my feet on the ground, be more like Maybelle and find a nice young man. But I think Maybelle should have had a little more fun before marrying. John Taylor is a nice man but he doesn't measure up to the gentleman

I'm going to marry. Now, Diary, this is a secret
and not a soul should know for a while, but
I believe that we'll be getting married before
long. I know Mama won't approve because of
the difference in our ages, and neither will
Maybelle, but they'll understand once they
see how happy we are. It will be wonderful!
No longer will we be separated by time and
distance while he's somewhere on the river
or down to Memphis. I shall travel with him
as his wife. I have such plans! And when I see
him again, we can share our plans together.

Several blank pages followed, and Jauncey wondered if it ended there. But on the fifth page the
handwriting continued.

She's so beautiful! And she's mine, only mine.
I hadn't planned it to be this way, but it is. I
will put behind me the despair and desola-
tion I felt when he told me he already had
a family. That he couldn't do more than take
me to a house where women knew how to
deal with this problem. That's where I am
now and have been for the past six months. I
refused to lose my baby, and the kindness of
the woman who runs the house has allowed
us to continue on without further payment.
I'm not sure how long I can continue to live
on her kindness, but I know I can never go
home.

Jauncey put the book down. She'd been born in
a bordello. How ironic that her life should come

full circle. She found herself wondering how many other women like Ginny, Maggie and her mother had turned to bordellos in fear and desperation. And could she honestly blame them?

She scanned through the blank pages following what she'd just read, but there weren't any other entries. She could only piece together what must have happened. Obviously, her mother had given her away before she'd left St. Louis. How long had she stayed before going west? There was no way of knowing and she wasn't sure it mattered anymore.

She closed the book and thought about how her mother must have felt as a young woman, alone and undoubtedly frightened, having to make a choice for herself and her child.

Remembering the letters in the attic that Maybelle had written, she realized how difficult it had to have been to cut the ties of motherhood. And making a promise to herself to read the rest of them, she allowed compassion and understanding to begin their work in her heart. Perhaps, forgiveness would not be so hard after all.

As impossible as it had been to accept Spicie and the life she'd lived, it was just as impossible not to see the goodness and love in Ginny and Maggie in spite of the fact that they, too, had lived in this house when it was managed as a bordello. Wasn't it the heart of the woman that counted?

With a lurch she remembered Maybelle's letters being addressed "Dear Sister," each one written with love and concern, not condemnation.

And hadn't both women acted in the best interests of her, as a baby, as a child and even as a young woman? Hadn't both women loved her?

A new peace settled over her. She had not been a misplaced child in a misplaced life and she didn't feel less loved, but precisely the opposite.

From this new position, this new outlook, she reviewed her feelings for Matt. She had been unfair to allow her own insecurities to interfere with what had happened between them, to mar the beauty of the blending of their souls. Her actions, she realized now, had been independent of her mother's influence; her actions had simply come from her heart. She also realized that she and she alone was responsible for the choices she made, good or bad. And that her choice to give her heart and body to Matt was not a predestined fact but a choice of love.

And it was plain to her now that she had loved him, indeed still did.

Yet did she love him enough to forgive him for exposing their one night of intimacy to another woman? And didn't that mean his loyalty, if not his love, was with Lottie?

The answers were undeniably evident.

Chapter Twenty-six

Once downstairs, Jauncey was greeted by the smells of the pine-scented tree in the parlor mingled with the spicy aroma of cinnamon in the kitchen.

Ginny hugged Jauncey, wishing her well, and Dan kissed her cheek. She tried her best to put on her cheeriest smile, and with the startling good news about Maggie and her new peace about Spicie, the effort wasn't difficult at all.

Breakfast consisted only of sugar-glazed cinnamon buns since making Christmas dinner would take so much time. Maggie and Ginny snatched pieces of the gooey confection while they hurried preparing the turkey and stuffing.

Jauncey toyed with the piece they'd insisted she eat, preferring to drink her coffee. This should have been the happiest day of the year for her with the boardinghouse full, the awful episode over J.T.'s murder behind them and the wonderful discovery of a sister. But her mind couldn't connect all the good things she ought to feel with the way she felt deep down inside: empty and adrift.

When the last of the boarders who had come down for breakfast had gone to the parlor, Jauncey gathered the dirty dishes and washed them. Across the room Ginny hummed a Christmas carol and Maggie joined in. Dan pulled on his coat, kissed the back of Ginny's neck and went out the back door for more wood.

Squinting, Jauncey glanced out the window where the sun reflected off the brilliant snow. In the glare she could see Dan's dark shape walking toward the woodpile, but he stopped before reaching his destination. Appearing beside him, silhouetted against the bright background, she could barely make out Matt's tall form. Together they turned and walked toward the house, Dan leading the way.

A moment of panic held Jauncey frozen, unable to move, unable to get away. What was he doing here? She couldn't see him now, especially not after what he'd done. She turned from the window, willing her feet to run, but they wouldn't obey her command.

When Dan opened the door, Matt stepped into the kitchen, filling it with his presence. His face was tight from the cold and his gloved hands were shoved deeply into his pockets, his broad shoulders hunched.

"Look who dropped by!" Dan called out.

"Merry Christmas, Matt," Ginny said with a smile. She glanced cautiously at Jauncey. "How about a cup of coffee to warm you up?"

"No. No, thanks." His eyes caught Jauncey's and held them. "I see you're feeling better," he said to her.

Absently, she wiped her hands on her apron. "Yes."

"I want—" he began.

"I can't—" she began at the same time.

Silence filled the room.

"Well," Dan said, clearing his throat. "I believe I was on my way to the woodpile. I guess I'd better get back to it if we want that turkey to cook." Then he escaped out the back door.

Matt blocked out everything around him and focused on the strained look on Jauncey's face, dropping his gaze to where her hands nervously twisted the edge of her apron. Perhaps he'd made a mistake coming here, but he had to know what she was really thinking.

In two great strides he was close enough to her to reach out and grasp her wrist, pulling her along with him toward the parlor. "Excuse us," he said to Maggie and Ginny, while both just nodded their heads without answering.

With her heart pounding, Jauncey followed as though she had a choice, crossing the entrance parlor to the larger parlor, where a bright fire crackled. Inside the room, two boarders sat half dozing on chairs.

"We hate to bother you," Matt said with some urgency in his voice. "But we'd like a little privacy."

"Sure thing," one man answered, and both of them got up to leave.

376

Matt closed the door behind them and turned to her. She watched him remove his hat and drop it on a chair; then he stripped the gloves from his large hands. She fought back the rising warmth she felt just seeing him again, having him close again.

"You shouldn't have come," she said, trying to add some conviction to her voice.

He shrugged out of his coat. "I don't give up easily."

"Maybe you should."

"You haven't exactly told me why."

Her resolve weakened now that he stood in front of her, his face grim, almost foreboding and very determined. She tried not to look at the thick ebony hair he always hid under his hat, or the unwavering intent in his dark eyes. He stood close, so close she only had to reach out to touch the silkiness of his mustache. If only he hadn't come, if only she'd been up in her room . . . it would have been so much easier to tell Maggie to send him away.

Her newly found identity and recent ability to cope with it suddenly felt shaky. When she looked at him she remembered the girl she'd been in his arms, but she was changed somehow. Changed by the love she felt for him and the trust he'd betrayed.

"Tell me why," he said gently.

Did she owe him an explanation? she wondered, trying to harden her heart. Wasn't he the one who owed her at least that much?

"I ought to ask you that question," she said.

His eyes probed her face for clues, searched her eyes for answers.

"Maybe I should be a little more specific," she went on. Unable to say everything in her heart, she said simply, "Lottie."

"What does she have to do with us?" He looked puzzled.

"More than you realize," she said, turning away from him and attempting to leave the room.

He caught hold of her arm and pulled her back. "Wait. What do you know about Lottie?"

"Everything. She has a way of getting around and letting her feelings be known."

"She came here? And talked to you?" Anger flared in his dark eyes.

"Yes."

"About me," he said, his voice full of regret. "Why didn't you tell me?"

She didn't answer, but stared at him.

"What did she tell you?"

"There's no point in discussing it," she said, feeling the color rise in her cheeks. Under his scrutiny the rawness of her hurt feelings felt exposed. She couldn't bring herself to repeat Lottie's words and feel anew the pain of embarrassment. Once more she attempted to get away from him, but he gently held her captive.

It nearly killed him to watch her try to control the quiver in her chin. He wanted to hold her but her eyes warned him not to.

"Jauncey. We have to talk about this."

"I can't," she whispered.

"Do you want me to apologize for what happened that night?" he asked, his voice low with intensity.

With misery in her eyes she looked away.

378

"I won't apologize for that," he said.

Turning her by the shoulders, he forced her to look at him. "This isn't the way I planned to say it, not with you angry at me, but I have to say it now and hope you believe me." He cupped her chin and bent close enough to feel her breath on his lips. "I love you," he said softly, urgently. "I have since the night we stood in the dark out there in the kitchen and you came into my arms. Something happened to me, inside, when I kissed you. I wanted it to be right for you and I'd never felt like that before. I can't explain it." He leaned closer and kissed her forehead, her cheek, then the hair at her temples, savoring the scent of her. Roses, always roses, he thought. "I love you, Jauncey Taylor. And I never loved you more than the night we spent together."

The words were husky in her ear. Welcome, wonderful words. As her eyes slid closed she tried to block out the reality of Lottie's words, but she couldn't. He had told another woman, a woman who loved him and wanted him. She could not leave that problem unanswered between them, whether she loved him or not.

"And what about Lottie?"

"She's a part of the past. You are my future."

"She still loves you."

"No, she only thought she did."

"Did you love her at all?" She held her breath, waiting for his answer.

Raising her face, he gazed into her eyes. "No."

"Then why did you tell her . . ." She couldn't go on.

"Tell her what?"

"About . . . us . . . that . . . night."

"I didn't. I would never do that. She guessed. I suppose it must have been plain on my face. Do you want to know what the conversation was about? Would that help you believe me?"

"No. I mean, no, I don't want to know." She saw the honesty in his eyes, felt it in his touch, heard it in his voice.

"Lottie left town on the same train as Mr. Natter. At least that's what Charlie said."

She looked at him a long time before speaking, her love for him welling up but unable to spill over, revelations from her own past holding it back. "There's something you should know about me. Something that's been difficult for me until today."

A puff of smoke burst into the room, bringing with it the pungent but sweet smell of burning wood.

"Spicie was my mother." She spoke the words aloud for the first time.

He looked at the auburn curls framing her beautiful oval face and the clear hazel eyes that reflected her recent turmoil. This wasn't news to him. He'd suspected it from the moment he'd first met her.

"She was a caring woman," he said gently. "You could have done worse for a mother." Matt took her into his arms and held her close. "She loved you enough to give you up because she thought it was the best thing for you, not her."

"I've come to realize that," she murmured against his shoulder while a new feeling of security settled over her.

From this new position, this new outlook, she

reviewed her feelings for Matt. She had been unfair to allow her own insecurities to interfere with what had happened between them. And the gentle but firm way he held her now made her feel safe, cared for and loved.

"There's just one thing that hasn't been settled," he said, nuzzling her hair.

"Mmm. What's that?"

Leaning back to get a better look at her face, he smiled and said, "I need to know if you'll marry me."

Laying her hand on his cheek where she could stroke his mustache, she answered, "Yes."

His smile broadened. "I love it when you do that."

"You do?"

"Mmhmm."

"Then I'll do it every chance I get after we're married."

"And will you wear that same nightgown after we're married?" he asked, grinning.

"Only if you insist," she said mischievously.

"Well, on second thought . . ." He lowered his face to hers, his lips grazing hers.

As she relaxed against his chest, her hands reached around him and clasped him to her.

Matt pulled away slightly, then nuzzled her ear. "I love you," he said huskily.

Jauncey's heart soared at his words and her breath caught inside her until she thought she wouldn't be able to get the words out. "I love you, too."

Again he touched his lips to hers. Instantly, the kiss became deep and caressing, full of longing, heating both of them as the fire snapping and popping beside them could never do.

Tentatively, she pulled away, but he continued to hold her tight. "Should we tell the others now?" she asked.

"The sooner the better," he said. "And that goes for the wedding, too."

The planning would be simple, she thought, as they made their way to the kitchen. Just a small gathering in the parlor. Then the two of them would be together forever.

Chapter Twenty-seven

January 8th, 1887 dawned dark and cloudy, but Jauncey hardly noticed.

She fussed with the ivory satin gown she'd just put on even though it fit perfectly. Ginny had found it in the attic and cleaned and ironed it. Jauncey stood in front of the mirror in her room where she could see only the top half of the dress. The neckline was modestly cut with a row of slightly ruffled lace as the only adornment. Three tiny pearl buttons at the wrists complimented the sleek satin sleeves. And the skirt, larger than she was accustomed to, took a little extra negotiating when she walked. It wasn't the latest fashion, but she didn't mind.

When Maggie came through the doorway, her mouth opened and her eyes widened. "Jauncey, you're so beautiful!" Then she, too, fussed with the skirt and the neckline.

Smiling, Jauncey replied, "Thank you, Maggie.

What do you think of my hair?" She put her hand up to the array of curls at the back of her head, held by what seemed like a hundred pins.

"Lovely. Ginny did it?" Maggie touched the curls gingerly.

"Yes."

Ginny popped her head in the doorway. "Did I just hear my name?"

"Come in, Ginny." Jauncey extended her hand. "I can't tell you how much I appreciate everything you've done."

Ginny waved her hand. "It was worth every minute and I enjoyed doing it."

"Is Matt here yet?" Jauncey asked nervously.

"As a matter of fact he is. And he looks as cool and calm as a pond on a spring day," Ginny said, smiling. "You're the one who looks nervous."

"I am." Jauncey plucked at her sleeve.

"Well, don't be. He's a good man and he'll take good care of you," Ginny said in earnest. Then she smiled again. "And he is the handsomest man I've ever seen. Besides Dan, of course."

Jauncey returned the smile, trying to calm the ecstatic butterflies in her stomach.

"The minister is here and everyone is waiting. Are you ready?" Ginny asked.

She took a deep breath and nodded, then followed the two women to the top of the stairs, where she stopped. Below she saw Matt dressed in a black suit, wearing a new Stetson that had been brushed to perfection. His boots looked freshly polished, shining like the leather on a new saddle. He stood speaking to the minister and Dan, and hadn't yet noticed her. Then the rustle of her skirts drew his attention. As their eyes locked, he removed his hat, revealing the ebony thick hair she loved. Slowly, she descended the stairs.

Staring at her, Matt was thankful that the herd of buffalo that had been trampling the inside of his stomach was gone instantly. She looked irresistibly beautiful; and she was going to be his. When she reached the bottom, he crooked his arm in invitation for her to take it, and she did.

"Hello," he said in a low whisper.

"Hello to you," she whispered back.

"Shall we begin?" the minister asked.

"Yes," Matt and Jauncey said at the same time.

Everyone took their places. Ginny and Dan stood near Jauncey, with Maggie and Andrew Collins close by. Sarah and Jeff stood near Matt, and his sister smiled approvingly at him. Charlie was absent. He'd told Matt he couldn't tolerate fancy doings and not to count on him, but the rest of the room was crowded with Jauncey's boarders.

Matt held her arm tucked close against his side, covering her hand with his opposite one. Then he tried to focus his attention on the words of the tall, slightly graying minister.

"We are gathered for this solemn occasion . . ."

Jauncey watched the minister's mouth move, but the words became a blur of sound, and she was aware only of the hand covering hers and the steady strong arm holding her up. Then she felt Matt turn toward her.

"I, Matthew Dawson, take thee, Jauncey, to be my wedded wife. To have and to hold, to love and to cherish, till death do us part." Then he took the

385

gold band from his pocket and placed it on her finger.

Jauncey gazed in surprise at the ring. The fit wasn't perfect, but it was close.

"Repeat after me . . ."

Jauncey stared into Matt's dark eyes and repeated the words from the bottom of her heart.

"I, Jauncey Devon Taylor, take thee, Matthew Dawson, to be my wedded husband. To have and to hold, to love and to cherish, until death do us part." She accepted the reassuring squeeze of Matt's hand.

"You may kiss your bride, Mr. Dawson."

Taking her by the shoulders, he leaned down to gently but firmly place his lips on hers. Her arms reached up his back, and she returned the kiss full measure, her heart full to overflowing with happiness.

A cheer and a round of applause arose as Matt and Jauncey backed away from each other smiling. Congratulations, hugs and handshakes were exchanged amidst laughter and talking.

"Well, are you two going to stay here all day?" Dan asked, grinning.

Jauncey flushed.

Matt asked about her bags, and went to get the small trunk and two handbags with the help of a boarder. Everything was quickly loaded into the sleigh that appeared to be almost weighed down with bells, which Jauncey learned hadn't been there when Matt drove up.

Then there was nothing to do but say their good-byes.

"I'm so happy for you," Ginny said, hugging her

tight. "Don't worry about a thing here."

"I won't." Jauncey returned her hug. She would miss Ginny after she and Dan left to go east in the spring, but she was happy for them.

By the time Ginny and Dan were gone, Maggie would be able to run the boardinghouse alone. Jauncey had seen Andrew to have the paperwork drawn up so that Maggie would be the sole owner. He had also told her that he would be leaving soon after her wedding, now that everything had turned out fine. She turned to him and whispered good-bye.

Then Jauncey moved toward Maggie and embraced her. "Maggie, I'm so glad we found each other."

"Me, too," Maggie said, on the verge of tears. "Don't worry about anything. Just be happy." At last Maggie let go of her. "You'd better go. The weather will be getting bad. I wouldn't want you to spend your honeymoon stranded in a blizzard."

Jauncey brushed the tears from her cheeks. "You're right." And they hugged briefly, again. "Bye."

Jauncey bundled up and Matt put on his heavy coat; then out they went into the brisk cold air. A leaden sky and a scattering of snowflakes spoke a dire forecast of what was soon to be. Placing a heavy robe around them, Matt called to the horses, and they were on their way amidst the merry jingle of bells.

She snuggled down into the robe, moving as near as she could to Matt, loving the feel of his warmth so close. With one hand on the reins, he tucked his free hand under the robe to find hers and squeezed it gently, fingering her wedding ring. "Matt, where did you get this ring on such short notice?" she asked, smiling at him.

"It was my mother's," he answered, then looked deeply into her eyes. "Mrs. Dawson?"

"Yes?" she answered playfully, loving the sound of her new name.

"Did you by chance bring that white gown I've grown so accustomed to?"

"Actually, Mr. Dawson, I didn't bring it." She smiled mischievously up at him, then focused her attention on the surrounding scenery of white.

They rode in silence for several miles, her mind on the future.

At last the sleigh came to a halt and Jauncey's eyes took in the long ranch house with the scattered buildings behind it. The expanse of surrounding land and sky gave the impression of going on forever.

"Here we are," Matt said as large feathery flakes began falling.

He helped her untangle herself from the robe and lifted her to the ground. Then out of the nearby barn came a man bundled against the weather. He spoke to Matt, nodded to Jauncey, then took the horses and sleigh.

The smell of wood smoke swept down from the roof, a welcome sign of the warmth inside. Wrapping his arm around her, Matt led her through the back door into the warm kitchen. Jauncey quickly spotted a pot of coffee, and a dutch oven filled with stew and a pan of biscuits. She presumed that Matt's ranch hands had eaten early in anticipation of their arrival.

"Oh, this feels wonderful," Jauncey said, removing her coat and gloves. She glanced around at the wooden walls aged to a golden yellow. This was her new home, but more than that, it was their home together.

He hung their coats side by side on the pegs near the door and dropped his hat on the table before scooping her up into his arms.

"Would you care to see the rest of your new home?" he asked, burying his face in her hair, which had fallen from its pins.

"Of course," she replied, her eyes sliding closed.

He firmly planted a heated kiss on her neck. "Or maybe we could . . ."

The only sound was the wind rattling down the stovepipe.

Jauncey raised her hand to her crushed curls. "I must look a sight," she said, feeling suddenly self-conscious.

He continued to stare. First at her face, then down her neck, to her breasts and back to her face. Her skin felt hot under his gaze.

"I like it when you do that," he said softly.

"Do what?" She dropped her hand to her hot cheek.

"Blush."

"It's not something I can control."

The wind rattled down the pipe again.

"Are you going to show me the rest of the house?"

"Well, as you can see, this is the kitchen." He kissed the tip of her nose. "Where we'll spend a good deal of our time. I hope it's to your liking."

She nodded approvingly. "Very much so."

"Good. Then we'll move on."

He walked down the long hall to an open door where the smell of leather was strong in the cold air.

"This is my office, and I probably will spend more time than I want to in here now that I have you." He kissed her cheek.

Next was a large room he called the fireplace room. And no wonder, she thought. It had the biggest fireplace she'd ever seen in a house. A fire blazed and crackled cheerily, adding a warm glow to the wood walls and ceiling.

"I love this house. It reminds me of you," she said.

"It's plain."

"I would hardly call you plain, Matt Dawson."

Matt grinned and kissed her teasingly on the lips. "Why, Mrs. Dawson, are you trying to flatter me?"

"Could be," she said, smiling.

"Would you like to see the rest?" he asked, leaning down to nibble on her ear.

"Right now?" She tipped her head to one side, enjoying the delicious shivers running down her spine.

"I don't see any reason to wait, do you?" He followed the line of her jaw to her mouth, where he stopped, waiting for her answer.

"No," she said, a little breathless.

"Then we'll go this way." He took her back into the hallway and on down to another door. He pushed it wide with his foot and stepped inside, hooking it with his heel to close it.

Jauncey looked around at the same wood interior

so prominent in the other rooms. A fire burned here also, creating a warmth that radiated off the walls. A bright quilt covered the large bed, and rag rugs were scattered around the room. A row of pegs near the door held numerous paraphernalia: a jacket, a heavy plaid shirt, a rope halter, a hat that had seen better days and several belts.

Matt released her legs so that her body slid down his while he continued to hold her tight.

"This is my room. I mean, our room. And I hope we'll spend a lot of time here," he said, lightly brushing his lips across hers. "Will it do?"

With her arms looped around his neck, she replied quietly, "It'll do very nicely." Banished forever were the earlier butterflies, replaced instead by a sense of belonging.

Matt reached for the pins in the tangle of curls.

"I'd better warn you," she said. "Ginny put in lots of them." She tilted her head, studying the concentration on his face. "Let me help you."

They each laid a handful of pins on the nearby table. Her hair haloed her face in a riot of curls, cascading around her shoulders in soft auburn waves.

"It's beautiful," he said, drawing her to him and burying his nose in the rose-scented depths. He looked forward to having the whole room smell like her. "Welcome home, Mrs. Dawson."

"Mmmm. That sounds nice," she said, nuzzling under his chin.

Tipping her head back, he gazed into her warm hazel eyes and quietly said, "I love you." Overcome with a sudden need, he pressed his lips to hers and she answered by holding nothing back.

Melody Morgan

Quickly, the heat built in both of them. Then, with scarcely a wasted movement, Matt's black coat landed haphazardly on the floor and was soon accompanied by his linen shirt. Jauncey's satin dress fell like rippling water to pool at her feet. Boots and shoes, stockings and trousers were strewn around them unnoticed.

He lifted her in his arms and carried her to the bed, where he carefully laid her down, then stretched his long frame beside her. Their arms entwined, their eyes silently spoke words of love.

And as the sharp cold wind pelted the house with snow outside, a fire glowed and burned inside, melting their two hearts into one.

A FIRE IN THE BLOOD — SHIRL HENKE

Bestselling Author of *White Apache's Woman*

When half-breed Jess Robbins rides into Cheyenne to chase down a gang of cattle thieves, he is sure of three things. The townsfolk will openly scorn him, the women will secretly want him, and the rustlers will definitely fear him. What he doesn't count on is a flame-haired spitfire named Lissa Jacobsen, who has her own manhunt in mind.

Dark, dangerous, and deadly with his Colt revolver, Jess is absolutely forbidden to the spoiled, pampered daughter of Cheyenne's richest rancher. But from the moment Lissa stumbles upon him in his bath, she decides she has to have the virile gunman. Pitting her innocence against his vast experience, Lissa knows she is playing with fire...but she never guesses that the raging inferno of desire will consume them both.

_3601-0 $4.99 US/$5.99 CAN

SHIRL HENKE

WHITE APACHE WOMAN

By the bestselling author of *Terms of Surrender*

Running from his past, Red Eagle has no desire to become entangled with the haughty beauty who hires him to guide her across the treacherous Camino Real to Santa Fe. Although Elise Louvois's cool violet eyes betray nothing, her warm, willing body comes alive beneath his masterful touch. She will risk imprisonment and death, but not her vulnerable heart. Mystified, Red Eagle is certain of but one thing—the spirits have destined Elise to be his woman.

_3498-0 $4.99 US/$5.99 CAN

Sage NORAH HESS

Winner Of The *Romantic Times* Lifetime Achievement Award!

"Norah Hess not only overwhelms you with characters who seem to be breathing right next to you, she transports you into their world!"
—*Romantic Times*

Jim LaTour isn't the marrying kind. With a wild past behind him, he plans to spend the rest of his days in peace, enjoying the favors of the local fancy ladies and running his bar. He doesn't realize what he is missing until an irresistible songbird threatens his cherished independence and opens his heart.

Pursued by the man who has murdered her husband, Sage Larkin faces an uncertain future on the rugged frontier. But when she lands a job singing at the Trail's End saloon, she hopes to start anew. And though love is the last thing Sage wants, she can't resist the sweet, seductive melody of Jim's passionate advances.

_3591-X $4.99 US/$5.99 CAN

Winner of 5 *Romantic Times* Awards!

Norah Hess's historical romances are "delightful, tender and heartwarming reads from a special storyteller!"

—Romantic Times

Spencer Atkins wants no part of a wife and children while he can live in his pa's backwoods cabin as a carefree bachelor. Fresh from the poorhouse, Gretchen Ames will marry no man refusing her a home and a family. Although they are the unlikeliest couple, Spencer and Gretchen find themselves grudgingly sharing a cabin, working side by side, and fighting an attraction neither can deny.

_3518-9 $4.99 US/$5.99 CAN

Connie Mason
Bestselling Author of *A Promise Of Thunder*

"Connie Mason tempts her readers with thrilling action and sizzling sensuality!"

—*Romantic Times*

When he sees Cassie Fenmore sneaking down the stairs of a fancy house, Cody Carter thinks her a tasty confection he can have for the asking—and ask he shall.

When she meets Carter on the Dodge City train, Cassie believes him a despicable blackguard capable of anything—like denying the two adorable urchins who claim to be his children.

When Cody and Cassie learn they are to share the inheritance of the Rocking C Ranch, they have no doubt trouble is brewing. But neither can guess that, when the dust has settled, all their assumptions will be gone with the wind—replaced by a love more precious than gold.

_3539-1 $4.99 US/$5.99 CAN

FIRE ACROSS TEXAS

SUSAN TANNER

Married to a fire-and-brimstone preacher, Hannah Barnes has given up all hope of love and happiness. Then three gunmen kill her husband, and she fears she will lose her life as well.

A former Texas Ranger, Jeb Welles is determined to save the tart-tongued widow and be on his way. But while Jeb only has rescue on his mind, his body aches with desire for the stunning redhead.

Courageous beauty and valiant loner, Hannah and Jeb have nothing in common, yet everything to share. And in the tender embrace of the rugged ex-lawman, Hannah finally finds a blazing passion that will start her own fire across Texas.

_3640-1 $4.99 US/$5.99 CAN

WINDS ACROSS TEXAS

Susan Tanner

Bestselling Author of *Exiled Heart*

The Comanches name her Fierce Tongue; Texans call her a white squaw. Once the captive of a great warrior, Katherine Bellamy finds herself shunned by decent society, yet unable to return to the Indians who have accepted her as their own.

Slade is a hard-riding, hard-hitting lawman, out to avenge the deaths of his wife and son. Blinded by anger and bitterness, he will do anything, use anyone to have his revenge.

Both Katherine and Slade see in the other a means to escape misery, but they never expect to fall in love. Yet as the sultry desert breezes caress their yearning bodies, neither can deny the sweet, soaring ecstasy of their reckless desire.

_3582-0 $4.99 US/$5.99 CAN